ALSO BY EDITH SCHEFFER

The Janie Chronicles

Saving Janie

Janie a Broad

Janie on Board

Janie vs. The Big Apple

* * *

Fallen Gracefully

* * *

Winged

THE JANIE CHRONICLES

EDITH SCHEFFER

SAVING JANIE
The Janie Chronicles, Book 1
ISBN 978-1-954174-01-6

Edited by Louise Zanotto

GIVING THANKS

I would like to thank my mother, Lynn Scheffer, (who is not accurately portrayed in this book, I should add) without whose positive feedback, love and urging, this book would never have been completed. I love you Meema. To my father, Gene Scheffer, who has passed on, I did it daddy. 1 for you and 1 for mom. I love you both. Also I'd like to thank Torrie Merriam, (my sister) Diane Osborne, Lydia Bacon, Sarra Bobbitt Hu, Marne Wible, Marcy Fellows, Keri Morales, Gail Almasi, Louise Zanotto, Alison Crouson, and (Mama) Laura Kelly, for always having my back and adding silver lining to every cloud. I'd like to thank my daughter, Brenna, for letting me have unlimited computer time. Which I know almost killed her social life. Thank you to Mike, for seeing the crazy and thinking, "Yep, gotta have me some of that!" And lastly, to all the strong women in my life, named and unnamed, here and passed on: You have been my inspiration to live, to love, to give thanks, to dance, and yes, to act a fool for those things when need be. I love you all.

If you've read any of my books and would like to send your thoughts my way, please find me on fb (fb.com/AuthorEdithScheffer).

1

THE TERMINAL

Oh my God! I'm late. I'm never late! What the hell? I thought. "Where are my keys?" I yelled to no one. I'm supposed to be on a plane at 3:00pm to Hawaii. I looked at my watch. It was 1:30pm now. I still have to make it to the airport and go through their Gestapo search, because I look like a terrorist. Every 5'10" blonde haired blue eyed woman does.

"Crap, crap, crap!" I yelled. I looked in the couch cushions again. I haven't been myself lately. Ever since my boyfriend of two years, John, decided to whisk me away to Hawaii I've been in a dream world. I haven't been able to keep my mind on my work. Not that my work is very demanding. I work at a coffee house. But even my friends have mentioned that I seem to be "off in the clouds" somewhere. What do they expect though? I've tried not to say it out loud (don't wanna jinx it) but, I think he's going to propose. So, of course I'm excited!

The cab driver laid on his horn outside. "I'm coming!" I yelled out the door. "Damn keys." Well, I'll just lock up and have the landlord let me in next week when I get back from beautiful Hawaii. I grabbed my bag, my carry on, and flew out to the cab. It wasn't till I got me and my bags in the car that I realized I left my sunglasses inside my now locked house. "Damn!" I yelled. The cab driver stared at me, "I'm sorry. I'm running late. I lost my keys and my glasses..."

"Yes, yes I heard," he said. "Where am I going?"

"LAX please. And hurry if you can!"

I think he took that as a challenge. He sped away from the curb at the speed of light. I was so nervous that I couldn't help fidgeting. I kept cracking my knuckles and wringing my hands. I was ready to see John. He had been in Boston for the last week on business and I was really missing him. I pictured him waiting there: Tall, tanned skin, light brown hair falling across his dark blue eyes. He would see me and smile sweetly. Maybe he would get down on one knee right there in the terminal.

A huge pothole ripped me from my daydream. My cab driver's name was taped to the partition, but I couldn't pronounce it if I tried. He yelled what I assumed was a curse word in a language I couldn't decipher. A beautiful language none the less, I thought to myself.

He started heading away from Hermosa Beach, inland, and I started to panic. "You do know where LAX is, right?" I asked. I couldn't imagine a cabby in Southern California that didn't, but I do have that kind of luck, sometimes. He looked at me the way teenagers do when you ask them if they remember what time their curfew is.

"Yes, yes," he said, "I'm going to the freeway!"

"Won't that take us miles out of the way?"

"You don't want to be on Peach. There was an accident. All but one lane closed. The freeway will be faster!" he said.

"What's peach?" I asked

"Peach, peach," he yelled at me, clearly agitated.

"Oh, P.C.H," I said. I let a flush of embarrassment rise on my face. I started to fidget, again. P.C.H. ran through all the beach cities in Southern California then inland somewhere up towards Palos Verdes. You could get damn-near anywhere you needed to go in the beach cities by taking P.C.H. Not today though, I guess. I decided to just zone out and go back to my daydream.

John and I had the perfect relationship. We loved to do all the same things. Well, not all the same things. He did have a love for extreme sports that I didn't quite share. My attempts at Mountain Bike Riding, Hiking Arizona and Rock Climbing had left me bruised, beaten, sunburned and a little more afraid of falling from heights than I once had been. But I tried none the less. We both loved to read, but with him being a proofreader for a publishing house, that was kind of his job. Sunday mornings, we sat together and read the paper from cover to cover. We love to swim and cook gourmet food, and even took a class together; French foods 101. Hawaii was going to be wonderful. We share a love of history and nature, too. So this trip was going to be perfect for us. "Perfect," I said out loud, "everything is perfect."

The cab did a hard lunge to the left and I realized this was my cabby's version of merging. Another swear word I couldn't comprehend escaped him. But judging from the hand gesture out the window, I was pretty sure of its meaning.

I did tell my friend Fitz, that I thought John was going to propose. She was the only one to whom I confided this little inkling.

Her name is Sarra Fitzpatrick, but everyone calls her Fitz. Even her parents called her Fitzy. We had been best friends since kindergarten. That's when she told me I needed a best friend and she was willing to be that for me. Turns out Kindergarten is a tough place, what with the whole sharing thing being foreign to some kids and cooties everywhere. Sometimes you need a little muscle. Fitz was about an inch and a half shorter than me, but she had four older brothers and a kick ass attitude that I assume she was born with.

"What would you say if he did?" she asked, looking a little too concerned.

I paused for a moment to feel her out. "Yes, of course. I love him!" I finally said.

"Enough to spend your life with him?" she made the face. The one that lets me know she's completely grossed out, or slightly gassy.

"No, I thought we'd live in separate houses and e-mail."

"That's not what I mean Janie," she said with a look of absolute wonder. "I'm just saying, you moved straight from your parent's house in Manhattan five miles away to Hermosa. You've had a slew of bad relationships since the tenth grade… he's the first guy you've even dated for over a year."

"We've been together for almost two years," I corrected.

She made the face again but kept going without missing a beat. "There's so much out there you haven't seen or done. Are you sure this is the 'forever' guy?"

I paused. "Of course," I said, trying to sound totally confident. "We can do our living together. Who says you have to experience life alone to get anything out of it? Not only that… if you've found the right one why continue searching?"

It was no secret that Fitz and John didn't always see eye to eye. Fitz had been raised by a fun loving Irish Catholic family whose blood line boasted almost all boys. Because of that she had four older brothers. The joke when she came along was that dad's sperm was too old to produce another strapping young lad, so a girl emerged in their wake. Somehow this was funny in the Fitzpatrick family instead of offensive. Probably because even though Da had his boys, and he loved them well, he was absolutely head over heels with his baby girl. Da was 40 years old at the time of her birth. Not only did her parents adore her,

her brothers were very protective of the little sister they once tried to get to parachute off the second story roof with a bed sheet.

John had been an overly pampered only child in Fitz's belief. She hated the fact that he wasn't into family as much as we were. That, unfortunately, was true. We saw his parents three times a year and they only lived forty-something miles away in Malibu. My family had Sunday dinner together every week. Which was usually a tragic event (my family is a train wreck of sorts) that John missed quite often. I too was an only child but pampered was not a word used to describe me.

Every New Year's Eve the Fitzpatrick's throw a huge party. I hadn't missed one since I was six. But last year we had to go to John's boss's house for a little schmoozing, as he called it. He and two other 'suits' were in the running for a huge promotion. He needed me to make the impression that we were a young 'go getter' kind of couple, so I agreed to go. I had been a little more than upset when John, without asking or even consulting me, began to embellish my career. I work at a coffee house and somehow I became a Jr. V.P. of a chain of coffee houses. We were supposed to show up to the Fitzpatrick's party after dinner, but we never made it. John seemed fine at his boss's, but then developed a blinding headache on the way home. He said I could go on without him but I wouldn't dream of leaving him alone when he wasn't feeling up to par, especially on New Year's Eve.

But Fitz thought that he didn't want to come because he didn't want to play Bobbing for Beers again. Fitz's family owned the biggest pub in Southern California. 'The Bottom of the Barrel' was a well-known Fitzpatrick tradition done every New Year's Eve, and of course, St. Patrick's day. It's exactly what it sounds like. You submerge your head in a barrel full of water and bottled beer and try to extract them using nothing but your teeth. He thought the game was ridiculous and barbaric, but tried none the less, saying that, "Any idiot could do it!" He wasn't doing so well though and on his fourth attempt, the Fitzpatrick brothers decided to help him. I guess they held him under a little too long for his liking. I had tried to reassure him that Fitz's brothers were trying to help him, not kill him, but he said, "That is debatable."

Anyway, John got the promotion and was well on his way to becoming the bigwig he had always hoped to be. He even offered to take Fitz with us to a celebratory dinner for the occasion. But she said, "Being a third wheel at that dinner would be worse than having my teeth cleaned by a naked, nearsighted, eighty year old man with Parkinsons." I just told John she said, "Maybe some other time." She always had a very colorful, cut-the-crap, way of putting things.

I felt myself moving forward quickly, but I couldn't stop. I hit the partition face first, and hard! My cabby was in the terminal coming up on the Hawaiian Airlines when an old lady wearing a purple dress and a red hat, just stepped out in front of him. Clearly she was taking advantage of her right-of-way status. She lugged an old blue suitcase behind her on a cart. Suddenly a whole gaggle of older ladies wearing purple dresses and red hats were in the crosswalk. He started to curse again. I think.

"It's ok," I said, grateful to be at the airport in one piece. "I'll just walk to the next terminal."

He threw the car in park and said, "That will be $48.25."

I handed him $60.00, grabbed my suit case and ran. I looked at my watch and it was 2pm. Just made it. I already had my ticket so all I had to do was get my bag tagged and go through the metal detector. I hated those things. I was absolutely sure that someday I'd have a law suit against all the airlines and court houses I had been in when they discovered that those things caused cancer. I stood in line looking around for John.

He would most likely already be at our gate ready to board. We both hated being late, we hated it when people were late, so we weren't those people. Unfortunately, today, I was running real close to being one of THEM. My turn: I put my purse on the conveyer belt and held my arms out to my sides. Here came the wand of cancer. One pass in front and one in back…

"Take off your shoes, please."

"What?" I asked.

The very round woman repeated herself, this time with a little more gusto. "Take your shoes off, please!"

"Ok," I said, kicking them off and handing them to her. I wondered just what she thought I could hide in a pair of open toed sling backs.

She grabbed my shoes and shook them. She handed them back and said, "Next please."

"Oh, just a moment please, I was wondering where gate 5J was..."

"I'm not a directory, ma'am," she said, pointing to a wall map of the airport. "Next Please."

She was right, she was not a directory… she was a bitch. I had a private laugh and found the gate on the map. As I headed away I yelled back at her, "Have a nice day!" Never hurts to wish someone well, especially when they are meanies.

I walked to my gate and looked around. No John. Well, he may have been in the rest room. I found a seat and waited. I was a little nervous, or excited, I couldn't decide. In just a few hours we'd be in Hawaii. Beautiful sunsets, eating incredible foods and I might even get a marriage proposal. I started to fidget again. Oh, God, I thought. I better check my makeup. I dug through my purse and found my compact. "Oh shit..." I had a huge red line down my forehead and cheekbone from hitting the partition in the cab. I started to powder, but it was no use. I would just have to wait this one out. But, what the hell... right there on my forehead…a zit…why not a zit? I wanted everything to be perfect, so of course a zit! It looked like the kind that planned on gaining momentum, too. I dug for my sunglasses knowing I wouldn't find them, but it was worth a try. They're probably somewhere with my keys having a laugh at my expense. I dumped my purse out on the chair next to me. A compact, a wallet, mints-oh good, one of those couldn't hurt. I popped one in my mouth. Cell phone, charger for cell phone, condoms, tampons, just in case. (My period did what it wanted) Nail clipper kit (wasn't confiscated, kind of made me wonder) make up bag, mini hair brush, (didn't expect to find keys and didn't find keys) small picture book containing a picture of me and John, one of Fitz and me, another of mom and dad., and a small card that read, "It's All You Babe," that came with the first flowers John had given me. Well, the only flowers John had ever given me to be correct. He said he felt bad for killing a living thing to show me that he loved me. I had agreed with him at the time, but secretly missed the scent of the Stargazer Lily, my favorite flower. Nope. No glasses. I guess I'll have to buy a pair in Hawaii. Where is John?

I got up and went to the ladies room. A huge mirror, backlit with neon light, is not the best way to see yourself when you have a big red line on your face and a quickly growing zit in the middle of your forehead. I tried to comb my hair over the zit and the red mark. But, thanks to growing out my bangs, I looked like the dog from Lady and the Tramp. I couldn't pull off this look. Well, John had seen me look worse. He had come over once when I was sick. He left pretty quickly, though. "Don't want to catch your cold," he said. Made sense to me, after all we didn't want to pass it back and forth. Also, he had seen me with the most horrible sunburn ever. It peeled so badly I looked like a snake, sloughing my skin. He could bear with a red mark and zit. The cab ride would make for a funny story on the plane.

I decided to wash my hands since I had touched the door and who knows what kind of germs run rampant in an airport. I turned on the faucet and… "Shit!" I yelled. The water pressure was so high that it hit the sink and splashed up out of the bowl all over my white gauze skirt. "Damn it!" I shut the faucet off and tried to assess the damage. "You've gotta be kidding me," I said. I was soaked all the way down the front. I started to grab napkins and dry it as much as I could, but it was no use. The gauze material, ankle length skirt had soaked up the water like a sponge. I looked at myself in the mirror and all I could see was… my underwear. Clear as a bell. As if I wasn't wearing anything over them at all. I tried to pull my tank top down a little. No... It wouldn't pull down enough. A little more, I thought to myself. It was supposed to be one of those form-fitting-built-in-bra-tank tops. So at best, I was pulling it down and it was ridding right back up where the package said it promised to STAY when I bought it. I pulled one more time... and my boobs popped out the top. I guess the hidden bra could only do so much. I started to put my C's back in my shirt when a lady with a little girl, about four, walked in. She stared at me with a look of horror then covered the child's eyes before rushing her to the biggest stall in the ladies room. I guess finding a woman in the bathroom, apparently fondling herself, wasn't something she wanted her child to see. I finished tucking myself in, put my purse in front of the giant wet spot on my skirt and left the bathroom before she and the child could emerge from the stall. The bathroom was directly across from my gate so I sat there with a magazine on my lap trying to be as inconspicuous as possible. A minute later, the woman emerged with a huge wet spot on the front of her pants and a child with wet hair, who hurried off in another direction.

"The 3:00 to Hawaii will be boarding in twenty minutes," a voice called out over a loud speaker.

Where is John? I started to thumb through the magazine on my lap. 'Liz Taylor's Life Story and the Loves of Her Life', was the title. How sad. She must have had so many unhappy relationships. I paused and thought of her in her mansion, servants everywhere, surrounded by everything money could buy... but alone and miserable. Just proves, money can't buy you love.

Just then, I caught John in my sights. He was walking down the hall towards me wearing khaki slacks a white button down shirt with blue pinstripes and his calf-hide loafers. He was so handsome. He didn't bring any carry on? Usually he brings a book on flights, a light jacket, and his lap top, but I guess that's only on business trips. When he saw me, he slowed a little, took a deep breath and continued his approach. I stood to greet him, forgetting about the wet spot on my skirt. He stopped a couple of feet before me and said, "What happened to you?"

"Oh," I said picking up the magazine to cover myself, "It's a funny story..."

"Wait, sit down," he said, cutting me off mid-sentence. I sat as he took the seat next to me and grabbed my hand. Oh my God, was this it? Was he's going to propose right here, right now?

"What is it," I said in a coy voice, trying to prepare for screaming "YES" at the top of my lungs.

"I can't get on the plane," he said.

We had been through this once before when he had to take his first trip to New York. But after that flight he went to New York all the time on business and it never seemed to bother him. In fact, he seemed to love flying now. He loved New York too, and said we would go there in the fall.

"Oh honey, are you nervous? I can get you a Dramamine or some..."

"No. I can't get on the plane because I need to talk to you

about something." He took a long breath in and let it out slowly. This was his panic breathing.

I started to get a sinking feeling in my stomach and a wave of panic left my head swimming. I only heard a few key phrases. He sounded very far away.

"Great girl, but... thought I loved you, but...just come full circle…it's not you... it's me!" I was so dizzy and nauseated. Then I heard something that brought me back.

"Her name is Janine and we didn't plan for it to happen, but….."

He said Janine. But my name is Jane. Janie for cutes and parents...who the hell is Janine? I would have known the whole story had I been listening instead of having an out of body experience.

He wasn't about to spare me the details. Once again I floated off and only heard bits and pieces.

"Party at boss's... drank too much... drove her home…one thing led to another… felt really bad the next day... wanted to tell you..."

Slowly I came back to myself and found my voice. "Are you telling me that you had a fling with some Janine, girl?"

"It didn't start out that way. In the beginning it was...."

"In the beginning…?" I cut him off. "What beginning? How long has this been going on?" I asked, starting to hyperventilate.

He stammered and looked at the floor. This was not a good sign. Tell him it doesn't matter! Tell him you don't want to know! You don't want to know! Then he said it…

"Six months."

Now I just stopped breathing completely. I felt a deep ache in my chest.

"Fifteen minutes till boarding," the voice rang overhead again.

He finally looked me in the eyes. "I'm so sorry," he said. "I didn't mean for this to happen. It's better that I told you now, isn't it?"

My mind was spinning. "What do you mean, you didn't mean for this to happen? You didn't mean to cheat on me? You didn't mean to start a relationship with the woman you cheated on me with? You didn't mean to keep seeing me, dating me and sleeping with me…WHILE YOU WERE WITH HER! Or, do you mean, better you told me now than at your wedding, or maybe on your honeymoon? How can you say you didn't MEAN for this to happen, when you were the only person who could have changed it, or dare I say, avoided it happening in the first place."

"We're not talking about marriage, Janie."

"Don't do that!" I flared, coming back to myself. "Don't cute up my name! You have no right to be nice to me NOW! I can't believe this," I rambled. "How could you?" I pictured my heart being served by John to this faceless Janine person, holding a mallet instead of a tennis racket.

"Jane, I am sorry. Janine said that..."

At the sound of her name on his lips, I turned and bore holes into him with my eyes. "Amazingly enough I don't want to hear what Janine said. This wasn't supposed to happen! We're supposed to be boarding a plane right now, if you haven't noticed."

"That's kind of the other thing.... I need to get your ticket back," he said.

"What? Are you friggin kidding me? You're gonna take her? On the trip that we planned together! And I'm supposed to be fine with this? You must be out of your goddamned mind!" I yelled.

Heads and eyes flew in our direction. I didn't care. Let them look.

"Well, I did pay for the ticket and I promised her..."

"Oh you promised HER something, did you? Well hell, that's a totally different story, mean, you promised HER something! She must be here then...I mean, if you plan on taking her on MY vacation. Where is she?"

"I don't think it's a good idea for her to..."

"No, you're right!" I burst in. "It's not a good idea! None of this was a good idea. If you had any balls at all, you little worm.... you would have at least had the decency to break up with me before this! But here?" I said, using my arms to display where we were, "and now? Right before we're supposed to board…YOU ASSHOLE!" I yelled.

Now everyone was staring. Everyone but a very beautiful brunette model looking type that seemed to be bored by the display.

"That's her, isn't it? The bored model," I said, extending my hand to where she was standing.

"I don't know who you're referring..."

"Hey Janine," I yelled.

She looked at me with bored detachment.

"You can have him!"

I went to grab my purse and John reached a hand out and touched my arm. "Don't even try to comfort me now," I said, pulling my arm from his grip. "It's too late and..."

"No…I still need your ticket," he broke in.

Our eyes locked and I saw nothing in his. Not even the slightest sign of love, or caring, or compassion towards me. It was like looking at a complete stranger. But he wasn't a stranger, I reminded myself. I had been in a committed relationship with this guy for almost two years. Well, I was committed, I reminded myself.

"You want my ticket?" I asked, shaking so hard I was worried I would lose all control and deck him. "You want MY ticket? Fine," I said. "Buy it from me!" I hit him where it hurt. Money was always his driving force.

"Well, I bought the ticket in the first place," he said, with a little apprehension.

"You sure did. But you gave the ticket to me! It's mine now! Hey," I said, with what I assume must have been a crazed look on my face, "maybe I'll go to Hawaii with Janine!"

His face showed clear irritation now. "It doesn't seem fair that I…"

"Fair? It doesn't seem FAIR?" I interrupted again. "It doesn't seem fair, hum, you're right. Something about all of this shit doesn't seem fair, but I can't believe you're the one who somehow feels mistreated."

"3:00pm flight to Hawaii is now boarding," announced the hidden voice in the ceiling.

"You better make up your mind really quickly. You said this flight was sold out. Maybe she can go on ahead of you, huh? She looks like the kind of girl you could trust on a millionaire drenched, tropical island, ALONE! There'll be another flight in nine, ten hours or so," I said, looking at my watch.

"Here!" He clenched his jaw. "Here's what I paid for the ticket," he said, handing me $700.00.

"Oh, no," I said. "I'm afraid this ticket is going to cost you $2000.00."

"That's ridiculous! You can't charge $2000.00 for that ticket."

"Oh, I think I can. See, I'm charging not only for the ticket, but for the affair, the lying, not to mention the piss-poor way you decided to end things. Truthfully, I think you're getting off light, you asshole."

"Can you please not call me names? I am sorry."

"You've been cheating on me. For six months," I said, trying to fight back humiliated tears. "How about rotten bastard then, or piece of lousy shit, is that better?"

"I only have $1800.00 in my wallet."

"I'll take it," I said, grabbing the $1800.00 dollars and stuffed it in my purse. "You can mail me the rest." I dug the ticket from my bag.

Janine then walked over to where we stood. The audacity was awe-inspiring. She was beautiful. Not as tall as me but what she lacked in height, she made up for in body and balls, apparently. She had long dark hair and eyelashes over caramel brown eyes. Her suit was Dolce, her shoes were Prada, and I hated her. I stood there huffing trying to control my breathing. She didn't look at me or acknowledge me at all. I was nothing more than an irritating insect to her.

"Deeds you get z teekit? Eetz time fer uzz to board," she said, in an accent I couldn't place. What the hell was she? French? Italian?

I had a quick lived fantasy of me hitting her so hard, her nose split like a piece of over ripe fruit.

"Almost Bits," he replied, and smiled at her.

He calls her Bits? What kind of dumb ass name was that? I wondered if in her language, it meant bitch. No that's probably Beech, I concluded. For one moment, I honestly thought he was going to introduce us. I can't even imagine how that conversation would go.

"Um, Bits, this is Janie, the taller and blonder version of female anatomy that I was screwing before I met you. Oh, wait... I mean, while I was screwing you."

I had the immediate desire to bathe in acid.

She sauntered away, without once looking at me. It was the first time since Rene Callahan in the tenth grade that I had wanted to hit someone so badly. She had pantsed me during a football game at halftime in front of the whole school. I did hit her though. I knocked her right on her ass. Didn't even know I had it in me. And boy did I catch hell from my parents. I was grounded for a month, had detention for two weeks and had to apologize to Rene. And let's not forget the guilt. I was riddled with the guilt every good Irish Catholic girl was supposed to feel. I hadn't raised a fist to anyone since.

No, even this Janine person, who was definitely was a Beech, I couldn't bring myself to be mad at her. After all, there's no telling what he told her about me. He may have said I was a crazy stalker or an ex-girlfriend that he couldn't shake. No, I was mad at him. Then he did something so low, (and, given the situation, he had to work very hard to sink any lower in my book) he actually watched her walk away. He watched her ass sway from side to side with some stupid little grin on his face. No doubt locked in some sexual fantasy or memory they shared while he was still my boyfriend. I could have popped him one, right in the grin, but I knew I wouldn't. As much as he deserved it, and as much as I wanted to, I couldn't bring myself to be violent.

He looked back at me and said holding out his hand, "The ticket, please."

Instead, I uncurled my fist and looked him right in the face, as I ripped up the ticket. Over and over again, into smaller and smaller pieces, then threw it in his face.

"I'm pretty sure they'll still honor it," I said, trying to make my voice sound cold instead of shaken. "If not, I'm sure they have tape, you lying, cheating, bastard!" I yelled at the top of my lungs.

With that, I walked off to the ladies room with all of terminal 5J applauding in my wake. I had never caused a scene before, and yet, I found it impossible not to. It felt like a volcano was threatening to erupt inside me. I held my composure until the restroom door closed. Then...I fell apart…Big time.

I cried and cried until I couldn't breathe. At the fear of someone walking in and seeing my pathetic display, I went into a stall almost too small for a normal sized human, and locked the door behind me. I put my purse on the hook, which promptly slid off and fell to the floor, dumping its contents everywhere. I let out a frustrated half growl, half scream. I quickly tried to open the door to retrieve what had fallen out of reach and instead, I hit myself in the head with it, damn near knocking myself out. "Damn it," I yelled, just as the door opened. I stood there holding my head, make-up running down my face, hair and eyes wild from crying. It was the same lady from before, with the same child. She covered the child's ears and stared at me appalled. This time I wasn't embarrassed or polite. I yelled, "Get the fuck out of here!"She opened her mouth in shock, grabbed the child and ran out. I dropped to my knees on the green linoleum floor and started to scoop things into my purse.

The door opened again and I took a quick glance up. Hovering above me was the security guard from the metal detector. The badge on her ample breast read, Yolanda. She was a black woman about 5'8", round, in her 40's I would imagine. She wore too much blue eye shadow, but I think it was to offset the bright pink lipstick. If she was thirty years older, and white, she could be my Nana.

"I know, I know, I'm going," I said.

One hand reached down to me, "Come on, let's get you cleaned up."

I let her help me to my feet. "I'm kind of having a bad day," I said, sniffling.

"I know," she said, bending over to pick up a runaway lipstick tube. "Everyone in terminals 4 and 5 are talking about it."

I was horrified. "You're kidding?"

"No, and if it helps, everyone's on your side. They think he's a complete dickwod."

Oddly enough, it did kind-of help. I let a little smile emerged on my raccoon face.

She dropped the runaway lipstick tube into my purse. I tried to say, "Thank you," through my sniffles, but it came out, "Ank u."

She wrapped her arm around me and handed me a ball of wadded up Kleenex from her pocket.

I took the wad and blew my nose trying to sniffle back a sob.

"I gather from the rumor mill, you're either Janine or Jane."

"I'm Jane," I said, dabbing my eyes.

"Well, you know Jane, if I was you," said Yolanda, "I woulda kicked him in the junk!"

I nodded and sniffed again.

"Right in his jewels, then we'd see how much fun he has in Hawaii with his little tart after that."

I couldn't help but smile a little, "Yeah I missed a golden opportunity there I guess, huh?"

"Right in the junk!" she repeated. "I woulda gotten a running start at that shit and everything!"

Now I had to laugh at the mental image of Yolanda running full boar to drop a knee into John's sack.

I grabbed more napkins from the wall dispenser and took a look in the mirror. Quickly I had gone from a raccoon to Alice Cooper. Oh Lord, I thought, trying to rub my mascara from my cheeks. I placed the napkin under the faucet and turned it on, once again getting completely soaked.

"Shit," I yelled, backing up. "What the hell is wrong with this place?"

Miss Yolanda came up and hugged me. I let her. I needed a hug.

"Do you want me to escort you to your car, honey?" she asked.

"I don't have a car here. I took the cab ride from hell," I said, trying to get my breathing back to whatever normal was. "Oh my God," I yelled, "my baggage is on its way to Hawaii!"

"Shh Shh Shh, don't worry about that. We'll get your luggage taken care of," she soothed like a mommy. "Do you need to call someone for a ride?"

I shook my head, "God no. I'll take a cab." The only people available to pick me up would want to talk about why I wasn't on a plane to Hawaii.

"I'll get you a cab. Wait here, I'll be right back. You try and get some of the make-up off of your face. She opened the door to leave and said, "Maybe you should put on some sunglasses, or something."

I just stared at her as she disappeared out the door. "Yeah, why didn't I think of that?" I said to no one.

Yolanda came back a few minutes later and said, "I have a cab waiting outside the Security Exit Door so you won't have to walk out in front of everyone. Also, I told the cab driver that you're here for your great aunt's funeral and you're distraught, so he won't wonder about the tears and all. You know men don't do well with tears." She walked me through an internal maze of 'off limits' corridors, out a private exit door where a cab was waiting.

"Here," she said handing me a phone number. "This is who you call about your baggage. They'll make sure it gets back to you."

I was so grateful for the kindness of this complete stranger, I gave her another hug and said a "Thank you again." I angled into the cab for what I hoped would be an uneventful ride home.

"You're gonna be alright girl," she said, winking at me before closing the door.

I told the cabby, whose name read Mr. Abobo on his license, that I was going to Monterey Blvd. in Hermosa Beach. We headed out of LAX when I could be herd to yell, "Oh Shit!"

I startled the cab driver from his peaceful fare, causing him to jump in his seat.

"Sorry, Sorry," I said, trying to sound as apologetic as possible. A new realization had set in. How the hell was I going to get in my house? I locked my keys and sunglasses somewhere in the house. Correction, I lost my keys and sunglasses somewhere in my house. Fitz had a key, and so did my mother, but I wasn't ready to explain what had happened. So...I decided to call my landlady, Betty.

By now it was almost 4pm which meant that she was already half way to drunk. She lived right on the strand in Hermosa Beach and thought it was her personal duty to catch every sunset. Of course, she was passed out shortly thereafter. She was a slight woman, maybe 5'2", in her sixty's with lots of bleach-blonde hair that she piled on top of her head or in a ponytail. She had the longest pink nails I had ever seen, and Cotton Candy was her signature color. Her skin had been tanned to a golden brown so many times, that she had a leathery, Marlboro Man hue about her. She chain smoked Benson and Hedges Ultra Light 100's, but she still looked good in a bikini and didn't care who knew it. Betty was from the Great South. The drunker she got the more pronounced her accent became. She was even known to let out Yee Ha's and Ya'lls. She always seemed genuinely happy to see me though, even if she did call me Sugar or Puddin, most of the time. I wondered if she even knew my real name without looking at my rental agreement.Once upon a time she had a wealthy husband, fifteen years her senior. Apparently, a few years ago, a sack ride with her had sent him to that great round up in the sky. But her Bubba had left her everything, so she loaded up the truck and headed west. She bought several properties in the area, including my house. I wasn't sure if she gave all of her renters a break, if she was too drunk to know the property value of said houses, or if she just didn't need the money, but I rented a two bedroom house, six blocks from the beach for $500.00 a month, water and garbage included. This was unheard of, so it was worth the little inconveniences. Like her forgetting to call the plumber when my shower backed up or paying the sanitation bill on time so my garbage got picked up every week. In truth, she was a nice woman from what I knew of her.

"Damn," I waited for her message machine to pick up.

"Hey ya'll," I heard, "I'm not home right now, but you leave me a message, sugar, and I'll get back to you as soon as I can. Yee Haw."

I swear there's a cow bell ringing in the background of that message. I slammed my cell shut. (Yes, I still have a flip phone. Don't judge)

"Shit!" I yelled again. My cabby looked back at me in the rear view mirror and gave me a disapproving look. "Sorry," I said, with a wave of my hand.

If all else failed mom still had a key, but I didn't want to talk to her yet. She had just as many 'high-hopes' for my relationship with John as I once had. My mother is a good... no...well she's a half-ass Catholic. She believes in the sanctity of marriage and children. Mass on Christmas Eve, is a given. "There is no reason for divorce," she had said my whole life. Not because it's a sin, but more of a "You made your bed," kind of thing. An unmarried woman in this day and age, "It's just too much temptation," as she put it. And, "If not for marriage why did God create us at all?" I loved her, but right now, I would have rather scooped out my own intestines with a rusty spoon than talk about where I, and the relationship, had gone so horribly wrong. I wanted to wallow, not self-examine. The truth is, the anger had worn off a little and now, I was just feeling humiliated, brokenhearted and dehydrated.

There was still Fitz. She had a key, too. Sometimes she would use my house to escape an obsessed boyfriend. That's if the guy was too nice for her to sick her brothers on. Truth was, Fitz didn't need her brother's help with unruly men. She was an acrobat and a first rate kickboxer. Growing up the only girl in a house of 'spirited Irish boys,' she needed an edge. Truth be told none of those boys, now grown men, wanted to piss her off. I think it's more likely that she stayed at my house so often because it's clean. Her roommate B.J. is just as messy as she is. They would wait each other out from time to time in the cleaning department. I wanted to call her but I didn't at the same time.

I knew when I told Fitz she would say, "Good riddance," yell at me for not hitting him, and then she would start plotting revenge. Every woman should have a friend like Fitz, but all I wanted... was to be alone. Curl up in my jammies and watch sad movies till I finally cried myself to sleep. Well, on the bright side, I had plenty of cash. I could just stay in this cab forever if it weren't for the smell; Kind of a garlic/curry/floral scent.

"Can you please take me to Second Street on the Hermosa Strand," I asked my cabby. I was going to search out Betty.

The cab driver waited for me with the meter running. As I skirted the stucco modern two story, that belonged to Betty, I could hear her talking. She was on her back patio that butted up to the 'The Strand' with some of the local boys. She saw me and yelled, "Well hells bells…it's Puddin!"

That's me, I thought. I'm Puddin. I attempted a smile.

"Hey Betty," I said walking up the stairs to her lower patio. "I was wondering if you..."

"My stars in heaven child! What the hell happened to you?"

I saw myself the way she must have. Hair messed, eye make-up all over, red mark down the middle of my face, (a souvenir from cab ride number one), a wet skirt, that was finally drying and the zit, don't forget the zit. Which had doubled in size, I'm sure.

"I, ugh... I've had kind of a bad day."

The guys sitting at the table all turned to look at me. By the looks on their faces, I could tell I wasn't going to win any beauty contests today. They were all in their thirties, tattooed, tanned, and having drinks with Betty. What the hell is wrong with this picture? I thought. Oh God! My mind went somewhere it shouldn't. Which one of these guy's was going to get drunk enough to sleep with a woman 25 years older than him? Well... more power to her, I concluded.

"I need the spare to my house. I locked my keys inside, so..."

"So you had a car drag you here behind it?" she asked in a whisper.

"I know. I look like hell," I said, resigned to the fact.

"Come inside, I'll find the key."

I followed her inside. I had never really been in Betty's house before. It was gorgeous. She had white carpet that was so thick, my feet sank when I walked. A redwood staircase led to the second floor and the observation deck. She walked into the gourmet kitchen and I followed behind her. It was spectacular. Redwood cupboards and green marble counter tops wrapped their way around the room. It was immaculate. It looked as if no one had ever cooked in there. I'm sure she had a maid but, there was nothing on the counters. Even the coffee pot looked unused. She started to riffle through a drawer.

"I know I have one, Puddin. I just have to give you the right key to the right house."

I moseyed into the dining room which had a wet bar. Now that had been used, I thought. Everywhere, were pictures of Betty and her Bubba, doing everything. In one they were hang gliding. Another was of the two of them at the Jack Daniels Distillery raising their glasses and smiling. There was one of them on horseback, at what I assumed had been their Ranch down South. Then I saw it. The two of them with one of the biggest Bubba's of all…Bill Clinton. They all looked hammered, toasting the camera. There was a disapproving looking Hillary, standing in the background with her hands on her hips. Funny, I had always pictured her as a stern and disapproving woman.

Betty came around the corner and saw me gaping at the picture.

"Yeah, he's a hoot," she said, smiling. "But that was taken when he was still a Governor. The pictures we got with him when he was president, well, the Secret Service destroyed those." I gave her a look of absolute horror.

"No, no honey. Not that! My stars!" she laughed.

"Then I don't know what you're talking about," I said, truly baffled.

"We all inhaled, Sugar," she said. "Everyone forgets about scandal number one since that Monica thing. But I gotta tell ya, I knew Hillary and because of that, I could never blame him for straying. That woman is a cold fish. Sad really," she said with a little, half drunk look of pity. "My husband said if he'd been stuck with a woman like her he woulda put his head in the oven."

I couldn't help but wonder if Hillary felt the same way about Bill. Were they going to find her someday with her head in the oven? No, more likely he'll have a hunting or boating accident. After all, Hell Hath No Fury, right?

She held up the key to my house. When I went to grab it, she put it behind her back and said, "Do you wanna tell me what happened?"

I let my eyes drop to the floor and shook my head no.

"Alright then," she said. "But if you ever wanna talk, Puddin, I'm a good listener." She held out her arms to embrace me, and I let her.

Soon, I was back in the cab with Mr. Abobo heading home. When we arrived he got out of the car and told me, "Cab ride $86.00 not including tip. He held out his hand. I searched my purse for my new found fortune. I handed him $120.00 and told him, "Keep the change."

Then Mr. Abobo hugged me and said, "Many apologies for your loss." He held me captive in the awkward hug for long enough to make me clearly uncomfortable, then let me go saying, "Put a tea bag on that zit." With that, he got in the cab and drove away leaving me standing in the street wishing a large truck would just run me over.

I entered my house and plopped down on the sofa. Pictures of John were staring at me from every direction. There was one of us on the bookshelf taken at our cooking class. One of us on our sailing trip sat on the desk. Not to mention the large one on the wall, the only picture on my walls, of him and the fish he caught on that fateful trip. And there I was, standing in the back-round, red as a lobster. I was his Hillary, I thought. Four hours ago I had a boyfriend, a trip to Hawaii and some self-esteem. Now, I was dumped in front of terminal 5, had a red line down my face and a zit which required its own zip code. Oh, and the $1680.00 I had left that I had blackmailed out of John for my plane ticket. Nope, by my calculations, I was still a loser.

With every bone in my body I wanted to call Fitz. I wasn't ready to talk about it though. I wasn't ready to say out loud that, "John dumped me." And I really wasn't ready to say that, "John had dumped me for another woman." Or how about the fact that he had been "Having an affair for six months." Six months, I thought to myself…all of the business trips…all of his deadlines and late nights at the office? Jesus, I was an idiot, an unsuspecting, trusting idiot.

I went and grabbed my comforter off my bed, drug it to the

kitchen and grabbed the open bottle of Merlot off my counter… no glass needed, and brought them back to the sofa that I intended to wallow on. I pulled the cork out with my teeth and turned on the TV. 'You've Got Mail' was on, one of my favorite movies. I took a long pull off the bottle and wished that I was Meg Ryan. She was so cute that even a man, destined to ruin her shop and take her lively-hood, fell in love with her. The 'happily-ever-after' was implied at the end of the movie. I remember grabbing the second bottle of wine from the fridge, mixing red and white. I remember opening it. I remember sitting on the floor and sobbing. I remember calling about my luggage and picturing it sitting on the beach with a Mai Tai, looking at a beautiful sunset. And then I remember... daylight.

2

SAT: DAY ONE OF DUMPED

I woke at 7a.m. and dragged my ass to the bathroom with the intention of shaving my tongue. Then I looked in the mirror. Yep, still a dumped raccoon with a huge zit. I hadn't even tried to take off the make-up last night, instead deciding to look as bad as I felt. I found one of my many toothbrushes that I always bought in a handy four pack. I proceeded to brush the wine away. Then I started to baby oil my face to remove the rest of the waterproof mascara off my cheeks. Won't smudge my ass, I thought. I had just started re-brushing my teeth when I heard my front door open with a click of a key. Oh shit, I thought. Please God, let it be a robber, I begged. Anyone but my mom! It was Fitz.

"What the hell? Who's here?" she growled.

She was coming towards the bathroom. With her unmistakable Irish accent and true gusto, she said, "I'll kick the shite out of anyone who's in here!" I knew she would, too. I tried to say something before she came around the corner, but I couldn't spit out the toothpaste from my cotton mouth fast enough. She threw a kick coming around the corner that caught me under the jaw. Toothpaste flew from my mouth as I was knocked backwards into the tub. I tried to catch myself on the shower curtain, but to no avail. I and the curtain went down hard. She came around the corner and saw me lying in the tub holding my raccoon face with the shower curtain in my lap.

"What the hell are ya doin' here?" she asked, racing to my side. "Yer supposed to be in Hawaii!"

All I could do was let out a heavy sigh before I started to cry. "He dumped me," I garbled through my tears. I let my aching jaw drop to my chest and began really sobbing.

Fitz climbed into the tub and wrapped her arms around me. "What? That bugger did what?" she asked, arching her eyebrows.

"He dumped me, Fitz," I said, making tiny fists of anger. "Right there in terminal 5. In front of what could have been the whole world for all I know!"

I explained the whole thing to her; Cab ride #1, to the terminal, to the break-up, to Janine, to the bathroom, to Yolanda, to the lost bag, to Betty's, to the very inappropriate cab ride #2. All the way up to the point where she kicked me in the jaw. After all was revealed all she could say was, "Ya make that zit sound a lot bigger than it is."

She helped me out of the tub and examined my jaw. "Didn't catch ya square…you're lucky! I coulda done some real damage instead of just a little bruise."

Did she just say that I was lucky? I thought.

"What?" I said, moving to the mirror to look at my quickly bruising jaw line. Great, now I had a red mark down my face, a huge zit on my forehead, and a bruise beginning across my jaw. "Shit," I slumped down on the toilet seat, "I'm starting to look as beat up as I feel!"

"When was the last time ya ate?" she asked.

I shook my head, "Yesterday morning, I guess. Unless you

count the two bottles of wine and a patch of carpet where I slept face down, food?"

"Let's get ya fed," said Fitz.

"I'm really not hungry Fitz. I just want to go back to bed."

"Well, I need food," she said, "and I'm not leavin' you here like this, to wallow! Let's get ya dressed. I'll pick out some clothes for you." She brought me back a pair of spandex work-out shorts and a halter top.

"Really?" I asked, taking the clothes from her and holding them up. "Are you kidding me with this? I'm not wearing this outside. I don't even know why I own spandex shorts."

"Suit yourself, but you're not gonna to find a new man dressed like a frump."

I just stared, wanting so badly to hate her.

She smiled, "Just kiddin'," and handed me my 501's and a T-shirt.

I checked out the zit and the bruise in the mirror. On the bright side, I couldn't look more like hell, nowhere to go but up from here.

We walked down towards Hermosa pier. I felt so conspicuous, like everyone knew I had been dumped. Maybe there was a scent I was putting off. Truth be told, I probably was. I hadn't showered since the day before. Unless you count my sink bath at the airport and I had been drinking and crying all night.

"Wait," I said as we passed a street vendor, "I need a pair of sunglasses. I can't find mine anywhere."

I tried on 5 or 6 pairs before I realized that it really didn't matter what they looked like. I didn't care. I bought a pair of the darkest $5.00 glasses I could find. They were "Mad Dog" knock-offs and I looked ridiculous in them. I took some comfort in the thought that no one would look good in these. We continued on our journey to my favorite little Italian bistro a block off the pier, Sarducci's.

It was a come-as-you-are kinda place. You know the kind of place where rich executive types would rub elbows with guys in surf gear and wet suits. They had kick ass cuisine at a reasonable price. On a Saturday morning they were slammed. Just what the doctor ordered. A place crammed to the rafters with the rich and beautiful. And today I was neither. We didn't wait for a seat inside. Instead we took a table on the patio. The size one, seventeen-if-she-was-a-day, year old waitress who sat us, said in her Italian accent, "Wouldz zou like to ear our speeecials?" I shook my head no. She handed us our menus and walked away.

"Does everybody have a fucking accent these days? Is no-one from the fuckin valley, anymore?" I asked, agitated.

"Don't blame the accent," Fitz said defending her own Irish accent. "It's not her fault that your Ex is a piece of lousy shite!"

"Yeah, I know," I said, looking towards the beach.

"Besides, as painful as it is for ya, I'd think you'd be happy to have him gone. He wasn't for you, Janie. He always did whatever he wanted without a thought to what you wanted or liked. There was a lot of take and not much give on his part. I opened up my mouth to defend, well... I think myself, but she interrupted.

"No Janie," she said, "Think about it! You took a cooking class together, it's true. But if I remember correctly you were already signed up for the Italian course. But he didn't want to take Italian Cooking so he talked you into taking the French food class, instead."

Hmmm, French I thought to myself. If I wasn't mistaken, he had been taking French for the last six months. "I learned how to make a great duck," was all I said out loud.

"Yes, yes, I know," she paused, but only for a moment. "And what about all those hikes? You wanted to do the

California Hikes, did ya not? Up in the forests with lakes and rivers? But he wanted to do all those hikes in Arizona." She shot me a side long look. "Ya know…the ones that almost killed ya. Ya dehydrated on that trip, did ya not? And then he got ya lost in a desert like a wandering Jew. Hell, even the wandering Jews we know thought that was stupid. And all that sailin', that fuckin' sailin'," she went on, "you hate bein' out on the water," she yelled. I noted that once again people were staring.

"I ended up liking it…kind of," I said, in what was supposed to be my defense.

"Yer scared to death of the ocean," she wailed. "And if I remember it correctly, you ended up in the fuckin' water after the boom got ya. Ya had a concussion, didn't ya? Jesus Janie, all I'm saying is, ya kinda lost yerrself there. You started carin' more about his wants, his needs than your own. You invested two years in becomin' nothin' more than his perfect Ex. I felt tears welling up behind my glasses.

She reached out and took my hand in hers. After a brief pause, she posed the question, "Do you know that you've been dumped 16 times in 10 years?"

"What the hell?" I said, shaking my head and dabbing under my glasses with my napkin. "What? Have you been keeping track of my pathetic love life?"

"No, no. I'm just countin' 'em up now. First was Dave, then Billy, then that Andre fellow with the green hair...," she went on.

"Great. Now I feel like a dumped slut."

"Oh, ya can't be a slut now, Janie," she chided. "Ya didn't even sleep with most of 'em. If I'm not mistakin', that's why Dave broke up with ya. He got tired of waitin' for your legs to open!"

"Did he tell you that?" I asked horrified.

"No, but I think the fact that he dumped you for Angie

Adams, the biggest slut in our town, may have given ya some indication."

"So, which am I then, a slut or a prude?" I said, with a heat rising in my face.

"You're neither. You've just had a bad row with men. It's like your cursed or somethin'."

"Hey, you aren't exactly in a relationship either."

"Yes, but I don't want to be, do I? I'm not the one who's been lookin' for true love and thinkin' of the kids the house and the dog. I'm not even sure I'll ever want those things. But you do, Janie! And, you've dated a slew of losers trying to find that very thing."

She stopped when she saw a tear run out from underneath my glasses. I couldn't speak anymore. She was right and nothing I could say would change that. There was a long pause where neither of us said a word.

Finally she spoke, "I'm sorry, Janie."

"Are you sorry for what you said? Or are you sorry for being right?"

"I hate to be right if it means I hurt you. I love you," she said, and squeezed my hand again.

She did love me… and I her. Besides, maybe she was right, in a way. I couldn't help but start adding it up in my head too. She was right. Sixteen failed relationships, all of which I was the one getting the "It's not you, it's me!" speech.

The young waitress came back and took our order. A half hour later, I had watched Fitz eat all the Spin Dip and I had finished my Bloody Mary. It took the edge off the headache behind my eyes. I couldn't figure out if it was the residual from the wine or all of the crying I had done the night before.

Fitz excused herself to the ladies room and came back with a piece of paper and a pen.

"What's the paper for?" I asked as she sat down.

"I want you to make a list."

"A list of what?" I asked.

"Of all the things you like. And on the opposite side, all the things you don't."

"What? Like about myself?" I asked.

"Sure," she said. "About yourself, or what you like in men or don't like, whatever. Find out what you want, Janie. What you need...what you care about."

"It's too soon for this," I said, backing away from the table.

"Fine," said Fitz, backing her own chair away from the table. "It's too soon. But promise me you will do it."

I extended my pinky finger and locked it with hers. A pinky promise was like a blood oath between us.

"I will, I promise," I said, standing. "But now, I've got to go tell my mother what happened and why she won't be having grandkids."

"You still haven't told your mother?" She asked, shocked.

"No, I wanted to wallow not self-examine," I said, shooting her a shitty look.

"I wondered why she wasn't there cleanin'. That's her M.O. isn't it? Well, I suppose I should go too and face the music with ya. After all, it's all due to my bad influence that you aren't married with children already, ya know."

I let out a little giggle at what she said, but it was true in a way. My mother had blamed everything that I had ever done wrong in my life on my friendship with Fitz.

When we were 12, Fitz had swiped two cigars from her dad and brought them to my play house. We smoked them and got really sick. If we had been smarter we wouldn't have blown the smoke out of the little window. Maybe then my mother wouldn't have called the fire department thinking the playhouse was a blaze. Then Fitz wouldn't have thrown up on my mother's new couch while she was reprimanding us. We hadn't been able to see each other outside of school for a month after that. Would have been longer but my father convinced mother that kids do dumb things and that's what childhood was all about. All these years later, we were still best friends and still doing dumb things together. And my mother still hated that we were.

We started back to my house. When we rounded the corner I stopped dead in my tracks. My mother's gold Caddy was in the driveway behind my silver Dodge Neon.

"Damn," I said, somewhat defeated. I dropped my head and continued walking to the house.

"Oh," said Fitz, looking at the car. "This should be loads more fun than ringing her." "Mom," I yelled. A mix of bleach and lemony disinfectant ambushed us as we entered.

Mom was in the kitchen cleaning the two glasses I had left in the sink. She turned, saw my face and fell apart. She started sobbing and I knew she was saying something but I couldn't make it out. She made her way over and wrapped her arms around me.

"What happened?" she started. "What went wrong? What did you do?" she asked.

What did I do? That's what she asked me? What did I do wrong? That thought bounced around in my head, as she rambled on, clinging to me. I turned towards Fitz with an exhausted hurt look that I couldn't hide. Fitz was wearing a sardonic smile on her face. The smile that said, "If you weren't her mother…I'd be kicking your ass right now."

"Oh I can't believe this happened," my mother wailed, burying her head in my hair.

"Maybe you two can work it out? Maybe you just need some time? Maybe you…"

"Mom, he dumped me for another woman," finally escaped my mouth.

She lifted her head and looked me in the eyes. "What? No, I talked to him and he didn't mention anything like that."

"What do you mean you talked to him? When?"

"I called last night to make sure you made it ok, but you never answered your phone. I started to get worried. So, after I called the airline and they told me that the flight had made it in ok, I called his cell phone. He didn't answer till this morning and then he told me you two broke up and you never went to Hawaii."

Of course he didn't answer the phone, I thought, he was getting laid on a white sandy beach, by a Beech.

I looked over at Fitz, who looked as exasperated as I felt. Mom was still talking. "Then I came here to find you but, you weren't here and your phone was, and I was so worried," she sobbed. "He didn't say he left you for another women. Not to me!"

"Mom, why would he?" I asked, doing a palms up. "If he's done with me, doesn't that mean he's done with you too?"

"Well, are you sure?"

"Actually mom"...I said, flopping down on my couch, "I had the pleasure of making her acquaintance. So, yeah, I'm sure."

"He brought her with him to...break-up with you?" She looked absolutely dumbfounded again.

I let my jaw unclench, "Well he kind of had to I guess....since she was using my ticket to go to Hawaii with him and all."

She stood there, solid as stone. Then finally she said, "He gave her your ticket?"

"Yes mom. He broke up with me and took her in my place."

"He took some chippy he barely knows."

I interrupted her. As fun as it was to go over all of this again, piece by piece and relive it, I had to let her in on the punch line. "He's been seeing her for six months."

Once again, she went stone faced. "And you didn't know?" she asked.

"Ahh come on, mom," I said, throwing my hands up in the air.

She did a palms up, indicating that she really didn't understand why what she had said was so wrong, "What did I say?"

"Of course I didn't know," my voice rising. "Do you honestly think if I had known it wouldn't have been OVER six months ago?"

Fitz, who was no longer amused by any of this, sat down on the couch and turned on the TV.

My mother and I both turned our heads to look at her. She looked up wide eyed and said as innocently as she could muster, 'You've Got Mail', is on. I love Meg Ryan."

After I explained the whole sorted, embarrassing and painfully humiliating story to my mother, she said, "I know a nice boy."

I put my hands in my hair and wondered just how much strength would it take to pull out every last blonde lock. Then I wondered if Sinead O' Conner had ripped her hair out after a conversation with her mother.

"I don't want to go on a date mom. I just want to be left alone. In fact, the whole male race can kiss my ass right now!"

"Janie that is not appropriate talk for a lady in such a delicate condition such as yours!"

"What delicate condition?" I yelled. "I got dumped! I'm not knocked up!"

"That's the kind of talk I would expect from other women," she said with a head tilt towards Fitz, "Not you!"

I turned my head towards Fitz in a questioning manner.

"Me! She means me." Fitz said, never taking her eyes from the TV. "Don't ya Mrs, O?" That was short for Mrs. O'Connelly, our last name. Fitz had been calling my mother Mrs.O since we were in the tenth grade. Somehow, mom never seemed to get the implication of what or who "O" was. Or why it was so damned funny, given my mom's stringent personality.

My mother let out a little huff and walked back to the sink.

Fitz sat there smiling from ear to ear, very amused with herself, indeed.

After my mother cleaned the house she left. She kissed me on the cheek and said, "Are you sure you don't want to stay with your dad and me for a few days? I can have your old room dusted and clean sheets put on the bed in no time."

"No mom, I'm okay. Or at least I will be," I said, giving her a kiss goodbye.

"Ok, but dinner tomorrow night, 6pm," she said with a nod.

For some reason, I thought being on vacation meant I wouldn't have to go to Sunday night dinner, but I wasn't in the mood to try and explain what I'm sure would end up in more tears and my eventual caving in anyway.

"Of course mom," I said, "dinner at six." I waved to her as she pulled her gold Caddy away from the curb. I didn't have the heart to tell her that her car looked like something a pimp would drive.

I walked back in the house and plopped down on the couch next to Fitz. "That was exhausting," I said. "Thanks for being here. It could have been much worse if you weren't."

"Worse than that?" Fitz asked, surprised.

"Yeah, she would have cried harder if you hadn't been here."

"Jesus-Mary and Joseph, I thought she'd never stop cryin' as it was. Not to change the subject mind you, but what are ya doin' tonight?" she asked.

"Nothing," I said. "I don't want to do anything except crawl in my jammies, watch sad movies and maybe eat a gallon of Ben & Jerry's."

"Well," said Fitz, "maybe you should pop down to the pub with me?"

I started to shake my head vigorously, "No, no. I'm not ready for that. Not people and laughter..."

"Just hear me out...you haven't been to the pub in a really long time. It'd do ya good if ya came along."

Fitz, her brothers and parents had moved here from Ireland when she was five. Thanks to some very skillful investing, they bought several homes, businesses and a bar right off the strand in Hermosa. Prime Real Estate, I believe is the term for it. My mother had always hinted at the fact that the Fitzpatrick's were connected, as in The Irish Mafia or some such nonsense. As for the bar, they turned it into the most successful pub in all of Southern California. Several movies, videos and such had been filmed there. It was a real tourist trap at times. Truth be told, Fitz didn't have to work a day in her life. Not only was she part owner of the pub, but her parents made her and the boys equal partners in a sixth of everything the family had invested in. She was also a local celebrity of sorts. Her long flaming red hair, white skin and green eyes had landed her the face of Fitzpatrick's. She was their cover girl since before she was old enough to legally be in the pub. Currently, she was modeling for huge companies and magazines as well as commercials and publicity for the pub. My mother had always said the Fitzpatrick brood should have moved to Beverly Hills, but Fitz's mom, (Mum, as I was to call her) wouldn't hear of being that far from the ocean or the pub.

"I don't feel like being around people," I said, pouting and feeling justified in doing so.

"We'll hole up in the pool room, but at least you'll be out of the house. I'll play you some stick for the money you took from dopey."

Normally, kicking her ass at pool would be right up my alley, but not tonight. "I just don't feel like it, Fitz."

"You can't sit here all night alone and watch Meg Ryan movies. You'll kill yerself! Plus…what about our tradition? We have to carry out the tradition!"

I was shaking my head no, but I knew she was right. Since Tommy Reynolds dumped me in the tenth grade we've had this tradition. I still remember us sitting on the floor in her room with a bottle of, as she called it, "Shitty champagne," that we swiped from her parent's fridge, and a black forest cake. When my boyfriend stood me up for my birthday dinner, I had shown up at her house with puffy make-up smeared eyes, and my birthday cake in tow. We sat there, half crocked, cake all over the place, me crying and her telling me what a bastard he was. She popped the tires on his Schwinn Cruiser the following Monday. We had been through several break-ups (most of them mine) and this was how we moved on, shitty Champagne and Black Forest Cake.

"Come on," she pleaded. "I'll pick up the cake and the champagne, everything. Just show up."

I wasn't going to win this one, and I knew it. One way or another, the tradition had to be carried out. I guess that was the part that really bothered me. After the cake and champagne, it meant that my relationship was really over and I had to accept it. I had really lost another one. I was the Doctor Kevorkian of relationships.

"What time should I arrive?" I said, with the most defeated tone anyone has ever heard.

"Be there at nine," she said. "I'll have everything ready to go by then." She gave me a quick hug then took off out the door saying, "Nine o'clock, Janie."

I made a half ass attempt at a smile then started to close the door. Suddenly, I was aware of what she had said. "I'll have everything ready by then?" I repeated it to myself. What the hell could that mean, I wondered? We wouldn't carry out the tradition at the pub. The tradition isn't complete until one of us passes out drunk and I had no desire to spend the night on Grandpa Fitzpatrick's pull out couch in the upstairs office. Not again.

I looked at the clock and it was just past one. It seemed like a whole day had gone by and it had only been a couple hours. Shit this was going be a long day. I plopped back down on the couch and turned on the TV. Sleepless in Seattle was just starting. I pulled the comforter over my head and went to sleep.

When I came to it was 6:30. I had to force myself off the couch and find something to wear to tonight's festivities. All the cute new outfits I bought for Hawaii were right where they were supposed to be. In Hawaii! I was having a worse vacation than my luggage. The thought actually amused me somehow. I found a pink and white dress that I may have worn if I had been feeling better about myself. But in the end, I grabbed my 501's and an old T-shirt. My most comfortable stand by. I jumped in the shower which I noted that my mother had cleaned. It wasn't dirty to begin with, but now it shined and a slight odor of bleach hung in the air. Irish Spring my ass! Irish mother's clean with bleach. I washed and shaved. Well, I shaved my legs up to the knee and my underarms. I had my first bikini wax the day before yesterday so that I would look well kept in and out of my suit. Fitz had been trying to get me to get a Brazilian wax for as long as I could remember, but I had no desire to look like a prepubescent girl. But Fitz had won that one argument too, saying, "You're gonna be in a swim suit sixty percent of the time and naked the other twenty percent. Do you really want to spend time shavin'?"

"I can't help but notice my coochie has no plans for the remaining twenty percent of the day."

"I'd like to think you'll have your coochie completely covered for meals," she laughed.

Now what did it matter? It cost me $75.00 to remove all the hair from a part of my body no one would even see. F.Y.I... A bikini wax does not remove the hair gently from the follicle as the teenage desk bimbo would have you believe. It rips it from your body the way a doctor might rip a stubborn child from your womb. I know, slightly exaggerated, but the aforementioned is slightly under exaggerated.

I came out of the shower reluctantly. I kept thinking, if I just kept my head raised, like a turkey when it rains, I would drowned and not have to go to the pub. Why didn't I just tell Fitz, "No?" Well, I guess I had. And then I gave in like I usually did when it came to her. I guess in some strange way, I trusted her to always make things right for me. After all, she had been doing it for a long time. She called at 7:30 just to make sure, as she put it, "That my ass was awake and getting ready."

"Do you want me to fetch ya?" she asked.

The pub was only eight blocks from home. "No," I said. "I'll walk."

"You're sure? I can come grab ya."

"No I'm fine. The walk will do me good."

"You'll be here at nine then?"

"Yes, I said I would. What the hell's going on, Fitz?" I asked.

"Nothing, don't be so paranoid."

"Ugh huh," I said, and hung up.

I pulled on my jeans and was grateful that I hadn't packed them for my trip. They were my favorite pair. I was tall for a woman, 5'10" in my bare feet. Finding comfortable jeans with a 36 inch in-seam was a real bitch. Fortunately I loved men's 501's, so it wasn't as hard as it could have been. But girly pants...were almost unheard of in my closet. I threw on an old Black Flag T-shirt that I had swiped from boyfriend #4 in high school and looked in the mirror. The bruise on my chin and the zit had grown considerably. Make-up, I thought to myself. I need make-up. I never wore cover-up, hated the smell of it. But for some reason every time I bought make-up, I bought cover-up, too. For the first time this little piece of personal weirdness would pay off. I took the bottle from under the sink and shook it vigorously. Then I opened the cap and applied the Peaches and Cream sludge to a sponge. I started rubbing it in trying desperately to cover the bruise without looking like I was wearing spackle. Another problem with cover-up is you then need to wear blush or you look dead. So, a little blush, eyeliner and my never smudge waterproof mascara, and my face was done. Tomorrow, I thought to myself, tomorrow I buy new mascara. My middle of the back length blonde hair was still wet. I ran a brush through it while I tried to decide whether to blow dry it, curl it, or what. I finally decided to put it in a ponytail still wet. I didn't care what I looked like. And the people at the pub wouldn't care what I looked like, either. I put on my favorite pair of old beat up, black Doc Marten boots. Then I transferred all the things I would need for the evening out of my carry on sack to my favorite black shoulder bag. Lip balm, wallet with cash and ID, keys (Betty's spare set). I found the tiny photo frame book I always carried with me. The first picture was of John and me. I took the picture out of its plastic holder and stared at it. "Six months," I said out loud, shaking my head. I ripped the picture in half, splitting us right down the middle. I shoved his half of the picture under the couch. Why not in the trash, I don't know.

I grabbed a light jacket, seeing as how summer nights in Southern Cal are almost never cold, and I headed for the door. I took a look at myself in the entryway mirror. In a city like L.A., where every day was a fashion show, I was on the 'What Not to Wear', list and didn't care. I looked back to make sure I had turned off the light in my bathroom. No point in running up a huge electric bill. Nope, it was completely black, and I was completely alone.

I walked south, just off the strand for the eight blocks that separated me and the pub. Fitzpatrick's Pub, the red and green sign blazed above the two story building. It was one of the oldest buildings in Hermosa and to me the most beautiful. It had once been a theater and ball room. Because of that, the ceilings were 25 feet high in some places with old tin roof tiles that were worth a fortune. The chandeliers that hung above the bar were over a hundred years old and brought here with the Fitzpatrick family when they came to America. All the walls were plastered with pictures of Ireland and of the family as far back as any photograph could go. My favorites were the wedding photos of Fitz's great-great-grandparents. No one ever smiled in old pictures, but the Fitzpatrick's did. In truth, they may have been crocked but the smiles were big and genuine. They had old yolks for cattle and antique farming equipment hanging on the walls. But the coolest thing was the 30 foot long mahogany wood bar that had to be shipped here in pieces from the family pub back home. The bottom of the back bar was also ornately hand carved, scroll worked mahogany. The top of the back bar consisted of a leaded-glass mirror stretching the length of the bar with seven rows of glass shelving. The top shelf, of course, was my favorite. It held all the Irish Whiskey. They never ran out of Bushmills or Jamesons in this bar. They also had an off-sale license. It was the only one still Grandfathered-In, in Hermosa Beach, which meant that they could sell bottles and beer to go. On more than one occasion that had been a godsend.

To the right of the bar they had shelves of wine from the cheapest bottle of Boones to some of the best, should you crave a glass of red with your Shepherd's Pie. They even carried a few bottles of Port, thanks to Andy, the second eldest son. His wife was form Italy so he kept bottles to offer his father-in-law when they came for dinner. Several taps of beer lined the bar as well. There were two Guinness and two Harp taps for the perfect 'Half and Half', or as we American's called it 'Black & Tan'. They never ran out of those, either. They also had a "home brew" tap that was changed every season. This season's beer was called 'Wiccan B', which boasted a 9% alcohol rating. Boddingtons and several other European beers in bottles or cans, and of course, the old American standbys were present and accounted for. Grandpa Fitzpatrick, who passed on to his maker earlier this year, had a humidor installed years ago so you could always purchase a fresh cigar. Further back was the dance floor and the stage sitting caddy corner up against the back wall. Small four person tables were scattered about the wall for sitting space near the band leaving an open dance floor, just in case the alcohol made you think you had rhythm. The back wall was covered with posters from several of the bands that had played there over the years, along with photos of family and good friends in various stages of drunkenness. Off to the left of this giant barroom, was a kitchen, a small restaurant,(that was almost never open to the public), the restrooms, a small banquet room rented out by the Rotary Club and other small businesses, and finally a small card room that was marked 'off limits' to anyone unless invited. Off to the right was a pool room that had two cherry wood tables lined with blood red felt and a couple dart boards. The upstairs consisted of an office and the flop room. The flop room had once been occupied by Grandpa Fitzpatrick when he had 'had' too much of the Old Irish Spirit or Home Brew, as he called it. That room had a couch that made out into a bed, its own bathroom and a small kitchenette. The Home Brew had knocked plenty of us onto that couch. No cover charge for the spins.

I walked up and looked past the neon beer signs into the window. I saw "The Spikes" van parked out front and nodded to the newest roadie unloading Gregor's drum set. "The Spikes" were a sort of punk/ska band that played here pretty regularly. Loved them. The music was loud and at times offending, but sometimes you just need that. The lead singer, Bacon, had the biggest crush on Fitz. He would write her punk love songs with titles like, "I Want to Share Your Toothbrush" and "I'd Let You Stick That Anywhere." He was cute, in his own way, adorned with an eight inch tall Mohawk that could be any color from week to week. Even though he didn't do any drugs, he always looked a little on the Heroin Sheik side for me. He was really skinny and as pale as plain yogurt. But Fitz didn't see him romantically. She liked her men "big enough to toss her around" a little, as she put it. After all, she was no pussy. I had once caught the eye of the delightful base player, Dillon. But no romance was to bloom there. He liked to throw up his food and play in the toilet with the mess. He was cute, non-the-less, just not my style. It could never have worked out between us. I like to keep my food down.I couldn't see Fitz from where I was standing. I could, however, see her brother, Andy, behind the bar. He saw me through the window and waved me in.

Andy had tortured us when we were young. He liked to chase us around with bugs and hold us down, pretending to spit on us. He'd let long hangers of loogies drip slowly towards our screaming faces before sucking them back up into his mouth. In short, brother stuff. I never had a sibling so I was an honorary sister. Not always by choice. It was hard to believe that he was a father of three boys himself. He was 6 years older than Fitz and me. Mary, his high school sweetheart, and Andy were married right after they graduated and are one of those happy couples you hear about. He looked like all of the Fitzpatrick boys. They were all about six foot, stalky, reddish brown hair, fair skinned with dark green eyes, compliments of Fitz's mom, or Mum as we all called her. Da, as we called her father, had the only blue eyes in the family. Good looking men each and every one of them.

Danny was the oldest. He was also the only one who didn't work the family business. He chose to follow another Irish tradition. He's a Sergeant in the Hermosa Beach police department and is the father of four boys himself. (All very rambunctious) Andy was the second oldest, then came Paul, married with two boys. (Also very rambunctious) His wife, unfortunately was a real bitch who would rather him do anything but work for the family. She, for some reason had always looked at me as a threat and seemed to enjoy finding new and clever ways of making me feel like shit about myself. She pointed out bad haircuts as if I didn't know I had received one, and regularly asked if I had put on weight. I wasn't sure what I ever did to deserve such venom, but I assume it was the fact that even though I wasn't a blood member of the Fitzpatrick's, nor was I married in, I was still more of a family member than she would ever be. She was a slight woman just over five feet tall with long dark hair and blue eyes, named Mona. She would always introduce herself the same way, "Mona", she would say, "as in the Mona Lisa." She ruled Pauly with an iron fist, but soon found out that whatever pull she thought she had over him was nothing compared to the pull of Mum. Mona and her constant bitching had to take a back seat when Mum put her fist down. And last but not least…was Barry. Ahhh Barry!

Barry was three years older than me, so when he was a senior, I was one of the geeky 9th graders that followed him around like a puppy. To say that I once had a crush on Barry was an understatement. There were pictures where it was his birthday or some such occasion, he would be holding up a new game for the camera, and there I was in the background, with a dopey smile on my face. Every girl in our school had a thing for Barry. He was funny, smart, gorgeous and kind. Unfortunately he always saw me the same way the other brothers did, another annoying little sister. My crush kind of died with that realization. Barry usually tended bar here during the daytime. Since he was the only unmarried son he needed his nights free to find the woman of his dreams, settle down, and have grandsons for Mum. The fact that he was approaching 30, unmarried, with no children made Mum worried that maybe, just maybe, he was a little light in the loafers. Oh God, I thought to myself…that would cause a day of mourning across Southern California. Girls became day drinkers to catch an eyeful of Barry.

I entered the bar and was quickly embraced by Andy.

"Where ya been, Janie?" he said, in his thick Irish accent that had never left him. "I haven't seen ya in months."

I returned the hug and let out a sigh, "I've been busy," I said.

"Yeah, I heard you got dumped again," he said with a tone of amazement.

I let go of the embrace and just stared at him. "Yep," I finally said, not quite knowing how to react to the comment.

He hurried back to the other side of the bar and said as he went, "Don't ya worry none Luv. They're gonna find ya a good one."

At that comment, I started up to the bar and said as calmly as I could, "What did you say?"

Andy didn't miss a beat. "Let me get you a drink. A Black and Tan, right?"

"Andy," I said, trying to get him to look at me. "What are you talking about? Who's gonna find me a good one?"

He went right on layering my beer. "Now Janie, you know how Mum feels about ya. She adores ya. And I'm sure she, Fitz, and Aunt Marble, are just tryin' to help ya."

"Oh shit," escaped my lips. "Mum AND Aunt Marble are here?" I asked.

He didn't answer me, but smiled.

Why? Why is Aunt Marble here? I thought to myself, panic rising.

He put the beer in front of me with an uncomfortable grin. "Maybe a wee bit of the good stuff for ya, too?" he said, pulling down the Bushmills bottle and pouring me a double.

"Where's Fitz?" I asked, staring at the shot.

"She's in the poker room. She's almost ready for ya."

I started for the poker room and Andy said, "Janie Luv… I'm to keep you out here until they're ready for ya." I began to say something in my defense, but he looked at me and said, "Ya haven't been invited yet. Ya know the rules."

I did know the rules, in fact. And they had never applied to me. But now I was being told to wait in the bar?

I planted myself back on the stool and debated leaving. I wanted to grab Andy by the collar and demand he tell me all he knows. I wanted to yell out, "What the hell is going on?" Really get medieval on his ass. And I would have too, if it weren't for the fact that it would be amusing to him, not intimidating. I was starting to fidget and my panic was doubling:

Fitz and Mum…that was one thing…but Aunt Marble? She was crazy! I mean truly nuts. She looked a lot like Mum. She was short and stout just like Mum. But Mum had kept her natural red mane while Aunt Marble had piles of dyed brown hair. Seriously, when she took her hair down it fell to her ass. None of us could figure out how her little neck held all that weight. She wore Hippie dresses or Moo Moos with sandals. She was blind as a bat and wore glasses so thick her eyes looked huge behind them. Diamonds dripped from her ears, fingers, neck, and God only knows where else.

When she was a young woman, she married Ira Goldstein, a

Jewish jeweler from Chicago, 12 years her senior. I think that made her an honorary Jew, but I wasn't really sure how that worked. He had made a very good living so she never had a job outside of her wifely duties. Unfortunately, Uncle Ira had some semen trouble that left them without children. After years of trying, and believe me we all heard about the trying they did, she decided to enlighten herself spiritually to pass the time. She studied the Kabbalah, The Torah, Astral Projection, Chakras, Numerology, White magic, Herb Magic and the most frightening of them all, Sex Magic! That's right...Tantric Sex. I knew more about her and Uncle Ira's acrobatic, limber, and prolonged lovemaking, than any one not sleeping in their bedroom should ever know. Uncle Ira, God rest his soul, passed on 10 years ago so Aunt Marble moved out to Hermosa to be closer to family. They were very supportive and stood by her while she started teaching her "Spirituality Classes."

When I was 17, I attended a class with my mother, Mum, Fitz, and about 10 other women. We all sat in a circle in little folding chairs and awaited the evening's format. I was more than a little horrified when Aunt Marble walked in and said, "Welcome all. Thank you for coming. Tonight's topic is "Getting to Know Your Vagina!" I could see the horror on my face mirrored in my mother's. Then...there were the pamphlets. They not only had pictures of the vagina in full, but had captions that said things like, "Please touch me here" and "Yes! That's it!" outlining the G-spot in all its glory.

As we were leaving that night, Aunt Marble pulled me aside and asked me if I had found my G-spot before. I stammered, red faced. She put her arm around me and said, "Honey, if ya don't know where it tis ya can't expect anyone else to find it."

The next ten minutes of my life went in slow motion as she described in detail which positions would best help me find the elusive spot, complete with which fingers or toys would be most helpful. Then she sent me home with a hug and homework to, "Learn Myself" as she put it. Even now, eight years later, I couldn't see her without blushing. Probably due in part because every time she did see me she would ask me quietly if I had "Found Myself" yet, and then wink at me as if we were talking in some kind of secret code.

My head was starting to spin. Aunt Marble was here, planning something in the back room. Planning something for the recently dumped, no, the once again dumped me! I took the shot of whiskey, all four fingers, and downed them. Andy saw this as his cue to pour me another. I started to object but he cut me off and said, "You may need this." I took a deep breath and motioned for a second pour. With enough booze in me I thought, I may just make it through the night.

I said "Hello" to the band as they made their way to the stage. I was grateful that they were running late as usual, and I wouldn't have to make small talk. I felt the heat rising to my head from round-one of the Bushmills. I took a good pull off of the Black and Tan. God I missed those.

Finally I saw Fitz talking to the band. She was in a weird little Hippie dress. I had never seen her wear anything like this. In fact, I had never seen her wear anything that didn't cling to every curve. That's if it covered the curves at all. She caught a glimpse of me and started over to the bar. Heads were turning as she walked by, but it wasn't the usual looks. Her long red hair was piled on top of her head in a bun. I swear I only saw her wear this 'do' when she was working out or washing her face. As she got closer, I noticed that she wasn't wearing any make-up. Not a drop. This was not the Fitz I had known for 20 years. The Fitz I knew would never leave the house this made down.

"Hey," she said, embracing me, "I'm glad you're here."

I looked her up and down and said, "This is a new look for you, isn't it? Who are you supposed to be?"

"I think I look comfortable," she said, with a spin so I could take in the whole get-up.

"Oh, cut the crap!" I said in a hushed tone. "What the hell is going on in the back room? I know that Aunt Marble's here."

Fitz shot Andy a look. He just shrugged his shoulders and moved further down the bar.

"Is this some kind of psycho ambush or what?" I asked, letting my agitation show.

"Don't get upset, Janie. Look, I told Mum what happened to you. As you know none of us had any real love loss where John was concerned, but we do however love you."

I did an eye-roll and a heavy sigh.

Fitz caught me by my bruised jaw to make me meet her eye to eye. I let out a wince of pain and pulled back. "Oh yeah," she said. "Sorry again about yer jaw."

"My jaw is fine, damn-it! What the hell are you guys planning for me? Look," I started, "I already know my vagina, okay. Please tell Aunt Marble that I KNOW MY VAGINA! I found the spot! I don't need any help with it, just.... please!" I said, in a tone that bordered on begging.

The two guys sitting behind me at the bar turned to look at us.

"Mind yer fuckin' business," said Fitz, with a wave of her hand. "This doesn't concern ya!"

They both promptly turned back to their drinks and conversation.

"This isn't about your Vagina," she began. "This is about you and your relationships. You're the dating impaired. Remember today when I said it was like you were cursed?"

"Yeah, I appreciated the hell out of that by the way."

"Well, what if ya were?" she asked quite seriously.

"Were what? Cursed? I stared at her with a look of true

confusion. "Are you kidding me with this shit?" I started to laugh. "I'm not cursed! There's no such thing as cursed!"

She sat there staring at me with this look of pity. I had seen that look too many times since yesterday, I thought.

"I will admit," I began, "that I have had a hard time in the boyfriend department. Everyone does from time to time. But it's nothing more than bad luck or bad choices or bad situations. I'm not cursed!"

Fitz started to shake her head at me.

I was getting really worked up. Fitz grabbed my hands and held them in hers. "Janie," she said, looking deep into my eyes, "you have never broken up with a man in your life."

I started to mentally go over the last ten years of relationships in my head.

Fitz kept right on going. "You've had a slew of relationships, and been dumped every time. You've made yourself emotionally, mentally and physically available. And for that, you've been a doormat for all of 'em."

My eyes grew huge. My best friend…in the world…just called me a doormat? I wanted to yell at her. Scream at her. But I couldn't move. I was in shock.

Her eyes softened, "They've all used ya, Janie, for whatever they could get from ya, because you were always more than willin' to give 'em anything they wanted. I think ya see it as yer duty to be their…everything. But what the hell did you get out of it? When was the last time ANY guy asked ya what ya needed, what ya wanted?" She let her voice drop to a whisper and searched out my tearing eyes, "When was the last time ya asked yerself any of those things?"

I sat there stone faced for a moment then I let my eyes fall to the floor. "Do you really think I'm a doormat?"

"Normally, I'd ask, what do you think? But this time," she shook her again, "this time, Janie, I think ya need help. I think ya need help from the strong women around ya, to find the strong woman inside ya."

I could have argued. I could have pointed out the fact that Fitz hadn't been in a serious relationship in years. I could have attacked. But the truth was she and I weren't the same. She didn't want marriage or kids. And if she had, most men would have cut off their testicles to be with her, and she knew it. She actually did possess a power that radiated, an inner strength that shined. I had always been a little jealous of her. She was the beautiful, sexy, strong one, and I was known as the smart, funny, cute one. But now, instead of being jealous of her, I was mad at me. I was mad at me because I knew she was right…again. I started to tear up and had to 'WILL' myself not to cry.

"I want to take ya in back now. I want ya to realize that we all love you and we're here to help and guide ya," she said. I just nodded. We started to walk towards the poker room, her arm around my shoulders, when I stopped her. "This isn't going to be like an intervention, is it? I mean, what kind of stuff are they going to do to me?"

"No one's gonna hurt ya, if that's what yer askin'," she said with a light laugh.

We started to walk again. "Your aunt's not gonna make me look for my G-spot again, is she? Because I still haven't gotten over that."

Fitz just laughed.

"No really," I said moving along. "I still have nightmares about not having my homework complete on that one."

"You'll be fine, Janie," she assured me again. "It's time."

There were three doors that led to the Poker Room: One from the bar, one from the kitchen, and one that led to the alley out back. We were coming in from the bar door. The Poker Room always smelled of old booze and cigars. It permeated the wood siding on the walls. I loved that smell. It made me feel like

I was home and safe, but tonight... it didn't smell right. A faint smell of sweet herbs and flowers hung in the air. The lights were dimmed so that my eyes were having a hard time adjusting. The poker table had been laid on its side and set up against the wall. In its stead sat a toddler's wading pool. The kind made of hard plastic. A small folding table, with bottles, jars and vials sat in the corner by the alley door. It also had a punch bowl that was full of what looked like cooking oil. Another folding table was set in the opposite corner with flowers, wreathes, candles and a strange something that looked like a big knife. I could almost make out the little huddle of women speaking in hushed tones in the corner. I didn't recognize any of them. Correction, I didn't KNOW any of these women.

"I thought it was just Mum, Aunt Marble and you," I said. "Who are all these women?"

"Shhh, pipe down! You'll be introduced soon," Fitz whispered. I

I did, however notice that I was the only woman not wearing some kind of Hippie dress and a wreath of flowers on her head.

Breathe, I told myself. It's not like they're gonna sacrifice you. I may have been telling myself that but part of me yelled back to myself, you don't know that for sure, do you? Fitz had moved away from me. Where the hell did she go? I wondered. I wasn't sure if I was allowed to talk or not. This was all a little too much like, "Secrets of the Ha' Ha's", or whatever the hell the name of that movie was. I saw Mum and Aunt Marble enter the room from the kitchen door. They too were dressed in the little Hippie frocks and barefooted. Aunt Marble and Mum made their way over to me and embraced me one by one.

Mum, all smiles, snatched me in an embrace and whispered, "Oh my little Janie, so good to see ya Luv."

Then she passed me off to Aunt Marble, who took me in her arms and said, "I know this has been a real hard time for ya,

Janie. I promise we'll take good care of ya." Letting go of me, she extended her hands to the women in the corner and said, "Ladies of the Moon, this is Janie."

Five women of all shapes and sizes came from the corner and one by one introduced themselves.

The first one was a very thin woman maybe 5 foot tall and about forty-five, I would guess. Her shoulder length brown hair fell across one side of her face as she walked. She blew the lock from her sight to reveal big brown eyes. She grabbed my hand and said, "I am Jasmine. I reduce stress and help with menses." I smiled at her and nodded my head, not sure how I was supposed to respond. She bowed and walked away.

Help with menses, always a good thing I thought.

The next woman emerged in her wake. She was taller, but not tall, and round, very round. She appeared to be in her fifties with blonde hair and blue eyes popping out from over round, very round, cheeks. "I am Anise," she said, taking my hand in hers. "I help quench thirst, sore throat and cough." She smiled and walked away.

Ok, I thought, I call her when I'm sick but not menstruating.

Next was a sixty-ish, Latin looking woman. She was tall like me. Thin. Okay, thinner than me. She had a very stately manner about her. "I am Chamomile," she announced in a voice that seemed to radiate. "I aid in headaches and produce a healthy sweat to clean the system of impurities." She nodded at me then joined the other women.

I call her if I fear I can't pass a drug test. Not really one of my problems. I hadn't gotten high since tenth grade. And even then, it wasn't what I had hoped it would be. It was actually kind of a let-down.

The fourth was a woman with a huge grey bun on her head. She had the bluest eyes I had ever seen. She was, I thought, beautiful. She seemed ageless to me. In fact, no matter how hard I tried I couldn't put her in an age group. One moment she seemed young, and the next older than the trees themselves. Like she had been here in this room, on this planet, in this world since the beginning of time! I shook my head like a puppy. Obviously the Bushmills was kicking in nicely, I thought. She grabbed my hand with a knowing smile and said, "I am Lavender. I comfort the heart and promote rational thinking." She too, bowed and moved aside.

Oh, a heart comforter, I thought, I am in need of one of those.

A round faced, red haired woman that could have been one of the Fitzpatrick brood, came next. "Hi," she said, a little awkwardly. "Hi," she said again, shaking my hand with a little giggle, and started to walk away but then caught herself. "Oh, yeah, that's right," she said waving her hand. "Sorry, I'm Violet and I strengthen the heart and lungs." She let out another little giggle then snorted and moved away.

Uh huh, was the only thought that emerged upon meeting her.

Then came Mum to take my hand in hers and said, "I am Vervain. I strengthen the womb." She bowed her head and moved off.

Yeah, I thought to myself, if any of these women could boast a strong womb, it would be Mum.

Then there was Aunt Marble. "I am Clary. I clear the Sight to promote true visions." She kissed my cheek and walked away.

My eyes grew wide. Really??? AUNT MARBLE is the bringer of clear Sight? I didn't think that was the end of the female anatomy she specialized in.

Then there was a woman I hadn't even seen earlier. She was a black woman with roses in her cheeks. When she smiled, a tiny glow inside of her became a huge beam of light. "I am

Rosemary," she announced. "I aid in mental awareness and pure memory." She gave my hands a reassuring squeeze before taking her place with the other women.

Oh, I thought, clear memory is not required here. Now clear liquids, I surmised…Vodka, Rum...my thoughts were cut short.

Finally Fitz walked up and took my hands in hers. She wasn't saying anything though. She just kind of stared at me and smiled.

"Well, go on," I said.

She looked confused. "What do ya mean, go on?"

"Well, what's your name?" I asked, being very serious.

"What do ya mean?"

"I mean...who the hell are you? Everyone has a name of an herb or flower...something."

"Oh," she said, with a little embarrassed smile. "I haven't been given one yet."

"Oh," I said in return, nodding and trying my best not to seem disappointed for her.

"It's no big deal," she said, trying to convince herself. "I'm new at this, ya know? It can take a long time to be given a name and a purpose, and all..."

"Yeah, yeah, of course," I said, with a wave of my hand, trying to sound supportive.

"Don't ya do that! Don't ya look at me that way!"

"What way?" I asked, with a palms-up, trying to look as innocently as I possibly could.

"Yer being down right condescending with me!" she hissed in a hushed, angry tone.

"No, no," I said, trying to calm her and taking her in an embrace. "You're good... you are doing a... great job!" I said, with forced enthusiasm.

"Yeah?" she asked slowly.

"Yeah, definitely, you are great at this! You…you are

Awesome!" I added, giving her a squeeze.

She seemed to calm down a little and finally said, "This stuff is really hard, Janie."

"Yeah," I nodded, in a reassuring way, not having any idea what the Hell she was talking about. "I bet it is."

"Ladies," I heard Aunt Marble call, "It's time to take your places."

Fitz moved over towards the other ladies and left me standing there in the corner wondering what I was supposed to do.

All the women started taking their hair down from the buns on their heads. Ones that weren't already barefoot slipped their shoes off and put them in the corner. Then, they all started to unhook their bras from the back. I started to get nervous. Oh God, this isn't going to be a 'naked thing' is it? I started telling myself, "You're not a prude. You are not a prude!" But then rational thought broke in and said, "It doesn't make you a prude to not want to stand naked with a bunch of women you don't know. Or in my case, the ones I did know either. I had at one time been somewhat forced to picture Aunt Marble naked. The memory of that still made me queasy. It didn't help that I had also unfortunately pictured Uncle Ira, 'au naturel'. I shook my head a little trying to clear the vision. One by one, each of them took one hand and put it up the opposite arm hole of their Hippie Dresses removing one strap at a time until the bras were off. Ah, the ancient womanly art of removing the bra but not the clothing on top, I thought. Not a naked thing. Good!

Aunt Marble motioned me forward. "Come Janie," she said with wave of her hand. "Come, take off your shoes."

I leaned against the wall with one hand and started untying a boot with the other. When I had removed my boots and socks, I stood there and awaited my next instructions.

"Come, stand in the pool of rebirth," said Aunt Marble,

gesturing towards the kiddy pool.

"Okay," I said, stepping into the empty, two foot high wading pool.

"Now dearest Janie," she rang, "remove your clothing!"

"What?" I paused. "No, wait a minute," I began. "I'm not uh...um...no…I... I don't want to.... see, I'm not big on the naked thing. Really, I'll do just about anything for you ladies," I said, extending my hand. "You," I said, and pointed, "Crimson or Clover or whoever you are again...great ladies, I'm sure. I know you're trying to help... but I…ugh...I...NO!" I said, shaking my head vigorously.

All the ladies started to laugh.

"We're just gonna get ya down to yer skivvies, Luv, and do a rebirthin' on ya," said Aunt Marble. "We don't wanna see ya naked, child," she laughed.

I put my hands over my eyes and began laughing. Finally I said, "I am so embarrassed. Really ladies, I am so sorry that I implied that..."

"Ya haven't even been initiated yet," Aunt Marble cut me off. "Ya can't expect to hold a naked rank in front of the Ladies of the Moon without being a member."

My embarrassed smile dropped. I needed to get this straight in my head. For them, this was a naked thing. But, because I wasn't a member, I didn't get the joy of being naked, or having them naked in front of me? Not the best way to make an outsider jealous of being on the outside. I also wasn't sure about this rebirthing thing. Were they going to find a crack in the wall and try to push me through it?

Aunt Marble and the other woman just kept laughing, "I admire yer gusto though kid," she said with a wink. "In time," she bellowed, "in time."

My ass! I thought. W.C. Fields had put it best, "I wouldn't be a part of any club that would have me as a member," or something to that extent. I was more than ready to agree with him. I was pretty sure this was my first and last Ladies of the Moon experience.

When the ladies finally got done with a grand laugh at my expense, Aunt Marble said, "Ok now dear, off with your pants and shirt."

I hesitated before I said, "You know I was supposed to be in Hawaii."

All the ladies stared at me. No doubt wondering what this had to do with the whole rebirthing thing they were trying to accomplish.

"Well, see…what I mean is," I started, "I packed all my good underwear for the trip, so I had to wear an old pair tonight. Hell, right now I'm just glad I wore underwear," I said with an uncomfortable giggle. "But, ugh...the underwear I have on… well...aren't…ya know, ones I would usually wear. I mean if I got in a car wreck...tonight...my mother would be so embarrassed!"

"Oh, for the love of Pete," Mum bellowed. "We don't care what your skivvies look like. Just drop the jeans already."

I pulled the Black Flag T-shirt off and threw it behind me on the floor. Then I let the jeans drop. Every woman in the room was trying to stifle a laugh. There I stood, in my bra with a pair of men's boxer shorts that had a picture of a frog on the crotch. The caption read, "Sometimes, you have to kiss a lot of frogs."

After a moment these wonderful, spiritual, and enlightened women, began to crack-up. I put my hands on my hips and said in my defense, "I told you, I packed all my good undies."

The black lady, known as Rosemary, said, "We're sorry honey, we were expecting some granny-panties, or maybe a pair with the elastic stretched out. But this," she said extending her hand towards my undies, "this is just a little too on the nose, don't you think?"

"Yeah," said Violet, the round redhead. "We're trying to get you into the right man's pants and it turns out, you're already wearing them," she giggled then snorted.I let out an exhausted sigh and let my shoulders fall, "I'm done," I said. "I give up."

"No," said Lavender, stepping forward. The grey haired woman looked at the other ladies and said, "Women, it's time we compose ourselves. There's work to be done."

With that, the women circled the pool I stood in and joined hands. I guess Lavender was the head Priestess or something because she took control of the ritual or ceremony, whatever you'd call it.

It's not like I was really on board with any of this and had no reservation about it. But Mum was someone I trusted with my life and figured I was safe in her presence. No matter how weird this all seemed to me.

"White Light from the North," began Lavender with a clear radiating voice, "Ruled by the Earth herself. Heal your child. Strengthen her with your undying and unwavering love. HEAL!" she commanded.

I jumped a little in my kiddy pool, waiting for her to smack my brow.

Then all the other women said, "Yes Mother, let it be so!"

I'm not sure exactly what I was expecting…maybe more Bibbitty-Bobbitty-Bo, or Eye-of-Newt, Wing-of Bat-stuff, but this was just as foreign to me, so I just went with it.

Then Aunt Marble spoke, "White Light from the East ruled by air, Clear the Sight of yer child, open her eyes and bring her clear vision."

Once again, all the other women chimed in, "Yes Mother, let it be so!"

And once again I found myself wondering who put Aunt Marble in charge of 'Clear Sight'? I mean literally her glasses were as thick as coke bottles. And metaphorically, bat-shit crazy came to mind when describing her.

I was starting to feel something though, something... strange. Yay, I thought. Maybe the Bushmills was taking effect. The room seemed to be moving, moving with my breath. This wasn't my normal Bushmills buzz. My head started to feel very lite, and my stomach…very heavy. Like it was trying to ground me to the Earth! (Or in my case, the little plastic kiddy pool) Deeper and deeper my breathing became. I felt as though my breath came up from my toes. I could feel it move through my whole body. There was a different rhythm to it. I let my eyes close. My head wanted to fall back, so I let it.

I heard Mum now, "White Light from the South ruled by fire, open the heart of yer child. Let true love find her."

The chorus rang out a third time, and the chanting of, "LET IT BE SO MOTHER, LET IT BE SO!" was repeated over and over. Louder and stronger, the voices grew.

I started to sway. I could see light behind my closed eyelids and see quick flashes of color. I could hear a strange humming in my head and a heat was rising from my stomach to the tips of my ears. I started to get a little scared and wondered if I should stop all of this, but I couldn't, I didn't want to. A surge of power shot through my body, through my mind. I was glowing from the inside, out. Time no longer existed. Was it only minutes that had passed while I stayed in this state of…I don't know what? Suddenly I was aware of a warm sensation starting at the top of head and running down my back and front, down my legs.

They were still chanting, "Let it be so Mother, let it be so! Let it be so Mother, let it be so!" Fevered, the voices melted together and became one.

The next voice sounded very far away, but I heard the fourth woman say with great power and authority, "White Light from of the West ruled by water, open the womb of your child, rebirth her Mother. Bring her again to your knee to learn of your never ending love and power!"

Now, I too chimed in with the women. "Let it be so Mother, Let it be so!" I chanted, not knowing for how long. Finally, the chanting stopped and I slowly opened my eyes. I was now aware of everything around me. I was aware of some substance running down my face. It was the herb infused oil that had been in the punch bowl. When did they put the oil on me? What was that sweet smell? I wondered, but I said nothing. Fitz came and handed me a towel. I wiped my face and wasn't the least bit surprised to see all the makeup I had worn was now on the towel. My hair was unbound, but for the life of me, I couldn't remember taking it out of the pony tail. My breathing was still deeper than normal. Finally I took a good look at my surroundings. There was a circle of salt around the outside of the little pool. In the pool where I was standing, were dried herbs, what looked like oil, salt and candle wax. I can't imagine how they got there. I don't really remember. I knew they weren't there when we started the ceremony. I felt a little light headed still, but chalked that up to the Whiskey.

Aunt Marble and the other women had been standing at the little table in the corner doing something with backs turned to me. I wasn't sure what I was supposed to do or say, so I just stood there dripping oil until I was spoken to. Aunt Marble walked to my side and with a huge smile said, "Would ya like to sit, darlin? Ritual can really take it out of ya."

I nodded, a little shaky.

"Okay," she said. "Stay right there. I'll get the Athame and cut ya out."

Normally, the words, "I'll cut you out," would have scared the living hell out of me. (Especially from Aunt Marble) But I felt completely safe, high in a way. That is, if you can be high and totally aware at the same time. I had a tiny headache between my eyebrows. It didn't hurt though, it pulsated.

Aunt Marble brought back a beautifully ornate knife and told all the other women, "Gather around ladies, it's time!"

They all circled the tiny pool and locked hands. Aunt Marble took the knife and cut the air around me, as she called it. I felt a little stir of wind.

"Okay child," she said, handing the knife to one of the other women then taking my hands in hers. "Once you pass the salt line…you've been reborn. Yer a new person Janie…with a new life and new responsibilities to yerself," she said, with a truly loving smile.

I took a deep breath, smiled, and let Aunt Marble assist me in my rebirth.

Aunt Marble held out her arm and wrapped it around my waist. I swayed a little and felt Fitz arm go round me from the other side. They directed me to one of the little folding chairs in the corner. Sitting, I realized that my head wasn't done swimming yet. Mum came to my side and handed me a cup.

"Drink this," she said smiling. "It'll soothe ya."

I looked in the cup, but couldn't see through the liquid. I smelled it. Whatever those sweet herbs were, I knew they had been steeped in whiskey. I started to drink, thirstily.

"Slow down," said Mum. "It's a wee bit more powerful than yer used to."

The mixture was sweet and bitter at the same time. It caused another quick rising heat in my chest and cheeks. I swear I could feel it move through my body, lighting me up as it went. "What is this?" I asked.

"Oh, that's the Nectar of the Goddess, Luv," Mum said.

She inclined her head to where the women had gathered. "Lavender makes it for us. She's very learned in herbs and such. You'll have more run-ins with her later. But right now, if yer steady, let's get ya dressed."

Mum helped me stand, but I assured her that I could dress

myself. I polished off what was left in the mug and sat it on the table. I was still pretty oily, as was the towel I was using. I grabbed my shirt and jeans and wandered off to find a private place to get out of my bra and boxers. Which I was sure, needed to be burned.

I knew the restaurant was closed, so no one would be in there. I tiptoed through the restaurant door. It was black and quiet in the kitchen. I peeled off my bra and the horrible frog boxers, and started to mop off the oil with a clean hand towel I had found on the linen rack. There I stood, naked as could be, toweling off my hair. I wasn't self conscious anymore or uncomfortable in the slightest, I noted. I was feeling damn good about myself. I did a little naked spin. I had always been so modest, so unsure. Well not anymore, I told myself. Today, that all changes. Today I learn to love myself, mind, soul and body I thought. I was so proud of me. I had enough of the oil off now, or rubbed in, either way that it wouldn't ruin my clothes. I got my jeans up and buttoned. I found my shirt and simultaneously, the bar door to the kitchen opened and the light clicked on. Barry stopped dead in his tracks when he saw me

I grabbed my shirt and turned my back to him as quickly as I could. But I noted, not quickly enough. Only me! I thought to myself. I was wrong, I take it back God. I'll never be naked again, NEVER, I promised. Whatever buzz I had from the Goddess Nectar was gone. I was now 100% sober and 50% naked.

"Hey, Janie," he said, smiling, "long time no see."

"Oh God," I said, trying to figure out where the hell the armhole in my T-shirt had gone. "I'm sorry. I didn't think anyone would be in here...."

He chuckled, apparently amused by watching me fumble, "No," he said, never missing a beat, "I just hadn't eaten dinner yet and...."

I knew he was talking but I wasn't paying any attention. I was freaking out.

As soon as I got the shirt pulled down, I turned to him and said, "I'm…I'm sorry, what did you say?"

He smiled again, raised his eyebrows and said, "I was just wonderin' what you were doin'… in the kitchen…naked," he added.

I put one hand down on the counter to steady myself and the other on my hip, trying to look calm, "I, ugh…I was just doing something for your mom."

His eyebrows furrowed and he said, "Excuse me? What'd ya say?"

"No, no, I mean," I stammered, trying to smile, "I was doing something WITH your mom…"

He folded his arms over his chest and stared at me with a quizzical look. "My mom's not around here somewhere naked, too, is she?"

He was torturing me and he was enjoying it.

I had become very aware of the fact that I was bra-less. I folded my arms over my chest and said, "I better find Mum and Aunt Marble."

"Oh," he said with a slow head nod. "Aunt Marble's here is she? Then…never mind! I'm pretty sure I don't wanna know."

I started to walk back to the Poker Room, totally embarrassed, when he said, "Janie, you forgot yer…"

I turned to look and he was holding up my oily bra and the frog boxers, inspecting them. "Boxer shorts?" he said, confused.

I walked back to him with my head down and held out my hand. He handed me the oily mess and I turned on my heels, retreating as quickly as I could.

A thought occurred to me: Someone up there, I looked to the Heavens, is having the best time watching me right now!

I passed back into the Poker Room and immediately

dropped my bra and boxers into the trash can by the door.

Back in the Poker Room, Mum, Aunt Marble and Fitz, who were in a huddle talking quietly, turned in my direction.

"Where did all the women go?" I asked.

"They had to rush off," Mum answered.

"I didn't get a chance to…um, thank them?" I said, as more of a question than a comment.

"Don't ya worry about that, you'll be getting' a chance. We did wonder where ya got off to though," Mum stated.

"I wanted to discard my bra and, well, you know, the skivvies so I went into the kitchen to disrobe."

"You always were a modest little creature," smiled Mum. "You used to wear a T-shirt over yer bathing suit when you were little. Went all the way to yer knees," she laughed. "That may have to be one of the things we need to work on?"

"Yes, after all," said Aunt Marble, "being comfortable with yer own body is the only way to be comfortable with someone else's, ya know? Remember me tellin' ya that?"

I nodded, hoping she wouldn't go into detail.

Fitz was laughing at me from behind their backs.

I mentally went over the past five minutes. "Yeah, about that," I started, "I thought that the ceremony or ritual we just did... would kinda take care of that?"

"What do ya mean, Luv?" asked Aunt Marble.

"I don't know. I'm not sure what I expected, but I thought that it was gonna be.... different. You know, like I was gonna be different. Like it would change me, or change the things about me that I didn't like, or weren't quite right," I said.

Aunt Marble and Mum looked at each other and smiled.

"Ah Janie," Aunt Marble began, taking my hand, "no one changes overnight. And no one changes against their own will. Nothin' we did here tonight, nothin' anyone can do, will change ya, unless YOU consciously want to change. We haven't bent ya to our will or some such nonsense. What we did here Luv, was to call upon the forces of nature and the Great Goddess so that they will give ya the strength, power, clarity and protection you'll need. Then you'll figure out what, and how, ya want to change. Then, you can start yer changin'. If it were an easy process, everyone would be walkin' around totally enlightened and glowin'. The fact is that it IS so difficult for us as humans to be honest with ourselves, and each other, it's what holds us back, dear."

I tried not to look bummed. I was now to understand that it wasn't going to be a snap of the fingers, or the flick of a wand. Damn it. Aunt Marble had given me homework…again. At least it wasn't about my vagina. Well, not totally.

Fitz, reading my thoughts loud and clear, said to her Mum and Aunt Marble, "Well, ladies, thank you for everything tonight, but Janie and I still have one tradition to carry out."

"Ah, yes the tradition," said Mum.

Aunt Marble turned a questioning look on Mum. "Tradition?" she asked.

"I'll tell ya all about it," said Mum, "over a pint. Barry was supposed to meet me here. We need to have a chat." Mum raised her eyebrows at Aunt Marble, who nodded knowingly. "I wonder if he's here yet?"

"Oh yeah, he's here," I said letting out a long sigh.

"Oh did you see him, Luv?" asked Mum.

"Yep, he saw me. I mean I saw him…I mean we saw each other," I stammered.

Fitz furrowed her brow, "What the hell's the matter with ya?"

"Nothing," I blushed. "We should go. Now!" I added.

We all exchanged hugs and Fitz directed me towards the ally door. Aunt Marble stopped me and said. "Oh, I almost forgot. There is one small side effect I should be mentionin to ya."

"Oh, that's right," Mum said, nodding her head to Aunt Marble. "You'd be remiss."

"Okay," I said, "what is it?"

"Well darlin', the Goddess works in mysterious ways," she started.

"I've heard something similar to that," I smiled.

"Well, it seems that she, like all mothers, has a protective side to her."

I nodded, "Yeah."

"If you find yourself in a situation, dear, one that's not right for ya, she'll give you a subtle sign. To get you back to the right track, so-to-speak."

"How subtle," I asked, a little concerned.

"Oh, little signs," Mum chimed in. "Nothin' to worry about. Hardly worth mentionin' really. Just think of it as havin' a little angel on your shoulder, directin' ya."

Both ladies stood there nodding and smiling.

"Oh, and dear," said Aunt Marble, "this is for you." She handed me a tiny vile with a murky yellow liquid inside.

"What's this?" I asked.

"It's for the zit, child," she smiled and walked off in the other direction.

I stood gaping after her. Hell, up until now I had completely forgotten about the zit.

When Fitz and I made it to the back door, I stopped and asked her, "How long have YOU been doing this Goddess stuff? I mean, you've never said anything about any of this."

"Well, truthfully," she admitted, "this was my first ritual, too. I guess the Ladies you met tonight have been meetin' each other for over ten years. Every Monday. Usually right here in the Poker Room."

"You didn't know about this?" I asked, baffled.

"Actually…no." She looked a little embarrassed. "We do

our family nights on Sunday, so every Monday night when Mum would disappear for a spell," she emphasized the word, "I just assumed that it was her quiet time. Ya know, get away from kids, work, and Da. Turns out that's exactly what it was. I didn't have any idea that she may have actually been doin' a spell or empowerment ritual or whatever they call it. Or that other people were involved. I've only been goin' to the gatherins' for about two months now. Two moons, as they call it. It's not what I was expectin' when I was first dragged along, and I was dragged. I thought it was gonna be a bunch of Hippie shite. You know how I hate the Peace, Love, Hippie Shite!"

I giggled, knowing that Fitz was the person least likely to enjoy a 70's flashback weekend.

"But it wasn't that at all. These women are all shop owners or business women of some kind or other. They have real lives and pressures, and come together to kinda be there for each other. They listen, allowing each women, if need be, to vent, to rage and then they take turns doin' healins' and prayers for each other. They do Empowerment Chanting and Release Dancin', which I' m learnin' can be very beneficial. They do energy work on each other and open or align each other's Chakra's, whatever they are. They're more of a support system than anything and they truly love and care for each other. They bond over the feminine and over being a female in this life."

"And you didn't tell me about this because....?"

"Did ya hear what I just bloody said? I sound crazy!"

I just gave her my best bullshit look.

"Okay, okay," she said. "Mum said not to say a word to ya. She said soon enough you would be invited."

I wondered if Mum had seen the break-up beforehand or if it was just my track record with men that made her think it was just a matter of time. "Do you think your mom has special powers? I mean, do you really think she gets visions of things to come?"

She wrapped her arm around me and said smiling, "I know she does, Janie. Of that, I'm sure."

We stepped out into the ally, our arms thrown over each other's shoulders and there she was... Baby! Oh sweet Baby! She was absolute 'Cherry' from bumper to bumper. I was no gear head. I could care less about most cars. In fact, no Porsche, no Corvette, no Ferrari could make me turn my head or even bat an eye. But Baby...Ohhh. She was a 1959 Cadillac convertible with suicide doors and Leopard skin interior, and I...was in love with her.

"Hello baby," I said, stroking the door as I got in. I always felt like a 1950's movie star riding in her. Suddenly, I was bold, daring and sexy, probably the only time I felt those things. She reminded me of a time long past when Hollywood was all about showing some class, not your ass. Baby had been Fitz's 16th birthday present from Grandma Fitzpatrick. In fact, it had once been Grandma's tooling around car. We had no such hand-me-downs in my family. My first car was a 1981 Grand Prix that we affectionately called "Rocky," because even though it was beat to shit, it ran.

I clicked my lap belt and we sped off towards my house. I'm glad she brought Baby. I didn't want to walk eight blocks without a bra.

"Did you get the stuff," I asked, like an addict.

"Yep, we have three bottles of shitty champagne in a cooler in the trunk..."

We used to require only one bottle, but as we became more experienced drinkers we required more booze to get the desired effect.

"...and the pink box in the backseat is from...Lorenzo's," she said, pronouncing it slowly for me.

"Oh my God!" I said, with real excitement.

Lorenzo's was our local bakery, but it was so much more than that. They had the best homemade bread, baked daily of course. But they also had the best pies, cakes, éclairs, cobblers, cheesecakes, you name it. They had won award after award for being the very best bakery in the South Bay.

"How'd you get a Black Forest Cake from Lorenzo's, with almost no notice at all?"

"I agreed to go out with Pete."

I just looked at her and shook my head. I had no idea who Pete was.

"Ya haven't seen Pete?"

"No," I said, still shaking my head and grinning.

"Oh my God, he's gorgeous. He's only been working there a few weeks, but I've already gained like five pounds. I've been going there almost daily."

If she had gained weight, I couldn't see it.

"He's 6'2", dark hair, brown eyes and a huge white smile," she continued, "and an Italian accent that makes my knees shaky. We flirt a little."

Which actually meant she flirted a lot, I gathered.

"So today, after I left ya, I decided to stop by and play the damsel in distress. I explained our tradition and how important it was..."

Great. She got a complete stranger to feel bad for the poor dumped wreck, I thought.

"...and he said, he'd have it for me by six, if I agreed to dinner."

"He blackmailed you for a cake?"

"He could have asked me for my liver and I'd have gone along with it."

"Oh, the things you're willing to do for our friendship," I said, giggling.

"Ya have no idea," she grinned.

I walked in and pushed 'play' on my answering machine. It clicked on....

"Hi, this is Annie, from Hawaiian Isle Airlines," said a very nasal voice. "First I wanted to extend my sympathies for the break-up. Everyone here is talking about it."

I nodded at Fitz, "Of course."

".......Anyway, your luggage left Hawaii on yesterday's flight. Unfortunately, it was sent to Paris, France. It's a horrible mistake. We apologize and were sending you 500 frequent flyer miles. I know it doesn't make-up for the inconvenience, but we are so sorry, and..."

She was still talking but I clicked the off button.

"I'm airport news," I said, sarcastically.

"That's great," Fitz nodded.

"I stared at her, "How exactly is that great?"

"Well, if they're talkin' about you," Fitz started, "they're not talkin' shit about me!" she smiled.

An hour later, we were sitting on the floor using my couch as a back support. We gave up on the glasses and decided to just pass bottle number three back and forth. On my table sat a half eaten Black Forest cake and two cake covered plastic forks.

The movie 'French Kiss' just started.

"Ah, I love this movie," I said.

"Ya say that about every Meg Ryan movie. What…is there a Meg Ryan-a-thon on? It's like the cable company knew you were gonna be dumped!" she tried not to laugh.

I was actually at a point in my drunkenness where I could laugh about it finally. "Thanks, Bitch," I retorted, grinning.

"No, really Janie, I am sorry this happened to ya. Ya know how much I love ya, right?" she said, her Irish accent beginning to thicken with booze.

I did the drunken head nod, before taking another huge

swig of the champagne.

"Yer my best friend in the whole world... I want the very best for ya," she slurred a little.

I nodded again.

"And he wasn't it."

Ah, here comes the part of the tradition where she bashes him, I thought. Give him a lickin', I don't care.

But she didn't. A short while passed where nothing was said.

Finally, she got very serious. She looked at me and said, "We're best friends, right?"

Oh no, I thought, she's stuck in drunk repeat mode. I took another pull off the bottle and handed it to Fitz. "Yes! Yes we are!

"This Goddess stuff," she began, "don't ya laugh at me, but...it makes me feel different about myself. Stronger."

"In what way?" I asked, taking the bottle back from her and swigging it. Fitz was already one of the strongest willed women I had ever met.

"I feel connected to everything," she said, growing serious. "I feel energy in everything. I feel it move around me."

I had experienced that very same feeling just a short while ago but I kept quiet. I wanted her to elaborate. Maybe she could put it into words for me, but she went silent and stared at the ceiling.

"Did they do that to you?" I asked. "I mean, did they put you in a kiddy tub and pour oil on you?"

She shook her head, "No. Until tonight, I had never seen an initiation or whatever that was. Mostly, they just tell stories and drink. My kind of club," she joked.

"So, it's not against God or this Goddess...spirit," I searched for a word, "to drink?"

Fitz shook her head, confused. "Why would it? This doesn't replace religion for these women. It's a belief that there is divinity in the feminine, as well as the masculine. And it should be celebrated. Actually, three of them are Catholic, another is a Buddhist, two are Christian, and one practices Hoodoo."

My brows arched. I had never known anyone who practiced Hoodoo and I found the thought interesting. I automatically assumed it was Rosemary, but that only goes to show why stereotyping will make you look like an ass. Turns out, the very round, blonde haired, white woman was the practitioner of Hoodoo. But that is a story for another time.

"It's about the Goddess within them," Fitz continued. "They all have their own beliefs, their own truths that they hold dear. By celebrating the feminine inside them, they are celebrating exactly what God made them…Women! We also give thanks for everything that was made for us."

"But aren't there rules to this or something?" I asked.

"Ya try to do your best, always. Treat others with respect and kindness and know that how you treat others is what will eventually come back to you."

"Isn't that the basis for almost every religion? I mean, it's not exactly rocket science, is it?" I stated.

She looked taken aback. "It shouldn't have to be, Janie. That's what these women are teachin' me. It's not hard to please God. He doesn't expect perfection, just the pursuit of it. These women wouldn't deny God. They embrace him. Like a parent, a forgiving, loving, and proud parent that only wants the best fer us.

I thought of my mother. Forgiving, loving and proud…these were not words I would use to describe her.

She took a long pull off the bottle and handed it to me as I mulled the thought over. I had experienced something tonight, something wonderful and awe-filled. It was easier for me to think of God as a parent rather than some ominous outer force that was judgmental and disapproving. I already had judgmental and disapproving in my life and could only force myself to spend one hour a week in her presence. I took another drink and handed Fitz the bottle.

"I don't understand the Goddess thing," I finally said. "Is she God or a totally different ...thing? I mean, I don't understand where she comes in at all!"

Fitz laughed at me. "I had the same question," she giggled. "This is how Mum explained it to me...It takes a man AND a woman to create life."

I waited for her to elaborate. I gave her the 'and' hand rotation.

"That's it, Janie. Ya can't have creation, or birth, or re-birth, without both. You were right the first time. It's not rocket science, its common sense."

I thought about that. It made perfect sense. And it was a simple, no bullshit way of thinking. I started to nod my head in understanding.

"But why does the church make it so difficult? I mean, why do they make women out to be the root of all evil?" I asked.

"If ya wanted to control someone…wouldn't the fear of offending God, be the best way to do it? She got serious and said, "Let's pretend you have two kids. Twins…one boy, one girl."

"Okay," I said, straightening myself up against the sofa.

"Ya tell both children," she said, "Don't be goin in the biscuit jar before dinner."

I nodded in understanding. "Alright."

"You leave the room."

I nodded again.

"When ya come back in the room, both children are holding half eaten biscuits, crumbs on both of their faces.

My eyes narrowed and I nodded again.

"Which child do ya punish?"

"Both," I said quickly.

"But the brother says that his sister was the one who grabbed the biscuit first," she looked at me sidelong. "So now who do ya punish?"

"Both," I repeated. "Both were told not to go in the biscuit jar, and both did."

"What if the brother says his sister MADE him do it?"

"I don't buy that crap," I said in wannabe mommy mode.

"And yet, we've been buying into it for thousands of years."

Fitz was not a thinker. She was smart, don't get me wrong. But that was more street smart, life lessons and all. But this was a deep thought easily summed up and gift wrapped for my approval. I still wasn't sure how I felt about the whole thing, but maybe drunk wasn't the way to ponder it.

I nodded again. "Holy crap," I finally said.

"Atta girl," she said, "great start," and took a long pull off the bottle. "Do you wanna drink off this before I finish it?" she asked, offering me the bottle.

"No, I want food," I said, swaying slightly as I stood.

"Okay," said Fitz, following me into the kitchen. "But it'll kill yer buzz."

We had gone through all the champagne and I was hungry for anything, but cake. We riffled through the kitchen. I grabbed some cheese and crackers, and a bottle of Chardonnay. Fitz went through the cupboard and pulled out a half-full Bushmills bottle.

"Ta da," she said, showing me the bottle like a magician's assistant.I shook my head, "No," I said gravely. "No shots for Janie!"

"One shot," she bellowed. "For yer Irish ancestors," she raised the bottle in a toasting fashion.

Let's see, I thought. I'm still sober enough to realize that Fitz is drunk, so I could probably have a shot. Drunk rationalizing. I grabbed two shot glasses, and said, "To our Irish ancestors!"

We headed back to the living room, arms full, and plopped on the couch for the long drunken haul. Before I knew it, "French Kiss" was almost ending. I was having trouble seeing straight but I knew from the hundred or so times I had seen the movie, that Meg was kissing Kevin Kline in the grape vineyard.

Fitz and I toasted the kiss with our shots. "To Meg!" I yelled, with my shot raised above my head to the heavens.

"To Kevin," she yelled back, with a raised hand and a defining head nod towards the TV.

We pounded the shots and did the Whiskey face. The one where your face squishes up and you let out a breath of flaming hot air.

Fitz was trying to catch her breath but finally asked, "Have ya given any thought to yer list?"

I watched her pour two more shots. "Do bad ideas come in threes?" I asked.

"What are ya talkin' about?"

"Taking a second shot, and that list," I said, trying to burp back shot number one.

"It's good for ya, all three of em," she said teetering. "Ya really should do the list. Mum and Aunt Marble say it's really important. It'll help ya...what's the word I'm lookin' for?"

I sat there shaking my head at her.

"It starts with an A," she kept going.

I raised my eyebrows, still shaking my head.

"Assess," she finally said. "That's it. It'll help you assess things."

"Ok, after this next shot we'll start assessing my list," I said.

"What should we toast to?" she asked.

I thought about it and finally said, "To Kevin Klein!"

She nodded her head, lifted her glass and said, "To Kevin!"

We downed our shots and pounded our glasses down on the table... that's the last thing I remember.

3

SUN: DAY TWO OF DUMPED

I woke up on the living room floor. I was conscious long before I actually opened my eyes. I ASSESSED the situation. I was lying on the paper-thin carpet. My back, neck and hips ached. My tongue gave off such a horrible taste that I thought it would probably be more effective to rip it out than to try and brush it. That's if I could pry it free from the roof of my overly dry mouth. My stomach seemed to be fine as long as I stayed perfectly still. Don't shake anything up, I told myself. I still had to open my eyes, which in my estimation was always the hardest part. It let in the light that burrowed a tiny burning hole in my brain. The whole point of the Tradition is to get so drunk, the only thing you focus on…is your hangover. According to my head and stomach we had accomplished our mission with great gusto. This, I thought to myself, this is why I shouldn't drink or date. I sat up and prepared myself. I took a deep breath and let it out slowly. I opened my eyes and was immediately faced with a picture of John. "Ah, yes," I said, extending my hand to the picture. "And that's why I DO drink…and still shouldn't date." I passed the picture on the way to the bathroom, or to 'The John,' I thought to myself. The thought that his name was used as a metaphor for a toilet made me very happy indeed. I knocked the picture of him on the chin and kept moving towards the bathroom.

I could hear the shower. "Fitz!" I called, as I walked through the bathroom door. "I have to pee."

"So pee then! Just don't flush yet! I'm almost out."

I sat down to go potty and realized that a tiny headache was starting behind my eyes.

"What do ya want for breakfast?" she asked me, in a singing tone.

I covered my eyes with my hands. "Death," I whined. "Food does not sound good at all. I just want to go back to sleep, preferably in my bed."

"We have tons of things to do today, Luv. Whether ya want to or not, you'll need something in your stomach to soak up last night."

I stood and looked at myself in the mirror. I had cake in my hair and down the front of me.

She grabbed the towel from the rack and I heard the shower go off. The curtain opened and she said, "I'll make ya breakfast. You, get in the shower. Go on get ready."

She's cooking? That thought was enough to scare the hell out of me and threaten to bring-up last night's festivities. Scared sober, I thought. There were very few things that Fitz could cook that wouldn't require a barf bag.

"I feel like shit, Fitz. I don't think food is going help."

"Well then, get in the shower and take care of the other."

"The other," I repeated. "What other?" I asked, shaking my head. "What are you talking about?"

She raised her eyebrows, nodded at me, "The other," she said looking down at her own midsection.

"What?" I made the ewww face. "Are you talking about....?"

"It helps relieve headaches, gets the blood flowing and all," she said, very matter-of-factly, with her hand on her hip. "Take it from me…it'll kick the crap out of a hangover."

We both stared at each other for a moment.

Finally I said, "I can't help but notice that you seem rather refreshed for someone who drank as much as we did last night."

She cocked her head, "I imagine I do," she smiled and walked off.

"Eww! Not in my shower?" I yelled. "Right? Not in my shower? At least tell me you were done before I came in here! Fitz...?"

After my shower, which by the way, I still felt like shit, (Draw your own conclusion) I came into the kitchen and Fitz had made eggs and potatoes. She had wanted to try her hand at Bangers and Mash, but I had no sausage. I was raised on traditional Irish dishes but rarely cooked them myself. And no matter what, no Blood Pudding would ever find its way into my home.

I had a horrible experience at the Wake for my Great Aunt. I was only five, so to me there were two kinds of pudding. (Black or white, otherwise known as Chocolate or Vanilla). As I tried to hold in a mouthful of what I thought was chocolate pudding, my cousin explained to me just exactly what I was eating. He laughed and laughed as I puked all over that poor deceased woman's house. Thank God for plastic couch covers. My Dad's sister was not so lucky. Since then, I could still have lots of the Traditional Irish Dishes as long as nobody told me what I was eating. I was more than reluctant to try Fitz's cooking, but figured if it killed me I'd probably feel better than I did right now, anyway. I braced myself for instant death and took a bite.

I was surprised, the food tasted....good.

With a mouth full of potato I asked Fitz, "What-cha reading?"

"The list," she said, squinting her eyes at the paper in her hand.

"What list?" I asked. "My list?"

"Yeah," she said slowly, never taking her eyes off of it.

"What's it say?" I asked. "Where was it?"

"I found it on the coffee table when I was cleanin' up the mess from the cake."

She cleaned? What the hell has gotten into Fitz, I wondered? But I said nothing.

"The problem is," she said, irritated, "I can't make the damn thing out. The worst part is, it looks like we spent a lot of time on it and its totally illegible! I've been sitting here goin' over it since ya got in the shower. I have yet to make sense of it."

"Well let me see it," I said. "After all, it's based on my shitty life. Maybe it'll make some sense to me."

She handed it over and said, "Good luck! By the way, do you remember writing any of this?"

"No," I said, shaking my head. Then after a moment, I said, "Not that it matters because I still don't remember any of this," showing her the list. "But this is your writing not mine."

"Oh thank God," she said, relieved. "I wouldn't have been able to read it anyway then," she laughed.

I started to mull over the words I could make out.

4

THE LIST

"Holy crap, what the hell? Does this say Group Sex?" I asked Fitz.

She just took a quick look at the list through squinted eyes and said, "That's what I thought it said, too. I know you haven't gotten that far off."

"Something tells me I better make a new list," I said, leaning back in the chair.

"Not right now," said Fitz. "We have lots of things to get done."

"What do I have to do today?" I asked, like I was being punished. "Remember, I'm on a really shitty vacation."

"We have to meet Mum and Aunt Marble at 2:00. We promised." She saw the confused look on my face and said, "Okay, I promised rather, when you were in kitchen at the pub yesterday. We were supposed to have the list done by then, but, oh well..."

I blushed a little remembering the Barry incident at the pub.

I just nodded, "Ok, what else?" I asked.

"Well, you have dinner with yer Dad and Mrs.O at 6:00," she giggled.

I nodded, like someone resigned to a death-row sentence. "So, we don't have to be anywhere for hours?" I asked. "I mean, it's 10am. I could go back to sleep!"

"No actually, by my account we need to do a bit of shopping."

"What for?" I said, starting to pout.

She stared at me. "Yer gonna sit there and pretend you don't know…really?" There was a moment of silence. She looked like she was a little pissed at me, and I was baffled. "Ya need new skivvies," she bellowed, seriously and wide eyed.

I started to laugh.

"No, I'm not kiddin'," she kept going. "It was downright embarrassin' to be yer friend last night. Yer a direct reflection on me, ya know," she said laughing. "Boxers and group sex, indeed. I'll be party to none of it."

"Okay," I said, raising my hands up in defeat. "But we need to make a stop off at my work."

"Why?" asked Fitz. "They're not expectin' ya back for another week."

"I just thought I should tell Nancy that I'm here in case she needs me."

"Oh, I stopped off and got a coffee when I left here yesterday. Nance was doin' the inventory. She asked me if I had heard from ya, yet, ya know… how your trip was goin' and all. So, I went ahead and spilled the beans. Get it?" she said, with a wink.

That was the name of the coffee shop I had worked at since I was fifteen, 'Spilled the Beans'. I know that working at a coffee shop doesn't sound very ambitious to most people, but truthfully, I loved the place. My boss, the people I work with, my regular customers, are all awesome. It's like having a third family, who tips. Fitz's family being first and mine a close second. Then there's the art work. We showcase some of the best new artists in the South Bay. The 25 foot high walls are covered in oil, pastel and charcoal works. Watching the art being hung, I knew that the next time that piece leaves the wall it's going home with a person who loves and adores it. They have to have it! If I had any balls at all, my artwork, my paintings, would have been on those walls years ago. I didn't fancy myself an artist though. I was just someone who loved to paint. I thought about my second bedroom. The one I needed to have when I was looking for a place to rent (The one that was supposed to be my painting studio). It had great lighting and my very expensive easel, which had now been reduced to a very expensive piece of furniture that needed to be dusted. I had barely stepped foot in there in the last eight months.

"What did Nance say?" I asked.

"You know Nance," said Fitz. "First she said how much she loved ya and how a man like him should have given his left nut to be with you. Then she asked if ya wanted him killed. She called him a lousy, greasy piece of shit spewed out of the ass, of an ass. I love her. She's so colorful."

"I should still drop by. Maybe tomorrow," I said, more to myself than Fitz. I started for the bedroom to find something to wear, when I stopped and turned on Fitz. "You did tell her NOT to have him killed, right?"

She sat there smiling at me.

"Never mind, I don't want to know."

Nancy Goldburg, or Nance as I had called her all these years, was an eccentric. Not exactly hard to find in L.A. but what made her stand out from the crowd was she was originally from New York. That made her a theatrical eccentric. She had a slight New York accent and attitude which gained momentum with drink or agitation.

Once, a man had hit her car while trying to park in front of the coffee shop. She very kindly let him know that the car he had hit, the one he wasn't leaving a note on, was in fact hers. He had refused to give her his name or insurance information, telling her instead to, "Call the cops, I'll be gone by the time they show up. Then it's your word against mine..." and so on. We had to call the police to stop the ass beating he was receiving at her tiny hands. She was old enough to be my mom, in her late forties, early fifties, but she could be vicious if provoked, and I suspected "connected." To whom, or what, I really didn't want to know. She had been a divorcee for as long as I had known her and had no desire to marry again, not that she didn't date. She was a slight woman, maybe a hundred pounds soaking wet on a five foot-one frame. Her brown hair with red highlights was kept at shoulder length and was always perfectly styled. She wore red glasses that were too big for her face at first glance, but after knowing her a while they just suited her. She was always impeccably dressed and favored Bohemian Prints. And of course, she loved rich coffee and great art. She never had kids, by choice. She said she loved children the way she loved tigers; "In cages and sedated!" In the last several years I had done all the managerial duties leaving her free time to travel and sculpt. Truth is, I ran her business and she thought of me as, "The closest thing to a daughter I'll ever have, or want." I loved her. Her down to Earth, tell it like it is, attitude, made it impossible not to.

I put on another pair of 501's, that didn't have cake all over them and a red baby T. Thanks to over packing for my Hawaii trip, I didn't have any underwear left, so I went 'commando'. I found a bra that I had to put the under wire back in. But like I said, everything I owned that was worth wearing was on vacation without me. I didn't feel like doing the make-up thing, instead deciding to wear the five dollar knock-off sunglasses. I pulled my hair into a pony tail as we walked out to Baby.

"Top down, I think," said Fitz.

"I don't really care," I said, putting on my sunglasses.

"Don't be such a gloomy Gus."

"I'm not," I replied. "I'm a 'Hungover Harriet'."

A few minutes later, we were on our way. Fitz had been right, the food had done wonders for my champagne, wine, and whiskey hangover.

"So, where are we heading?" I asked.

I figured that we were going to some cute little boutique. I was a little surprised when we pulled up at the mall. I hated the mall. There were always too many people. And, for some reason, no one could figure out a flow of traffic. You had several different kinds of people, too. First, was the Mossier: This was the person who knew you were behind them, but wouldn't move over and let you 'pass'. Instead they walk in the middle of the flow and stop at every window, only gaining speed when you try to go around them. Next was the Heel Walker. These people are on your ass, no matter which way you move. They never say "excuse me," choosing instead to practically run you down no matter how hard you try to get out of their way. They always seem to be in a violent hurry to get to the food court.

Last are the Baby People: These people see all the madness the mall has to offer. The 'Mossier' and the 'Heel Walker', and somehow still thought that this is the best place for their small children to take their first steps. Even if there were no escalators, no men with huge carts delivering packages and no old people in wheel chairs, this would still seem like a bad idea to me.

We stepped into the madness. People were rushing everywhere.

"Where to?" I asked.

"Right there," said Fitz, directing me to a store that was ironically named, The Boutique.

When we walked in a waft of perfume met us. Mannequins lined the walls in seductive poses. They modeled frilly bra and panty sets complete with garter and hose. There were round tables set about strewn with lace and satin thongs and bikini underwear. Fitz started thumbing through the merchandise and pulling pairs she thought I would like.

"These are nice," she said, showing me the smallest pair of panties I had ever seen.

I made a face at her. "Do you know me at all? I don't wear things like that. Short of porn stars, who does?"

She shot me a shitty look and pulled the side of her thong out of the top of her jeans to reveal the exact same pair.

I made a look like when you step on a snail barefoot, "Sorry," I said, embarrassed for her…or me. I wasn't really sure. "I just, you know, wear regular underwear…comfy underwear."

"Granny panties," she shot back. "I know you prefer your white cotton undies. But we're trying to make some necessary changes here. These," she held up the panties, "are sexy. Your underwear says something about you. And unfortunately, although your underwear are comfy for you, they scream matronly to anyone else who pries you out of your jeans," she said, with an offended smile.

"Ok," I sighed, with my hands up. "But can they be a little less sexy and a little more comfy?"

"Fine," she said, dropping the panties back on the table. "We'll keep lookin'."

We finally found a few pairs that had a little back support, but could still be considered sexy.

I looked at the price tags. "Is this for one pair?" I asked in shock.

Fitz nodded at me. "Yes, they price them separately," she said sarcastically.

"Sixteen dollars for one pair?" I asked. She nodded. "I usually get 12 pairs for that price."

"Yes, and they look like you buy them in bulk at one of those price club stores."

"This is ridiculous, I mean, who can afford these?"

"You can," she grinned. "Yer gonna use some of that money ya got from dopey, yer last conquest," she grinned, "to entice yer next."

When she put it like that, I had to smile. "You're right," I said. "I deserve pretty panties.

Expensive pretty panties" We both grinned and the shopping was on. After all, I did have $1,600.00 left over that I had extorted from John. Not to mention all the money I had saved to go on the trip to begin with. The way I saw it, it wasn't the vacation I expected but I could still shop like it was.

After we found what would be my everyday panties, we shopped for bra and panty sets for a special occasion, should one arise.

Fitz held up a very padded ultra lift and separate, bra. I shook my head no.

"Why?" she wanted to know.

"Because," I said, "it's like false advertisement."

She giggled. "What the hell are ya talking about?"

"At some point the bra has to come off. I know some men are stupid or unschooled in women's things, but the one thing they know is boob size. If you're a full hand-full with the bra on, you should be a full, hand full with the bra off. I don't mind lifting but I don't believe in padding. It's like starting out a relationship with a lie," I said, laughing. "And I'm a full hand-full already, depending on the size of the hand, thank you very much."

"Okay," said Fitz, shaking her head and laughing back.

"No really, what if men padded? How disappointing would that be?"

She pondered and nodded. "It's a logical question," she added, "and yes, I'd be put off!"

I guess we were being a little loud. I noticed that we were getting some pretty dirty looks. Mostly from flat-chested women, holding horribly padded bras.

After I had spent hundreds of dollars in The Boutique, we went to find me some more 501's.

Fitz tried her best to get me to try on some overpriced girly jeans saying, "Ya can't even see your curves in these things? Ya have good hips, Janie. You should be showin' em off!" But I stood firm on comfort there. My 501's were my happy place.

I found some very girly camisoles though, and tank tops, some strappy sandals, two light sweaters, and a red & white polka-dot sundress that had a 'pin-up' feel to it. I stopped off at the Sun's Rays to get some decent sunglasses. Not a really expensive pair, not the way I go through them, but a nice pair that suited me.

Then I had to get a corn dog from the food court. Truthfully, I didn't really like hot dogs and almost never eat them, but anytime I went to the mall I absolutely had to have a corn dog from Stick Dog.

"We should get tattoos," said Fitz, out of nowhere.

"What? Like the temporary ones we used to buy at the accessories shop when we were in our teens?"

"No, real ones."

Fitz already had a tattoo. It was a beautiful butterfly on her ankle. I went with her to get said tattoo. She's one of the toughest women I know, and it had reduced her to tears. I thought Blade, the tattoo artist, who looked like he studied his art in prison, was going to have to knock her out to finish it.

"No," I shook my head, "I've made it to twenty-five..."

"Almost twenty-six," Fitz interrupted.

"Yes," I said, "a few weeks to twenty-six, without succumbing to what has become a huge fad. I'm not caving now. Plus, I don't even know what permanent image I'd want on my body."

"Just say you'll think about it?"

This was her way. She knew she had just tried to program me to think of nothing else. She thinks she knows me so well. And she does.

We were supposed to be going over to meet Mum and Aunt Marble, but I noticed that we weren't heading towards either of their houses.

"Where are we meeting them?" I asked, as we pulled onto Hawthorne Blvd. heading towards Palos Verdes.

"Remember the woman ya met the other night, Lavender?"

"Yeah, the grey haired woman, right?"

"Yep, were goin' to her house," said Fitz. "Wait till ya see it...you'll be amazed."

We wound around the turns climbing the cliffs. To my right was the Pacific. The sun was bright and warmed my flesh. I took a deep breath of the ocean air. I was so relaxed that I hardly noticed how badly Fitz drove, or the fact that the car had stopped.

We had pulled up in front of a beautiful old Victorian home, nestled so that you couldn't see it from the road. The huge white house had a wrap-around garden with a wrought iron fence. I didn't know too much about flowers, but I could obviously identify the Roses, Irises and Lilies. I could also see that a garden such as this one would be a labor of love. A cobblestone path led us past a flower covered trellis that hung above the large patio area. Marble benches and tables were set up for entertaining. We continued up the cobblestone path to the leaded glass French doors. Fitz knocked.

Mum answered the door in one of her vibrantly colored moo-moos. "Oh, my babies are here," yelled Mum, to someone in another room. I loved that I was one of her children in her eyes. She hugged Fitz and then turned to me for another. "Well, move your tooshies, girls."

She hurried us inside. I took a look around and was flabbergasted.

The foyer was surrounded by windows and was big enough to be my living room. Straight ahead was a long hallway leading off to an unknown destination. To the right, there were four stairs leading down into the open Great Room. The ceilings must have been twelve feet high. Cherrywood bookshelves lined one whole wall, the floors matched and stretched throughout the house. On the opposite wall, was a huge brick fireplace with a cherrywood mantel. The couches looked like overstuffed white clouds that you could sink into. I was surrounded by antique furniture and elegance. All of the sudden, I was scared to death that I would break or spill something with my constant fidgeting and downright clumsiness. I made a conscious effort to stifle my busy hands. There were seven lit candles on the coffee table. Because of last night's events, I couldn't help but wonder if the number of candles was significant in some way.

"Hello Luv's," called Aunt Marble coming from the kitchen wearing what looked like an African ceremonial dress, carrying a pitcher of lemonade. "I noticed that Fitz drove, so I'm glad to see you made it in one piece."

Fitz put her hands on her hips and said, "One time I crashed the car. And it was ten years ago. I hadn't even had drivers training yet. You bring it up every time I see ya!"

"I know dear," said Aunt Marble. "That way every time ya drive, you'll think about it and be safer. It's pure logic, Luv."

Fitz shook her head and turned her attention to me, "Am I a bad driver?"

"Of course not," I said, biting my lip and trying not to think about all the curbs and poles she had taken out since we were sixteen. Thank God Baby was all steel and heavily insured.

In came Lavender. Her long grey hair pulled up in a high bun on her head, wearing white slacks and a button-up light blue shirt, and barefoot of course. She was carrying a tray of homemade cookies and cakes. "Hello girls," her voice rang. "Welcome to my home," she said looking at me.

I couldn't help thinking how Mum and Aunt Marble looked like the gypsies that read tarot cards and palms at the psychic fairs and festivals. But Lavender... she looked like Jackie O on vacation in the Hampton's.

"It's absolutely gorgeous," I said. "Thank you for having me."

She smiled, "Thank you for coming. Please sit," she said, extending her hand towards one of the cloud sofas.

"We'll be in the garden," Mum said, grabbing her lemonade. Fitz and Aunt Marble followed quickly at her heals before I could protest.

"They don't need to leave. I mean, they know me almost as well as I know myself. Mum bought me my first bra, for God sakes."

"I wanted a chance to get to know you without anyone else's input. And since Mum and Marble are famous for... input, I thought maybe we could go it alone."

I nodded, understanding exactly what she meant, but still wondering why this woman wanted a sit down with me. "Okay," I said.

"Are you comfortable?" she asked.

"Yes, thank you."

She sat down across from me and smiled. She didn't say anything, though.

Finally I asked, "What should I call you? Is it Lavender or Mrs....someone?"

"You may call me by my real name if you like. I'm Diana or Diane, either way."

I'm sure I looked a little surprised. I guess I knew she and the other women would all have real names. I mean seriously, Valerian, or whatever, who names their kid that? I just hadn't given it enough thought. But, she definitely looked more like a Diana than Lavender.

We sat on the sofa facing each other.

I don't know why, but I got a little more nervous and started to fidget again.

She reached out a hand to my jumping fingers and said, "No need for that, relax."

It sounded almost like she was commanding my body, and it listened.

"So Janie," she started, "do you have your list?"

I took a deep breath and said, "No." I started to ramble on about me and Fitz's drunken evening and she laughed.

"It's fine," she said. "It's just used as a tool, one of many actually. I want you to feel secure with me, safe."

I nodded knowing that my breathing had changed. It was slower, deeper.

"Tell me about yourself," she inquired.

It was a quick and somewhat vague editorial on me; just the basics.

"I don't want an obituary," she said, with her gentle smile. "Tell me how you feel about the relationships in your life. From mother to lover, as I always say."

I took another deep breath. I wasn't really accustomed to sharing my life with strangers. Truth was, I was kind of shy and a little closed off until I felt a bond of some sort. But then I started talking. Before I knew it I told her about everyone in my life. Good, bad or indifferent. Things came spilling out of me that I hadn't really known had even affected me. From my relationship with my mom and dad, to Fitz and her family, to my work and Nance, to the men I had dated and been dumped by. I couldn't stop talking, and crying and laughing. I finally came to the present tense and she looked at me with those loving eyes and said, "The journey can be rough at times."

She then told me a little of her childhood. An alcoholic mom and an absent dad made for a difficult adolescence. She made her way to Berkeley College in San Francisco on grants. What they didn't cover she made up for by flipping burgers. She majored in psychology and minored in art. She met her now deceased husband, Oliver, there. They graduated together and were never apart again. They joined the Peace Corps where they spent years and years in foreign and under developed countries. They helped build bridges, dams, and whole villages. She said that Africa had been their favorite adventure of all. She had become a mother there. Their daughter, they named Arinna after the Goddess known as the Queen of Heaven. But, every Country they spent time in had been an amazing and eye opening experience.

"We moved back to the states when Arinna was ten," she said. "It was hard for her. She too, fell in love with Africa. But it was time to come home. We three rebuilt this place together," she said, with a wave of her hand. "It was so run down I never thought we would finish. It took years but we finally did. It was our dream home. Now it's just my dream home. Arinna is grown and lives on the East coast with her high-powered attorney husband, Paul. And my Oliver, well, he passed away two years ago. I miss him in my everyday life. I miss his touch, his voice. I even miss him ribbing me constantly. But every night I talk to him and tell him all the things that I would if he were sitting right next to me, in body. I know he hears me and listens. Sometimes I ask him for signs. And, I do receive them in ways that may only make sense to me, to us. You see, I know that I was well loved then and I still am. He wouldn't let me forget that."

I had tears running down my face when she finished her story. I reached for a tissue and blew my running nose. I wanted to beg God to send Oliver back to her. They had true love, the kind that should never be allowed to be severed. I felt so bad for her. But, I noticed she wasn't crying. She looked at the candles on the table in front us. Six were completely still and one was flickering and dancing. She smiled at it, then at me. I caught my breath and looked from it to her, awestruck, a chill running down my spine.

"There are no small signs, when it comes to love!" she whispered, taking my hand in hers.

After I composed myself, she grabbed the note book and pen off the table and said, "Tell me your birth date."

"Oh," I said, dabbing at my runny nose. "It's June 28th."

"Coming up quickly," she smiled.

"Yeah," I said, with very little enthusiasm.

"You don't like your birthday?" she inquired, with a raise of her eyebrow.

"It's just... I haven't done all the things I was supposed to do by twenty-five. And twenty-five is almost gone."

"Like what? What accomplishments do you feel you're lacking?" she asked, cocking her head.

Yep, I thought to myself, definitely a psychologist. "I thought by now," I began, "I would have sold one of my paintings. Or published the cookbook I wrote. I should be more than," I paused looking for the right word, "this!" I finally concluded. "I'm supposed to be married with children," I said, pulling my fingers through my hair. "Not dumped again."

"Who says you're supposed to be married with children right now?"

"Well, my mom for one."

"Who else?" she asked.

I thought for a moment. "I guess just my mom. But I have been raised to believe that a happy woman is married with children. And, the older you get, and the more men you date, the more undesirable you become. Twenty-five is like the cut-off. My mom was twenty-two when I was born. I mean, I don't want to blame my mother, that's so cliché..." I trailed off.

"Ah," she said, nodding her head. "So is it possible that you've been trying to make a man 'Mr. Right' so that you could meet a deadline that you set for yourself?"

Damn it, I thought. Truth was I was more than prepared to blame my crazy mother. Was almost looking forward to it, but now the ball was in my court. And an ugly court it was. "I guess it's possible," I said, in a non-committed way.

"Have you ever tried to sell one of your paintings?"

The immediate change of subject threw me. "Not really," I said. "I mean, I could ask to display them at my work."

"But you haven't?"

"No," I said slowly.

"And this book, you say it's done?"

"Yes," I began to fidget again, mentally going over my Manicotti recipe.

"Have you tried to find a publisher?"

I shook my head. "No, I haven't." When she put it this way, I was starting to see the point she was making.

"Are you proud of your paintings, of your book?"

"I am," I said. She watched me and waited for me to

continue. I let out a sigh, "But what if no one else likes them or every publisher shoots me down?"

She smiled and nodded, like she was seeing me in a new light. A pathetic one.

"My dear," she began. "It sounds like you're afraid of failure."

"Isn't everyone," I asked in a desperate tone, covering my face with my hands.

"Yes, we are. Everyone is at some time. But to never try is to have failed already. Maybe this is why you put so much work into relationships, you know are destined to fail."

"What? Why would I do that?" I asked, baffled at the thought. I was seeing a slight connection…okay, a huge connection and I didn't like it.

"Maybe it's easier to put all of your attention into a relationship than it is to put into yourself. Maybe you think your being selfish by putting yourself first."

"Well, isn't it selfish? I mean, isn't that what selfish is?"

"Only if you always put yourself first," she said gently. There was a long pause. "Have you ever asked a man out on a date?"

She was all over the place with her questioning. I laughed. "Yeah, I must have at some point," I said, trying to figure out what this had to do with anything.

"Think," she said. "When have you asked a man out?"

I tried to think of a time. But if I was being honest, I couldn't. For the life of me, I couldn't remember even one man that I had ever approached first. Even the Sadie Hawkins dance in ninth grade, I had to go with Willy Price, a chess geek, because I couldn't bring myself to ask a boy out. "You know, I can't say that I have. What does that mean?" I asked very seriously.

"Well, it could mean that you've only been interested in men that show an interest in you first. The fact that they showed an interest may have been what attracted you to them.

Ok, I thought, is there another word more pathetic than pathetic? Cause I was that. If I was hearing her right, and I knew I was, it meant that it was possible that I settled for whoever liked me. My attraction to them was based SOLELY on the fact that they liked me!

"Have you ever been interested in a man who didn't approach you?" she asked, digging deeper.

My mind, totally against my will, went immediately to Barry. I nodded but wouldn't say his name.

"But you didn't approach him?" she asked.

"No," I said, with a nervous laugh, shaking my head trying to clear last night's embarrassing moment with Barry from my mind. "I don't think he thinks of me that way."

"How do you know?"

"He's never said anything. I mean, I've known this guy for years," I emitted an uncomfortable laugh, "and he's never shown the slightest interest in me. He would have said something by now, or done…something."

"You do have feelings for this gentleman?" she inquired.

I nodded, "Well...yeah."

"You're attracted to him?" she asked.

I thought for a moment, "Yes." I was starting to feel nauseated again.

"So, you're afraid to put yourself and your feelings out there?"

I nodded at her, "Ugh, yeah. It's a little complicated."

"So what makes you think he's not afraid to approach you? If it's complicated for you, couldn't it also be for him?"

I mulled this over in my head. Was it possible that some men were so scared of being shot down, they wouldn't make a move? "I thought having a penis made you immune to having fears like that," I stated.

She smiled at me. "We're human, all of us. We all have

fears…even people with a penis," she joked back and grinned before continuing on. "For some of us, rejection, even the thought of it is so painful, we settle for whoever shows an interest. The 'sure thing' so to speak. What you have to remember is first attraction is almost always based on the physical. Although our bodies may work well together it's our minds that keep us together. You see dear, opposites do attract. But attraction may fade. Compatibility," she said, "is more than a passing fancy. Now back to your birthday."

Again the change of focus had my mind spinning. I was still stuck on my pitiful dating life.

"Birthdays are mile stones to be proud of," she went on. With them comes wisdom and knowledge. They're worth every wrinkle. Now, you wouldn't know what time you were born, by chance?"

Feeling quite schooled, I said, "Yeah, I do actually." I explained how my mother told the story almost every year, about how I had been born at eight o'clock p.m. on the dot. My father had been waiting to see a boxing match for weeks. My mother managed to get him tickets and then I went into labor. Not her, me! She never mentions that I was an easy birth. One hour is all I took escaping her womb.

"You know she loves you very much," she said, nodding at me. "She just wants you to be happy. But what makes her a happy woman may not be what you want out of your life."

"Yeah, I guess," I said, exhausted from mulling.

"You don't get to choose how your parents are taught to love or show love. You do however get to choose how you accept to be loved by a partner."

I thought this over a little.

"You see, you can decide what you want from a partner. What you require. And, what is worth accepting to you. My Oliver used to smoke cigars, and I hated them. But, this bad habit he had was something I was willing to accept. It was something I could live with. And now, every time I smell a cigar burning I smile. He, in return, would put up with some of my less favorable habits. But he never tried to change me, or I him."

I wondered what her unfavorable habits could possibly be, being right?

She continued, "I fell in love with the man he really was. Not what I could turn him into and vice-versa. Part of that comes from being honest with each other up front. Some people say, he or she changed while I was with them. Most likely, they didn't really change. The real "Them" finally emerged. Or they hid the real "Them" for selfish reasons. Usually people with an unfavorable past will embellish who they are to be with the person they want. They are of the mindset that no one could possibly love the real them.I knew this type of person to be a sociopath, but stayed silent.She waited to see how this affected me before going on. "It's more likely they had different desires and interests that finally needed to be met. They say things like 'we just grew apart'. Usually, that's not it at all."

I nodded, trying to take this in, knowing that I had heard this break up speech before, and had only bought it to save myself some humiliation.

"Then there are people who want to be the right person for their partner so badly, they try to emulate what they think their partner wants and needs." Her eyes softened and I knew she was putting me into this category as gently as she could. "They may have even changed their needs and wants to be that person for their partner. Unlike the first type of person, this is the unselfish act of a person who wants to please their partner, not to deceive. But then they can lose sight of who they are and what they want and need. Then they're just going through the motions, lost in a way. To really know yourself, and like yourself, and be yourself, is the only way to find someone who likes you. The real you, just the way you are. I'm not saying you shouldn't work on qualities you have that you may not be fond of. I believe that self-examination and exploration of one's self is necessary. Very few people ever take the time to examine what they would like to change about themselves. And even fewer ever make those changes."

I nodded, mentally applying that to my relationship with John. Going over in my head how many things I had wanted to do with him. And, how he always backed out or changed our plans without even consulting me. I had to admit to myself, I had done things (many of which I didn't enjoy at all) simply to be with him, and to spend time with him. I felt like a dumb ass.

"This," she said, showing me a book titled 'The Cancer Woman' "is about you. I'm sure the book won't be dead on, how could it be? You really are one of a kind. Once I find out your Rising and Moon signs, you'll be receiving two more books. Do you enjoy reading?" she asked me.

I nodded. She was now speaking Quantum Physics with the 'rising moon sign' stuff to me, but I didn't want to interrupt.

"Good," she smiled. "I want you to read through it, if you'd like. Decide what applies to you. Then, write down the things that you would like to change," she smiled at me, judging my apprehension. "Also, I would like you to write down your strengths. What you're good at. What you're proud of. This is an important part of the exercise. Once on paper, you'll find so many things you are proud of yourself for accomplishing that you may have taken for granted."

I thought of writing down, "I love my mother." That was my greatest feat at times, but I just nodded like a little kid who had been struck dumb.

"This Rune," she showed it to me. It was a little flat stone that had what looked like a symbol of a lightning bolt on it. "I want you to keep with you. You can keep it in your purse but, on your body is better."

I had no idea why carrying the tiny stone would have any effect on my life, but decided to just roll with it, I mean, obviously, it couldn't hurt me either.

"In this pouch," she held up a Mojo Bag, "are some herbs. Jasmine, lavender, red rose petals, dragon's blood…"

"What?" I said, looking at the bag with obvious concern.

"It's just a name," she laughed and let her attention move back to the mojo bag "...a copper coin, a silver moon and a rose quartz and a few other things I've picked for you. Keep this with you too. You don't have to wear it, but some people do. These candles," she said, "are your Chakra colors, this tiny pamphlet here, it will tell you when, and how, to use them."

"I don't mean to sound rude, but I wouldn't have expected a psychologist to be so into this spiritual stuff."

"There are four levels on which I believe people can connect: mental, emotional, physical and spiritual. I don't expect to connect to everyone I meet, on every level. The truth for me is, the diversity of our disconnections can be very enlightening and thought provoking. But my job is to understand people, even if I don't see the world the way they do. To be 'well rounded' and 'grounded', so to speak, helps me connect to people more easily, and them to me."

I smiled at her. I didn't quite understand, but she gave me plenty to think about.

I looked at my watch, it was 4:45. "I hate to do this, but I have to run. I have to be at my parent's house for dinner at six. If I'm late my mom calls everyone I know then starts calling hospitals. (Unless she knows that I'm with Fitz. Then she starts with the city jail, I thought.)

"She loves you, Janie," said Diane, with a wink and a pat on the hand.

I nodded and stood to leave, then stopped dead in my tracks and turned to her. "I had one more question or...comment, um, last night, I felt... something."

"I know you did," she said, smiling.

Neither of us elaborated. Maybe because she knew at this stage, I really couldn't. I wasn't sure what I thought or even how I felt about it.

Diane walked me out to her side garden to find Fitz, Mum and Aunt Marble sitting and enjoying the sun at her large marble table.

"How was it dear?" asked Mum, hugging me.

"It was great," I said, realizing that I really did feel lighter. "I've got some work to do though."

Aunt Marble winked at me and said, "You won't go it alone, Luv. We'll be here for ya!"

I know that she was trying to be supportive but that thought scared the hell out of me.

Mum asked, "Janie, say you'll come for dinner tomorrow night?"

"But it's Monday. Don't you do your Ladies of the Moon thing on Mondays?"

"Most of the ladies are going to a Men's review, but, Marble and I begged out on account of her pulling her back Salsa dancing," she said, patting Marble's shoulder.

"Yeah, no reason for me to go if I can't grind on the dancers," said Marble.

I nodded as straight faced as I could, and said a silent prayer for male strippers everywhere. At least they would be safe from Aunt Marble…this time. "You bet," I said. I smiled trying not to look frightened and quickly took my leave.

Mum was a great cook, one of the best, but I always had to worry about what part of what animal I was eating. Best not to think about it.

Fitz and I jumped back in Baby and flew back to my house. We didn't talk much. Instead we sang along to Social Distortion. Twenty minutes later, we carried in my new clothes and stuff from the mall.

I hit the answering machine as I passed it. One call from mom, I heard, "Don't forget, dinner at...," I hit the skip button. Another message, from Nance, "Call me honey, when you can, that is. Love you!" Next message was from Betty, "Puddin? I was hopin' you could bring me back that spare key. I just like to keep track of 'em. Give me a ring, sugar or just drop by. I'd love to see you." The fourth call was from the airport. "Hi, Miss O'Connelly this is Annie from Hawaiian Airlines, again. Um... your luggage...somehow...well..."

I screamed at the answering machine, "Spit it out Annie!"

"It's in London," the voice said, as though she was responding to me.

"You have got to be kidding me!" I yelled.

"We're keeping track of it. I don't know how this happened. We really are sorry. We're sending you 1000 more frequent flier miles on top of the 500 we've already sent."

"That's pretty good," said Fitz, joining me at the machine.

"Yeah," I said, "it would be, if I believed they would ever make it here. They're probably on their way to Sri Lanka, or Budapest. My luggage has seen Hawaii, France and now London... without me!" I turned the machine off. "Aaaahhhh," I yelled.

Fitz laughed and said, "Don't let yourself get too emotionally exhausted you still have to dine with Mrs.O."

I shot her a shit look and a heavy sigh. Then a thought came to me. "Hey, what are you doing tonight? Maybe you could...."

"Oh no," said Fitz cutting me off. "As much fun as it sounds to torture your mother with my very presence, I have a date. Pete, remember? I'm missing our family night for this date."

"Oh yeah, well call me later and tell me how it went."

"Hopefully, I won't be able to call until tomorrow morn," she grinned. "Bye." She looked back at me, "Do you have a spare to your car?"

"Yeah, it's in the kitchen cupboard," I said.

"Why's it in there?"

"I don't know. Where do you keep your spares?"

"My bedside drawer."

"Huh," I said as she left. That's not what I expected to find in her bedside table.

5

MOM'S SURPRISE

I drove to my parent's house in Manhattan. They lived in the same house on Ardmore, a one way street where I had learned to ride a bike as a kid. Thanks to the hill leading up from the beach you could see the ocean from their patio, even though they were still three blocks up from the sand. I made it with ten minutes to spare.

"Mom," I yelled, coming through the front door. I could smell the roast cooking. I followed the old shag green carpet down the long hallway, to the linoleum floor. I walked into the kitchen to see her standing over the stove wearing a frilly apron, her hair pulled back in a tight red bun.

"Hi Mom," I said.

"Oh, you're here. Good, and on time!"

"Mom, I'm always on time," I said, trying not to sound defensive and reminding myself to breathe. I did that a lot in her presence. "Can I help you with anything?"

"No, I have this all under control," she said pouring flour into the drippings for gravy. "But, you could set the table."

"Done," I said, grabbing the plates.

"Oh, there'll be four of us for dinner tonight," she said nonchalantly.

My parents never had company. My Aunt Kate and Uncle Morty came for dinner from time to time. But that's not company, that's family.

"Who's coming to dinner?" I asked, suspiciously.

The doorbell rang.

"Get the door, Tom, will you?" she yelled at my father. I heard him grumble from the living room.

"Who'd you invite to dinner, Mom," I asked, a little worried.

She began to whip the lumps out of the gravy.

"Mom," I said again, with less patience, "who's coming to dinner?"

"Lenny," my mother said, blankly.

"Lenny who?" I asked.

"Aunt Kate's son."

"Why? Are Aunt Kate and Uncle Morty on another cruise?"

Last time they went on a cruise my mother had to cook for Lenny every night for a week. Seems he's not allowed to use the stove.

"I just thought it would be a nice change for him. After all, I'm a much better cook than Kate."

It seemed odd to me that he would accept an invitation to dinner. He didn't really like people, from what I remembered, and family fell into that category in the broadest sense of the word.

As children, I didn't like Lenny. He was allergic to everything, so I had to play inside when he was over so he wouldn't feel left out. He was a pasty-faced gangly kid with red hair and freckles to match. His horn-rimmed glasses were rarely seen since he usually had his head stuck in a book. That's when he wasn't studying his mail-ordered bug collection. He gave me the creeps. I hadn't seen him in two years, but he hadn't changed much as of then.

I walked into the dining room and began setting the table. I could see Lenny through the doorway that led to the living room. He was sitting on the couch reading a book. My father was in his easy chair watching the fights. Neither one of them acknowledged the other's existence. My father had always been the strong silent type. Before he retired he was a machinist for an airline company. He was used to sitting alone for hours and never having to make small talk. But he was my sanity growing up and I loved him well. I resisted the urge to kiss my father "hello" seeing as that would mean I'd have to talk Lenny as well.

Mom yelled from the kitchen, "Dinner's ready, time to eat."

We sat at the table in silence for a long time. I sat across from Lenny and tried not to watch him dissect his meat. I wasn't sure how he could eat. His deviated septum made it impossible for him to breathe through his nose. My mother finally got the ball rolling.

"So Lenny, your mother says you got a new pet, a dog right? I thought you were allergic to animals?"

"I am," he said, as matter of fact, "When they're alive that is."

I gave my mom a concerned raise of my eyebrows. He was going to elaborate on the subject. I just knew it.

"I do taxidermy as a hobby," he said, never looking up from his plate where he was separating meat from fat with frightening precision. "I now have a cat, a dog, a blue bird and a squirrel."

My mother nodded and said, "Isn't that nice," forcing a smile, as if this was a completely normal dinner topic.

I sat there trying not to look as sickened as I was. But I couldn't help picturing him in his room, stroking a dead cat while he planned world domination. A shiver ran up my spine.

"So Janie, did you know that Lenny works at the hospital?" Mom asked.

I stabbed a carrot with my fork. "No, um, what do you do there?" I asked, trying to sound interested.

"I work in the lab." he said, still not looking up from his plate.

"It's a great job," said Mom, nodding at me.

"Yeah, it, ugh, sounds very... interesting," I searched for a word, other than disgusting.

Out of nowhere, he asked, "Do you know how many parasites and bacteria can live in fecal matter?"

My jaw dropped, and I shot my mother a look of horror. My father, who had been quietly trying to ignore the conversation, stopped his fork half way to his mouth and stared at his pot roast, before putting it back on the plate. Lenny seemed unfazed by everyone else's reaction and kept talking.

"E. coli is particularly rampant."

My mother, sensing discomfort, tried to change the subject.

"So, Lenny, your mother tells me you're not dating at the moment."

He shoveled the pot roast into his mouth and shook his head no.

"Our Janie here isn't seeing any one right now, either."

I looked at my mother, totally confused. Why would he care if I was dating? I wondered. I sure as hell didn't want to think about the kind of woman that would date Lenny.

"Janie's just been through a bad break-up. That's why I thought the two of you should get together," she said.

A look of terror flashed across my face. My eyes widened, my brows arched even higher. Was I understanding her? Did she want me and sick-boy to console each other? To hang out? Be buddies?

"Um, Mom, I think we need more gravy," I said, standing up and grabbing the gravy boat.

"Nonsense," she said, "there's plenty of gravy."

"No, Mom, I think we need more and..." I clenched my teeth, "and I think you should come with me to get it." I walked into the kitchen with her in tow.

"What are ya doing, Janie?" she hissed as we entered the kitchen. "You're being very rude. Making ridiculous excuses to leave the room!" she barked.

"Are you kidding me? I'm not going to introduce him to any of my friends, Mom! Or hang out with him! I can't even stand to be around the little weasel!"

"I didn't invite him here to meet your friends," she huffed and turned her back to me.

"Then what the hell is all of this about?" I asked.

"Don't curse Janie! It's unbecoming of a lady," she sniped. "I just thought," she began "that maybe the two of you... you know... could go to dinner sometime or see a movie..." she trailed off.

I was trying to wrap my head around the thought. "Wait a minute," I finally spat, "are you trying to set ME up with Lenny?" I asked, dismayed.

"Well, neither of you are seeing anyone..." she began, "you two have known each other for years, so..."

"Of course we have Mom...He's my cousin!" I hissed, as quietly as I could.

"Oh, I swear you overreact to everything, Janie"

I stood there like a stone. My head was spinning, my stomach sloshing. "He's my cousin!" I repeated. "That's not only sick, Mom, but I think it's illegal." I thought I was going to throw up. I could feel what little dinner I actually got down, coming back.

"There's not a drop of blood between you!" she insisted.

"Aunt Kate married your Uncle Morty when Lenny was two. You know perfectly well that Lenny was from her first marriage and Uncle Morty adopted him. You don't even have the same last name! That makes it legal!"

I stared at my mother wide eyed and dumbfounded. Has she lost her mind, I wondered? "Even if he had not been raised as my cousin, and even if you didn't make us bathe together until we were six, I would never go out with Lenny. He's a freak, Mom! A taxidermy-ing, fecal-labbing-freak, that still lives with his parents, who just happen to be my Aunt and Uncle!" I yelled with eyes bulging now.

She let out a forced sigh, the one that lets me know that she's exasperated with me.

"How do you think he's going feel when he finds out WHY you invited him here?" I snapped.

"Well smarty-pants, he knows why he's here and he's very interested in you," she snapped back.

I stood there staring at her, mouth a gape, mortified. At first, I couldn't find words. Finally with a shudder, I emitted the only thing that would come out of my mouth, "Eewww…I'm outta here."

I walked back into the dining room, kissed my father on the cheek, and said goodbye.

"What? Your leaving?" my father asked, with a look of concern.

"Yeah, I'm not big on fix-up's, especially with family members," I huffed.

Dad's face went blank as he considered this new piece of information. "Your mother tried to set you up.... with him?" he asked shocked, pointing his fork in Lenny's direction.

"Yep, and I've gotta go now, Dad. I'm sorry, but I can't even begin to deal with this," I said, sickened. "This is morbidly wrong."

"Your mother must have lost her damned mind. He's your cousin," Dad interjected, doing a shudder himself.

Looking up from his plate for the first time, Lenny said to my father, "There's no blood between us."

With that, I said," Eeewww," again and ran towards the door. I heard my father say to Lenny before I closed the door, "You're not right, son."

I drove home in a state of shock. What the hell was that crazy old bat thinking? Most people go to their parents for comfort, support. Not me though. No I have the only mother in the world that would rather have grandkids that were a limerick than none at all. I may have had some bad relationships, but, like I said, even if Lenny wasn't my cousin, I would have to be bound and gagged to be caught dead with him. That thought brought up a whole new batch of scary. He's exactly the kind of sick-o that probably had a bound and gagged woman in my Aunt and Uncle's basement. And he was interested in me? When I got home I made sure all the doors were locked. I wanted to call Fitz, but she was on her date with Pete, the gorgeous baker. After putting a chair in front of the door I fell asleep on the couch. I had a horrible dream of Lenny in a powder blue tuxedo waiting at the front of an alter, and me in a white wedding gown, bound and gagged, on a conveyer belt leading me to my future husband…and taxidermist.

6

MON: DUMPED DAY 3

I woke with a start and sat up immediately. My heart was pounding out of my chest. It took a moment to find my bearings. I looked around, grateful to be unbound and in my living room. I gathered my senses and headed for the shower to disinfect myself when I caught the flashing light of my answering machine. I stood over it a moment, wondering, "Where was my luggage now?" I pushed the play button and heard my Mother's voice.

"I hope you're happy! Your father and I were up half the night fighting because of you!"

I stood there shaking my head, wondering if she truly had lost her mind and ... whether it was an inherited trait.

"I just don't see what the big deal is," she went on. "I mean, neither of you is seeing anyone… If you weren't interested, you could have just said so. You didn't have to be so rude..." I turned the message off and thought, yep, bat shit crazy.

I jumped in the shower and tried to wash off the 'yuck' from the dream. When I got out, I did my lotion/oil routine and brushed my teeth. I grabbed the vial Aunt Marble had given me.

"Zit Juice," I said out loud. It was a murky yellow and slightly thick gel of some kind. Well, it couldn't do any real damage, I thought. I was still worried, but the zit showed no sign of going away if not forced. So I unscrewed the top. A waft of flowers mixed with a camphor scent emerged. I dabbed a little on my finger and reluctantly applied it to the volcano on my forehead. It tingled slightly and warmed. But, my skin hadn't turned green or anything. Not yet at least. I put on a pair of my new undies and decided that they were going take some getting used to. They kept riding up into places they shouldn't be. I put on the new bra and it fit like a glove. A happy woman is the woman who is comfortable in her undergarments. I'd have to settle for 50/50. After I towel dried my hair and brushed it out, I pulled on a pair of 501's and a "Social Distortion" T-shirt. I had errands to run.

7

SPILLED THE BEANS

I jumped into my Neon and headed off. My first stop was my work, 'Spilled the Beans'.

Nance had bought the building during the early 80's. It was a time when people wanted to invest in new places, not put love into an old one. This building was an old loft style. It had the high ceilings, exposed brick and duct work you can't find in new construction. Because of its age it needed some revitalization. New flooring, separate bathrooms and a bigger kitchen were just the beginning. But she got it dirt cheap, made it her own, and could sell it today for more than ten times what she paid for it.

When I walked in Nance was showing two men where she wanted a new painting to hang. She had her back to me and I heard her say, "Higher and to the left." I walked up and scratched her upper left shoulder.

Turning to me, she smiled and said, "Never mind guys, we'll get back to it in a little while. Help yourself to some coffee and pastries. "How about you?" she asked me, "Coffee?"

"Please."

She yelled to Dante behind the counter, "Triple Non-Fat

Latte for Janie, please." He nodded, and said hello to me. I returned the pleasantries.

"Sit," Nance said. We took two chairs near the front window. "So, the bastard dumped you?"

She always cut right to the chase.

I nodded, "Yep, right there in the terminal in front of everyone…at least everyone that was flying from L.A. to Hawaii on Hawaiian Isle Airlines at 3pm on Friday," I grinned. "I hear I'm still big news though. The lady from the airline, who calls periodically to let me know what new adventure my lost luggage has been on, let's me know that I'm still a topic of much gossip. I have become the Urban Legend of bad dating."

Nance and I had always been close. She was one of those rare people I just connected to. She used to say that we would have been family, if you got to pick your family that is.

Nance smiled. "Well, it's good to see the humor has come back," she said, smiling wryly.

"Come back? It never left. It's been forced on me." I told her about the whole mess: the break-up, the bathroom, Yolanda, the cab rides, Betty's, Fitz's jaw breaker kick. She couldn't help but laugh with me. I had to admit, nothing that happened in my life was ever boring. I told her about dinner the night before and she was horrified.

"Your mother's crazy," she said, sounding truly astonished. "I really thought after all these years nothing she pulled or said could shock me."

"And now?" I asked.

"She still blows my mind!" she shook her head. "Somewhere there's a padded cell with her name on the door!"

"Yeah, I've already come to that conclusion. I'm thinking maybe I shouldn't have kids just in case senility sets in with childbirth," I grinned. "I have to assume she was normal once."

Dante brought me my second coffee in a to-go cup. "I'm

sorry to hear about the break-up," he said. I gave Nance a look of, thanks a lot.

"I didn't tell him," she said, with her hands up.

"Fitz told me the day before yesterday," he said.

"Of course she did," I said, sullen. I had forgotten that Dante had a huge crush on Fitz and would ask her anything to keep a conversation going, even about me.

I said, "thank you," and expected him to depart. But, he stood there staring at me. "Did you want something else?"

"I just wondered when Fitz would be back by. I made a new drink and named it after her. I can't wait for her to try it. It's got tons of cinnamon and nutmeg in it, so it has a lot of spice," he said grinning.

"I'm not sure, but I'll let her know you have something for her, okay?" I said.

"That'll be great," he said, and practically skipped away. Nance and me watched him, and laughed.

"You know," said Nance, "I shouldn't let Fitz in here while Dante's on shift. He doesn't get any work done!"

"About work, Nance, do you have any room on the wall for a new artist?"

She took in a deep breath, "You're finally ready!" she exclaimed. "I've been waiting since you were in high school to ask me." She threw her arms around my neck. "Of course I have room. Hell, if I didn't I'd make room."

I was a little surprised. "Why didn't you ever say anything?" I asked.

"I was waiting for you to be ready. Art is like your child," she said hugging herself dramatically. "If you weren't ready to display it or sell it, I would never force the subject. It had to be your decision."

I thought about that and it made sense, except the part about selling your child. But I knew what she meant. I told her I would be back in a couple of days with three paintings. I hugged her and headed back to my car, Latte in hand.

I was so excited. I could hardly wait to tell Fitz. But it was only ten o'clock and I figured she'd be asleep, possibly even asleep at someone else's house (Although, that wasn't her M.O.) As soon as I sat down my cell rang. Shit, I thought. Now I had to locate it in the purse that organization had forgotten. No matter which inside pocket I put it in it always ended up in the bottom somewhere. I finally fished it out on the fourth ring. Any second now it would go to voicemail. Since I was screening my calls, heaven forbid I have to talk to my Mom, and try, yet again, to explain why what she did was so wrong, I didn't have time to check the caller I.D. before it clicked over. I flipped the phone open, one missed call from Fitz's cell. I hit the redial and she picked up immediately.

"Come get me," she whispered.

"What, where are you?"

"I'm at Pete's house."

"Where's Baby?"

"I let Pete pick me up," she said, starting to sound agitated. "Come get me," she repeated.

"Ok. Once again, where are you?" I asked.

She gave me an address right off of Manhattan Beach Blvd. "Ok, I'll be there in five minutes."

"I'll be outside," she said, almost inaudibly then hung up.

I rushed to Manhattan Beach. A million thoughts ran through my mind. Fitz never let some guy take her to his place, not without her own transportation. She usually wouldn't go to a man's house unless she had known him for a while. What the hell had happened? It was exactly what I was thinking when I ran a red light. "Shit!" I said out loud, as I looked behind me to see if red swirling lights were gaining. No cop, good. Then my mind went back to Fitz. I took a right on Manhattan and began looking for the address. I didn't have to look long. There was Fitz standing on the curb waving her arms at me, heels in hands, hair crazy, looking a wreck. I pulled over and she jumped in.

"Go, GO!" she instructed.

I pulled away like a bat out of hell. "What the Hell is going on?" I shouted.

She was shaking. She reached in her purse and pulled out a pack of cigarettes. I was shocked. She and I had quit smoking almost two years ago. It had been the hardest three weeks. Not only of our lives, but also for anyone dumb enough to be around us. She took a long drag and started to calm down.

"Smoking? Really? What happened?" I yelled. "Are you okay?"

She nodded and blew out a puff of smoke. "I'm okay Janie," she reassured me.

Oh God I wanted that cigarette, I thought.

"What Happened?" I repeated, becoming angered by her silence. Had he hurt her? Raped her? I decided right there and then, if he had…he would die horribly.

She took another long drag and let it plume out. "We were having a great time. He took me to Tony's on the pier for dinner. I love Tony's. They have the best crab puffs."

"I know," I said, trying to move the conversation forward.

"Well, we had dinner and drinks. Then we went to that new Salsa dance club on Fifth. Ya really have to go with sometime. You'd love it."

"Fitz", I said, "if you don't get on with it, I'm driving back there," I threatened.

"I'm getting' there!" she shouted. "Everything was going fine. He was a great kisser. Ya know I'm a sucker for a great kisser?"

I nodded, rolling my wrist, "Go on."

"Well, when the bar closed at two neither of us wanted to

call it a night. But B.J. had a date last night and asked me if I would clear out. I intended to stay at Mum's but I wouldn't take a date there. He suggested a night cap at his house. I never do that," she insisted.

I knew this to be true, but said nothing.

"So we went to Pete's. His house is very nice. He brought some beautiful things from Italy when he moved here. One very beautiful thing," she said.

There was a long pause.

I mulled this comment over. "You mean a wife?" I yelled.

"Not quite," she said, timidly, "not a woman at least."

"Then I don't know what the Hell you're..." I stopped. "You mean…a man?" I spat out.

She nodded slowly, tongue in cheek.

I started to laugh uncontrollably, "Pete's Gay?"

"It's not funny," she shrieked, "and I think 'Bi' is more accurate."

"Oh, it's funny," I bellowed, laughing harder.

"Ya haven't heard the worst part." she said, seriously.

"Oh, I gotta hear this!" I said, and pulled the car to a curb so I could give her my full attention.

She remained silent until I agreed to stop laughing.

Finally she told me: They hadn't had sex. Just made out then passed out. Half of an hour before she called me, his lover who lives there by the way, entered the apartment and found her bra on the sofa. He started yelling. Her Italian being not so good, she didn't know what he was saying but she did know he was pissed. Pete told her that his lover was very jealous and violent. He begged her to hide while he was frantically trying to shove her and her shoes under the bed. She told him that she was utterly humiliated and refused to hide. She intended to meet this man eye to eye and explain how they had both been duped. Then she heard things, breaking and crashing in the living room.

Pete's boyfriend was freaking out. She quickly decided that maybe she didn't want to have a run-in with the jilted boyfriend after all. She had just made it under the bed, when Pete's lover burst in and started to advance on Pete. He flung Fitz's bra at Pete's face. Fitz recognized the word, "Stronzo," and thought that either she or Pete had just been called a bitch.

I didn't want to interject that I was pretty sure that Stronzo was Italian for 'Turd'. Seeing as how it still would have been offensive, I just let her continue.

So Pete started rambling. Something in his defense, she imagined. He sounded as if he were pleading his case. The next thing Fitz could see, was Pete's lover trying on her bra, and she thinks, thanking Pete for the gift the lovely gift. They started to make out and moved to the bed Fitz was hiding under. She had to pull on her jeans, grab her shoes as quietly as she could, shimmy her way across the floor, and escape the house. She called me when she made it safely outside.

By the time she finished the story I thought I was going to pee my pants. After I stopped laughing, I couldn't help but ask her if this meant, "No more cake from Lorenzo's?"

She said nothing. Just sat there fuming with her arms folded across her chest.

"I guess you're lucky that Pete's lover was a cross dresser, too, huh?" I asked, adding fuel to the fire.

She shot me a shitty look and said, "Shut up Janie... I loved that bra."

I felt a little bad for laughing at Fitz. She was sitting in the passenger seat looking sullen as we headed to Betty's. I had to throw her a line. So, I told her about what my mother had tried to do the night before. Her jaw did 'the drop'.

"The little Geek?" she asked astonished. "Ewww, he's a frickin' weirdo! I mean it! No, I'm serious Janie," she said, as if I was unaware of his being a complete freak. "Someday neighbors will be on the television saying things like, "He was a quiet boy...ya never would have expected he was capable of it. And "IT" will be the police finding dead women in his basement. Stuffed and dressed in his mother's undies!" she did a shudder. "Ya do know your mother is a nut-job, right?" she asked.

I nodded, "Yep, bat-shit crazy!" I said.

"Bat shit," Fitz agreed, nodding her head.

Fitz had a run-in with Lenny when we were young. She caught him leering at her through the bathroom window while she was peeing. It was probably the only time he ever went outside. He had stacked some of dad's firewood against the house, as a makeshift stand and waited for her. I heard her let out a scream. Fitz came running out of the bathroom just as Lenny came running in through the back door. He tried to make it into the kitchen to my mother but Fitz caught him with a right hook. He went down, Fitz on top of him, beating at him with tiny fists. My mother pulled her off and told her to go home. She never believed Fitz's urination story. Even though, as my father pointed out that night, there was wood stacked at the bathroom window. From then on, Fitz wasn't allowed to come over when Lenny was there. And I made sure the shower curtain was pulled closed when I went potty.

We stopped at Fitz's condo so she could put on a bra and then we headed to Betty's.

We pulled up in front of Betty's and plugged the meter.

"Will an hour be enough?" Fitz asked.

"I'm hoping to do a, run-in/run-out kinda thing," I said.

We walked around to the back patio that butted up to the Strand. No Betty. Her sliding glass door was standing wide open, and a Hank William's song was pouring out. 'Lonesome Blues', if I remembered correctly. I leaned my head in through the doorway. "Betty?" I called.

"Maybe she's hard of hearing?" Fitz said.

"No, she's not that old, Fitz," I said in a whisper.

"Well, then yell again," Fitz insisted.

I yelled a little louder this time, "Betty its Janie!"

"Tell her it's Puddin," Fitz said, straight faced.

I shot her a look. I was starting to worry. Betty wasn't hard of hearing. I didn't know her too well, but I couldn't imagine anyone leaving a door open and leaving the house, especially on the Strand. There was too much foot traffic outside.

"I'm going in to check the house," I said. "Wait here."

I walked into the living room. No Betty. I walked through the dining room to the kitchen. No Betty there, either. What if she had had a heart attack or fell in the shower? "I'm going to check upstairs," I whispered to Fitz.

She nodded at me.

I started up the stairs. I wanted to yell out Betty's name, but what if there was a burglar inside. I sure as Hell didn't want to give him a heads-up. As I slowly climbed, I wondered if maybe I should have had Fitz be the look-around and I stand guard at the front door. At least she could defend herself, well against everyone but an angry gay man, I thought. But I was more likely to pee myself or pass out, if confronted. At the top of the stairs, I looked back at Fitz. She was checking out her manicure. Apparently, she didn't seem to think we were in too much danger. From where I was standing, I could see into a bedroom, bathroom and the study. There was only one other room, the Master suite and the door was shut. I gathered my nerves, set my jaw and threw open the door. A man jumped from the bed and quickly and covered his naked body with a pillow revealing a naked Betty, spread eagle on the bed.

"Holy crap!" I yelled, quickly stepping back out of the room and pulling the door closed behind me. "Oh my God, I'm so sorry," I yelled. "I'm so sorry!" Fitz, hearing my scream started up the stairs, but I met her half way and tried to shoo her back down. "Go, oh my God, oh my God," I rambled, panicking.

Betty started out of the room, fastening her bathrobe around her. "Puddin wait," she called.

I stopped at the bottom of the stairs and faced her, blushing. "I am so sorry," I began. "It's just…" I stammered, "the door was open and I yelled for you. Twice," I said, looking at Fitz for back-up. She nodded, grinning up towards Betty, "I didn't mean to..."

"Honey, calm yourself," Betty said, as she made her way down to us. "I think you got the worst of that shock," she said, grinning. "Now breathe Puddin!"A man came down the stairs buttoning his shirt. He was about fifty and in great shape from what I saw, and knew I would relive in nightmares. As he passed me, I put my head down and said, "Sorry again, Sir."

"Oh no worries, Luv," he said in an Australian accent. "And you can call me Larry," he winked, extending his hand to me. I shook his hand and introduced him to Fitz, who was still grinning. "Lovely to meet you both, but I'm afraid I must be off." He walked over to Betty and put a kiss on her cheek. "I'll be back around seven tonight."

She nodded, smiling like a school girl.

"I'll bring dinner?" he winked again.

She nodded, "I'll have dessert ready."

He blew past us, "Have a good day, ladies."

Fitz turned to me and whispered, "I wanna be Betty when I grow up."

I nodded at her. "I'm sure you do."

"Well, come on in the kitchen. I'll make coffee and you can introduce me to your friend," Betty said.

We sat down and I introduced Fitz and Betty. I apologized again for bursting in on her and her friend.

"Oh hell, honey, I'm just glad it was you, and not his wife."

I sat there blankly staring at her.

"I'm just kiddin'," she said, when she saw the look on my face. "We've actually been datin for quite some time now. The young tattooed boys you saw on the back deck the other day are his sons."

I nodded, feeling horrible for assuming Betty was a cradle robber.

We sat and had coffee with Betty, talking about nothing in particular for a long time. Finally she asked me what I knew she had been waiting to ask for days. "What happened with you and John?"

Betty didn't know 'either one of us very well. But she had met him a couple of times.

"What do you mean?" I asked, trying to avoid making eye contact.

She gave me the look, the one that says: If you don't want talk about it you don't have to, but I'm not dumb. Or in Betty's case: Don't blow smoke up my ass.

I broke down and told her the whole story, after which she said, "They can be big, dumb animals at times. But you mark my words, he'll be back," she insisted.

I hadn't thought of that. Would he try to come back? After all of this?

Betty then let me know that she was going to be having some work done on my house and to expect laborers to be there for a few days. I asked what she was having done to the place.

"I'm having a patio poured in the back yard and maybe a fence put up. You know, make it more private."

I started to worry. Usually, landlord's only fixed things when they planned on selling the place.

Then she confirmed my fears. "You know, it'll add value to the house if I ever decide to sell."

I didn't ask anymore. I told her, "Thank you," for the coffee and said we had to get going.

Fitz and I started outside. "I like Betty," Fitz said.

"Yeah, she's something else."

"So, when you burst in on them...did ya see anything?" she asked as we got into the car.

"Let's just say, I'm trying not to see anything as we speak".

"I really do want to be Betty when I grow up," she said, again.

"You will be Fitz," I patted her hand. "Of that, I have no doubt. Just do me a favor... shut and lock the doors when you're having sex. All of them!"

We spent the rest of the afternoon sunbathing and reading Cosmo. If you can call spf 5000 sunbathing for Fitz.

"How to Keep Your Man Satisfied," was the article I was reading. I couldn't help but wonder why men's magazines didn't have anything in them that didn't relate to sex? Then I realized that the article I was reading was all about sex, too. Is that really all there is between men and women? Our only common bond? I didn't want to think about John and what areas of our relationship he was dissatisfied with. I mean, didn't an affair mean you weren't happy with your sex life, or was there more to it? I was pretty adventurous sexually when we first got together. Sex outdoors, (not anywhere that we would be caught) or dress up from time to time and play little games. But for the last year he seemed disinterested in me no matter what I tried. I thought the relationship was just calming down or getting comfortable. And since John was the longest relationship I had ever had, I had nothing to compare it to really. The truth was, I was dissatisfied with our sex life and had brought it up as gently as I could. It hadn't helped though, and six months later, I was dumped. Maybe it wasn't just sex? Maybe he left me because I was boring, or too predictable, or not driven enough. We never fought.

Truthfully he did lots of things that hurt me or made me angry, but I just didn't want to talk about them. Why, I wondered, had I never told him? I knew why. I tried to make our relationship one big bubble of happiness where whatever he wanted was good for me, even if it wasn't. DOORMAT, I thought. The thought bummed me out so I decided to go ahead and read the cheap romance novel instead. The one with a half-naked man on the front cover…his hair blowing in the wind and eyes that burned into...well, maybe your soul, via somewhere else first. Then it was off to Mum's for dinner.

I loved Mum and Da's house. Even though they had money to throw around, even though it was a huge house filled with antiques, it had a down-home feel to it. It looked a lot like the pub. You couldn't help but be comfortable there. Then there was Mum and Da themselves. Everyone who walked through their front door was treated like family. I was fortunate enough to have grown up with this place, this family, as my escape from my mother and her constant craziness.

I wasn't sure what Mum was cooking but it smelled wonderful. My stomach started growling the minute we walked in. Fitz and I made our way through the living room, through the dining room and into the kitchen. Aunt Marble and Mum stood together over a large cast iron pot. It looked a little like a cauldron. They both jumped when we walked in. Turning, they promptly stood side by side to hide from our view, whatever was cooking on the stove. I figured it was some kind of critter we were having for dinner that they didn't want me to see. Fitz would eat anything put in front of her. But I was picky about what kind of road-kill I ate. They knew that I'd eat it as long as I didn't know what it was, but they were acting especially odd. They practically ran us out of the kitchen. This must be one hell of a disgusting critter, I concluded. One with tentacles or fangs maybe.

Fitz and I went into the family room and found Da sitting reading the paper. He stood when I came in. He was six foot tall and still a nicely built man. His hair was red, but graying a little at the temples. I loved that his blue eyes always seemed to sparkle with true warmth.

"Janie girl," he said, embracing me.

"Hi Da," I said, returning the hug.

"It's been too long since I last laid eyes on ya. You're lookin' lovely, my dear." His Irish accent, though still very prominent, was no longer hard for me to understand. I had grown accustomed to it. All four of the boy's had it, although not as thick as Da. Mum was from another part of Ireland, so her accent had always been a little easier for me.

"Do you know what we're havin' for dinner?" Da asked Fitz and me.

I shook my head. Fitz said, "No, is it some kind of secret?"

"Well, they won't let me in there. I went to grab a beer and was all but shoved out. Those two hens are actin' oddly if I do say so myself," he said, with a head nod.

Rugby was on the TV. so Da was reading, watching the match, reading, watching the match. Every time the announcer got excited, Da would drop his paper and say, "Damn, I missed it!"

I heard the doorbell ring. I figured that the rest of the Fitzpatrick brood would be coming for dinner, but I never knew any of them to ring the bell before entering. After all, they had been raised here.

"That'll be Scotty," Da said, with a wink, as he headed to get the door.

I looked at Fitz, "Who's Scotty?"

She shook her head at me. "The only Scotty I know is the one who delivers the beer shipment each week."

It wasn't odd to have extra company at Mum and Da's house.

They loved to entertain and threw legendary parties. After which, it could take days to recover.

"Girls," we heard Mum yell, "time to eat. Move your tooshies!"

Fitz and I filed into the dining room where usually there was a huge dinner table able to seat twelve to accommodate the Fitzpatrick brood. Two of the leaves had been removed to make the table smaller. Fitz too, looked surprised.

"What did ya do to the table?" she asked Mum.

"We made it a little more intimate is all," she replied, without glancing in our direction.

Aunt Marble was coming down the hall carrying in a serving dish. She had a man in tow, carrying another dish.

Fitz's face showed a look of surprise. "Well, what do ya know," she said, suspiciously, "It is Scotty."

"Hello," he said, putting down the plate then extending his hand. His accent was thick. I wondered what part of Ireland he was from.

I reached out and shook his hand. "Hi, I'm Jane," I said.

He looked to Fitz with a quick head nod and said, "Hello Miss Fitz."

"Uh huh," she responded rather cool.

I looked from him to Mum and Aunt Marble. The two older ladies stood there smiling and nodding their heads at me.

I let out a sigh and sat down. I smelled a fix up coming. Two in two days I thought. I wonder what's wrong with this guy. He is Irish, so I could be related to him somehow. Although that's not Mum's style. Fitz's mom isn't nuts. Well, not the same kind of nuts as my mom.

"So, Mum, where are the boys at tonight, the grand-children?" I asked.

"Oh, they all had other plans, couldn't make it Luv. But

never ya worry dear, we're havin' a BarBQ this Saturday and you'll see them all then if you'll come?" she asked.

"Certainly," I said

"Oh, she's so polite," said Aunt Marble, looking at Scotty. "And a great cook, too, from what I understand. That's an important quality in a woman ya know? So many women these days don't know their way around a kitchen. It's shameful!" she concluded, nodding her head towards Fitz.

Fitz let out a sigh, "I'm learning Auntie."

They were laying it on a bit thick, I thought.

"You sit right here across from Janie," Mum said, pulling the chair out for him. Fitz took the seat next to me.

Scotty was certainly a handsome man. He was 6 foot, blonde and tan with big blue eyes and a strong upper body from what I could tell through his shirt. At least I could be grateful for that. And, after some polite conversation, I found out that I indeed wasn't related to him. I never thought that 'that' would be on the list of selling points but it was now.

I tried to get Fitz's attention, but she was busy giving Scotty the look of death. She was so protective of me, I thought. It warmed my heart to see how she took an ambush on me as an ambush on herself, as well.

The food had been passed around and I was delighted to see that we were eating chicken. I could easily identify chicken. I helped myself to the roasted potatoes and steamed asparagus. We all began to eat heartily when Mum started the conversation going.

"So Janie, have ya done much paintin' lately? She's a brilliant artist," she said, smiling at Scotty.

"Ah, not really," I said. "But I did get clearance to display a few paintings at my work." Now that I had said it out loud, I felt a surge of pride for having the guts to finally follow through with it. Fitz turned and looked at me.

"Ya didn't say a word to me, Janie. I'm so proud of ya!" she turned to hug me.

"Quite an accomplishment," said Da, nodding to me. "I'm very proud of you! And your parents must be thrilled," he added.

"Let's hope so," I said. "I haven't told them yet. This just happened today, so..."

I tried to make it sound as if I just hadn't had the chance to tell them, instead of telling Fitz's family that I was avoiding my mother like the plague for trying to set me up with my cousin. Her family already thought my mother was weird enough.

"Scotty here is a beer distributor," said Aunt Marble. "Aren't ya, dear?"

He had a mouth full of chicken, so he just nodded.

He had a healthy appetite, and I loved to cook for good eaters.

Fitz had gone back to scowling at Scotty.

Mum came around the table and brought me a glass. "I've made some wine, Janie. Mulled it myself, would ya like a taste?"

"Sure, thank you," I said.

"And how about you, Scotty?" she asked. "Would ya fancy a glass?"

"Don't mind if I do," he said. "Thank you, Mrs. Fitzpatrick."

"I wouldn't mind tryin' some of that wine," Da said to Mum.

"No, you wouldn't like it dear." she said. "Drink your beer."

"I like wine," he bellowed. "I'm not as uncouth as all of that, ya know."

She stared at him with the 'not-in-front-of-company' glare.

He held the stare a moment before saying somewhat put off, "Fine, I'll drink my beer."

Mum softened her tone towards her husband. "It's just we

didn't have enough to go the round," she smiled. Her gentle voice seemed to appease Da. He gave her a wink.

I looked around the table and noticed that Scotty and I were the only ones with wine. I started to get an uneasy feeling. I couldn't help but remember the two of them, Mum and Aunt Marble, over the pot. They wouldn't drug me. Would they?

"Fitz, you're not having a glass either?" I asked.

"Oh, I'm afraid I gave Scotty the last of it," Mum interjected.

"Oh, well that's fine," I said, "Fitz can have some of mine. I'm not afraid of cooties, or anything."

I started to hand Fitz the glass when Aunt Marble said quickly, "No dear, Fitz wouldn't like it. Uh, it has....uh...black licorice in it!" she finally spat out.

"Ew," Fitz said, and handed me back the glass. "I hate Anise."

I was starting to get a strange lift from the hairs on the back of my neck. Staring at the wine, I could see the sediment trying to settle in the bottom of the glass. "Oh Mum, I'm so sorry, but I can't drink it either," I said, raising my eyebrows. "I'm allergic to Anise," I blurted out.

Mum narrowed her eyes at me, like she was sizing me up. "I didn't know that, Luv," she said suspiciously. "Well, I wouldn't want you to get sick, or anything."

"I love Anise," chimed Scotty and downed the wine.

Fitz was eyeing me. She knew the only thing I was allergic to was Penicillin. But she didn't say anything. She just shot me a questioning glance then turned her attention back to Scotty. She began the evil-eye again.

Da asked, "Well if no one is goin to drink the damn wine, can I have it?"

Aunt Marble winced and shook her head ever so slightly, at Mum.

Mum looked worried, too. But after a moment, Mum said, with a wave of her hand, "Oh for the love of Pete, go ahead."

Aunt Marble turned and watched Da take down the wine in one gulp. I thought I saw her cringe a little.

Mum looked at me and smiled wryly. "Eat yer chicken dear."

We ate in silence for a short time. Mum and Aunt Marble were taking side long looks at Da and Scotty, who both kept shaking their heads like puppies. All of the sudden, Da looked up from his plate and said to Scotty, "Tell me about yerself, Son. I want to know everything about ya."

Aunt Marble dropped her fork and her jaw. Mum let out a sigh and looked up at the ceiling, "Oh crap."

Scotty turned to Da and said, "I'm so glad you're saying this. I feel so close to you right now. I can't even describe it." Then the two of them stood and hugged each other.

"I have something I have to tell ya, I can't keep it from ya any longer," admitted Scotty. He gulped hard, like he was worried about making his confession then said, "I want to sleep with your daughter."

Mum and Aunt Marble shot appalled looks at Fitz, who, with an embarrassed smile, gave a palms-up.

Da was still holding Scotty. The room was deathly quiet. Now Da may not have been as young as he once was, but he was a first rate pugilist. He even held titles back in Ireland for Bare Knuckle Boxing. If Da had been in his right mind at all, this guy wouldn't have had a tooth left in his head.

Scotty shook his head again and said, "No, I mean, I want to marry your daughter and then sleep with her!"

Fitz's jaw dropped.

There was another moment of silence, then all of the sudden, Da began to sob, "I can't wait for you to be my son-in-law," he said, hugging Scotty tighter.

Scotty began to cry, too. "Thank you Mr. Fitzpatrick. I would be honored if I could call ya Dad?"

"Please call me Da, Son, just like one of my own offspring."

"That means the world to me. I promise I'll treat her right." They kept right on hugging and crying, as if no one else was in the room.

"Ah damn!" Mum said, as she and Aunt Marble gathered up their plates and headed to the kitchen. Fitz and I followed swiftly at their heels.

"What happens now?" Aunt Marble was asking Mum in a hushed voice as we came into the kitchen.

"Oh," said Mum, exasperated, "it'll wear off by the morn...I think."

"What'll wear off?" Fitz asked.

"The potion," said Aunt Marble, nodding matter-of-factly, her eyes huge behind her glasses.

"So I was right?" I asked Mum. "You two were trying to drug me?"

Fitz's mouth fell open again. "What? You tried to drug Janie?"

"Yes, yes," fumed Mum, waving her hand. "And it's not a drug," she continued, "It was a potion. Drugs are illegal!" she asserted. "And this stuff," she held up a vial, "doesn't impair your will at all, it just gives you a little push in the right direction."

"Da sure as hell looks impaired!" yelled Fitz.

Mum made a 'shooing' hand gesture and then turned on Fitz. "By the way little girl, we could have avoided all of this," she pointed towards the dining room, "if I had known that you two were bangin' boots!"

"Oh no ya don't," Fitz spat, "you're not gonna blame this on me! You said you didn't want to know about my sex life," she dropped her voice to a whisper, "and I've kept it from ya. And by the way, we're not bangin' boots, we didn't get that far," a slight blush lighting her cheeks. "I had no reason to discuss it with ya, Mum. I didn't think that you'd drag him here under false pretenses and then drug him!"

Now I remembered the Scotty incident. He and Fitz had gone out a few times, but he showed no interest in it going further than friendship, or so it seemed to Fitz. "He won't even touch me!" she bellowed. And this whole time he was head over heels for her.

"Well, look at the fine mess we're in now," Mum retorted.

"We're in?" Fitz yelled. "I just became engaged to a man I barely know." Fitz was freaking out and really, who could blame her? "What were ya thinkin' Mum?" she asked.

"Well, I talked to him today," Mum started, "he said he had a little crush on someone but it wasn't going well. So, I invited him to dinner. I told him I had a girl for him. He accepted so quickly…and now I know why," she said, "he thought I was settin' up the two of you!"

Fitz was rubbing her head like it ached.

I just stood there shaking mine, and thought, drugged! That's one for the books.

Just then, Da and Scotty entered the kitchen with their arms wrapped around each other's necks.

"Ladies," Da started, "I don't know what all the fightin' is about, but this is a happy occasion. Mum," he said, turning his attention to his wife, "break out the champagne so we can toast to our daughter's weddin'."

Scotty leaned forward and put a kiss on Fitz's cheek. "Gonna talk over some weddin' arrangements with Da, Luv."

With that, the two men turned on their heels and made their exit, leaving us staring after them.

"I'm goin to go clear up your mess," Fitz said to her Mom, and started toward the hall.

Mum stopped her, "Ya can't do that Fitzy, not yet at least."

"Why the hell not?" Fitz looked half crazed.

Aunt Marble broke in, "We're not sure what will happen if you try to break a love potion. "It could go badly."

"Worse than this?" Fitz asked pointed to the dining room.

Mum and Aunt Marble exchanged worried looks. Finally Mum said, "Potentially."

"So what the hell am I supposed to do?"

"Wait it out," Aunt Marble suggested, shrugging her shoulders. "I mean, it's bound to wear off sooner or later."

"Sooner or later," Fitz huffed, "as in I could be married by the time it does?"

Mum and Aunt Marble both did a palms-up.

"Do love potions wear off?" I asked.

"Well, this one was just a Push, not a full spell," said Aunt Marble.

"I don't understand," I said.

"Well," started Mum, "you see a Push just encourages ya to want to get to know each other a bit more."

"So basically, it doesn't make you fall in love?" I asked.

"No, of course not!" Mum stated indignantly. "That's meddlin', and it's frowned upon. Plus, it has the ability to go horribly wrong."

Mum and Marble exchanged looks again that I caught, but really didn't want them to elaborate on.

I needed to get this right in my head, a Love Spell: meddling, frowned upon, and potentially dangerous. A Push: a totally acceptable form of drugging.

"But, if Scotty really is in love with Fitz," I started, "doesn't it mean it won't wear off?"

Mum and Aunt Marble exchanged looks of concern. "We don't have any information on that," Mum admitted. "We honestly don't know."

Again Fitz huffed. "You two had better figure this out, and quickly!" she added.

"If you don't mind," I said, grabbing a beer from the fridge, "I'll only drink unopened things from this house for a while."

"Gee, Janie," Mum said, looking down at her shoes like a scolded child, "I'm really sorry we tried to drug ya and all." Mum moved in to hug me, and let her voice fall to a whisper, "It was Marble's idea, Luv." she added seriously.

I patted her on the shoulder. "It's ok Mum."

I tried to exit the kitchen via the backdoor. I was desperately in need of air, or something. Aunt Marble caught me in an embrace. "It was all Mum's idea!" she said, almost inaudibly.

I let out a sigh and said, "I know." I returned the hug to assure her that there was no ill will on my part. After all, I had gotten off light. Fitz was the one who was now engaged to a man she barely knew, and I knew the truth. They both did it. Aunt Marble is insane and Mum is crazy. They both just kind of.... feed off of each other. A thought did frighten me though. In another thirty years, or so, they'd be like those crazy old sisters in Arsenic and Old Lace. Then we'd really have to keep our eyes on them.

I swiped a smoke and lighter from Fitz's purse, leaving Fitz, Mum and Aunt Marble in a huddle of confusion, and headed out on the back porch.

I hated the idea of smoking, but the act of it...was wonderful. I knew I had plenty of time alone. Fitz and the Scary Sisters were in the house, appeasing Da and his new best friend. I sat down on the double sized porch swing and lit up. I had been through hell the last few days. But, I thought to myself, at least I wasn't drugged.

I wondered how Da would feel tomorrow. Then I wondered if the potion would wear off by tomorrow.

"Smokin's bad for ya," I heard a voice say from behind me. I knew who it was, but I turned to look anyway.

"Hi Barry," I said.

He came and sat beside me on the swing. "Can I get one of those from ya?" he asked.

"I swiped this one from Fitz's purse," I said, handing him the cigarette.

He took a long drag and handed it back. "I thought you quit?"

"I did. But I did it for all the wrong reasons." I took another drag and handed it back to him.

"So, not for your health, huh?" he asked, taking another drag.

"Nope, did it for John. He hated me smoking. It was easier to quit than to put up with his disapproving looks and comments."

"Ah," he said, handing it back to me. "Where's Fitzy?"

"Oh, she's inside with the family toasting to your new brother-in-law."

"What?" he asked confused.

"It's a really long story, Barry," I smiled.

There was a short pause as we finished our communal smoke. "Ya look like you could use a real drink," he said, "Maybe a Bushmills?"

"Now you're talking,"

"Come on, we'll go to the bar for a night cap." We both stood. "Did ya want to tell Fitz where you're goin'?"

I looked back towards the house. "No," I said, shaking my head. "I'm not going back in there. After everything that's happened tonight, Fitz knows where she can find me."

We walked down to the Pub. The sun hadn't even set yet, so, I guessed that it was around eight o'clock. When we walked in, Andy greeted us with a surprised smile.

"What are you two doin here?" he asked.

I knew what he meant was, "What are you two doing here, together?"

He poured us each a Bushmills, three fingers high, and a Black and Tan.

My shot went down in one gulp.

Barry looked at me with questioning eyes. "I guess you really did need a drink. You wanna talk about it?"

I shook my head no. But a minute later, I was slowly spilling my guts. I was doing a lot of that lately.

"I knew about the break-up with John," he said. "That was a bastard way to end things, Janie. You have to know that."

"Oh, I guess Fitz told you all about it, huh?"

"No, it was on the six o'clock news," he said, straight faced.

I started laughing. "Well, that's not the half of it. I started to tell him about the cab, and his sister kicking me in the jaw, my mother trying to set me up with my cousin...

"Oh, that's so wrong!" he laughed.

"Right," I said, doing a palms-up. "And, the fact that she doesn't understand WHY what she did was so wrong, scares me to death," I shook my head. "It makes me want to check our family tree, you know, to see if it forks."

"No, that's truly sick, Janie," he added. "Yer Mom is a different kind of, not okay."

I told him about trying to save my landlady from sex. I didn't tell him about Fitz's little encounter with Pete. It wasn't my story to tell. But I did tell him about Mum and Aunt Marble trying to drug me and the poor unsuspecting beer distributor.

"Mum's crazy ya know?" he interjected. "Good hearted, but crazy. And Aunt Marble...well," he trailed off, and took a sip of his beer, never finishing his thought out loud. "It sounds like it's been one hell of a week for ya."

I smiled and said, "It hasn't even been a week, Barry. At this rate, I'm scared to think of what tomorrow holds in store."

"Try not to think about it. You know," he started, "you've explained almost everything. Except...what you were doin' in the kitchen…naked."

I grinned sidelong at him. "Sorry," I shook my head, "for the time being... it's still my little secret."

"Okay. For the time being," he said, nodding.

We were both silent for a minute, enjoying our Black and Tan's. Finally, I had to ask. "You didn't, um…you didn't really SEE anything the other night, did you?"

He grinned at me. "When?"

I let out sigh. "When we were in the kitchen... did you see anything?"

He kept grinning. "Like what?"

He was torturing me, and he loved it. "Never mind," I said, grinning back at him.

Andy brought us two more Bushmills. We sat in silence for a minute before he said, "You look good, Janie."

"Yeah, not too bad for all the crap that's happened," I took a swig of my beer.

"No, I mean the other night," he dropped his head.

My heart began to pound out of my chest.

He looked up at me and caught my stare. "Ya looked really good," he repeated, then turned his head towards the bandstand.

I was dumbfounded. I looked at the back bar and tried to steady my breathing. I needed a focal point. If I had any balls at all I would kiss him right now. After all, even if he pulled away, it wouldn't be the most humiliating thing I've been through this week. Yet, oddly enough, somehow, it would be the most painful. God, it would be so much easier if he would just kiss me. Where's that damn potion now? Ok I can do this, I thought, trying to work up my nerve. I was almost there. Seconds from taking my leap of faith when I heard from behind me.....

"So this is the stupid bitch you left me for?"

I turned to see a tiny woman staring at me and huffing through her nose like an angry bull.

She was all of five-four, skinny, with dark ratted hair and way too much make-up. She was dressed like an eighty's reject: Mini skirt, a cut T-shirt hanging off one shoulder to reveal a bra strap, high heeled black boots, so she must have been just around 5 foot tall.

Oh, Barry. You didn't, I thought to myself.

Barry hung his head and let out a sigh.

"This," she pointed at me, "this is what you left me for? Are you on drugs Barry?" she chided.

Barry got off his stool and stood to face her.

"Look," I started politely, "I don't know who you are but...."

"I'll tell you who I am," she said, rolling her head at me. "I'm Barry's ex."

I guess this was supposed to hold water for me. "Oh?" I said, trying not to look shocked.

"Oh? Oh, is all you have to say?"

I tried to suppress an uncomfortable laugh. "I'm not following," I said. "What does this have to do with me?"

"He broke up with me for someone else! You! Bitch!" she said, leaning in and pointing at me.

"Please don't put your finger in my face," I requested, as calmly as I could.

Barry moved in between us. "Look," he began, "I already told ya, there was no one else. I just don't think we're a good match."

"And this Bitch is?" she asked.

"Look, I don't know what you think is going on between

Barry and me, but you've got to stop calling me a bitch!" I warned, starting to lose my patience.

"Or what, bitch?" she asked, trying to throw a punch at me around Barry.

"Of all the women in the world," I began, "you can be sure I would never be the OTHER woman, and if you were listening to him, he said there was NO other woman."

Her eyes narrowed at me as she pondered the thought that maybe I was just some nobody Barry sat next to while having a drink.

Finally she said, "That's exactly what the other woman would say, isn't it? Profess her innocence!"

I let out a heavy sigh, somewhere between complete exhaustion and irritation. "Look, I've had a really bad couple of days and I'm not in the mood for this."

"You shoulda thought of that before you tried to steal another women's man," she yelled.

She tried to throw another punch around Barry and it landed on top of my shoulder.

"Ouch!" I yelled, and rubbed what I was sure would be a new bruise. "That hurt!"

"You think that hurt?" she threw another punch around Barry's other side, and hit my other arm.

"That's it!" I announced, getting off my stool to face her. I lunged at her, but went nowhere.

Barry scooped her up and I felt myself being restrained by my T-shirt. "Let me go Andy!" I yelled. "I'm gonna knock her little head off her little shoulders! Come here you angry midget! I'll fight you on my knees," I roared.

"It's not gonna happen, Lass," Andy said to me. "Calm yerself!"

Barry's voice became stern, but not raised. "She's not my girlfriend. She's a friend of my little sister. I'm just bein' a good person to someone who's had a really bad week. Now, if you want to talk, we'll do it out back. Not here! Not in my parents bar!" I watched them walk towards the Poker Room.

She looked back at me and said, "I'm not gonna forget you, bitch!"

"Right back at ya!" I yelled.

Barry's face was flushed, but I couldn't tell if he was mad or embarrassed. Over his shoulder he said, "Sorry Janie, I have to deal with this."

"You don't have to explain anything to her," I heard the midget say, as they disappeared behind the door.

Andy finally let go of me. I was shaking so hard I could barely hold my beer as I downed it and walked out of the bar. Andy came running after me. "Janie, are you ok?"

I'm fine." I said. "When, or if, Barry comes back in, tell him thanks for the drinks."

"Can I at least call ya a cab?"

I shook my head. "No, I need to walk this off," and turned away. With that, I headed home.

Even after walking for eight blocks, I was still shaking so hard I could barely get my key out of my pocket. When I did manage to pull it out the Rune Diane gave me, fell to the ground. I reached down and picked it up. I was sure I hadn't put it my pocket. How did it get in there? I stared at the little stone with the Lightning Bolt shape carved into it. I rubbed it between my fingers then palmed it tightly. Little signs, huh…well she was little, I thought.

When I walked in the answering machine was flashing. I stood over it and wondered, "Who is it this time?" Only one way to find out, I pushed play.

"Janie O'Connelly," I heard my mother fume, "you pick up this phone right now! You're being ridiculous!" I hit skip.

"Hi, Miss O 'Connelly? This is Annie from Hawaiian Isle

Airlines. Do you remember me? Of course you do." The voice rattled on... "I have some, well, kind of good news. You'll be happy to hear that your luggage in back in the U.S. We tried to send it to L.A. the city, you know, LAX, but it went to La, Louisiana, instead. I guess they mixed the city airport with the state. You know the La with the L.A. Any who, the good news is that we're sending you one thousand more..." I hit the skip button again and covered my face with my hands to muffle a scream. I guess the good thing was I had a free flight coming. The bad news was it was on their airline.

Next was Fitz. "You should see this," she said laughing. "Da and Scotty are singing 'Oh Danny Boy' to each other. Ya know…Scotty's kinda cute, in a drugged out sort of way." She paused again to laugh at them. I could hear them through the phone, singing their hearts out. "Hey, are you ok?" she asked. "Andy called and told me about what happened. Ya' shoulda clocked the bitch. I woulda if I'd been there. Anyway, call me tomorrow or tonight if ya want. I'm staying at Mum's until this... ya know, 'Push' thing, wears off. I love you," she said, and hung up.

I guess she had made peace with the whole drugging thing.

I walked into the kitchen and opened the fridge. I had three bottles of wine, a six pack of Guinness, a six pack of Diet Coke and a box with a chunk of cake left in it. I reminded myself, why would I have gone shopping? I wasn't supposed to be here. I grabbed a diet coke and headed for the couch. I turned on the TV. Not really to watch it, just for background noise to drown out my thoughts. I couldn't stop thinking about Barry and how I almost got up the nerve to kiss him. Boy, that would have been a mistake, I thought. He said it: "She's a friend of my little sister. I'm just being a good person to someone who's had a really bad couple of days." The words echoed in my head. Well, I thought, at least now I know how he really feels. Oh, I feel so stupid. I can't believe that I actually thought we had a moment there. And, he was just being nice to me. At least I didn't have to totally humiliate myself to find out. It could have been so much worse. I had a vision of me coming at him, all lips, and him pulling away with a look of horror and disgust on his face. Yeah, I concluded, that would have been worse.

I laid the Rune on the table and stared at it some more. Maybe it was a sign. I went to my makeshift desk and grabbed a pad of paper and a pen. I sat back on the couch and wrote at the top of the page. MY LIST. Great start! Now what? I sat there drumming the pen against the pad. I decided to start with my wants. Starting with what I didn't like about myself, right now, seemed like a form of self-mutilation.

I wrote #1. I wrote down Barry. Seeing it in black and white bothered me, so I scratched it out. Number one, I started again. I want to sell my paintings. All of them, I added. Hell why not, it was my list. I could dream big if I wanted to.

#2, I went on. I want to have my cookbook published. Oh, and teach a cooking class! Should that be number three, I wondered, or just an 'add on', to number two. Who cares? No one's going to read this but me.

Ok, #3. I want to buy my own house. Renting from Betty has been great. But what if she sold this house? I'd be out on my ass. No, I want a place I can call MY home, not just where I live.

#4, I want to travel. I want to see Europe. I want to eat Italian food in Italy.

#5, I want to get in shape. Well, kind-of, I thought. I wasn't overweight to begin with, just a little...squishy. Toning up a little couldn't hurt, I thought, looking down at the little roll over the top of my pants. Why did that always happen when I sat down? I wondered. It wasn't there when I stood up. I looked down at my list. It felt complete. Those were the things I wanted. Everything I wanted in black and white. Ok I needed an add-on.

#6, A pair of Prada sling backs. Yes NOW it was complete. It was only then when I realized, I hadn't put down husband or children. I mulled this over, but truth be told, I didn't want to examine why those things hadn't made the cut. In the end, I left the list 'as is' and set it on the coffee table next to the Rune.

I grabbed the Goddess book that Diane had given me. Maybe reading would take my mind off of tonight and help me sleep. I lay back on the couch and got comfortable. I expected it to start with: IN THE BEGINNING.... But it didn't.

An hour later, I still hadn't put the book down. It had all this stuff about positive energies and people. The next chapter was about negative energy and people, and how we should avoid them. I wondered if that argument would 'stand-up' with my mother. I could hear the conversation now; "Mom, I can't be around you because you're a sucker of positive energy and a manufacturer of negative energy." No, I thought, probably not going work.

The next few chapters were on meditation and visualization. They even had some exercises at the end of the chapters. I decided to try one. I got as comfortable as I could. I lay on my back, hands out to my sides and began the 'breathing' they had outlined. Deep breathing…in through the nose, out through the mouth. I let my eyes fall closed... and before I knew it, I fell asleep.

8

TUESDAY: DAY 4 OF DUMPED

I was dreaming that a truck was about to back up over me. Beep, beep, beep, it went in back-up mode. Beep, beep, beep, it got closer. I sat up quickly, and was even more alarmed to still hear the beeping. I looked out the windows and saw the workers guiding back a cement truck into my driveway.

Oh thank God, I thought. When my heart stopped threatening to jump from my chest, I made some coffee. I was a little disappointed that I had fallen asleep while trying to meditate. On the other hand, it was the best night of sleep I'd had in months. It was only nine o'clock, but I decided to try to call Fitz at Mum's house. Mum answered on the third ring. She sounded so groggy. I knew Mum to be an early riser and hang-over proof. "Ello," She mumbled.

"Mum, its Janie. Is Fitz there?"

"Uh huh, hold the line dear," she said.

"Hello," Fitz's voice rang, "Where ya at?"

"I'm at home. What's wrong with Mum?" I asked. "She sounds horrible!"

"Fitz started laughing. "Turns out, that potion they made

had another side effect. Works better than Viagra, from what I couldn't help over hearin'."

I started to laugh, too. "Maybe they should bottle that stuff."

"From the way Mum looks this mornin', women wouldn't appreciate it at all," she giggled. "You know the expression 'rode hard and put away wet'? It applies," she said. "Hey, by the way, ya left yer car here last night. Are ya gonna come get it? I need to talk to ya."

"I guess so," I said. "You know the worker's Betty said were coming? Well, they're here."

"So?" she asked.

"Well, I don't know what the protocol is for leaving them here on the property."

"Whatda ya mean?"

"What if one of them, has to go to the restroom?" I asked. "I mean, do I leave the door unlocked or tell them to hit the coffee shop, a block away?"

"Oh, I get ya," she said. "Well, in that case, I'll come over there. I'll bring you a goody from the coffee house. I need coffee."

"You know I have coffee, Fitz," I said defensively.

"No offense Luv, but unless you can make me a quad-mocha, you don't have coffee," she said, and hung up.

She was right in a way. I worked at a fine coffee house and loved coffee. I drank more coffee than damn near anyone I knew, except maybe Fitz. There were definitely days where it would be easier to just hook up a drip line to my arm so why haven't I invested in an espresso machine?

I knew Fitz would take her sweet time getting here, so I went to take a shower. I looked in the mirror and was shocked. The zit! The horrible zit, it was gone! Not a trace of it. I picked up the vial of murky oily gel. "Shit! They should market this, too," I said to no one. There isn't a sixteen year old virgin boy, or hormonal woman, that wouldn't pay a fortune for this. I jumped in the shower. I was washing my hair when the water went off.

"Ah, Damn it," I said. The workers must have shut off the main water valve. I hopped out of the shower and threw on my fluffy yellow robe. The one that made me look like a Giant Easter Peep, and stomped out the front door.

"Hey," I yelled, crossing the front lawn to my driveway. No one seemed to hear me. I walked up to a guy who had his back to me. "Hey," I yelled again over the noise of the truck. Still nothing. So I tapped him on the shoulder. He turned around and I was awe-struck. He was beyond handsome. Dark hair and eyes, when he saw me he smiled. Oh, great smile, I thought. He almost struck me dumb.

"I'm guessing you were in the shower?" he said, with a wince. "We were told to look for your silver Neon in the driveway. If it was here I was told to knock on the door and let you know we were starting." He was rambling. "I'm sorry. We didn't think anyone was home. We had to shut off the main water valve. Seems we hit a water pipe during the dig out. We'll have it fixed as soon as we can, but it could be an hour or so. I'd turn it on, but it will flood your driveway. Oh, is that shampoo in your hair?" he asked timidly, and winced again.

"Yeah, it is," I said loudly, to be heard over the cement truck, realizing I sounded more upset than I wanted to.

"Here, come with me to my truck," he said. "I think I can fix that for you."

I followed him over to the huge Ford F150. "I keep a couple of gallons of water in a cooler so the guys don't get dehydrated. If you'll put your head under this spout," he said, pulling the cooler down towards to the open tail gate, "I'll hold the water on for you. It may be a little cold though," he warned. "The ice hasn't had a chance to melt completely."

"It'll work," I said, smiling. "I just want to get this stuff out of my hair."

He smiled back and said, "Well then, lean over ma'am, and we'll get you cleaned up."

I leaned over into the stream of water and began using my hands to work the shampoo out of my hair.

"You missed a spot," he said.

"Where?"

"Right here on the back of your neck."

I moved my hand. "Did I get it?"

"No, not quite," he said. "Let me."

His huge hand began massaging the shampoo left on my neck. I assumed he'd have the rough hands of a construction worker, but they were smooth and strong.

"Almost out," he said.

I didn't care anymore. I was enjoying the scalp rub.

"Ok, it looks like I got it all," he said, flashing that amazing smile of his.

I was still bent over when Fitz pulled up. She stepped out of the car, pastry bag in hand, and gawked at us.

"Thank you, ugh, I don't know your name," I said.

Fitz came up to stand beside me.

"Henry," he said, extending his hand.

"Janie," I said, shaking his hand. We both stared at each other for a moment.

"Oh, this is Fitz," I finally said.

"Hellooo," she said, shaking his hand and grinning like the 'Cat Who Ate the Canary'.

"Well, I better go get dressed," I said, looking down at my Peep bathrobe. I moved towards the house with Fitz in tow. At my front door, I turned and yelled back to Henry, "Thanks again."

He waved, "Any time!"

When we walked into the house, Fitz said, "Wow! He's gorgeous!"

"You don't usually "wow" over men," I said, tying a towel around my wet head.

"I don't usually see men that good looking," she said, peeking from behind my pulled drapes.

"You work with male models," I pointed out.

"Yes." she said. "But they're usually gay or really conceited. They kinda lose the wow factor for me."

"Really, I thought you were into gay men," I giggled.

"Oh, I knew you couldn't hold out forever. I knew that eventually you'd have to bring that up," she huffed.

"Ok," I said, "I'm done tormenting you." I changed the conversation. "So what happened after I left last night?"

Fitz began to giggle. "You shoulda seen it. Da and Scotty were arm and arm singing to each other. Turns out, Scotty's from a well-to-do Irish family. In fact to make matters weirder, Scotty's father, who still lives back home, was one of Da's school-boy pals. Apparently, they used to raise quite a bit of hell together."

"So, if Scotty's family is so "well-to-do," why is he working as a Beer Distributor here?" I asked.

She grinned. "His daddy owns the company. They've expanded to the U.S. so he's runnin' the company on this side of the pond," she said with a palms-up. Also, he wants to learn the business from the ground up. They're trying to break into a mass distribution. You know the seasonal beer we carry? Wiccan B?"

I nodded, "Good beer."

"Well, that's his father's brew."

She looked different to me. Giddy. I was starting to understand.

"Did you and Scotty have a moment or something?" I asked, grinning at her.

She smiled and raised her eyebrows. "A true lady never tells," she answered.

"Yeah, a true lady wouldn't...so, spill it," I said grinning.

She jumped on the couch with her legs underneath her, like a teenager would. "Ok," she began

I came and sat next to her. I got in gossip position, sitting Indian Style, facing her.

"Ya know," she started, "from the moment he walked into the house, all I could think of was how to get rid of him."

She was glowing. I had never seen her this way. "But..." I asked, rolling my hand at her.

"It was amazin'," she began. "He was so sweet, professing his love to me. And, he's so gentle and kind."

I remembered his build. He was a big boy to be seen as gentle, I thought.

She went on. "He was so cute with Da. Listening to all his stories. And hearing ones about his own father, he'd never heard before. Well, I had no intention of being drawn in."

She was using the 'so' word a bunch. Knowing Fitz the way I do, this was a clear sign for me. "But..." I asked again, trying to keep her going.

"I had the best time! We laughed, danced and sang," she giggled. "Then...around one o'clock, Mum and Da went bed, and it was just Scotty and me," she grinned.

"What did you do?" I asked.

"Nothing." she replied.

"Nothing?" I asked.

"Well, not 'that' I mean. I am a lady, ya know? We talked. We talked for hours. About everything..., favorite places, music, food...and about nothing," she said. "I laid curled up in his arms for over an hour. Neither of us said a word, Janie. And I was completely comfortable. It was 5a.m. before he kissed me. I still haven't slept yet!" she exclaimed.

"And the kiss?" I asked, because for us the kiss is a big deal.

"It was..." she searched for a word, "Amazin'!"

"So did he tell you why he was so stand-offish when you two went out before?"

"He said he was nervous and didn't want to offend me by being oaf-ish…he didn't want me to think the only reason he liked me was for my body. But he said, he had to concentrate so hard to keep his hands off me, he couldn't think straight."

She left herself open for another gay joke, but I refrained, like a good friend should from time to time.

"He said, he had wanted to kiss me so badly that it almost drove him insane," she blushed

A moment passed before I said, "I'm shocked, Fitz. It almost sounds like you're...smitten?"

"Ya know," she said dreamily, "I think I am."

I reached out and hugged her. I had never seen her so happy and I had never been so happy for her. When I pulled back, she had tears in her eyes she was desperately trying to wipe away. Fitz wasn't given to petty crushes and thought of men as great company and very good for what they offered physically, but she wasn't the type to get swept away. This was blowing my mind.

"Okay, okay," she said sniffling, "on to new business. Who's the hottie in the front yard and why was her washing yer hair?"

I grinned at her. "Oh, he's just one of the guys working on the house. I guess they hit a water pipe and needed to shut off the main valve, so my yard didn't flood. Unfortunately, I was washing my hair at the time, so he let me wash out the shampoo in his water cooler."

"Looked like HE was washing yer hair from where I was standing," she gave me a sly look.

"It wasn't that interesting," I said. "I just missed a spot and he helped me get it."

"I don't know," she chided. "His stare coulda burned a hole through ya!"

I made a dismissive gesture and went to fill up my coffee mug and raid the pastry bag Fitz brought.

Fitz joined me in the kitchen. "So, what's on the agenda today?" she asked.

I took a long drink off my coffee, "I need to pick out a few paintings to take down to work. I looked at her timidly, "It would be a lot easier to transfer them in Baby, than it would be in my car. Not to mention my car isn't here.

"No problem," she said.

"And, I would like to invest in an espresso machine. So, I want to go shopping for one of those."

She nodded, "That would be a lot easier for me. I wouldn't have to drink any more of Dante's inventions. He's a sweet kid, Janie. But that drink he made me this morn, was undrinkable. I had to stop at another shop to get my quad mocha."

I grinned and tried not to laugh. "You know, he named it after you. As he put it, 'It's got a lot of spice. Just like Fitz!"

She winced and shook her head.

"And lastly...I want to join a gym," I said, hoping she wouldn't laugh too hard.

"Oh, that's great," she said. "I know just the place."

We mulled over our coffee a little longer while I told her everything that happened at the pub the night before. At the end of which she raised one eyebrow and asked, "What were you doin' there with Barry?"

"Oh," I waved my hand. "He was taking pity on me, treated me to a few 'well needed' drinks."

"Hum," she said suspiciously, and nodded. Then we dropped the subject.

She had known for years that I had crush on Barry when we were younger. But when I started dating in high school the crush had faded, or at least I was otherwise occupied. Truthfully, it hadn't been a topic of conversation since the tenth grade.

I picked out the three paintings that I wanted to display. Two of them were relatively small, two foot by three foot. But, the other, my favorite, was a three foot wide, by six foot tall, painting of Fitz as a pin-up. She wore a black and white polka-dot fifty's bathing suit, doing the 'one hand on the hip and one hand behind the head' pose, on a red flame background. It had a kind-of 'Betty Page' quality to it.

"You really want to display this one, Janie?" she asked glowing.

I smiled, "This is the one I'm most proud of," I said, turning to her.

She hugged me. "You know," she said in a heartfelt tone, "I think you're my biggest fan.... and I am definitely yours."

We wrapped the paintings carefully in the mover's tarp I had in the closet. "Well, they're ready," I said, and took a deep breath. "I hope I am."

I got dressed quickly and began loading the paintings into Baby. Henry saw us lugging the huge painting and came running across the lawn.

"Let me help you with that," he said. "What? Are you moving out?"

"No, our Janie here," Fitz said, with a nod towards me, "is a brilliant artist. We're takin' them to her work to be displayed."

"Wow," he said, turning to me. "That's impressive." Again he flashed that smile that made my legs go all rubbery.

I started to say something humble when Fitz broke in again.

"Don't let her fool ya," she said. "She's great."

"I don't doubt it," he looked at me and grinned.

I was blushing again. I hated that. I had too many 'tells', as we called them. If my eyes didn't give me away, my damn blush or fidgeting hands would. I got in the passenger seat and tried to avoid looking Henry in those deep brown eyes.

"I'd love to see them sometime," he said, squatting down next to the car to look me in the eyes.

Fitz answered again. "They'll be on the wall at Spilled the Beans. Or maybe, Janie can give you a private showing," she said, with a head tilt.

I shot her a death-to-you look.

"I'd love that. Here," he said, handing me a business card. "Call me sometime," then he walked away.

I looked back at Fitz, "I should kill you!"

She smiled, watching him walk away. "You should send me a gift basket."

9

MY PAINTINGS

Nance saw us pull up out front and start unloading the paintings. She and two huge men came out to help. Once they were inside I removed the tarps. Nance caught her breath. The first one was a view of 'Hollywood at Night' I had done from a vantage point off Mulholland Drive.

It's beautiful," she said. "All the lights…and that skyline…It's perfect."

I smiled like a proud parent. I was still a little apprehensive about finally displaying my work but I had taken the first step on my list. Well, half of the first step.

The next was also a skyline. It was a view from the Crow's Nest in Palos Verdes. The Crow's Nest had been developed over years ago. But I had painted what it once looked like. As a teenager it was known as a make-out spot, but I actually went there for the view.

Nance shook her head. "It's gorgeous Janie," she concluded. "What the hell are you doing working here?" she asked, hugging me. "You have real talent! More than I knew. I'm so proud of you!"

I smiled and rocked back and forth on my heels. I was so excited but not in the fidgety nervous way I usually was.

The final one was unwrapped and stood up for approval. There was Fitz, in all her glory...immortalized in oil. A loud crashing sound emerged from behind us. We all turned to see Dante gaping at the picture with an empty tray in his hand and a pile of broken mugs at his feet.

"Well, I think that says it all," Nance said, hugging Fitz. "So, should I dock him for those, or you?" she chided.

I watched the men hang my paintings. I had such an unbelievable feeling of satisfaction. I knew I was overly critical of myself, picked myself and my decisions apart constantly. But this...this felt right.

After a while I thanked Nance then Fitz and I left. We headed for the 'Home Store' to buy an espresso maker. I didn't care what happened or what went wrong the rest of the day. This would still be the greatest day of my life. "No matter what," I told myself.

We pulled up in front of the Home Store. When we walked in, we went to the far right hand side of the store where home appliances were displayed. I was eyeing a huge industrial copper Cappuccino maker, so lovely, but way out of my price range, when I heard from behind me...

"I knew I'd see you again, bitch!" I turned to see Barry's ex running at me and yelling, "You're in my house now!"

I barely had time to think. But I'm sure F.M.L. jumped quickly into my head, as I put out one hand to stop her from colliding with me. She was even shorter than last night. No boots, I thought. Quickly I had both of her hands in mine, trying to hold her off. She was screaming like a tiny Banshee.

Fitz turned and said, "What the Hell are ya doin', ya crazy bitch?"

Barry's ex was flailing, trying to get her hands free from me.

It was like being attacked by a mad midget. I towered ten inches over her head. I couldn't bring myself to hit her even though holding her off seemed to be ineffective.

"Who the Hell is this?" yelled Fitz.

"This is Barry's ex," I yelled back, agitated at the fact that we were having a dialog at the moment.

"Yer MY Barry's ex?" she asked, with real surprise.

"I'm not his Ex, and he's not YOUR BARRY, he's mine! And if you're thinking of taking a stab at him, you'll get the same as this bitch here!" she yelled, at the top of her lungs. She was grunting now.

"Oh, is that true?" Fitz asked, her eyes narrowing.

I was still holding both her hands and we had become quite a spectacle by now. People were looking down the aisle at us. But, I noticed, no one was coming to rip the crazed employee off of me. Not even Fitz.

"Listen here ya bloody little Leprechaun, I have more pull with Barry than you'll ever have," said Fitz, antagonizing her further.

"You think so?" she blazed. "Then I guess you're next! I'll fight you both! One at a time! As soon as I take care of this bitch, your mine!" she screamed.

"Seriously, is bitch the only word you know?" I asked.

She became even more agitated, yanking harder on me to pull herself free. She was growling now, like a little rabid pit bull and trying to kick me with her tiny legs.

Fitz, who had finally had enough of this, said, "No that's fine, I'll wait my turn. In the meantime, I'll call my brother."

"Call whatever back-up you need!" she huffed.

Fitz pulled out her cell phone and hit speed dial. "Hello, Barry?" she said. "I'm at your psychotic ex-girlfriend's work. Well apparently, she's tryin' to attack Janie."

At first she seemed unconcerned with the conversation Fitz

was having, then several key words started to sink in: Brother named Barry…We're at his Ex's work…her struggle to beat my ass was subsiding.

Fitz went on, "I haven't given Janie the go ahead to beat her ass yet." A pause…then, "Well, I don't want her to hurt someone ya may have feelins' for, but I don't know how much longer I can hold Janie back. Ya know she's an absolute beast when she's pissed. There wouldn't be anything left of the poor girl."

"You're Barry's sister Fitz?" the angry midget questioned, her eyes threatening to pop out of her head.

"Yes," said Fitz, pulling the receiver away from her mouth. "And you've just made a grave mistake," she added, smiling viciously.

Finally, a man wearing a yellow 'Home Store' vest came to a pull the psychotic employee off me.

"What are you doing Shelia?" he yelled at the woman I now knew to be named Shelia. "Have you lost your mind? These are grounds for termination!"

She started to say something in her defense but the man, who I assumed was her manager, shook his head. "I saw the whole thing on the video camera, Shelia. You attacked this woman," he said, gesturing to me. "Are you alright Miss?" he asked.

"I'm fine," I said, leering at Fitz.

I heard her say, "I love you, too," and hung up her cell phone.

"Miss, I am so sorry." the man began. "She will be seriously reprimanded, if not fired. It's not for me to decide, but here at The Home Store, we don't tolerate such outbursts of violence. You," he pointed at Shelia, "Wait in my office."

She wasn't looking at her manager, though. She was still staring at Fitz, with wide frightened eyes. And Fitz was smiling back, ear to ear, like an evil redheaded Fairy.

She nodded and walked away without a word, looking back over her shoulder as she went.

"Miss," said the manager, whose name tag I now noticed read, MANAGER BOB.... "What were you shopping for today?"

"I was looking for an espresso machine," I said, still trying to calm my breathing back to normal.

"Well, Miss," said Manager Bob, "Which of these fine models were you looking to take home with you today?"

I started to point to a mid-priced version, when Fitz interrupted.

"She wants the copper one. The big one! Over there," she pointed to the display.

I furrowed my brow. I wasn't gonna spend that kind of money on an espresso machine. I wasn't even sure I had that kind of money. I started to say, "No," but Fitz waved me off.

"Of course," manager Bob nodded. "You know…if you'd be kind enough to sign some quick legal papers, just saying that you have no intention of suing the store, The Home Store would be more than happy to buy that espresso maker for you." He flashed his best salesman smile.

"Well," Fitz said, "my friend has been through an awful lot. She's still in shock, aren't ya now?"

I nodded, not sure what the hell I was supposed to say.

"But, I think that would be okay. Don't ya Janie?" she asked. "We can cut this nice gentleman a break, can't we?" she asked, turning to me. "I mean all that horrible paper work? Whatdaya say?" she grinned.

I was afraid to speak, so I just nodded again.

Half of an hour later, my new espresso machine was being loaded into the back of Baby.

When we took off, I looked at Fitz. "I can't believe you," I said, still in shock. "This thing is worth thousands of dollars. I feel like we took advantage of MANAGER BOB!"

"Relax your overworked conscience. A law suit woulda cost him more," she said calmly.

I shook my head, feeling very uncomfortable with the whole incident.

Fitz read my mind and body language the way only she could and said, "Look…his company woulda fired him for sure if you pressed charges and ya had every right to do so."

"But I wasn't going to press charges," I began.

"Hear me out," she said. "Manager Bob HAS to pass on the tape as an incident to his boss."

I nodded, knowing that this was probably true.

"This way, he looks like he averted some great catastrophe and bad publicity for them. He's their new hero," she exclaimed. "I mean, seriously Janie, as long as it took someone to come to yer aid and all..."

"Yeah, about that," I asked, being drawn back to yet another reason I should be angry with her, "What the hell? Why didn't you pull that bitch off of me? Even as mad as I was last night, and she DID hit me by the way, even if it was only on my shoulder, you know me. I can't bring myself to hit anyone. And," I added, "I'm almost a foot taller than her! It would look like I was midget bashing!"

"Oh, Janie," she scoffed, "I knew she couldn't hurt ya. And this way nobody has to go to jail for assault, manager Bob looks good to the muckety-mucks, and you have a free top of the line espresso maker," she smiled.

I rolled all of this around in my head before concluding, "I think you're the Devil,"

"Well, that's just because of that whole, 'The Devil comes in beautiful wrapping' thing."

I couldn't help but shake my head and laugh finally. "We're a horrible twenty-first century version of Lucy and Ethel," I said. "But how come I'm always the one who gets hit or attacked?"

"Ya know Janie…someday, your fists are gonna curl in anger, and I do fear for the person who receives the unloadin' of all the shite you push down inside yerself."

I was quiet for a moment, thinking about how good/bad it would feel to just unload.

"So, what did Barry say about the whole thing?" I asked, as nonchalantly as possible.

"Oh, it was his answerin' machine I was talkin' to. I guess I'll have some splainin' to do later," she said, mimicking Ricky Ricardo.

We weren't going to make it to the gym today and I didn't care. I had a new espresso machine to hook up. We pulled up out in front of the house since they were still working on my driveway. When Henry saw Fitz and me trying to lug the huge box out of the back seat he ran over to help.

He saw the picture on the front of the box. "Nice, I wanted one like this but couldn't afford it."

"I can't either," I said, straining.

We carried it in the house and cut open the box. It was beautiful. It had two steam stems, one on each side. And it could make four shots at the same time. Eight shots, if you set it for doubles. It came with two copper frothing cups to make steamed milk or foam and a book with recipes to make the perfect espresso or latte.

"The directions are in Italian," whined Fitz.

I laughed, "Yeah you're not good with Italian."

She gave me an 'eat shit' smile and an exaggerated laugh, "Oh yer so funny Janie!"

"I work in a coffee house, Fitz," I said. "I'm sure I can figure it out."

"Or I can read it for you," said Henry.

"You speak Italian?" Fitz and I asked, in dreamy unison.

"Yeah, my family is from Palermo. We still speak only Italian in front of my grandmother."

An hour later, Henry said, "Finito! Okay, you have a drip cord here," he showed me, "where you can set this machine up directly to the pluming. But until you get it installed you can load water from the top," he smiled.

"Thank you so much," I said. I didn't know if I was thanking him for setting up the machine or for reading everything in Italian the whole time, then translating it to English. It made me, and Fitz I noted, a little weak in the knees. "I want to pay you for doing this for me. I really appreciate it." I started to dig for my wallet in the purse that organization forgot.

"No, I was glad to be of assistance," he said.

"No really, I've taken up too much of your time. I feel guilty."

"Nonsense," he said. "It's no big deal."

"But it's not your job to.....

"Oh, for Pete sakes," Fitz interjected. "Why don't ya cook him dinner tonight to make up for it? She's a great cook. She loves to cook. So, cook for the man, already!"

I shot her a look.

Henry saw the look and laughed. "I haven't had a home cooked meal in a while. It does sound good." He patted his washboard tummy.

I hesitated for a moment before saying, "Okay," I was a little embarrassed at Fitz's blatant attempt at a set-up of her own. "Seven o'clock, then?"

"Seven sounds great," he said with a smile. "See you then." He turned and walked out.

I really did enjoy watching him walk away. I turned to Fitz and shook my head at her.

"Yer welcome," she said grinning.

"What should I make?" I said out loud, more to myself than Fitz. "Do you think I should do an Italian dish?" I asked her.

"Funny, I was gonna suggest you 'DO' the Italian dish," she giggled.

"Subtle Fitz," I said, "very subtle."

Fitz took me to the grocery store, since my car was still on vacation in Mum's driveway. I had decided to make Chicken Marsala and Artichoke Bruschetta. I bought a Tiramisu Cake, instead of making one on such short notice. It wouldn't have enough time to chill. I grabbed a beautiful baguette of French bread and a good bottle of red wine. Fitz was on her cell. I wondered if it was Barry, but I couldn't hear her. And honestly, I didn't like the thought of him laughing at me over today's escapades. When she hung up I asked her who she had been talking to. I wasn't too surprised to hear that it was Scotty. They had a date tonight, as well. Fitz wouldn't be cooking the meal though. Not unless she wanted to run this guy off.

We got back to my house and the workers were gone. I had two and a half hours to cook a great meal and look breathtaking. Fitz helped me inside with the groceries then took her leave so she could make herself lovely, as well. Not that it would take her nearly as long.

I started pounding the chicken breast and had to sauté the mushrooms and sweet onions in the Marsala Wine. I decided to put the Chicken Marsala over pasta instead of Italian rice. It was a personal choice. I had ground up the artichoke hearts and was mixing in the final ingredients. I looked around. A quick reheat was all that was left to be done. I had an hour and a half to finish ME. No time to lollygag, I thought. After all, finishing me was the hardest part.

I jumped in the shower, grateful that my water was back on. I washed, exfoliated and shaved everything that needed shaving because, what if? 'What if' never happened because I didn't fall into bed that quickly, but just…what if? Jumping out of the shower, I did the women's oil and lotion routine, blew my hair dry and put it up in a loose bun with a fancy clip. I raced to my closet. I was going to wear the red and white polka-dot pin-up dress. I put it on but my bra strap was showing. "Tacky," I said out loud. I tried on a different cut bra. "Nope," still showed. "Third time's a charm," I thought. After trying on all my new bras I came to the conclusion that I didn't have a bra to wear with this dress. Maybe they didn't even make one. I was gonna have to go braless or wear something else. In the end, I wore a blue cotton sun dress. I didn't feel as pretty in it, but I did feel a lot less naked. I put on some 'night time' eye make-up. Fitz says there's a difference between night and day make-up. Night make-up should be slightly bolder, smoky. Day time make-up should look bright and clean. I clearly had some advantages to having a best friend who was a model. I went to put on a pair of panty hose and realized that I didn't own one pair without runs. Why the hell did I have a drawer of hose with runs? It's not like I'll ever wear them again. I tossed all eight pairs in the garbage and looked at the clock.

"Too late to make a store run," I said to no one. It was no big deal. I didn't even have to wear shoes if I didn't want to. After all, this is my home, not a restaurant. I looked at myself in the full length mirror in my room. "Not bad."

I uncorked the wine so it would have time to breathe. Time was counting down quickly. Hurriedly, I cut the baguette into rounds and started browning them. I made a quick Caesar Salad from a pre-made bag, and started re-warming the Chicken Marsala. The doorbell rang at seven on the dot.

I was like a nervous teenager as I went to open the door. There he stood, wearing jeans, a button down black shirt two buttons open at the top with a sport coat. He looked so handsome and smelled of Polo Cologne, one of my favorites.

"Bella," he said, kissing each cheek and handing me a bunch of wild flowers.

"Hello," I said, my knees shaking so hard I thought he would hear them knocking.

He stepped inside and the 'dinger' went off on the stove. "Oh, perfect timing," I said. "Dinner's ready."

I went into the kitchen to remove the toasted rounds from the oven and put the flowers in a vase.

"Can I help with anything?" he asked.

I was dumbfounded. A man offered to help me in the kitchen? "You could pour the wine, if you'd like. The glasses are already on the dining room table, in there," I pointed.

He grabbed the bottle of wine. "For the center piece," he said, grabbing the vase of flowers, and placed them on the dining table.

I served our salads and bruschetta at the same time. He ate heartily and made happy noises. It was so nice to cook for someone, I thought. I served the Chicken Marsala and we made idle conversation. It was your typical 'getting to know you' stuff. Where did you grow up? Where'd you go to school? What are your hobbies? Do you have any brothers or sisters? (He had many siblings, I of course, none. My mother's craziness would have been easier to handle if it was distributed among more than one child. I did avoid the whole 'my mother is insane and tried to set me up with my cousin' conversation. That was more of a warning spoken right before they meet her, kind of thing. I held that off with most prospective boyfriends as long as I could.) We were so compatible. We both had a deep love of art, poetry, old movies and nature. Soon enough, I offered dessert but he patted his washboard stomach and said he was too full at the moment.

"You know what I'd like to do?" he asked.

"My knees began to knock again, "No…what?"

"I'd love to see your paintings," he said.

I smiled kind of relieved that he wasn't making a move. I wasn't quite ready yet. "Yeah?" I asked. "Alright, they're in here," I said, walking with him in tow to my studio. I really wasn't used to people viewing my work. Truth was, I always worried that they would find it necessary to find something nice to say but he took his time and eyed them all carefully. He talked about the light, color and brush stokes used. I gave him a surprised smile. He knew art very well.

"This one," he said, 'The Blue Woman', this isn't a self portrait is it?"

I nodded. "Yes, it is. I did it last year."

"There's so much...sadness. A real loneliness to it," he said turning to me. "I don't see you that way at all."

"It was a different time in my life. I'm not that person anymore," I said, knowing that the statement was true. If I had been honest with myself, my work would have told me how I felt about my relationship with John. But I pushed that out of my mind.

Our eyes locked. He took a step into my personal space and brought a hand to my cheek. A shiver ran down my spine. Bending his head, softly he kissed the spot on my neck that turns me to Jell-O. His breath was hot, and it sent another chill that ran to an undisclosed part of me. My skin was coming alive with goose bumps under his lips. Now I was ready. His hand reached behind my head and tilted it up slightly, my eyes fell closed. His lips brushed mine and he kissed me, gently. I returned the kiss, melting into it. My arms circled his neck as one small kiss turned into a passionately long surrendering. This was the way all women wanted to be kissed. Something I actually hadn't felt in a long time. His arms circled my waist and his hands pulled my body closer to his. He pulled the clip from my hair, and he let out a half moan as it fell down my back, his fingers running through it. I was so glad I shaved because maybe......Ding Dong went the doorbell.

I looked at Henry and wondered if we should just ignore it but, then it rang again. Ding Dong! And now whoever it was… was now knocking too. I made it half way to the door and I heard Barry yell.

"Janie, are ya in there? I need to explain!"

I opened the door, "Barry?"

"Oh, I'm so glad you were home. I just got Fitz's message. I'm so sorry about…." he trailed off.

Henry had come up beside me and put his arm around me. Like a dog protecting his bone. "Janie is there a problem?" he asked, glaring at Barry.

"No," I said, with a wave of my hand. "Henry this is Barry," I introduced them. "And, Barry this is Henry."

Barry extended his hand but was met with an icy stare. Barry looked caught off guard. I wasn't sure if it was because of Henry's very presence, or his rudeness. "I'm sorry. I didn't think you'd be on a date after…."

"Well, she is on date," Henry said, and squeezed me tighter. "So why don't you just say what you have to say, so we can get back to it."

I was dumbfounded, and my brow furrowed with confusion as I turned to Henry, "It's okay." I looked back to Barry. "I'm just a friend of his little sister, right Barry?" I said, trying not to sound hurt.

"Uh yeah," he said slowly, nodding his head. "She's a friend of my little sister," he repeated, staring at me. "Look," he began, "I just wanted to apologize for, well...the misunderstandin' last night, and for what Sheila's been puttin' ya through. I'm very sorry for both." We just looked at each other for a moment.

My face and voice softened. "It's alright Barry. It's not your fault."

"Well, if that's all?" Henry said abruptly, and tried to move me so he could close the door.

I put my arm on the door to keep it from shutting in Barry's face, and glared at Henry.

Barry started to say something else then stopped. He looked from me, to Henry, then back to me, "Never mind." He looked back at Henry, "Take good care of her," he said, and walked off.

"I will," Henry said, moving me back inside and closing the door.

I was in shock. Did Barry want to tell me something important? Was he just apologizing or was there something more? Henry woke me up from my zone-out.

"I hope I'm not going to have to run men away from you all the time," he said, and tried to hug me.

I pulled away. "What the hell was that all about?" I questioned. "Why were you so…rude? He's a friend of mine."

"Hey, all these other guys are going to have to realize that I'm in the picture now."

"What 'in the picture'? I fumed. "You had no right to do that. And, you never will have the right to throw anyone out of my house or bar someone…especially not someone who's been a friend of mine since we were kids!"

"Maybe I overreacted," said Henry, reaching out to touch my arm. "But, I'm not gonna want other guys thinking they can just drop by and see 'My Lady' any time they want."

I was almost struck dumb, but my 'Crazy' detector was going off the charts. He reached out to me, but I recoiled from him and huffed, "I am not your lady! And you are not my boyfriend! We just had our first kiss not even five minutes ago!"

"Alright, alright," he said, raising his hands like he was admitting defeat. "That was wrong of me, I guess. But I know what I want, and when I get it…it's mine."

"What about what I want? Do I get a say in this?"

"Look, don't be dramatic…plus, that kiss…told me that you wanted me too."

My eyes rounded at his audacity, "You have some nerve," I hissed, then I raised my hands and took a deep breath. "But you know what, you're right…"

He grinned and folded his arms across his chest.

"I did want you," I said, nodding my head, "…but then YOU turned into WHOEVER the hell that just was, and I sure as hell don't want him."

He laughed at me as though I was being ridiculous.

This made me angry, my voice and temper escalating. "And just so you know," I went on, "I am not a doormat…so desperate to be loved that I'll do, or say, or allow whatever some guy wants me to, to make him happy, Oh no!" I said, shaking my head. "Not me!"

I knew he didn't understand the last part. I didn't expect him to. I also didn't expect everything to come blurting out of me. But, I had said it. And whether or not it made sense to him, some part deep inside of me yelled, IT'S ABOUT TIME!

He did a "palms up" and laughed, "Honey, I don't want to play games…."

I cut him off, "I'm not your honey," I said calmly, "and I'm not playing any games, not now, or ever!"

I pulled the door open so hard, the knob stuck in the wall.

"Now, get out of my house!" I said, pointing the way.

As he moved past me, he started to say something, but I pointed again and said more firmly, "Go!"

As he headed to his truck I yelled, "And don't come back!"

I wanted to slam the door after him, but first I'd have to free it from the wall. I waited for him to pull away and then I grabbed the doorknob and yanked and yanked till it came free. The hole would have to be patched, preferably before Betty saw it. I guess I do have something to do tomorrow, I thought, and slammed the door shut.

"Oh my God," I thought, pacing with my hands over my eyes. What the hell just happened? I just let some lunatic practically run Barry out of my house. Scarier still, I just let a lunatic in my house. Oh God I almost..."Ew, ew, ew!" I yelled jumping up and down. Then it hit me, Oh God… I've got to call Barry!

I walked to the phone and picked it up before I realized I didn't have his phone number. I couldn't call Fitz and ask for his number. She would want to know why and that was a can of worms I wasn't ready to open yet. I quickly changed into a pair of 501's, threw on a tee shirt, and headed down to the pub to look for him. With every block I told myself that I was going to tell Barry how I felt about him. No chickening out. I even rehearsed it in my head.

I knew Andy was on shift, but I didn't want him to know I was looking for Barry. I wanted to be as nonchalant as I could but, how can I be inconspicuous in the pub? I walked in and slowly made my way through the bottom floor, looking into the Poker and Pool Rooms. When I finished my rounds I noticed Andy was eyeing me and said, "Janie girl, can I get ya something?"

I took a stool and ordered a Black and Tan. "So Andy, what's going on tonight?" I asked. "Bands…anything?"

He looked at me suspiciously, "It's Tuesday, Janie. You know we don't have a band on Tuesday."

So much for nonchalant, I thought. Finally, I just blurted out, "Have you seen Barry?"

"He was here about an hour ago. He prattled on about havin' to make something' right then he bolted outta here. Why?" he asked.

"Oh, no reason," I squirmed. "Could you, uh, give me his cell number?"

"What's goin' on with the two of ya?" Andy asked.

"What do you mean?"

"I mean," Andy began, "when Barry was here, he asked if we had your number lyin' around. I told him to call Fitz or Mum, but he said, "Never mind." That's when he started ramblin' and took off out the door."

"Shit," I said under my breath.

Andy eyes narrowed. "Barry doesn't have a cell," he finally said.

"What?" I said, concern rising. "Everyone has a cell phone."

"Not Barry," said Andy. "I'm not sure why? Mum's been barkin' at 'em for years to get one. Hey..." Andy said, laughing, "that's probably why he doesn't have one! It's because of Mum and all of her crazy fix-ups, I'll bet. Ya know," he chuckled, "he almost had Mum convinced that he was gay just so she'd stop her meddlin'. Boy am I glad I'm already married."

I bit my lower lip and furrowed my brow.

He went on, "Ya know, that one...that was in here last night, the one that was freaking out and tryin' to pick a fight with ya?"

A nod of the head was all I could muster.

"That was one of Mum's."

"No," I said, shaking my head.

"Yeah, yeah," he said, nodding. "It's a friend's granddaughter, or some such nonsense. Barry didn't want to go out with her, so Mum ambushed him," he nodded again, "invited him to dinner."

"No," I said again, sounding more anxious.

"Yep, the little ding bat was there. Barry said she hadn't seemed all that 'right' with the fix-up either. She was kinda cold towards him and all. But, by the end of dinner, she was practically throwing herself at him. He almost had to fight her off. She's been hasslin' and tormentin' him ever since."

"Shit," I said under my breath. "You don't know if Mum MADE wine for that dinner, do you?"

He looked confused. "Haven't a clue. If she did, it would have been wasted on Barry. He hates wine. Mum had to come just short of beatin' him to get him to take the Holy Sacrament when we were young," Andy laughed.

I rubbed my temples, "Oh God, Mum," I said out loud. My stomach was spinning. Had she tried to drug Barry, too, and succeeded with the psycho bitch? I wondered. Was that WHY she was a psycho bitch?

Andy was still watching me with concern. "Janie? Are ya ok?"

I nodded.

"Ya look ill. I can give ya his home number. I don't know if he's left yet. I could call Mum for ya. She was his ride. She'd know."

These words dragged me back from a horrible vision. "Left yet?" I repeated. "Where... where is he going?" I stammered, having trouble finding and steadying my voice. I had a sinking feeling now along with the stomach spins. Oh, this Black and Tan is coming back, I thought.

"Ireland," said Andy, starting to look really worried for me. "Janie, ya really don't look good. Are ya gonna get sick?"

My eyes bugged out. I shook my head no, but I really wasn't sure. "Why is he going to Ireland?" I finally managed.

"His best friend's getting' hitched."

"His best friend?" I repeated.

"Yeah from childhood, before we moved to the States. They've been pen pals for years. Barry's his best man."

Barry's a pen pal? I couldn't picture it. "When will he be back?" I asked, trying not to sound as desperate as I felt.

"Oh, the lucky bastard, he's goin' home for ten days. "

"Ten days," I repeated, looking down at the bar to try and stop the room from spinning. I remembered this feeling. Once, when I was young, I had to stand for an hour with the church choir. I had this same feeling. The next thing I knew, I woke up on the floor with people hovering above me. Apparently I had passed out cold.

Andy handed me a piece of paper with Barry's home phone number. I rubbed my eyes and tried to gain back my balance. I willed myself through a breathing technique I had read the night before. When I could speak again I told Andy thank you, and put the number in my pocket. I felt something else in there. I grabbed the tiny object and pulled it out. Even before looking at it, I knew it was the Rune. I rubbed it again between my fingers then shoved it and the number, back in my pocket.

I left the bar, and my beer, and took my spinning stomach home. On the way, I dug my cell out of the bottom of my bag and tried to call Barry's house. I got the answering machine. "I'm not in," I heard him say. "If you'd be kind enough to leave your name and number, I'll ring you as soon as I can." BEEP, went the machine and I hung up. What was I supposed to say? I had finally gotten the balls to tell him how I feel, face to face, like an adult. I was ready to take a leap of faith and deal with whatever humiliation lay ahead, and Barry was gone…to Ireland! I hung up and tried to think positively. It was only ten days. Maybe I'd still have the courage in ten days.

I got home and saw the answering machine light blinking away. I stood over it hoping that maybe, just maybe, Barry had called me. No, I thought to myself. That stuff only happens in movies, and after what I had allowed Henry to do, why would he call me? More likely, it was the crazy women in my life calling to torture me. I hit play anyway and crossed my fingers.

The first was my mother. "Janie, I'm sorry for what I've done to you. Your father made me realize that what I did…well, it was wrong. Well, your father and the fact that Lenny was fired from the hospital yesterday for stealing Fecal Specimens."

I cringed and shook my head. Great now the little freak was unemployed and had plenty of time to stuff poor, unsuspecting animals. Or, I thought with a shudder, women.

She went on... "I guess the real question is, what was he going to do with them?"

Oh, people were really testing my gag reflex, I thought.

"….I think he IS a little...touched," she searched for a word. "The next time I fix you up, I swear, it'll be better."

I skipped the message. She almost had me. But, she had to go and say she still planned on meddling in my love life. Why can't she just be a normal mom? With that, I thought of Mum meddling in Barry's life, my life, and inadvertently, in Fitz's. Maybe this is what normal moms do? I wondered. Not cousins though, I reminded myself, never cousins. Not normal!

I hit play for the second message.

"Hi honey. It's Nance. Look, I have some really important news for you but, I don't want to leave it on the answering machine. Call me back. I don't even care how late it is! Okay? I love you, chow."

I hit play for the third message.

"Hi dear," rang Mum's voice. I was callin' to invite ya to a special gatherin' of the women tomorrow night. It's a full moon, and all, so we'll be headin' to Lavender's house. I mean, Diane's. Why do I keep doin' that? Anyway, we hope to see you then."

"Yeah, I bet they do!" I thought. What kind of crazy crap were they gonna try now? They had already stood me in a kiddy tub and baptized me with oil. Then Mum and Aunt Marble tried to drug me. What next, a crucification-purification maybe…an herbal colonic…or how about a ritual where they shave my head and just lobotomize me already? That may be the best idea of all, I thought. That way, I'd never have to think for myself again.

One more message: Please be Barry, I begged, as I hit play.

"Puddin?" said Betty.

No such luck, I thought.

"It's Betty," she slurred.

Like anyone else in the world called me Puddin. I thought she was talking really slowly. Drunk, I concluded.

"How'd ya like the gift I sent ya? He's a looker, ain't he? I hope you two are having a great night. Call me tomorrow sugar and tell me all about it, okay?"

The line went dead, but I wasn't sure if she hung up or passed out. If I was to understand her drunken message, she set me up with Henry. I mean, it seemed like I was asking him out, but in all reality, he was here on a 'fix up' of sorts. She had sent him here to 'hook up' with me. And, he must have reported back to her that we had a date. Oh, my head was spinning again.

I sat down and tried to collect my thoughts. First, I was dumped by my boyfriend of two years in an airport terminal, in the most humiliating and offensive way possible. Then, Fitz drags me to a ritual, where strange women want to rebirth me because my dating life is so bad they need to remove my curse. Humiliating again! Then, at said ritual, I wind up flashing her brother, who, I just happen to have had the biggest crush on for practically my whole life. What I assumed was the pinnacle of humiliation. Then, my crazy mother tries to set me up with my seriously demented cousin. Not just sick but also humiliating when you consider the fact that she, no matter how crazy, thought we would be a good match. Then, Mum and Aunt Marble, or the 'Scary Sisters' as I had taken to calling them, tried to drug some poor guy to make him like me...pathetically humiliating. Then my landlady, who barely knows me, tries to set me up with a cute all be it, but also insanely jealous, possessive (not to mention somewhat delusional) man, using home construction as a guise. Ah, the cherry on the top of the humiliation sundae, I thought.

I pulled a pillow off my couch, buried my head and screamed into it, again and again. These crazy women were ruining my life. It took me a bit more yelling into the pillow, but eventually I tuckered myself out.

I went to change into my jammies. When I pulled my 501's off, the tiny Rune fell out again. "I wonder exactly what you're supposed to do?" I asked it, like it would respond. "You certainly don't keep crazy away," I told it. I put it back on the coffee table and turned on the TV. I was too exhausted to read. I was asleep before my head hit the armrest.

I had the best dream of Barry. He was dressed like a prince in a fairytale. He had a crown of gold on his head and was toasting his new bride. "I love ya with all my heart," he said. I was just raising my glass to him to return his vow of love, when I heard some other woman say, "And I you, my dearest." I turned to my right and saw a beautiful woman in a white wedding gown, glowing. He had married someone else? This woman, glowing in white, was Barry's wife? He came to her, the whole kingdom watching, and kissed her passionately. "No!" I tried to scream, but no words would come out. I was unable to speak. Unable to tell him that I was the one he was supposed to marry. They passed by me, hand in hand, and were ferried away in a horse drawn carriage.

I woke screaming, "No!" Seems I had finally found my voice again. My heart was pounding out of my chest. It was a dream, I told myself. Just a horrible, horrible dream!

10

WEDNESDAY: DAY 5 OF DUMPED

6am, wide awake. Even on vacation I couldn't sleep in. The dream of my 'dream guy' marrying another didn't help, I'm sure. I went and splashed cold water on my face. I needed coffee. When I passed by my side window I heard the construction workers beginning their day in my front yard. I hoped Henry wasn't with them. Upon further inspection, or snooping from behind a drawn curtain, I noticed he wasn't out there. Thank God, I told myself. I had no desire for a run in with that weirdo.

I finally used my new espresso maker. I loved it. I made myself a triple non-fat latte and plopped back down on the couch. I should call Betty today and tell her to please not meddle in my life. Oh no, I remembered, I was supposed to call Nance. She had said that it was important. I hope she didn't need me to work today, we opened at 5am. I ran to the phone and called Spilled the Beans. Dante answered and promptly handed the phone to Nance. "Janie?"

"Yeah Nance, it's me. I'm so sorry I didn't call...."

"It's fine, it's fine," she interrupted impatiently. "Are you sitting down?"

This question caught me off guard. "Ugh, yeah," I said, backing up to sit on the couch.

"Last night," she began, "the owner from the Rien Gallery, Micca Rien, stopped in for a coffee." She paused and took a deep breath. "He was so impressed with your paintings he asked if you would be interested in having them displayed at his Gallery Auction this Sunday night."

Now I was having trouble breathing. "Are you kidding?" I finally yelled into the receiver.

"No, I'm not!" she yelled back loudly.

"Oh my God, tell him yes. Yes, yes, yes!" I yelled, jumping up and down.

"Well, that's the other part," she said. "I couldn't get a hold of you last night so I told him yes without asking you. I'm sorry if I overstepped my bounds."

A woman in my life who was worried about overstepping her bounds? I loved Nance for so many reasons. And now there was one more.

"No, you did the right thing, Nance," I said. "You did exactly the right thing."

"Honey, I am so proud of you," she said. "There's only one other thing."

"What?" I asked, worried that this is where I would wake-up.

"Well, you only get six tickets. I probably could have finagled one from Mr. Rien, but I wanted to go with the artist."

"Of course," I said, beaming. "I'm going to need you there for moral support."

"Great," she yelled with real enthusiasm. "I'll give you the other five tickets when you come in. Bye honey."

"Bye, Nance!" I yelled before hanging up the phone.

I decided to call my mother first. I knew Mrs. O would also be up with the sunrise…bleaching something. It was still too early for Fitz. My mother rambled from the second she picked up the phone. I could hardly get a word in edgewise. Finally I had to tell her to please stop talking so I could give her some important news. After I told her everything about putting the paintings up on the wall at the coffee house, to Mr. Rien, and then to Nance's call, I said, "What do you think of that, mom?"

"Your little paintings are going to be in a Gallery?"

I let out a deep sigh. "Yes mom. The Gallery owner wants them in his Auction. He really likes them."

"What day is this happening?" she asked.

"Actually, mom, it's this Sunday night so…"

She cut me off midsentence. "So you're gonna miss dinner with your father and me?"

"Uh, yeah mom," I said, slapping my forehead. "This is kind of a big honor. I mean, this kind of opportunity doesn't come around often. If it goes well, it could launch a whole new career for me."

"Well, just don't get your hopes up Janie. I'd hate to see you set yourself up for a fall."

"Well, thanks mom," I said, and made some lame excuse to get off the phone.

This was the most important, the most exciting moment of my life, and she had managed to suck it away. "Good-Energy-Sucker," I yelled at the phone. On a more positive note, I had found a way out of dinner at mom and dad's. Yay me, I smiled.

I sure as hell wasn't inviting her so she could tell potential buyers how she thought my painting's looked exactly the same as the scribbling I had done on the wall as a toddler. It hurt a little, her inability to be happy for me. Was it too much for her to at least fake being excited when something good happened in my life? But, sadly, I was more than used to it. I wanted to call Fitz so badly, but settled for Mum. She too would be awake…not bleaching anything.

Mum was truly excited for me. She was screaming to the rest of the brood. Whoever was there and awake at least.

"Can I come to the Auction?" she asked.

"Definitely," I said "you'll be my guest. It'll be you, Nance, Fitz and me."

"Yer mom's not comin'?"

"Um no…she and Dad already had plans." It wasn't really a lie. They did have plans. Dad would be watching Sunday Night Fights, and mom would be quilting, cooking or bleaching something.

Mum just said, "Well, okay then, Luv. We'll be there with bells on. Oh, can I bring Da and Marble?"

I only had two tickets left but who the hell else was I going to invite?

"Sure you can," I said.

"Are ya coming tonight? To Diane's?"

Oh yeah, I thought. That's why I wasn't supposed to call Mum. "Uh, is Fitz coming?"

"Well of course,"

"Well...yeah, I'll come," I finally said.

When we hung up, I felt so good about myself. I didn't even care that I may have put myself back in the hands of the lunatics. I'd just be really careful about what I ate or drank. It's not like they'd try to drug me again, I concluded. I jumped in the shower and dressed as quickly as I could. I wanted to pick up those tickets from Nance, and scope out the Gallery. I also had to try my hand at spackling the hole in the wall from the doorknob. I opened the door to check the knob for any damage and let out an, "Aaaahhhhh!"

I ran face to face with Fitz. Quad mocha flew in the air and went tumbling to the ground with an un-ceremonious thud. I was just so relieved she didn't clock me this time.

"What the hell are you doing on my doorstep at 6am?" I asked, trying to steady my heartbeat.

"I couldn't sleep when Scotty went to work," she pouted. "And I knew you'd be up," she said, holding her chest and looking agonizingly at her spilled Mocha.

"Come in, I'll make you a coffee. I have news for you anyway."

After I told her my great news, we stood in my living room jumping up and down and screaming, "Yay," until we wore ourselves out.

"That's amazing news, Janie! I'm so proud of ya!" she replied, out of breath. "I knew if you tried…somethin' good would come of it," she beamed. "So, where are we off to today?"

"I need to see Nance, and go to the hardware store." I pointed to the hole in the wall.

She started ask what happened, but I put my hand up to stop her. "I'll explain in the car."

I hurried up and threw on a pair of 501's, a T-shirt, and grabbed a sweater then headed out to Baby.

Spilled the Beans, was only a few minutes away, so I ran down the 'Henry' story as quickly as I could. After I had explained, Fitz said, "That guy's got some nerve talkin' to my brother like that! Who does he think he is?"

"Ahem," I cleared my throat, and stared at her, as we pulled to the curb.

"Oh yeah, and you too, Janie," she added as an afterthought. "He shouldn't have treated you that way, either."

I smiled at her. I knew she loved me, but her brothers…were a different story. She was just as protective of them as they were of her. "Ya know what really bothers me?" she asked.

I shook my head, not really sure what she was thinking.

"Why did Barry allow himself be ran off? It's not like him not to stand his ground and all."

She was right about that. Barry never looked for trouble. It wasn't his demeanor. But, if it came after him, Barry was first rate at ending it.

"Maybe he thought it wasn't his ground to be makin' a stand," Fitz finally said.

There was that nausea again. I was mentally kicking myself in the ass. I should have made my feelings known to Barry. I should have kicked Henry out on his ass, right there and then. The fact that I didn't sent Barry the wrong message. Truth was, even if Barry and I were never anything more than friends, I never should have let some guy treat him that way. To my credit, I did kick Henry out and I did try to find Barry and explain. But I was too late. Oh, I'm gonna be sick, I thought. Fitz brought me back from the bashing I was giving myself.

"I'm really sorry about that Henry guy, Janie. I practically threw you to 'em," she said.

"Well, not really," I said. "Turns out, Henry was a fix up courtesy of Betty."

"Yer kiddin' me?" She paused to roll this new information around in her head. "She must love the Hell out of ya?"

"What? How did you come to that assumption?"

"Think about it Janie. She picked a gorgeous, talented, hard-working man with a great body…one who's punctual, speaks Italian and knows art."

I started to say something, but Fitz cut me off.

"I know things weren't ideal, but how could she have known that he would be crazy when it came to relationships of the heart? Unless of course..." she trailed off with a head tilt.

"Eeewww! I don't want to think about that," I pleaded.

"All I'm sayin' Janie, is she must care for ya very much to have gone to such trouble. She must think rather highly of ya."

Well, in a way Fitz made sense. I mean, look who my own

mother picked for me? That pretty much said it all. If my worth was based solely on that...well then, thank you Betty!

I saw Nance looking out the window motioning to me to get my butt inside. Seems she had told every 'regular' that walked in the good news. She handed me the tickets and hugged me over and over again. This was the reaction I wanted from my mom.

When Fitz and I got back in the car, I handed her the tickets for her, Mum, Da and Aunt Marble. She stared at them.

"Is that all ya got?" she asked. "Mrs. O and your Dad aren't coming?"

I did a deep sigh and stared at her.

"I get it," she said, and reached out to squeeze my hand. After a moment, she pulled Baby away from the curb and asked, "Can you get more tickets?"

"I'm not sure. Why?"

"Well, Scotty's dad is comin' to town on business and I thought he might like to see yer work."

"Oh, I get it. You want me there for moral support, a buffer."

"Well, kinda."

"You're meeting his family?" I chided in a playful tone. "That's a big step for you."

"I know, I can't believe I agreed to it, but... I just can't tell Scotty no. I really like him, Janie," she said, shaking her head in disbelief. "For the first time in my life, I feel like I've found somethin'....that I didn't even know I was missin'. Is that weird?"

I shook my head. "No Fitzy. It's wonderful. And I am completely jealous," I added, laughing. I really was happy for her.

"What if his father doesn't like me?" she asked seriously.

"Impossible Fitz," I assured her.

We pulled up to Dan's Hardware at 7am.

"Do you even know what you need to fix the wall?" Fitz asked.

She brought up a really good question. I knew more about cars than I did about home repairs. And that wasn't saying much. I had seen women construction workers on HGTV and figured that if they could do it…I could screw it up. I decided that I should ask for some advice from a professional. We walked in and it was like being in a gynecologist's office. They had all kind of tools and gadgets. I had no idea how they worked and wasn't sure I wanted to.

"Can I help you find something?" we heard from behind us.

Fitz and I turned...and looked down. The gentleman that stood before us, smiling, was not quite five foot tall and almost as wide. He had black wavy hair, and sparkling brown eyes set deep in his round face. He was like a happy, 'Um-pa Loom-pa'.

"Hi," I said, and nudged Fitz so she would close her jaw. "I need some help. I've got a hole in my wall that I need to patch."

"Okay," he said nodding, and putting his little hands on where his hips should be. "So, how deep is this hole?" he began.

I tried to measure it up with my fingers. "It's about this deep," I showed him,

"Okay, so about three inches, or so?"

I nodded, "Yeah, that's about right."

"And how big around?" he asked.

I looked at Fitz. "Uh, your standard doorknob size," I said.

His brows arched, "Okay, well that hole is too deep to just spackle. You're going to have to use some drywall to adhere the spackle to. We sell it in all different sizes. But you'll only need a small piece for that," he said, waddling off and waving to us to follow.

We walked down an isle that housed six foot pieces of drywall, and sheet rock. I had no idea what the difference was between the two. We worked our way down to the precut pieces.

The size I needed, unfortunately, was on the top shelf. The man pointed to it and said, "That's the size you need. I'll get the step ladder."

As he waddled off to get the ladder Fitz and I just stared at each other. I knew she was reading my mind. The thought of that round man on a little ladder scared the hell out of both of us. He set up the ladder and began to climb while I held my breath watching the medal rung 'give' slightly. He grabbed the piece and started to descend. I prayed for him all the way down. By the time he reached the ground, he was huffing and puffing. I noticed sweat running down his face. Now I was worried that he was going to have a heart attack.

He was kind enough to walk us through the whole process and picked out everything we would need for the job. It didn't sound too difficult, so we said "thank you" and headed off to conquer the wall.

Back at my house, the workers were loading their trucks. They had come back to pull up the concrete forms and seal the new patio.

"Looks like their done," said Fitz. "I don't see Henry anywhere."

"Good. I really do want to listen politely while he makes excuses for last night and tries to convince me that I overreacted."

"Wow! It's like you've been through this before or something," she kidded.

I looked at the hole in the wall. I was still going to have to cut the drywall piece I had purchased.

I didn't have a saw, per sey, so I used my electric carving knife and began trimming the edges. I finally worked it down to the desired size and maneuvered it into the hole. Next was spackle. I dipped the putty knife in the can and pulled out a glob of the thick paste. I smeared it over the drywall and tried to smooth it out as well as I could. I stood back to admire my work while Fitz raided my fridge. Not bad, I thought. Now all I had to do was wait for it to dry, then sand it flush with the wall.

Fitz walked up beside me, "Oks grt," she said, with a full mouth.

"What are you eating?" I asked. "Ir-ama-u aak," she mumbled.

I shook my head at her, "Did you leave me any Tirimisu Cake?" I asked

She nodded with fat cheeks.

"Chew Fitz," I laughed.

I heard a car pull up in front of my house. I looked out the window and saw Betty in the passenger side of a new Candy Apple Red Cadillac.

"Holy shit Betty's here!" I hissed to Fitz.

Fitz looked confused. "So," she said, wrinkling her face at me.

"The hole," I reminded her. "She's going to see the hole in the wall," I began to panic.

"Ya fixed the hole, Janie. It'll be fine. Calm yerself."

The truth was I felt bad about the hole. But, that wasn't the part that had me acting oddly. Betty, in all my years living in her rental, had never come to the house. Never did a 'drop by' or an inspection of any kind, so why now?

"I just know she's going to sell my house, Fitz. Do you know how hard it is to find rentals around here, in my price range? Most the rentals around here are going for three times what I pay a month. Hell, I might have to move as far away as Lomita to find something I can afford.

I now saw that Larry had come from the driver's side to assist Betty. They were walking towards the side of the house. No doubt to see the new patio and privacy fencing.

I looked at Fitz, "My car's not in the driveway. Maybe they'll think I'm not home?"

"Yer being ridiculous, Janie. Anyway, if worst came to worst, you could bunk with me and B.J."

Oh, the thought of that was almost too much to bear. Picking up after both of them… cooking all the meals so that neither of them accidentally poisoned the other. Not to mention, fighting B.J.'s drunken boyfriend's friends for the couch. The image of all this made the commute from Lomita seem a lot shorter and almost bearable.

"When are ya gonna pick up yer car, anyway? It's been sitting in Mum's driveway for two days?"

"Ssshhh, they'll hear us."

I looked outside as they were coming to the front door.

"Crap," I said, more to myself than Fitz.

Ding Dong.

I took a deep breath and opened the door.

"Hi Betty," I said, with a tense painted smile.

"Hi, Puddin!" she said, stepping forward to embrace me. "You remember my ..." she giggled, "friend." "Yes, ugh, Larry," I said, extending my hand. "Oh, and you both remember Fitz?" I asked.

He nodded to both of us. Fitz had come from the couch to hug Betty. She had become very fond of Betty, thinking of herself as Betty's underling.

"So Puddin, can I talk to you alone for a minute?"

I shot Fitz a look. I was going off to 'Renter's Death Row'.

We stepped outside then Betty and I began to wander out of ear shot of Larry and Fitz.

"Puddin," she began. "I'm so sorry I set you up with Henry. Ya know, he told me about the date," she paused. "What he did." She shot me a sideways glance. "I shoulda kept my big nose out of your business. It's just… the other day when I found out about you and John...," she trailed off.

"It's okay Betty," I began, but she cut me off.

"No, no, sugar," she said shaking her head. "I had no right to think that I knew what was best for you. It's just"...she stopped and took my hand... "I see so many wonderful things in you. I just wanted you to be as happy as I am."

I gave her a heartfelt hug and told her, "Thank you, Betty. Thank you for caring about me." I was amazed that I said it, and even more amazed that I really meant it.

We held the hug for a moment until Betty said, "I did have one other question for ya, Puddin."

"Okay," I said, visibly moved by her genuine concern for me, "Shoot."

"That guy...the one that Henry acted like such an ass in front of..."

"Barry," I informed her.

"Barry," she repeated, nodding. "Is there somethin' goin' on between the two of you?"

I felt heat rising up from my stomach. I shook my head, "No. I'm like a little sister to Barry," I said, without trying to sound bitter. "Why do you ask?"

"Oh, I just thought I picked up on somethin' when Henry was relayin' the story." She was eyeing me closely, almost like she could read my mind. "Must of had worked it out wrong in my noggin. Happens sometimes at my age," she said, smiling gently and wrapping her arm around me. "Come on. Let's go see the new patio and fence."

We walked over to the new patio. I hadn't seen it yet. It wasn't just a plain concrete patio like I imagined it would be. It was beautiful and I was awestruck. It had 'Used Brick' inlay done in a compass design.

"Didn't this turn out lovely?" Betty asked.

I nodded. "Where did you come up with the idea of a compass design?"

She grinned at me. "I love to travel, Puddin. To the ends of the four corners of the world and back!" she exclaimed. "But home…is always somewhere in the middle. Kinda like a center," she said, making a circle with her hands. "I figured this patio should be a center, a home base, a place where a person could relax and get grounded."

I wondered how long I had to get 'grounded' here.

The seven foot redwood fence was perfect. I'd be able to sun bathe out here without feeling like I was being watched by Mr. Mendlebaum.

Mrs. Mendlebaum had alerted me to this odd quirk her husband had of looking in on people when they were unaware of his presence. She said he was just nosey. I don't know where she was raised, but where I come from, that's a pervert. Guess that was why I always keep my curtains closed.

"Ya know, Puddin," said Betty, "Henry told me that you were displayin' a few of your paintins' at your work. But Larry and I drove over there today, and I didn't see em!"

"Well, that's because a local Gallery owner saw them and decided he wanted them for his auction on Sunday," I beamed with pride.

"Oh, Sugar!" she yelled, taking my hand in hers again. "That's incredible! I am so proud of you!" she elated. "So, which Gallery is it?"

"The Rien Gallery on Fourth," I replied, still giddy. "I've been there. It's very upscale. Your work must be amazin', Puddin."

I tried to suppress a smile.

"So," she said, after a moment, "Can I see your other paintins'?"

I was mentally dragged back to the newly patched hole in the wall. Finally I decided to just come clean.

"Betty, the other night, when I kicked Henry out...well, I threw the door open kinda hard and...well...I put a hole in the wall with the doorknob. I'm really sorry. I mean, I've already patched it and it looks pretty good. But, if you want to have it fixed by a professional, I'll pay for it and everything."

Betty was laughing. "Oh Puddin, don't you worry about that. I remember this one time," she started, "a date getting so out of line that I threw a fryin' pan at him."

I stood there, wide eyed. The thought of a 'Pissed-Off Betty' was actually frightening to me.

"It whizzed past his head and hit the glass sliding door," she laughed at the memory. "Shattered the damn thing! Shards of glass everywhere!" she rolled. "I learned to be more controlled after that. Now, if a man gets outta line, I pull the snub nosed thirty-eight my late husband gave me and give it a good wave around, that pretty much puts an end to it."

"Yeah, I guess so," I said, laughing.

"After you shove a gun in a man's face, Puddin, they don't have to ask if they've offended you. And," she added, "they think you're as crazy as a rabid squirrel. They don't even bother to call to apologize," she laughed again. "And I haven't had to replace one window since."

It was the kind of Hillbilly Logic I was starting to grow rather fond of. I could see why Fitz wanted to be Betty when she grew-up. I was starting to wish I was so ballsy.

We walked into the house and I showed her my patch work. Larry said it looked really good, especially for a first attempt.

We walked into my studio where all my paintings were housed. Betty looked at each one like it was a Monet, or a Picasso, or dare I say it, a Van Gogh. He was my favorite of all the painters.

"Why haven't you hung any of these?" Betty asked. "Your walls in the living room are bare as a bone."

"I didn't want to put holes in your walls," I said, honestly. "Some of them are pretty heavy. They might even require molly's to properly mount them."

Fitz laughed, "She patched one hole and now she's a master builder."

I gave her a sarcastic smile.

"Well Puddin," Betty said, "I'd rather see those hung," she pointed at my paintings, "than worry about a few little holes. Plus, you know how to patch now," she smiled. "You should treat this house like it's your own. Paint it if you want to! It's not like it can't be painted over!"

I was getting some mixed signals. Was she keeping the house? Selling the house? I decided not to ask. For however long I was here Betty wanted me to feel at home, and the thought of that... was wonderful. I mentally started to pick out colors, and an accomplice. I smiled at Fitz.

Betty and Larry had other errands to run so they said their goodbyes and took their leave.

"So Fitz," I began, "if you were going to paint this room...."

She smiled at me and said, "But I'm not."

"Can't blame me for trying."

"So now what?" Fitz asked.

"I think we should go to the Gallery to see if we can get some more tickets for Sunday."

We jumped back in Baby and were on the go again.

We headed south to Fourth Street. There was the Gallery. It was another beautiful old building that had been completely restored. I had actually been here a couple of times before. Once I had the pleasure of seeing a Georgia O' Keefe showing. I took a gentleman I had just started to date, who, after his third glass of wine, announced very loudly: "These flower paintings look like giant vaginas. Look this one follows you wherever you go." The memory of it made me wish I would have had Betty's gun then (Especially at the end of our date when he asked if he was going to get to see any other vaginas that night.)

"I don't understand... if we don't have to buy the tickets, why do we have to have the tickets?" Fitz said.

I shrugged, "I really don't know. Maybe it's to keep track of people or a city ordinance of some kind?"

Fitz shrugged back, "Your guess is as good as mine."

"Really, what was your guess?" I asked.

She smiled at me, "Didn't have one, and your guess was just as good."

"You're kind of an asshole."

"And just think, I'm not even tryin'," she grinned.

We walked in and waited for someone to approach us. There was another couple there, who I assumed were doing the same thing. We looked at every picture in the Gallery while we waited. Twenty minutes had passed and still no one had come to help us.

Fitz said, "I guess art buyers are more used to waiting?"

To this question, I did an obligatory 'palms up'. "I don't know. How do you sell anything without a sales person?" I walked over to the other couple to ask if they had at least seen a salesperson since they entered. The two were having a conversation about a photo of an orange. It was named, 'The Orange'. This probably passed for many as clever or ironic. To me, it was as ridiculous as the photo.

"Excuse me," I said.

The couple turned to look at me, then went right back to their conversation.

I looked back at Fitz with a 'Can you believe this shit' smile.

Fitz walked over and said, "Excuse me, but ya wouldn't happen to know if someone works here, would ya?"

The lady of the duo was tall and thin with a black 'mod' haircut, and dressed impeccably in a black pantsuit. She turned to Fitz looking her up and down like she was some kind of peon. Finally, with an almost bored expression, she said, "I work here."

"I think ya may be exaggeratin' what ya do here," Fitz said smiling, and trying not to lose her temper. "I mean, if you won't even acknowledge yer customers, can ya really say yer workin'?"

The woman retorted smugly, "All of our artwork is very expensive.... If I thought for a moment you were an actual customer..." she trailed off. "I mean ARE you customers?" she asked snidely.

"No, yer right," Fitz said, shaking her head. "I won't be a customer, just an art lover."

The lady turned to her friend and gave him an arrogant smile. "So then, what did you need help with, exactly?"

"We just wanted to get three tickets to this Sunday's Art Auction," Fitz said, in an almost apologetic tone.

Now to anyone who didn't know Fitz, this smile would have said, I'm so sorry for bothering you. But I knew better. She was about to make this woman feel as small and insignificant as she tried to make us feel. I just stood back and let Fitz have at her.

The woman gave an irritated sigh, saying to her male friend as if we weren't even there, "This is why Art Galleries should charge for showings." She walked over to the desk and pulled out the ticket book.

"You said three, right?"

Fitz nodded, "Please."

"There is a dress code for the evening," said the woman. "You may want to re-think your shorts and T-shirts." She gave us another disapproving once over.

"Oh, I'm sure I have an evening gown, or somthin' layin' around," Fitz replied.

"Your name?" she said, without looking up.

"Sarra Fitzpatrick," said Fitz. Her family's name was well known in this town. Hell, her name was well known in this town. Young girls wanted to be her. And young boys...well we all know what young boy's wanted to do with her. And middle aged men, old men, specific kinds of women...

"Are you related to the Fitzpatrick's who own the pub?" she asked, slowly looking up at Fitz.

"Oh, yeah, the Pub....." she said holding up her fingers and counting on them, "rental properties...storefronts...oh, and some places in Ireland," she said, with a wave of her hand as if the last was of no concern.

The thin lady looked as though she would throw-up. Fitz or her family, either one, could buy any piece of work on the wall. Hell, they could buy the wall if they wanted.

"Oh and this..." she said, extending her hand to me..."this is one of yer featured artists for the evening, Miss Janie O'Connelly."

This didn't seem to help the woman's apparent stomach spin.

Her attitude and tone did a 180. "Oh it's so nice to meet you. I'm Madaline and I can help you with whatever you may need."

She handed us the tickets and said to Fitz with a wide, sticky smile, "Well, I hope you find a piece of art you can't live without, Miss Fitzpatrick."

"Unlikely," said Fitz. "As I already stated, I will not be a customer here."

"May I ask why not?" she had the audacity to pose the question.

Fitz smiled broadly at her, "Because...I refuse to pay yer salary." With that, Fitz grinned broadly and we walked out.

It had warmed up considerably. It was always hot in Southern California during the summer. But this was a scorcher. I had sweat gathering everywhere that skin touched skin. Fitz took me by Mum's house to pick up my car then we headed back to my house. We had several hours till we expected at Diane's, so Fitz took this opportunity to tempt me.

"Ya wanna go to the beach?" she asked.

"Nah, it's too hot for that." I couldn't see just laying around and baking in the sun.

"Oh," she said, nodding her head. "Well, I wasn't talkin' about just any beach." She gave me a sly grin and rocked back and forth on her heels.

I smiled back. She meant my favorite beach of all. The beach where you could sun bathe and swim and so much more...you could see guys jugging chainsaws, break dancers, have your Tarot Cards read, get a tattoo, watch steroid pumped men work out, find any kind of food you might crave, and shop to your heart's content. She was talking about Venice Beach Strand.

I squealed with joy and half a second later we were on our way. We climbed in Baby, and hit the 405 freeway heading north towards Hollywood. I was in charge of music. Being raised in such a diverse city, I had a love of music that spanned all types and all eras, from Big Band to Punk Rock. But my first pick was always my favorite. I grabbed the "Los Angeles" titled CD by "X" and hit play. I always believed that Exene and John Doe were the greatest singing duo of all time (next to Jonny and June, rest their souls.) They worked in perfect harmony and they catered to every state of mind, from sexy or mellow, to hard and fast. I sat back in my seat and enjoyed the sunshine and music.

Twenty-five minutes later we were exiting the freeway. We drove a few more miles inland then parked in the beach lot. We never tried to park on the street. Too much of a hassle to find a spot and, if we did, it would take Fitz forever to parallel park.

That's if she even tried. Half of the time, she just got out and told me do it.

We started down by Muscle Beach and headed north. I was caught off guard when I noticed that Fitz wasn't ogling the men pumping iron. Usually, this sweaty display of testosterone is good for at least one or two derogatory comments that were meant for my ears, but seemed to 'carry'. Damn, she must really like this Scotty guy, I thought.

The vendors were in full swing hawking their wares. I bought some hand rolled Vanilla incense, another purse (as if I needed one) a couple of new tank tops, a hippie skirt, a sundress and an amethyst crystal necklace. I also had my fortune read by a large woman named Madame Zorra.

She had Flaming Red tresses of hair falling out of her swami wrapped head dress, rings on every finger and one in her nose. Her hippy style dress fell to her ankles. Her covered stand smelled of Patchouli and Opium. Zorra said I had recently suffered a humiliating heartbreak, but it was in my best interest that the stars had removed this person from my life. Not a far stretch, I thought. I felt like I radiated 'break up.' Then she moved closer to her crystal ball and said that she saw me traveling overseas with a red head. I thought, No, the 'red head' I wanted took my heart and went overseas without me. I didn't offer this information though. Big news on the career front; a change was heading my way quickly and would be very prosperous. And apparently, a 'new man' was coming into my life from afar and would cast more confusion on my love life. I laughed thinking what love life. But her enlightened look into my future was entertaining none the less.

Fitz bought some rain incense, a new hat and scarf, and a Scorpio Pendant for Scotty.

"You'll never guess what Scorpio men are famous for," she giggled.

I looked at her grin and I said, "I'm gonna guess...Sex."

We were almost tuckered out from the shopping and the blazing heat when the Break-Dancers began getting their groove on. We watched them and clapped along while they bent their bodies in unnatural ways. I dropped a couple of dollars into their donation hat when they finished. After getting a soft serve ice cream we headed back home with our goods.

Leaving Venice, I was always relaxed. I reclined back in the passenger seat and fell asleep. Fitz nudged me awake when we got to my driveway. I came to and was happy as a kitten, all warm and comfy.

"Do ya wanna drive with me tonight?" Fitz asked. I thought about her taking those turns through Palos Verdes again. It made my comfy-kitty-feeling melt away, but there was no nice way to say no, so I said, "sure."

"Ok then…I'm having dinner with Scotty at 4, so I'll pick you up around 7," she said.

"Boy, that's early for dinner."

She smiled, "Hopefully, we'll have time for dessert."

"Ah, I get ya," I said, opening the car door. "I've cracked the master code…Sex right? You're gonna have sex." I began to yell for the amusement of my neighbors. "Gonna ride the White Pony, or how about, Polish the Knob," I said, laughing.

She threw her hat at me, smiled, and drove away.

I saw Mr. Mendlebaum staring at me through his bushes.

"She's gonna do the Reverse-Cow-Girl!" I said to him, rolling my head and slapping my ass as I galloped up to the front door.

He quickly pulled his head back through the bushes and disappeared.

I laughed at the top of my lungs as I walked into my house. I had to mess with the old pervert. Hell, If I had Betty's gun, I'd be able to leave my curtains open again.

I had hours to spare. I asked myself if I was hungry. No, I thought. That huge ice cream cone was still occupying too much tummy space. I sat down and tried to think of what to do. I grabbed the Goddess book and began to read.

Visualization Exercise #1: Get into a relaxed position. Picture yourself lying in a hammock.

I couldn't picture a hammock being comfortable, so I pictured myself on a chaise lounge.

Next, feel the sun warm you, energize you.

Ok, I thought, that's working for me.

Picture all the things you really want.

Ok, I can do this. Picture my paintings being sold, one at a time. No, I scolded myself, don't picture Barry. Get back to the paintings, I commanded.

Now picture your new house, I told myself. I visualized a mansion I had seen in Home and Garden. I shook my head to clear the thought. "Now try being realistic," I said, slowly. I saw a house with two bedrooms which both contained Barry, stretched out on the bed, beckoning me to come to him. Again I told myself, "Focus, damn it!" I continued on. Oh, what a beautiful kitchen. Granite counter tops. Yeah I liked those. Stainless Steel appliances...Oh, those are nice…Hardwood floors leading to the breakfast nook where Barry was reading the morning paper... "Crap, crap, crap," I yelled, and sat straight up. It was no use. My desire for Barry wouldn't quiet itself. So much for Visualization Number #1.

I decided to watch TV. for a while so I could veg-out, and not have to think of anything. I flipped through the channels. "Oh, Meg Ryan," I said, and stopped the incessant flipping. It was one of my least favorite Meg Ryan films, and that still made it better than a great movie by someone else. After all, it definitely wasn't her acting I didn't like, but the story line. I watched until she was reunited with her husband and her soul was back in her own body.

The movie had burned off two hours of wait time. I showered and put on my new skirt and a tank top. My long blonde hair went into a pony tail. I didn't bother with make-up, just in case they oiled me again. I was ready to go. All I had to do now was wait for Fitz to pick me up. I couldn't help but wonder what the women had in store for me tonight. "A full moon ritual," Mum had said. I understood all of the words separately, but what they meant together? I had no idea.

When Fitz came to pick me up, well, let's just say she had time for dessert. Eye make-up was smeared across one side of her face, and the back of her head looked like a rat's nest. I smiled at her. "I know what you were doing," I sang, in a mocking tone, "and…I know who was on the bottom."

She giggled. "I need to clean up a bit before we leave. Can I pop in your shower?"

"Yeah, have at it," I said, and sank back onto my couch.

Ten minutes later, I could hear Fitz mumbling and grumbling and cussing. "Ahh!" she yelled. She came walking out of the bathroom with my brush stuck in her hair.

"Why do you use a round brush? I mean, ya have long hair! Most people with long hair use a flat brush," she said, trying to free it from her head. She was having a tantrum, stomping her feet and pulling harder and harder. I couldn't help but picture Mum trying to work a brush through her wavy red mane when she was a girl. "Come here," I said. She sat down in front of me on the floor and I started unwinding the hair from the brush. It took a little while, but I finally freed her.

11

BREAKING BARRIERS

We jumped in Baby and headed south toward Palos Verdes. Within the next hour or so the sun would be setting, making its slow descent into the ocean. I could never tell which I thought was more beautiful, the setting sun, or the waves it would disappear behind. We wound the cliff, higher and higher. I was starting to get motion sickness. Fitz apparently took the 'Caution: Twenty Mile an Hour Turn Ahead' sign, as a challenge.

"Look," she said, as we screeched around a bend, "I took that one at forty. Who the Hell makes these signs? I guess they want you to slow to a crawl to make the turn. It's ridiculous!" she barked.

How was I even able to relax on our first trip up the cliff? I wondered.

By the time we reached Diane's I practically crawled out of Baby. My stomach was doing back flips and my shoulders were tight. The cobblestones that led to the garden were lined with lanterns that illuminated our path. As we rounded the corner to the garden I caught my breath. Every tree was a glow with tiny white lights. Everywhere you looked candles were dancing and flickering in storm vases. Her mature English garden, although beautiful to begin with, had been turned into something straight out of a fairytale. From out of the French Doors that led to the garden patio filed women with glasses in hand. Now this is my kind of "Full Moon" party, I thought to myself. The ladies saw Fitz and me approaching and yelled "Hellos," while coming to embrace us. I didn't know any of these women's real names, so I tried to remember their flower or herb names. Mum pulled Fitz and me into the mix.

"What are ya drinkin', girls?" she asked.

I could use something to steady my nerves. I was a little worried about what the evening held in store. "I'll take a Whiskey, please," I said to Mum.

"Oh no, darlin' we don't drink at Full Moon Ritual," Mum said.

I shot Fitz a look of questioning.

"We have fresh fruit smoothies. We have mango, pineapple, orange, strawberry, blueberry," Mum threw up her hands. "There's too many to name. Come see fer yerself!"

We walked into Diane's kitchen and I was flabbergasted. The kitchen was a hexagon shape with a window seat in one corner that looked out over the garden. There was an herb garden in the widow box above the sink. All the cupboards were antique white. The counters were white marble. The appliances were all stainless steel. My eyes were drawn up to the domed glass ceiling looming fifteen feet above. This was the house I should have pictured in Visualization #1, I thought. This kitchen was a gourmet's dream. Diane stood at the center island, manning the blender.

"Hello, it's nice to see you both," she said, with that gentle smile that somehow made me calm. "What can I make for you?"

"I'll have whatever you're making," I said. Fitz nodded, "Me too," she added.

She made us a concoction of oranges, pineapple and coconut, then the three of us headed back into the garden.

The other women were seated and engaging in lively conversation. We found seats and joined right in.

Violet had been saying something about her son. He was overseas in the military. She said she worried about him every day. So in addition to praying for his safety, and that of everyone else in the world, she had sent him a protection Mojo bag. All of the ladies nodded and seemed to agree that this was a good idea. Diane had given me a Mojo bag that I kept in my purse. I wondered where Violets son would keep his.

Next was the beautiful black woman I knew as Rosemary. She was talking about her two year old granddaughter and how she had learned to say, "No," with real authority. "She's making her mom crazy," said Rosemary. "I hope that girl doesn't turn out to be the handful her mother was for me," she laughed.

Aunt Marble shocked me by saying she had met a gentleman and was thinking about going on a date.

I don't know why it caught me off guard. It's not like she was 'Rest Home' bound. I laughed a little at the thought of Aunt Marble teaching all the women at the 'Home' about their vaginas and G spots.

Chamomile, the Latin woman in her sixties, said she finally had to put her grandmother in a rest home. She was having a hard time with the decision.

I added it up in my head. If she was in her sixties, her mother would be at around eighty, or close to it. That would make her grandmother in her very late nineties if not closer to the one hundred mark. Wow, I thought. If I made it to eighty I'm sure I'd have to find someone to help me change my Depends. I was starting to feel very comfortable with these women. I enjoyed their banter and the way they connected to each other.

Then it was Mum's turn. I figured she'd vent about one of Da's new inventions. He was always tinkering with something or another, or maybe the grand kids. Maybe she would regale us with the story of how she had drugged some guy and found her daughter a new boyfriend.

"I got a call from my Barry today," she began.

I perked up at the sound of his name.

"He's my youngest son," she reminded the ladies. "Anyway, he's gone home to Ireland for his best friend's weddin' and…he's finally met a woman of his own.

The air was pulled from my body. I couldn't breathe and a sharp pain ran though my chest.

"Her name is Calle," Mum went on. "He says she's quite lovely, and smart. He's smitten!" Mum announced, elated. I could hear my heart pounding in my ears. It felt as though my chest was caving in. I tried to steady myself.

Mum was still talking about the woman's attributes but, I didn't hear anything but my own tortured thoughts. He hadn't even been in Ireland for twenty-four hours, and he's found someone? I was trying to keep from passing out, or hyperventilating. How could he have found someone so quickly? Oh God, if I had told him, found him in time, would it have made a difference? Would he have cared or just let me down easy before going to Ireland and finding the love of his life. Oh God, the dream, I remembered. He was taking a bride! Sick, I was going to be sick.

All the women were happily toasting to Mum's news. I raised my glass and tried to compose myself. I noticed Fitz was eyeing me suspiciously from behind her raised glass, and ....she wasn't the only one.

The ladies had gone back to their idle chatter about the

weather, when Fitz turned and said, "Janie has some incredible news. Tell the ladies what's happening Sunday night, Janie!"

I didn't feel much like talking. Wasn't even sure I could make sound without sobbing, but thought it would seem odd if I didn't. I told them about the Gallery's Art Auction and how I would be a featured artist. All of the women cheered for me and toasted to my good fortune. Diane smiled gently and nodded to me. I couldn't help but smile back and nod to her. After all, I may never have attempted to display my painting if it weren't for her.

"Ladies," Diane asked, "are we ready to begin?"

All of the women agreed and we headed around the back of the house. I hadn't been this far into the garden and wondered what it held in store. We rounded the path and came into a clearing. There, sat a huge circular platform made of stone. It was about fifteen feet high and big enough around for all of us women to stand in a large circle. Stairs lead up to what looked like a massive gazebo. A ring of fire was ablaze in the center. I noticed that the gazebo had no roof, but was opened to reveal the night sky. "Wow," I said out loud.

Fitz smiled at my reaction. "I forgot you hadn't been back here before. It is something, isn't it?"

I nodded.

"Come on!" she said, and took me by the hand.

The other women had taken their places by the time we reached the top. Poor Violet was still huffing and puffing.

"Whew," she breathed. "What are you gonna do, Diane, when you get too old to make it up those stairs?" she joked.

"God and Goddess willing," said Diane, "that day will never come."

All of the women laughed.

I had no idea where to stand, or what to do, so I waited for Diane to instruct me. She had me stand with my back to the west, so I was facing the full moon that was now reaching its way higher into the night sky. I turned my back to the women, took down my skirt and pulled my tank top off over my head revealing red panties and a matching bra. I wasn't about to give them anything to laugh at this time. No more men's boxers for me! When I turned around I noticed that once again, I was the only one in her skivvies. There wasn't even a pile of removed bras at the women's feet. Mum was the first to respond, although they were all sniggering and trying to fight back laughter. "We all remain fully dressed for the Full-Moon-Rites, dear," she said.

I blushed and tried to redress as quickly as possible. I shot a look at Fitz and said, "You could have told me!"

"I'm sorry," she replied, stifling a giggle, herself.

"I see you bought some new undies," said Violet. All of the women finally roared with laughter. "Red is my favorite color!"

After another good hearted laugh at my expense, Diane began with a smile, "When we were all ready, ladies."

"Thank you so much for coming, ladies. First I'd like to say that we are enjoying June's Full Moon, also known as the Mead Moon."

All of the women nodded. I sat there wondering where the Mead was. I mean, that was some kind of wine, right?

Diane went on, "The Mead Moon is also known as the Lover's Moon. It's a time to focus on protection, personal strength and growth," she looked at me, and nodded again. "It's also a time of decision making. To finally ascertain and attain the things we want and need…to make known, our heart's desire."

With these words, I was panicked. I didn't know if we were going to have to say these wishes, or wants, whatever they were, out loud. If so, I didn't want to say Barry's name out loud. Not in front of Mum, Aunt Marble and Fitz. At the same time, I didn't want to leave him out. This seemed like the 'now or never' moment to me.

"Now, as the Moon ascends, ever higher into the night sky," Diane continued, "we call God and The Goddess to come. Protect us! Bless us! Hear us sing your praises!"

"Yes, Lord and Lady!" chimed Rosemary.

"Be with us and guide us!" Diane said. "Are we ready ladies?"

The group cheered.

"Oh Mother Moon," Diane began, "we love you, with your horns pointing West.

In unison the ladies chanted back to her, "Wane, be at rest!"

"Oh Mother Moon," Diane said again, "we love you, with your horns pointing East.

"Shine be increased!" the women rang back.

"Oh Mother Moon," expelled Diane, growing louder, "we love you, fertile and round!"

"Blessings be abound!" exclaimed the others.

"Join hands ladies." Diane instructed.

I joined hands with Fitz and Vervain, I think. We began to sway.

Diane's head fell back, face to the sky. Her blue eyes closed. Arms raised to the heavens, she implored the Watch Towers. The other women followed in suit. She was still speaking, but I wasn't paying attention to the words. I watched in quiet awe as a gentle wind came from nowhere. It seemed to swirl around her and dance in her hair. My eyes threatened to fall closed. To succumb to the energy around us, but I desperately wanted to see what was happening. A glow began to emit from Diane, like a gold mist. She was enwrapped. It began to reach out. In ripples, folds and waves, it wrapped its way around me. My eyes closed. I felt once again, like I was being filled from head to toe with liquid gold. I was at peace, as if the world and this body couldn't hold me, I was in flight! I could see all around me, from behind closed eyes. From above, I was really starting to like this feeling and wondered if it came bottled. Then, I realized I wasn't alone. Someone…or something…was there. I had a knowing of a 'presence' that I couldn't see, but I felt as if I stood in a flood of unbelievable and unexplainable love and acceptance. It was all around me, inside me!

The next thing I knew, I was back in my body and on the ground. "Again…really?" was the only thought that came to mind, as I came to. Diane was holding something to my mouth and telling me to drink. The faces of all the other women hovered above. They looked concerned.

"She's going to be fine," said Diane, stroking my brow.

Fitz was by my side, holding my head on her lap. I tried to speak but couldn't make a sound. I took a sip of the 'fire liquid' Diane was offering. It warmed my insides as it went down. I finally noticed my teeth were chattering. Despite the fact that it wasn't cold outside, and a fire was raging just feet in front of me, I was chilled to the bone. Jasmine came from nowhere with a blanket and wrapped it around my shoulders. What the hell happened? I wondered. Had I locked my knees and passes out? Did I have a stroke? That would explain not being able to speak. I let the ladies help me up and back down to Diane's living room. They laid me on the couch. Fitz was still at my side, giving me another drink of the hot, spiced liquid. Diane asked if she could speak to me alone. Fitz looked reluctantly at me, but then handed Diane the cup and put a kiss on my cheek before taking her exit.

Diane looked at me with questioning eyes. "Are you feeling better?" she asked.

I nodded and said in a very weak and scratchy voice, "Yes. At least, I think so."

"Are you feeling up to talking?"

I nodded to her, blankly. But the truth was it hurt to talk.

"What do you remember about the ritual?" she inquired.

I remembered everything, until I ended up on the ground. "Most of it," I answered, realizing that my voice didn't sound like my own. "I don't understand it, though."

"No, I'm sure you don't," she said quietly. "Did you feel like you were floating, out of your body…or, high above everything, looking down?"

I nodded, grateful that she seemed to know what I had experienced.

"Did you feel warm? Like you were glowing?"

I nodded again and slowly sat up.

"You, my dear, were engaged in what I refer to as a Spirit Walk."

I shook my head wondering what the hell that was. "I don't know what that means," I rasped.

"Let me see if I can explain this to you." She took a deep breath and said, "Your Spirit left its body."

At this comment my eyes bugged out. "What?" I tried to say, but squeaked the word instead.

She raised her hand to quiet the fear rising from my gut to my face.

"We are all spirits in our true form. The spirit is known to leave the body quite often when we sleep. Some people do this while they're awake, or in a meditative state. This is called Astral Projection."

My brow furrowed. I had seen this crap on a daytime talk show and didn't believe a word of it.

"I believe," she continued, "every person in the world is capable of it, but for most, leaving the body is difficult. Sometimes the thought is so uncomfortable, that fear can keep someone from even trying. There are old beliefs that you can leave your body for too long and be unable to find your way back. Or even worse, another spirit could jump into your abandoned body, and take it over, leaving you stuck in spirit."

I gave her a horrified look. What the hell was she trying to tell me? Was I possessed now? Was that why I couldn't talk? I casually pinched my leg. No, I was definitely me and that would definitely leave a bruise.

She shook her head, "I don't believe either of these things has ever occurred."

Information that would have better served me thirty seconds earlier!

"The biggest change you undergo when you leave your body is that your heart rate slows.... just as it does in any meditative state. Death while in this practice," my eyebrows went to my hairline, "well, I've never heard of it."

I let out a sigh of relief, although still not as calmed as I had hoped.

"And I have had the pleasure to be 'front and center' for hundreds of people during Astral Travels. The cold, I believe, comes from your energy going with you on your journey. Not to mention that your heart isn't beating as quickly, so the blood flow slows."

I nodded like this made some sense, trying to remember seventh grade Anatomy class.

"It's like when people exercise to stay warm. How you can go for a run on a bitter cold day and halfway through you're peeling off your sweatshirt because you're burning up from energy being created and expended."

Even though I no longer ran, not since high school, I did know what she was talking about.

"May I ask," she sat down next to me on the couch, "did you ...feel... someone or something else with you?"

My eyes went wide and I nodded slowly, hoping she

wouldn't ask me to try and put the experience into words. I really had none at the moment.

She nodded and smiled, as though I passed some test I wasn't expected to pass.

"There are two rules of thought on this," she began, "some people refer to this 'Presence' as your Spirit Guide."

I furrowed my brow again and shook my head trying to indicate that I had no idea what she was talking about.

"Okay," she rephrased, "it's like a Guardian Angel."

This I understood. Being raised as a Catholic, we were told we had Guardian Angeles around us at all times, watching us. That thought had kept me from the sin of masturbation through my teen years. But I had to admit, until now I had never felt one or the presence of one.

"The truth is," she continued, "many people, from all faiths and religious backgrounds, believe that they have a personal Guardian, and sometimes refer to them as Spirit Guides or Angels. Basically, it's a spirit sent from the other side, if you will, that is here to protect and guide us through the hardest times of our lives. Some people have even been known to speak to them, hear them…even see them."

I couldn't hide the fear in my eyes. I had no desire to hear my Guardian Angel and even less to see him, or her, or it. Diane had noticed and responded in turn.

"Were you scared when you were in 'Its' presence?"

I thought for a moment and shook my head. I wasn't scared. I had no fear at all actually.

"Do you remember what you did feel?"

I smiled broadly and nodded. Goose pimples raised on my flesh.

"Would you tell me?"

I nodded again then realized that she was waiting for me to speak. "I felt," I began, my voice raspy and dry, trying to come back to me, "I felt..." I paused again trying to decide on the words I would use, "Unbelievable love."

Diane was beaming, "Anything else?" she asked.

"I felt safe...at peace. Like my life was a beautiful gift... not the chore I've made it out to be." I started to tear up. Not tears of pain, not tears of anger or fear, but of joy, true unadulterated, overwhelming joy. I hated to cry in front of anyone but I felt like I was bubbling over.

Diane handed me a tissue and I dabbed my eyes and blew my nose.

"What's the other school of thought on this?" I asked, still rasping. "You said there were two?"

She smiled even broader. "Ahhh, the other school of thought," she said glowing, "was that you were in the presence of God, itself."

I went awe struck again. The thought that God and I stood together? That was just too much to believe. I mean, from what I had learned of God in Catholic school and church, was that he was too busy to make house calls, hence the Guardian Angel. I said as much to Diane.

"Don't you believe God is with you at all times?" she questioned.

I nodded, "That's what I've always been told."

"So would it be so odd if he made Himself 'known' to you?"

I thought about that. It was definitely something I would have to ponder. And on a related topic, I was back to never masturbating again.

"Can I ask you a question, Diane?"

"You may ask me anything."

"If you believe in the Goddess, why do you keep calling it God? Isn't there a difference between them?'

She smiled that calm warm smile again and asked me, "When you were in spirit, and you felt the Presence...?"

"Yeah?"

"Did you know whether it was a male or a female? Was there any distinction at all?"

I thought for a moment and realized that I honestly couldn't. I specifically remembered not being able to tell who or what was with me. I shook my head. "I guess not."

"What I have come to believe, after studying several religions, beliefs and superstitions, is that by 'Whatever' name you call God... it is still God, who answers."

My eyes narrowed and I mulled this over.

She went on, "If you had been raised a Buddhist, your love of the higher power would be no less, than if you had been raised to call it God. You see dear, what we refer to as God has been called several different names throughout history. Elohim, Christ, Buddha, Ceridwen, the Great Spirit, the Holy Spirit, 'The Goddess' and many others have all been used as names for the greater power. I don't believe that our creator, our protector, cares by what name it is called... so long as we do call."

Yeah, I thought, you tell my mom that. I didn't understand totally but I remembered... Once, as a child, I had asked one of the Priests at my church what it meant by, "I was made in God's Image." He gave me a lame explanation that made no sense. I told him, "If God was a man, I couldn't have been made in his Image...I'm a girl!" The memory made me laugh. I was pretty sure the Priests used to draw straws to see which one of them would have to talk to me. I had been a precocious child. I wondered exactly when it was that I stopped asking questions and started letting other people do my thinking for me?

Diane smiled, "These are just my thoughts, my opinions, and my beliefs that I'm sharing with you. I urge you to think about what you believe. What makes sense to you, brings you peace, and touches you deeply. Because your relationship with the higher power, regardless of what name you use, should do just that."

She leaned over and put a kiss between my eyebrows, the way a loving mother would, not that I was an authority on what loving mothers did. She took my face in her hands and looked deep into my eyes, "You'll be fine Janie."

Hearing her say it, I actually believed I would be. I smiled and hugged her. She really did have a calming and loving way about her that I was really starting to enjoy.

"Diane, I didn't have a chance to tell...God or the Goddess or whatever, my heart's desire."

She smiled and tilted her head slightly. With questioning eyes she said, "Do you think that God does not know what your heart desires, child?"

She patted my hand and I smiled, knowing that I didn't have to say anything aloud.

I rejoined the ladies long enough to say my goodbyes and assure them that I was alright before Fitz drove me home. We didn't talk much on the drive. I did, however, convince Fitz that my stomach was still a little queasy and asked her to take it easy on the turns. She obliged as best she could. I couldn't help but ponder what Diane had said. Did I leave my body? Or was hearing that Barry had found someone, taken its toll on me not only mentally but physically as well? Or, and this was just a thought, was I drugged again? I mean, I did drink the cool-aid, or the smoothie as it was. I decided that the latter was probably not the case. But I still wasn't ready to take the great leap that God was standing beside me during a Full Moon ritual. In all truth, I did know what I had felt, even if I couldn't quite explain what I had felt. I knew that the love, acceptance and pure joy I felt, was overwhelmingly beautiful and calming. I also knew, I wanted that feeling again. But now, back from wherever I was, the thought scared me a little.

Although I didn't know why, had I been so programmed to fear everything I couldn't explain, that I would think this amazing feeling had to be wrong? I was tired of thinking in circles. After pondering and coming to no conclusion, I told Fitz how sorry I was that she had to cut her evening short to drive me home.

"Like I'd leave ya alone," she replied, and reached out for my hand to give it a squeeze. We rode in silence a while longer. Finally Fitz asked, "Would you like to get a night cap? Maybe one where the fruit is diluted by alcohol?"

"God yes!" I said, like I had just been waiting for her to ask. We dropped Baby off at my house and I checked my messages.

The first was my mother. "Janie," she called. "Pick up the phone if you're there. It's your mother! Hellloooo! I had a question to ask you, but I'll ask you later. You know, you sort of screwed up our plans for dinner this Sunday. I had a nice gentleman I wanted you to meet. I guess we can reschedule. You may remember him. He makes the donuts at Holy Dough-Donuts.

Great, she's trying to fix me up with the donut guy. We used to get donuts every Sunday morning when I lived at home. I always had a hard time eating a donut shaped like a crucifix.

"Fitz," I said, "If he's the same guy who was making the donuts when I was young, he'd have to be in his fifties by now." I hit skip.

She gave me a look of compassion and rubbed my back. "I'm so sorry your mom is crazy, Janie," she said. "But at least this guy isn't related to ya."

"Yeah, that's a plus," I agreed.

The second message began. "Miss O'Connelly, this is Annie from... Oh hell, you know who it is! How could you not?"

My eyebrows arched.

The voice on the machine continued. "I have a whiney, nasal

voice that even grates on my nerves. Truth is, lately I've had a hard time trying to find anything I like about myself."

I furrowed my brow and looked at Fitz. Apparently, Annie had turned her business call, into a call-in talk show.

"It's not like I don't try," she went on. "but I just don't like anything about me...I hate my hair...thin and completely limp. My eyes are too far apart...and far too big for my face. My lips are too thin…almost non-existent…like a lizard."

I stuck my tongue in my cheek and tried to get a mental image of her.

"I tried that plumping lipstick...but I was allergic to it, so then my lips blew up so big, they cracked. It looked like I had Herpes for a month...I'm too thin. But, I just can't gain weight..."

I wondered if she thought she would get sympathy from me in that department.

"I know all women say that they wish they had this problem..."

I nodded at the phone.

"…but there's a difference between being thin and looking like you were just let out of a Concentration Camp. Oh crap, I hope you're not Jewish. I didn't mean to offend you. Great now I cursed, too. Grounds or termination in this job."

Suddenly the machine went quiet. Fitz and I looked at each other wondering if she hung up, then…

"My period's late again, but at least I know I'm not pregnant. You have to have sex to be pregnant. The last time I had sex, Northern Exposure was still on the air..."

My brow furrowed as I tried to add up how many years Annie had been 'without'.

"I got a cat just so there would be something else living in my house, since I killed all my plants, but it ran away. Probably thought it was going to meet the same end. Or maybe I bored him." A long heavy sigh was emitted from the machine.

"Anyway...I have your luggage and you can come pick it up tomorrow. Bye," she hung up.

"Wow," said Fitz, wide eyed, "she's just one introduction to your mother from committin' suicide."

I nodded my head slowly. "Yeah, that would do it."

The next message was from Betty. "Puddin…It's Betty…I have a surprise for ya!"

"God I hope it's not another fix-up," I said to Fitz.

"Don't worry, Puddin. It's not a fix-up."

I looked at Fitz alarmed. "Did she hear me or something?" I asked.

"You'll get it on Friday. I'll see ya later. Bye for now, Sugar," Betty hung up.

From what I was learning of Betty, this 'surprise' could be anything. I pictured opening a box and seeing a small but effective handgun engraved with the name Puddin.

12

STICKS AND STONES

Fitz and I walked to the pub. Pauly was on shift and I hadn't seen him in months. He and Andy were working around the clock covering for Barry while he was in Ireland. When he saw me he came around the bar and scooped me up in a huge bear hug, spinning me.

"There's our little Janie!" he said. "I've missed ya Petal!"

"I missed you too," I sang, as we spun around and around.

He put me down and Fitz cleared her throat, hands on her hips, "How about one for your little sister?"

Paul picked her up and swung her around like a red headed rag doll.

We took a few minutes to catch up then sat down at the bar. I couldn't get Annie's call out of my head. After Fitz and I had drinks in hand, I said, "How about that Annie lady?"

Fitz took a drink and nodded, "I know."

"I feel so bad for her, Fitz. I mean, I've been dumped... a lot! And far too recently that I shouldn't feel devastated inside," we both grinned. "Let's face it, I've had some rotten luck but at least I could always find one thing I liked about myself. Even at the worst of times. And, there's always the fact that I've had sex in the last fifteen plus years."

"Ya know how they say…ya never forget…sex is like ridin' a bike?" Fitz asked.

"Yeah," I said, trying to follow what seemed like a derailment of thought.

"Well, at this point… ridin' a bike would be the closest thing she's had to sex." She zoned out for a moment. "Is that ironic?" she asked.

I nodded, "Yeah, and kinda sad, too. Do you think she'll be there tomorrow?"

"Unless she takes her own life tonight, I'm guessing, yes."

"Fitz, I have never been miserable enough to vent my personal life to a total stranger."

"I know. It's heartbreakin'."

I thought about my personal life. It was a roller coaster, especially now. Lately, it seemed like every time something good happened, something bad was close at it heels. I went over the last few days in my head. I had been dumped. Possibly in the most humiliating way anyone has ever been dumped. And at the time, it seemed like the end of the world, but a few days later I was pining over another guy who left and went to Ireland. There was always the thought that maybe I was obsessing over Barry, to get over John. Like maybe he was a distraction, but I knew this wasn't the case. I had these feelings for Barry almost all of my life. And now I needed to let them go. The thought of that hurt worse than any of the break-ups I'd ever had. But if I cared about him, I needed to be happy for him. After all, that's what you wish for someone you care about, right? I thought about the Auction. I couldn't believe that in a few days, my art, my paintings, were going to be displayed at a renowned Gallery. Maybe I was thinking of all this wrong. Maybe, every time something bad happened, something good was waiting. If I looked at it that way I felt a lot better. I tried to add up in my head. Was it time for something good, or bad, to happen next? I wondered.

Fitz broke me from my thoughts, "Yer thinkin' too much!"

I took a sip off of my Black & Tan and nodded at her.

"Are ya thinkin' about what happened tonight? With the Ritual?" she asked, seriously.

I took a deep breath and started to tell her about the things that I could explain. Like… how I felt during the ritual. Leaving my body. I was a little afraid that she would laugh at me or think I was weird, but I knew better than that.

She nodded, trying to follow.

Then I told her about Diane's interpretation of what happened, her theories on God and the Goddess.

Fitz was adding all of this up in her head. "So does this mean you get to make a wish or something?" she asked.

I couldn't help but laugh. "I don't know if a Spirit Guide is like a Genie."

"Well, this whole ritual was about personal growth, inner strength and your heart's desire. Shouldn't you make your desires known to the higher power?"

This was a good question. I myself had asked Diane this very question. "I think they (my Spirit Guide, Angel, God, whoever) already know my heart's desire? I don't have to say it out loud according to Diane."

She shrugged. "I don't know how it works. I just pray," she said. "I guess I feel that my Guardian Angel is always with me, so it knows what my wants and needs are. And, at night, I pray to God and say Thank You for all the things I've been blessed with. Everything…from my family…to you…to a great cup of coffee."

I laughed again. She did love her coffee. "I didn't know you prayed so often," I said, surprised.

"Of course I do, Janie. I have a lot to be thankful for. Even if I didn't, I'd still be grateful for the life I had been givin'. It's a gift, ya know?"

Her wording was perfect. That was exactly the same word I had used to describe it to Diane. How I felt when I was out of body. But I had known Fitz almost my whole life, and never knew she had such a deep spiritual side. I nodded at her and said, "You're right Fitz. We both have a lot to be thankful for."

With that she said, "Don't sound so surprised. Every once in a while I shock the livin' hell outta myself, as well. Now come on, the band's getting ready to start. Let's get some more drinks and move closer to the stage."

We sat at a table closest to the stage and listened as the Spikes played their first set. It was hard, loud and fast. Fitz got up and started to dance. She held out her hand to me to come join her. I shook my head no. I didn't dance in public, usually. Oh, there was the drunken occasion, just like everyone who didn't really dance. But, I wasn't drunk. She grabbed my hands and pulled me up. Now, too many people were watching not to at least pretend to move. I just sort of...bopped along. She was shaking her head at me. "Dance!" she yelled. We were becoming a spectacle. She started to do the well known dance scene from the cult classic Pulp Fiction. Now we had done this dance in my living room every time we watched the movie. And thanks to Fitz's crush on John Travolta, we had seen it hundreds of times. This dance I knew I could do. All I had to do now was get up the guts to do it in front of other people. She yelled at me again, doing the 'Batman' eyes dance, "Come on!"

I looked around and thought, screw it! I don't care what these people think. I began to do the 'Batman' with her. Then we did the twist, the shake and the shimmy. I was dancing. In public! And, I didn't care. I really started to let myself go. The guys in the band played the song twice through for Fitz, who yelled, "One more time!" I was having the most fun. I lost myself in the music. I danced most of the night, apparently wearing Fitz out. She was sitting in the corner laughing and shaking her head at me. I took the seat next to her.

"I'm having a great time," I yelled over the music. My breathing was hard, but I was still dancing in my seat.

She yelled back to me, "I don't know what's gotten into ya, but I'm lovin' it! You should get dumped more often," she teased.

"I'm not sure that's even possible," I said, taking one on the chin with true humor.

At the band's next break, they came and sat with us. Pauly brought us all a round of Bushmills shots which we raised up in a toast and shot down in unison.

After the band finished their smokes in the Poker Room, we headed back out for the last set of the night. I was ready to dance some more. I was backing on to the dance floor, calling Fitz to come join me, when my butt ran into someone.

I turned to see an angry woman wearing the drink I had just spilled on her. I cringed. She was my height but a little bigger around. She was wearing a floral print peasant top, and spandex pants. Her brown hair was in such a tight ponytail, it pulled her eyes and brows back in a mock facelift. And the face it was lifting, was wearing too much green eye shadow and hot pink lipstick.

"I'm so sorry!" I yelled over the music. "Can I buy you another drink?"

"Why? So you can spill that one all over me, too?" she yelled back.

"I really am sorry, I'm a horrible klutz."

"No shit!" she yelled.

Taken aback by her hostility, I wondered if I should offer to pay for the dry-cleaning of her polyester shirt. "I don't know what else I can say or do, I really am sorry," I said again.

"I oughta kick your skinny ass," she said, setting down her empty glass on the table.

"Look," I said, starting to get a little panicked, "I really didn't mean to."

"Your dumb ass has been all over this floor all night. You had to know you were gonna knock into someone, flailing around like that!"

"Hey," I said, trying not to be as offended as I was. "I know I'm not a great dancer. I'm just trying to have some fun." I held my hands up, in what was supposed to be a submissive maneuver.

Fitz finally stood up and said, "Hey, I'll get ya another round. This is my parent's pub. Whatever ya want, it's on the house."

"Oh, and I guess that makes you feel special? Like a big shot or something?" she said to Fitz, putting her hands on her ample hips.

"Ya know what, lady," Fitz began, hands now resting on her less than ample hips, "I'm tryin' to be polite, here. It was a simple accident. It's not like she can go back in time and change it, so how about ya find a way to get over it."

"Why don't you just keep your big mouth shut?" she flared back.

"Why don't ya just leave then?" Fitz asked. "If a fight is what yer looking for, find another bar. We don't do that here."

"That's the pussy in you talking," she said to Fitz. "Lucky for you, you aren't the one I have a problem with, shorty. My fight is with Skinny Bitch, here," she looked me up and down.

I finally get called skinny, I thought, and it has to be immediately followed by bitch.

One of the girl's friends, who looked like a miniature version of her, came and stood by her side, 'mad dogging' Fitz.

The short one said, "You take the tall, skinny one, I got the red headed bitch!"

"You're kidding me?" I broke in. "You really want to fight over this? It was an accident!" I yelled, finally allowing myself to lose my humor.

Pauly walked over and said to the two women, "I think it's time for ya to leave." He had a few words with them as they were heading back towards the bar. Now, I knew it was common practice in a bar to never call the police unless something small turns into something the bartender can't handle. Pauly had escorted several people 'OUT' over his lifetime in the bar and usually without incident. This was not going to be one of those times. Big scary girl and her twin were yelling at him and refusing to leave. Fitz and I had every intention of letting Pauly handle it without any further involvement.

We stayed down by the stage and watched. Then, it happened. The big one, tried to deck Paul. He stepped back out of reach, but then both girls lunged to attack him. Within seconds, I was heading for the Big Girl and Fitz was aimed at her friend. I pulled Big Girl off Pauly and stood back as fast as I could when she turned her attention to me. She waved me forward, daring me to take a shot. There I stood, still as a statue wondering what the hell I was supposed to do now. She advanced in my direction and I'm sure my eyes showed genuine fear: Fear of the ass beating I knew was coming...fear of the pain...fear of her sitting on me.

"I'll give you the first punch," she said, tapping her jaw with her fingers.

I didn't want to hit her, didn't want to fight at all. I looked at Fitz, and did a palms-up. "What do I do?" I asked.

"Clock the bitch!" yelled Fitz.

I closed my eyes and I threw a right cross that connected with her jaw. It was on then. The small one turned and charged at Fitz. Fitz threw a kick and caught mini bitch under the chin, knocking her out cold. Her battle was over. Mine was just beginning.

Andy grabbed the out-cold-mini-bitch and sat her up in a chair.

The bigger woman threw a punch that hit me in the chest. "Hey!" I yelled. "That was my boob!"

The B.B. (Big Bitch) got into a boxing stance and put up her dukes.

Oh shit, I thought to myself. Of course MINE, would turn out to be a boxer.

"Come on pussy!" she yelled at me, throwing air uppercuts. I had watched Fitz box all of my life, but I had never tried it. I got into a stance similar to the one I had seen Fitz do. I put up my dukes and braced myself. She threw a punch, and I blocked it with my forearm. I felt pain run from my elbow to my fingertips. I knew right then, I couldn't let her land another one of those, anywhere on my body. She threw another and I blocked that one, too.

"Crap!" I yelled, pain radiating again. Okay, I was doing fine with blocking, but if I didn't throw a punch, and soon, I was gonna run out of luck. I threw a left, and it was easily blocked. She batted it away the way someone would bat at a fly. I noticed that I was now mimicking her footwork. I didn't even know I could do footwork. Both of us were dancing and circling each other. The band had stopped playing and the whole bar had gathered around us. Fitz was yelling directions to me like she was my trainer.

"Throw a combo," Fitz yelled.

So the other woman, the B.B., did.

I did a little duck and dance to avoid any of them landing in my face.

She was using Fitz's directions, to give me an ass kicking. She caught me in the side with the left, but I blocked another face shot. Pain flared again, this time, through my whole rib cage. "Son of a…" is all I could muster though my clenched jaw. I threw one back as hard as I could and hit her square in the cheekbone.

"Damn it," I yelled. My punch didn't seem to affect her, but my hand hurt like hell.

She threw again and missed. Maybe I was skinny, I thought. I was starting to notice a rhythm to her throws and blocks. I waited for the right moment, and threw again. I hit her square in the jaw. I couldn't contain my excitement with actually having landed a punch where I wanted it to go. "Yes!" I yelled.

She growled, "You're dead bitch," and threw another punch. I ducked it and hit her square in the nose with my right. Blood squirted out. The woman stopped. Not hurt so much, but stunned by the warm liquid oozing down her face. She wiped the blood from her nose and looked at it. "Now you die! I'm not playing with you anymore!" she yelled. My last clear thought before she let out a grunt and ran at me, was, 'Oh crap, you were playing with me'? We locked arms as she ran me backwards and into a table.

Pauly moved forward to break it up, but Fitz stopped him. "Janie's got this. Back off!"

I hit the table hard. We rolled off with me on top of her. She threw a punch from below that caught me under my chin. I could taste blood. The next thing that happened was a blur that was relayed to me over and over again at every Fitzpatrick family gathering, for the rest of my life.

I sat up on top of her spitting the pooling blood from my mouth onto the floor. Then I began pounding her. Left first…

then right…then left…then right again, until I was pulled off of her by Fitz, Pauly and Bacon, from the band. The girl was helped up and asked to leave once she gathered her wits about her again. Her friend had 'come to' by then and both women left with homemade ice packs and their tails between their legs.

Fitz was beaming like a proud parent. Pauly poured me a double and I took a seat. Adrenaline still pumped through my whole body. My hands were shaking and my knuckles hurt like hell. The first taste of whiskey burned the cut inside my swelling mouth. The more I calmed down, the more my jaw began to ache. Pauly brought me some ice in a zip lock baggy. I put it to my jaw and winced.

"Yeah," said Fitz, "hurts like hell to get hit!"

"You didn't get hit," I reminded her.

"That's why I threw a kick. Better chance of endin' the fight without havin' to take a punch," she said, like it was a well known fact.

"Nice 'ground and pound', by the way," said Bacon.

"Nice what?" I asked.

"Ground and Pound," he repeated, as if this would sum it all up for me.

Fitz broke in, "It's a fighting maneuver used in the MMA."

I shook my head, still not understanding. "What's MMA?" I asked.

"Mixed Martial Arts?" Bacon said, like he couldn't believe that I didn't know what it was. "It's only the greatest of all 'one on one' fighting in the world. Well, at least the best that's televised."

Fitz laughed, "Its cage fighting, Janie! And the Ground and Pound," she went on, "is where you mount your opponent and beat them senseless. I wouldn't expect you to know, dating all those Nancy boys, instead of real men."

I gave her a shitty grin and said, "God that sounds so

violent."

"It's what ya just did," Pauly interjected. "And yes, it was violent."

I sat there staring at my drink.

"Ah, crap," Fitz said. "Yer gonna spend the next three days feelin horrible for what you've done, aren't ya?"

I raised my eyebrows and nodded my head.

"You and your overactive conscience!" she yelled. "Look," Fitz began, "These girls weren't leavin' without a fight. There are people out there like that, Janie. They're bullies! They seek out people they think are weaker than them and pick on 'em. Ya saw that crazy bitch. She hit Pauly," she nodded, in her brother's direction. "Now the odds were in her favor that he would be too much of a real man to hit a woman. So, her taking a punch at him was a desperate attempt to look tough and take her aggression out on someone, without any real fear of retaliation. Hopefully, what she learned here tonight will save her ass in the future."

"Oh, come on. Save her ass?" I asked. "I refuse to make it sound as if I've done her some great favor."

"Janie, she needs to learn two things…#1 Bullies, all bullies, eventually get their ass beat, and #2, best not to judge a book by its cover. She saw ya...shorter...skinner than herself...overly apologetic…she thought ya posed her no threat. That's exactly why she tried to escalate a ridiculous situation to somethin major. But just so ya know, if we hadn't pulled ya off, there's no tellin' how far ya would have gone," she said. "Ya kinda unloaded on her. And she kinda deserved the hell out of it."

I shook my head. I felt horrible, and as so often was the case, my face showed it.

"Well, I'm proud of ya, Janie," said Pauly. "That bitch had a mean right. I'm glad I didn't catch it," he said, looking at my jaw.

I couldn't believe that I could do any real damage. I was, for lack of a better term, a pussy. But I had kinda blacked out there. It scared me to think I was capable of losing it. Truth was, had she not tried to hit Pauly, I would never have raised a finger towards her. I went into 'brother protecting' mode.

Bacon said, "We need to give you a fighting name. Ya know, like a nickname."

I shook my head no, but suggestions were flying fast and furious. I couldn't help but laugh at some of the names they came up with. But they finally decided on Bacon's. For the rest of my life, I was to be known in jest, as 'Janie, The Ground and Pound O'Connelly'!

We closed down the bar with the boys from the band and helped Pauly clean up before walking home.

I was tired and sore, but I knew I would have trouble falling asleep so I gave Fitz my bed. She was out as soon as her head hit the pillow.

I sat on the couch for a while going over tonight's events, staring at my swollen hands. I felt really bad for what had happened. But, in the end, I knew Fitz was right. I never thought I was really the type to get in a fight, except for that one time in the tenth grade. Oh, and that little thing with Barry's ex. I wouldn't refer to either of them as a real fight though…not like this at least. What I learned tonight was, anyone was capable of anything, given the right, or wrong, situation. I didn't want to feel proud for what I had done, but I couldn't help but admit it, if I got mad enough, I wasn't too bad of a boxer.

My mother will be so embarrassed when she finds out, I thought. The really sad part was, somehow it would be all Fitz's fault. I shook my head at the thought. I curled up and fell fast asleep. It had been a really long couple days and I could only hope tomorrow would be better.

13

THURSDAY: DAY 6 OF DUMPED, AND NOT GIVING A S#!T

I woke to Fitz screaming. A stream of woven obscenities was flowing from the kitchen. I jumped up and ran in the direction of the cursing. My espresso machine was raining scalding hot water. Fitz was holding a large bath towel as a shield, trying to get close enough to shut the machine down.

"What the hell? How much water did you put in it?" I yelled, diving under the towel with her.

"You know where the fill line is?" she yelled.

"Yeah!" I shot back.

"A little over that!"

"A little?"

"Okay, a lot!"

I stared at her and shook my head.

"I wanted extra foam!" she exclaimed.

The machine sounded like it was ready for lift off. The steam stems were whistling a threatening tune.

"Is this thing gonna blow?" she asked.

I shook my head, "I don't think so."

"Should we unplug it?"

"The plug's behind the machine."

"Should I try to close the 'steam thing-ies'?"

"God no!" I yelled. "The only thing that's keeping it from taking off like a rocket is that the steam valves are open. Try hitting the brew button. It should relieve some of the pressure."

The two of us moved forward with the towel as our shelter. She reached out her hand and the steam attacked. She shrieked and pulled her hand back, "Damn it! That's hot!"

"I have an idea, wait here!" I yelled. "Where the hell am I gonna go?" she yelled over her shoulder to me, while kissing her boo-boo.

I ran in to my bathroom and grabbed a hand towel. I wrapped it around my wrist and ran back under the towel with Fitz. I held out my wrapped hand and moved the switch to 'doubles' then hit both brew buttons. Coffee spewed from the machine onto the floor. I grabbed a coffee cup and shoved it under the streaming spout, then pushed the foam stems back towards the ground. It began losing steam quickly. I let out a breath I had been holding and pulled the towel off my head. "You can come out now Fitz," I said to her.

I pulled the towel off her head and threw it on the floor. I used my foot to push it around like a mop to clean up the puddle of coffee.

Fitz moved to the corner of the room and stood there staring at me. "I'm sorry," she said.

I shook my head. "I have one question. Why did you move the steam stems to face up?"

She said, slowly, "I didn't want to get water on the floor."

I shook my head and started to laugh. "Get me another towel."

We cleaned the kitchen and decided that the Espresso

Machine had been through too much, and was probably still too hot to make coffee. So, we'd have to go to the coffee house.

I took a shower, although it seemed redundant in a way. Throwing on a pair of 501's and a tank top, I was ready to go.

"Ready," I yelled, walking back into the living room. I couldn't find Fitz. I called her name as I walked around the house. But there was no Fitz. I put my hands on my hips and wondered where the hell she went. Maybe she felt guilty about turning my Espresso maker into Old Faithful and went to go get me a coffee. I opened the front door to see if Baby was gone, and there was Fitz. She was in my 'Peep' bathrobe, making out with Scotty on my front lawn. They were really into it, too. I turned to walk back inside so they could have their privacy (if you could call my front lawn private), when I saw Mr. Mendlebaum watching them through his bushes. It looked as though he had been watering his lawn and moved to the bushes so as not to spook the horny duo. I yelled as loud as I could, "Good morning Mr Mendlebaum!"

He jumped and ran back inside his house. Scotty also jumped, like a kid who got caught with his hand in the cookie jar.

"Good mornin' Janie," he said, blushing and stammering.

"Good morning Scotty," I said back with a grin. I walked back inside and closed the door.

A few minutes later Fitz, in full glow, stepped back inside. "He called me on his way to work and just stopped by for a kiss," she beamed.

"A kiss?" I said "I thought Mr. Mendlebaum was about to get free porn."

"We get kinda carried away sometimes," she said, with her embarrassed little smile.

I smiled back. "When you're with the right person, you should get carried away."

We headed down to Spilled the Beans.

"Who's workin' today?" Fitz asked.

I shrugged. "I'm not sure, probably Dante."

Fitz winced. "Will you go in and get my coffee? He's a nice kid Janie, but his concoctions are horrid, and I really need MY coffee today."

I looked at her and shook my head, "Quad Mocha, coming up."

She parked halfway down the block so Dante wouldn't see her or Baby.

I walked inside and Dante was manning the Espresso Machine. I ordered my usual Triple-Non-Fat-Latte, and Fitz's Quad-Mocha.

"Is Fitz with you?" Dante asked, with wide eyes looking around me out the front window.

"Yeah, but she had to run an errand at the drug store so she won't be in. We're kinda in a hurry.

"I made this new drink for her. It's got ginger and cinnamon...."

"She's allergic to ginger," I cut him off. "She just wants her usual today."

"I'll make it for her next time," he said. "Without the ginger," he added.

"I nodded at him, "I'm sure she'll love that."

I grabbed our coffee and headed back to Baby.

I saw Baby, but no Fitz. Where the hell did she go now? Out of pure instinct, I looked around for Scotty's work truck. Were they somewhere around here, making out? The only thing open was a bookstore. Fitz wasn't much of a reader, but I guess to avoid poor little infatuated Dante, she may have ducked in there. I used my butt to push the door open. I walked in and saw a poster board that read: "New Swimsuit Calendar Now Available!"

Fitz was in the back of the store looking at the calendar. She saw me and started jumping up and down. "Look, look," she yelled. "It's out."

Fitz had done a swimsuit spread for the calendar last winter. I handed over her coffee and grabbed the calendar from her. There she was, Miss January for the upcoming year. She was sitting on an iceberg, clad in a shimmering diamond bikini and a white fur coat. She looked amazing.

"You look fantastic!"

"Thank ya," she said doing a curtsey. "But look at Miss June," she instructed.

I flipped to June and caught my breath. "It's Marne," I exclaimed. "Was she on the shoot with you?"

"No, I didn't even know we were doing the same spread. We definitely weren't shot in the same locales. Look, hers was shot on a white sand beach, and mine was done in a warehouse. "Lucky Girl!"

Marne was wearing a ruby encrusted thong bikini, toned from head to toe. Damn, that looked uncomfortable, I thought. Drop dead gorgeous, but uncomfortable.

Marne was a friend of ours from high school. She had been modeling in Paris for the past eight years. Living in London most of the time, she rarely made it back to the states. Born in England, she moved here with her dad when we were in the ninth grade. He was an architect specializing in restoring old buildings. During our twelfth grade year, her father's project was complete so they moved back home. We had done a pretty good job of keeping in touch though. Speaking every couple of months or so, it was always like we had seen each other yesterday.

"She looks so different now," I said. "I mean, since high school."

I had seen her in Vogue and gracing the cover of Cosmo several times, but it always blew me away.

She had always been very pretty. Six foot tall in her bare feet, she had the longest legs I had ever seen. Thanks to being our school's track star and on the dive team, she didn't have an ounce of fat on her. She was actually considered gangly as a teen. She was probably the only model ever that needed to be fattened up. Her agent made her eat nothing but cheeseburgers a week before one shoot. But she had blossomed into a striking woman with caramel brown eyes and skin, long black hair, full lips, and a perfect white smile to match her perfect body. She and Fitz had done a few shoots together in Europe, but I hadn't seen her since she came for my twenty-first birthday. In fact, she was my birthday present from Fitz that year. I let out a sigh, "I miss her."

"Me too," said Fitz.

"I need to buy one of those," I said, grabbing a calendar off the stack.

"I need to buy..." Fitz was counting them up..."eight!"

We took them up to the front to pay for them. The kid behind the counter was about eighteen, I would guess. He was about five-eight, skinny with unremarkable brown hair, wearing big square glasses and a Return of the Jedi T-shirt. When he saw Fitz his jaw dropped.

"You're Miss January!" he exclaimed almost breathless.

Fitz nodded to him. "That's me," she said with a wink.

"Oh my God," gushed the young man. "Will you sign my calendar?" he pulled a well worn copy from his book bag.

"Sure," said Fitz, beaming.

He looked like he was going to have a stroke. She signed her picture, "Lots of love, Sarra Fitzpatrick" then she drew X's and O's.

The overworked boy asked excitedly, "Can I get a picture with you?"

Fitz giggled, "Sure."

The boy ran to get his camera, then thrust it at me on his way back by. "Can you take the picture for me? Just push that button on the top," he said, not waiting for an answer from me.I was more than used to the way men acted around Fitz, and Marne, for that matter. They just seemed to emit a raw sexual beauty and energy that for years I hoped would rub off. As of today, still no 'rub off' had been attained.

I took three pictures of him. Including one where Fitz was putting a kiss on his cheek. He was starting to hyperventilate, and I was a little worried that the boy would pass out cold. Or maybe, if he was smart, fake it so he could try his luck at a mouth to mouth encounter. We left him, face pressed against the glass, staring after Fitz.

We got back in Baby and Fitz asked, "Where to?"

I shook my head. "I guess I'll have to pick up my luggage from the airport eventually. Before they accidently send it somewhere else! But, I can get it tomorrow. I'm not ready yet to see Annie."

"Well then, ya said you wanted to join a gym?"

I patted my thigh and it gave a little wiggle. "It couldn't hurt."

"Ya up to it?" she asked.

I let out a deep breath, "Why not?" I answered. "These thighs can't wait much longer for medical science to find a pill for cellulite." I thought to myself, if I were a scientist I would make that my life's work. If I succeeded, a statue would be erected in my honor and every woman in the world would sing my praises.

We drove back to my house so I could change. When I came out of the bedroom Fitz started laughing at me.

"What?" I asked, truly confused by what the hell was so funny.

"You're gonna wear that?"

"What's wrong with what I'm wearing?" I asked, holding my arms out to my sides. "I'm going to the gym not a fashion show."

I had on a pair of grey sweat pants and a matching sweatshirt. They had been standard issue in our high school gym class, and I noticed, barely worn. "What do you wear to the gym?" I asked.

Fitz smiled and shook her head, unable to get her laughter under control. We drove inland on Manhattan Beach Blvd, then hung a left on Hawthorne Blvd. There were possibly a hundred gyms in Manhattan Beach, but we just kept driving. I wondered just where the hell her gym was.

We pulled around the back side of a huge building that looked like a warehouse from the outside, and swung Baby into a parking space. When we walked in, Fitz and her gym bag headed for the locker room door that read: BAD ASS BITCHES. I took a quick look around and realized that I wouldn't be on a treadmill or exercise bike. Not at this gym. There were eight boxing rings in the center of the room, twenty body bags (or heavy bags, as I was told to call them) hanging from the rafters, chained about a foot off the ground. They were supposedly full body sized. A much bigger body than mine, I noted. Twenty speed bags lined two walls. Medicine balls, free weights, jump ropes, and mats took up the other two. This was not the kind of gym I had in mind. Fitz stepped out from the dressing room and it was my turn to guffaw at her attire. She was wearing a pair of spandex black 'boy' shorts and what looked like a red sports bra as a top.

"That's what you wear?' I gaped.

She nodded at me, "Yeah. Why?"

"You were wearing more in your bikini spread," I pointed out.

"I get hot when I work out," she retorted. "At least I'm not dressed like the Michelin Man."

I looked down. Shit, I thought. I do look like the Michelin Man.

Four of the rings were occupied by men beating each other's brains out. This was not the sport for me, I assessed, as I watched a man crumble to the ground from a vicious blow to the head. When the guys saw Fitz, the conscious ones stopped to say their 'Hellos', then they went back to pummeling each other.

She introduced me to Nate and Kurt at the furthest ring. They had concluded their work-out for the day. Both men were covered in sweat and trying to catch their breath as they toweled off

These were both big boys. I guessed they were in the heavyweight division.

Nate had sandy blonde hair and a great smile. Kurt had dark hair and looked like he had been hit in the nose one too many times.

I followed behind Fitz towards an empty ring. To my horror, Fitz started to climb into the ring.

"I'm not gonna spar with you Fitz," I said with absolute certainty.

"Why not?" she pouted. "You're a pretty good boxer. They'll give us headgear.

I shook my head. "In the last six days, I've smashed my face into a partition in the cab, I hit myself in the head with a door at the airport," I began to count on my fingers, "you kicked me in the jaw. I fell and hit my head during the ritual. Then, I got hit in the jaw again during the fight last night. Call me a wimp, but I'm tired of getting the crap knocked out of me," I finished.

"Ok, ya big baby!" she said sullen. "We'll work on the heavy bags."

She handed me a pair of gloves and helped me tie them up.

After she positioned my stance and guard, she walked behind the heavy bag and said, "Ok, I'm gonna hold the bag, you give it your best shot."

I felt kinda ridiculous. Not to mention the fact that I couldn't understand how me throwing a couple of punches at a heavy bag was a real work out. I threw a half hearted punch.

Fitz said, "Whenever you're ready!"

I threw another punch, a little harder this time and the bag didn't move an inch.

"Go ahead," Fitz yelled at me. "Throw one!"

"I have thrown one. Two, to be exact," I said.

"The bag hasn't moved an inch," Fitz said.

I made a face, "Believe me, I know!" I said frustrated. I threw another punch, trying to hit the bag as hard as I could.

"What the Hell?" yelled Fitz. "Put your ass into it!"

"What?" I asked her, beginning to huff and puff. Was she inferring that I had a big ass?

"I said put your ass into it!" she yelled again.

I threw a combo…as hard as I could. Right…left…right, but still nothing. The damn bag responded the way it would if a fly had landed on it.

"Stop already," Fitz said. "Let me show ya."

She came around to my side of the bag.

"Follow my stance," she said.

She got into her stance, and I followed. Now hold your hands like this. I made my fists just like hers.

"Good," she said. "Now, when you throw yer punch, I want you to step into it and throw from your shoulder, like this." She threw a punch and the bag swayed away from the hit. "You want to picture your hand going all the way through the bag, that way you won't pull your punch. You'll follow through and have more power behind it. Ok?" she asked.

I nodded, "Okay." I was now more determined than ever.

She walked over to the other side of the bag and held it for me. I got back in my stance, made my fists into little balls and threw another punch with everything I had. The bag didn't move. I was getting really frustrated and wearing myself out. I threw combo after combo. Still, the damned thing wouldn't move. I was exhausted and panting. My hair was plastered to my head by the sweat that began pouring from me.

Finally I walked around the bag, and saw Nate holding it. He and Fitz started to laugh when they saw me.

"You asshole," I wheezed to Fitz "Have you been holding the bag the whole time?" I asked Nate.

He smiled and said, "Yeah, but don't be mad at Fitz. It's a hazing thing we do to all the newcomers."

I gave him a crooked smile before I fell to the floor in a corpse pose of exhaustion.

"You forgive me?" he asked, grinning down at me.

I thought a moment. "Yeah," I said, nodding my head. "You're off the hook…but only because I'm too tired. Not to mention totally incapable…of beating your ass." I said between pants, "Also because you may need to carry me to the car."

"But you," I pointed my gloved hand at Fitz, "I owe you one…as soon as I'm again."

"Bring it on!" she said, and started her footwork with her dukes up. "Fly like a butterfly...sting like a bee."

Nate looked at me and said, "I'd be happy to help you with your stance and footwork, Janie."

"Oh, Fitz is showing me," I said. "Plus, I'm not sure how good of a student I'd be."

"No, No, Janie. You should let Nate help ya. He's a professional," Fitz said with a sly grin.

I caught her little grin, and thought, please don't throw me at another guy. Even if he is gorgeous, built and funny, I'm done.

"Ok, you're on, but don't say I didn't warn you," I smiled.

Fitz attacked the heavy bag, while Nate showed me how to throw a punch and properly hold my guard. We worked a little on my footwork and breathing. Apparently, you want to breathe out while throwing a punch. Not hold your breath, like I'd been doing. After two hours of direction, I had learned that I could throw a punch if I didn't move my feet, and I could do foot work if I wasn't punching. Apparently boxing took rhythm I didn't have. I was pooped and more than ready to call it a day.

Fitz and I headed back to my house so I could shower and change. I was already starting to stiffen up. Anyone one who thinks shadow boxing is not an exercise...is an idiot. I openly admit to being that idiot until just now. I was sore in places that I never even knew were there. The muscles under my armpits (I believe they were called wing muscles) hurt like hell. Until now, it never occurred to me how often I used those muscles in daily activity. Washing my hair was a bitch. Getting out of the shower I winced, reaching for my towel. In the end, I opted for my Peep bathrobe instead of trying to get dressed, then I joined Fitz on the couch. She seemed no worse for the two hour work out. I wasn't even sure she broke a sweat.

"Jesus, are you ok?" she asked.

Trying not to hate her, I replied, "I'm really sore. I feel like I was run over by a truck." I rubbed my aching neck.

"Ya know ya may even be sore from last night."

"I guess I was a little sore this morning." I rubbed my jaw. "But nothing like this!"

"Is there anything ya need to do today?"

"Aside from getting my luggage back from Hawaiian Isle Airline? No," I replied wondering why I had been putting it off.

"Maybe you should just take it easy tonight. Ya kinda look like shit."

"Thanks a lot," I said, shooting her a pained look. "I can always count on you to tell it just like it is."

"Come on, I'll build you a bed on the couch and order ya some Chinese takeout."

I was grateful to have Fitz suggest a night at home. I didn't even try to resist letting her baby me, which was almost never accepted without some grumbling. I curled up on the couch and she brought me Wang's take-out menu.

"What do ya want?" she asked all smiles.

She ordered me Honey Chicken, Crab Puffs, Fried Rice, Egg Rolls, and Hot & Sour Soup. By the time the food arrived, I was asleep.

I was having the strangest dream of me and Nell Carter singing together on a Las Vegas stage. Moments later, I was more awake and realized that Fitz had left the TV. on, and a rerun of 'Gimme a Break' was playing. That explained the bizarre dream. I found a note on the table from Fitz.

It read: Janie, I have a date, so I had to run. Chinese food is in the fridge. I took naked pictures of you while you slept, to hand out at the gym. Nate said he would love to see under your Michelin Man suit. See you tomorrow, Love Fitz. I shook my head, but it actually hurt my neck. I decided to find some Ibuprofen. I had the family sized bottle in the bathroom for family sized hangovers. Or, I thought with a giggle, the hangovers you get from drinking too much while trying to be around your family. My family gatherings had been responsible for several bottles of Ibuprofen.

I took three tablets from the bottle and drug my ass to the kitchen to get a diet coke. While I was at it, I grabbed the bag of Chinese food and headed back to the couch. The nice thing about Chinese food was, it's just as good cold as it is hot, so I dug in. I flipped through the channels. The movie 'Inner Space' was just starting. Another Meg Ryan film? Maybe the broadcasting network did know I was getting dumped, after all.

After I was done eating I curled back up. It felt so good to not have to be anywhere or do anything. If it weren't for this crick in my neck, I would be almost completely content. My thoughts went back to Barry. I so wanted to be happy for him, but I just couldn't believe that he had already found someone and was head over heels. John crept into my mind, and an odd realization hit me, I hadn't really thought about him at all. I hadn't wondered if he was having a good time, or pined over him, or anything. My loss had been being dumped, not being dumped by him. "Huh," I said out loud. I was more worried about my luggage than John. I knew right then and there, I was completely over him. I shook my head in disbelief. Just days ago, I had been prepared to marry that guy? It hadn't even been a week, but, I thought, what a crazy few days it had been. All the weirdness? And weirder yet, the people! Some of these people, I didn't want in my life. And some, I couldn't get rid of if I tried.

I thought to myself. My mother…I had to love my mother. I was pretty sure it was a law or something. I didn't have to like her, but I had to love her. Then there's Mum. She had actually been a second mother to me all of my life. She was the mom I probably would have chosen for myself if we were given that choice. Crazy Aunt Marble? Well? She was just that. She was MY crazy Aunt Marble, too. These women were my family. If not by a blood bond so to speak, then by a life bond. Now Betty, I thought. Betty wasn't all that close to me. She really had no reason to meddle in my life. Then again, I had no right to bust in on her and the handsome Aussie, either. No, I was worried about her when I did that. Truth was, I had been prepared to attack a burglar, or fight off a psychotic mad man to make sure she was okay. Would I have done that for someone I had no bond with? I did care for Betty, I concluded. She meant something to me. All of these women, crazy, deranged, demented and strange…I loved every one of them. And, in their own way, the only way they knew how, they loved me, too.

Diane's words came flooding back to me. "You don't get to choose how people show love or are taught to love." These women weren't trying to hurt me. If I really thought about it, I knew that. Deep down, they just wanted me to be happy. How could I blame them for not knowing what makes me happy, when I had been screwing it up myself, for years? These women had tried to help me the best way they knew how. Yeah, they had stepped over some boundaries. But don't we all, when it comes to people we love?

With that, I fell asleep.

14

FRIDAY: A "WEAK" OF DUMPED

I woke up to someone banging on my door. I could see light trying to creep in from behind my pulled shade. Morning I thought, not exactly thrilled with the realization. When I tried to stand, the pain came flooding back. "Holy crap," I yelled! I felt like I had been beaten. Then I passed by a mirror and realized that apparently I had been, with a really ugly stick. I felt like shit and my face showed my pain.

The knocking had continued.

"Hang on!" I yelled, trying to make it to the door and wondering what would appear if I just yelled, 'come in'. Rapists, murders, burglars, and my mother wouldn't knock. I was getting closer to the door and the knocking started again.

"Hang on," I yelled again, to whoever was on the other side.

I pulled open the door feeling every muscle working hard to achieve this pathetic goal. There stood two young 'carbon copy' boys in white button up shirts with blue ties and black slacks. They were holding pamphlets. Crap, I thought again. Had it been a burglar at least he would have let me stay on the couch, while he riffled through my new unmentionables and my valueless home.

"Good morning, ma'am," one of them said, in a cheery tone. "Have you heard the word of God?" he asked.

I stood there staring at him. I never wanted to put down anyone's religion (especially now since I wasn't sure how I felt about my own beliefs). But one thing I knew for sure… If trained priests and nuns couldn't answer my questions, no fifteen year old missionary could either.

"Yes, I've heard the word. Thank you for dropping by," I said politely, and started to close the door.

"Ma'am," the second boy began, "we'd like to offer you this pamphlet," he said stopping the door with his foot.

I looked down at his foot and narrowed my eyes. This was a little too bold, I thought. I opened the door and took the little booklet from him. "Thank you again," I said, and tried to shut the door, but the first of the carbon copies began to speak again.

"Have you heard the truth about Armageddon, ma'am?" he asked, in a very serious tone.

I opened the door wide and said with an exhausted sigh, "Yep, the end of the world, the coming of the beast, all of it. I've heard it. Pretty scary stuff," I said slowly.

"Did you know," started the second one, "you can safeguard yourself from being one of the ones left behind?" he asked, raising his eyebrows.

"Look, no offense guys, I don't mean to sound rude, but I already have a religion," I said, trying to sound as inflexible as possible. "Now if you don't mind..."

"But your beliefs may not safeguard you from the inevitable!" said the other boy.

I felt like I was being religiously tag-teamed. I kept looking from one to the other, as they served the unwanted conversation back and forth.

"But our religion guarantees you a place in Heaven," said the first boy.

I started to get a little annoyed. "I'm not really shopping for a new religion."

"This isn't a new religion. It's the only religion!" stated the boy with absolute certainty.

They weren't giving up. And I was in too much pain to stand here and listen to them ramble on like they were brain washed. They were still talking, although to be honest, I had stopped listening. They were exhausting my ability to be polite.

"Where do you boys live?" I interrupted the first boy mid-sentence.

"Excuse me, ma'am?" said the boys in unison.

"Where do you live?" I asked again. "You see, I don't have time right now to go over this pamphlet with you. But maybe later, me, a couple of priests, a few of the nuns from my old school and some of the women I've just made the acquaintance of, I think they may be a coven of some kind, well, one may be a witch possibly, and I think another is a Mobo, if that's the right word, I'm really not positive, oh, and my mother, I'll definitely bring my mother, because no one can tell you, YOU ARE WRONG, like my mother," I rambled, "we could come to your house, barge in on you, and try to ram our religions down your throats. How does that sound?"

Both boys stared at me with dropped jaws.

"Seven-ish?" I asked, as if this should be a completely normal request.

The boys turned to look at each other, before quickly walking away.

I hated to do that, but I had been polite enough to take their damn pamphlet. I couldn't help but wonder if they worked on a commission of sorts. You convert so many souls...you get a new stereo or something. The 'hard sell' wasn't working for me. I went to my make shift desk and grabbed a piece of paper and a black Sharpie Pen. I wrote in big bold letters: 'NO SOLICITATION OF RELIGION!!!' then taped it to my front door.

I no sooner sat down when my phone began to ring. I stared at it, all the way across the room. There was no way in hell I was getting back up to answer it. I heard the message click on.

"Puddin? It's Betty. I wanted to see if you were home, but I guess not. Anyway, I'll be dropping by later. Make sure you check out your back patio when you get home tonight. Ta, for now." She hung up.

No doubt she was having more work done on the house for when she sold it. I love this house I thought, looking around. "Oh well," I said out loud. Maybe I'll love my place in Lomita, too.

I decided to go take a hot bath and see if I could relax my aching muscles. I got the water as hot as I could stand it and sunk in. I almost never took baths anymore. But, I had to admit I loved them. I was drifting into pure calm when I heard the front door open. Had I locked the door after scaring off the missionaries? I wondered. Were they here for revenge? Like little children of the corn. Finally, I heard Fitz yell my name.

"I'm in here," I yelled back.

She came in and sat on the toilet seat. "Ya feeling any better?" she asked.

"No, I don't."

"I'm glad to hear that," she said.

I gave her a confused look, "Why would you say that?"

"Because ya look like shit. I'd hate to think ya felt better but still looked like that."

"Thanks."

"What's up with the sign on the door?" she asked me.

I explained my run in with the young boys. "I swear that crap could make an atheist out of me."

Fitz laughed dismissively.

"No really," I said seriously. "Who sends people to your door to solicit religion? It's not right," I shook my head. I was quiet for a moment and then asked, "So what's on your agenda for today?"

"Ya still need to go get yer luggage, don't ya?" she asked rummaging through my drawer.

"Yeah, I should." I replied, resigned to the thought that I'd have to do it eventually. "What are you looking for?" I asked her.

"Oh, I broke a nail on Scotty's back, and I need to straighten it out. Probably wouldn't hurt to file the rest of them down so I don't claw him to death."

I nodded my head. "So things with Scotty are going well I take it?"

She beamed. "I think I'm in love with him, Janie."

I had never heard Fitz use those words pertaining to a man. A pair of heels or a cake from Lorenzo's, or Baby, yes. But this… this was a first.

I stared at her. "You're serious aren't you?" I asked, shocked.

She grinned and nodded.

"Well son of a bitch," I exclaimed, "so much for atheism!"

I made us some coffee then went to get dressed. I didn't want anything that was a pain in the ass to get on and off. I picked out a sundress and huffed and puffed, wincing as I tried to get it over my head. I wondered if my Peep bathrobe was a bad fashion statement. Hugh Heffner wore one all the time and no one talked smack to him for it. Hell, I think he lives in his pajamas. Lucky S.O.B.

Fitz was holding Baby's door open. A faint whimper emerged from me as I sat down. Putting on the seat belt was a whole new fresh hell. We headed up Aviation Blvd towards LAX.

I hated driving through the airport. It reminded me of the game Frogger. Only we were the car and there were hundreds of little brave (or stupid) frogs. I couldn't make up my mind, but kept waiting to hear SPLAT!

Our second time around the airport, we finally got in the right lane to go to the right parking lot. There was a sign posted on the ticket meter that outlined the parking prices: $5 for half of an hour, or $8 for a whole hour or $25 for the day. It was a form of robbery to me. They lost my luggage for a week. During which time it was sent to a whole other continent. Now, when they finally got it back to the right country, state, town, and airport, I had to pay for the privilege of picking it up. They should have had a Sorry-we-screwed-you lane, and gave people like me cupcakes and beer.

We found a parking space on the third floor and headed to The Hawaiian Isle Terminal. We walked in, and my eyes were quickly drawn to the large woman standing by the metal detector. Yolanda saw me and smiled.

"Hey Janie," she said, hugging me.

"Hi," I said, and I introduced her to Fitz.

"Are you just now coming to get your luggage?" she asked.

"Yeah, apparently it just got in the night before last."

Yolanda shook her head, "That's ridiculous! We run four flights a day to and from Hawaii. What the hell is their problem?"

"Well it seems my luggage went on a vacation of its own."

She furrowed her brow, "Where?" she asked with a sideways glance.

"Let's see, it went to Hawaii, Paris, London and finally Louisiana."

Yolanda shook her head again, "Only this place," she said.

She pointed us in the right direction to find Annie.

We walked through the terminals, passed the bathrooms and

down a long hallway that looked like it led to an exit. At the very end was a small room with a door that read Lost Luggage. There behind a small green Formica counter stood Annie.

She was exactly what I had pictured. She was Fitz's height, about 5'9" or so, but that's where the similarities ended. She was so thin that her neck looked too small to hold up her head, and her clavicles protruded. Her mousey brown 'page boy' haircut lay completely flat. Her blue eyes looked like they were set on the side of her face rather than the front, somewhat lizard like. This was exactly the way she had described herself. Also, the name tag on her tropical vest read Annie. But for all of her self-loathing the other night, she seemed to be beaming.

I walked up to the counter with a confused look. "Hello. Are you the Annie who's been calling me about my lost luggage? I'm Janie O'Connelly."

"Oh yes," she said, moving to retrieve my bag from under the counter. "Here it is. I'm so sorry about all the mix-ups with your luggage. It seems this little guy went on one heck of a vacation," she said, patting my baggage like it was a dog.

I said "thank you," and was prepared to leave, but I had a deep-seated need to know that she was okay before I could leave. When I turned to confront her with my concerns I saw a heavy set security guard, graying and balding, give her butt a squeeze. She jumped and blushed before playfully reprimanding him. I heard her say, "Save it for tonight big boy." Then they both made growling noises at each other.

Fitz came to stand by my side and said, "Looks like this is a whole new millennium for Annie."

I stood there nodding my head not sure if I should feel good for Annie, or worried about the visions I knew were already brewing in my head.

Fitz grabbed my bag for me and we backed out of Lost Baggage. I went to say goodbye to Yolanda.

Yolanda said, "You know that dog of an ex-boyfriend of yours is flying back in today. I'm thinking he may be a drug mule. We might have to do a cavity search on him or something."

I laughed, "How do you know when his flight is coming in?"

"Nothin' around here is a secret, honey!" she said, with a head roll. "I know everything about everyone. After that bullshit he pulled on you, I pulled up his flight info."

I couldn't help but laugh, "Then maybe you can tell me what happened with Annie? She called my house the other night to tell me about my luggage and kinda went off the deep end a little." I went on, "But I see her today, and she's better than fine."

"That's because of Carl, the Security Guard." She leaned in to give me the low-down, "Turns out honey, he's had a thing for her for years but never said anything."

I rolled this around in my mind. It sounded horribly familiar.

"She had a thing for him, too," Yolonda went on, "but because he never said anything... she never said anything. You know how it is?"

Yes, I did KNOW how it was, I nodded.

"So last night I set them up together," she said. "I got so tired of seeing them pining away. Neither of them had the guts to make the first move, so I made it for them. I invited both of them to a bar for a small after work party, and then I just let drinks and a little privacy do the rest. Hell, they left together. Now I don't know what happened," she winked, "but they seem damn happy this morning," she clapped her hands.

"Well that's great," I grinned. "I'm very happy for them."

I hugged Yolanda goodbye, then Fitz and I headed off.

When we got back to Baby, I asked Fitz, "Isn't that amazing?

I mean, the two of them liked each other all along and didn't even know it."

She stared at me for a moment like she was trying to size something up in her head.

"What?" I asked.

"Nothing," she said innocently. "What are ya doin' tonight?"

"Nothing! I still hurt so bad, I don't plan on doing anything unless you can find a Nubian God to smear me down with Icy Hot."

"Sexy!" Fitz said, joking.

"Why? What did you have in mind?"

"You should come with me and Scotty to the pub."

I started shaking my head, but she just kept right on talking.

"There's a great band tonight. 'The Blow Hards'. They're a British band.

I was still shaking my head. "Don't take this the wrong way Fitz... I love you, and I love you with Scotty, but I don't want to be a third wheel."

"Oh, you won't be. Scotty's brother is here. He flew in from South America today to meet up with his dad tomorrow."

I shook my head some more, "I don't think so Fitz," is what I said, but she knew she could usually guilt me into almost anything. She just had to find the right button for the right occasion.

She begged all the way home.

Finally, I said, "He doesn't think this is a fix-up, right? I'm just a friend of yours...going to have drinks with your new boyfriend and his brother, right?"

"I swear it Janie!" she gave me the 'Scouts Honor' sign. Since neither of us was ever a Scout, or even a Brownie, we 'Pinky Swore' instead.

"I have to meet Scotty and Cecil at nine. Can you be ready by nine?"

"Fitz, it's not even five o'clock," I said in a hurt tone. "If I can't be ready in over four hours, I shouldn't be going out at all."

"You're right," she nodded. "I'm sorry I implied that you're a hag."

"Was that so hard?" I asked her, smiling. "You're a complete bitch, by the way."

"Definitely," she said, as she turned Baby's grill towards home.

I was on music duty again. Fitz had asked me if we could play anything but 'X'.

"Fine," I said sullen.

I dug through her CDs and found Social Distortion. Fitz let out a yell of approval when she heard 'Ball and Chain' start up.

As we pulled in the drive, I saw a giant red bow on the gate to the new patio.

"What's all this about?" Fitz asked.

I shook my head, "Betty said she had a surprise for me. I have no idea what it could be."

We walked to the back gate and opened her up. Both of us stood there, gaping. Betty had done more than just put in a new patio set. In one corner was a free standing fire pit and in the other was a free standing marble fountain with a lion's head perched on top. She had brought in two huge marble flower urns that were placed opposite to the fountain and fire pit. Both were filled with, well, I didn't know what kind of flowers they were. But they were beautiful. I found a card on the table that said: To Janie. I opened it. It said how grateful she was to have a renter and a friend like me, and of course, how sorry she was about the 'Henry' thing.

I read on: I thought you deserved a little slice of heaven for yourself. Enjoy Puddin, Love Betty.

"Damn," Fitz said. "She must really feel bad about that 'Henry' thing."

I stood there nodding and looking around. "It's like an Italian Garden," I said. "It's exactly what I would have picked for myself, Fitz."

"I'm coming to the conclusion that Betty knows you better than you think she does," Fits said, looking around.

"This is for me?" I asked stunned, like the thought was just occurring to me. "Maybe she's not planning on kicking me out?"

"Would you listen to yerself?" Fitz said, raising her brows. "Yes, she did this for you! Have you ever considered the fact that Betty thinks of you as more than a renter?"

"Not before this," I said. I thought about that as Fitz went on.

"You said yerself that you never saw any other women around…and she was so concerned about your break-up with John and how it affected ya. Then, the other day, you bust into her home because you think she may be in danger. Janie….I think you may be missing the fact that you are Betty's only real friend!"

I was still mulling this over.

"She's been making excuses to come see you. She calls almost every night. She tried to find you Mr. Perfect, for God sake. People don't do things like this," she used her hands to acknowledge the patio, "unless they care about you," she finished.

I gave her a look of contemplation.

"Have you ever considered the fact that she was scared that you were goin' to leave her?"

"What?" I blurted out, bewildered.

"She comes to yer house. You don't have anything on the walls. Except of one picture of John, which by the way, should come down...soon," she threw that in. "Not even yer own artwork is displayed. Then, she tells you to think of this place as yer home. Tells you to paint or make whatever changes you want. What landlord does that?" she asked, as if I weren't thinking at all.

I nodded, "You're right."

"What? Is that so hard to believe?" Fitz asked.

"No, I believe you. I'm just always shocked when you're right," I said with a smile. "I need to go call Betty."

Fitz nodded, "Yes. I think you do."

I walked inside to make the call. Fitz stayed behind to try out my new patio furniture. I heard her yell to me. "If Betty's in the market for another friend to spoil, I'm available."

I made the call but no one answered. When her message beeped, I left a gushing and heartfelt thank you.

Fitz left me to go get ready for her date. Ironically, I had to go get ready for Fitz's date, too.

I did the shower thing. When I stepped out I could hear my phone ringing. Thinking it was Betty, I ran to answer it.

It was Fitz. "Can you please dress like a girl tonight?"

"What the hell does that mean?" I asked, offended.

"Just anything but jeans," she said. "For the love of Pete, yer gonna be buried in those things, aren't ya?"

"Why does it matter? And yes, by the way. You said this wasn't a date. Why shouldn't I be comfortable?"

"No, it's not a date. But, I'm dressin' up a bit. Oh, and don't wear heels, they make you gargantuan."

"Fitz, I'll wear whatever I want!" I said irritated.

"Fine," she barked, and hung up.

I stood there shaking my head. I mumbled all the way back to my closet. "Tell me what to wear...could you please dress like a girl?" I mimicked. I had half a mind to wear my painting overalls.

In the end, I wore a pair of 501's with a camisole top, a pair of high heeled boots and a black blazer to 'dress it up' a bit. I pulled my long hair into a loose ponytail and applied some make-up. I took a look in my bedroom mirror. Not Bad, I concluded.

I grabbed my purse and headed down to the pub. I walked the eight blocks and was reminded why I almost never wore these boots. My feet were aching. Penance for trying to girl-up.

15

SIBLING RIVALRY

Into the Pub, I strode, and made my way to the bar. It was a Friday night so the bar was packed to the gills. Andy saw me and yelled, "Hey, it's Ground and Pound O' Connelly. Get ya a beer, luv?"

I nodded, "Thank you," I said over the crowd. Great, the nickname had taken, I thought.Fitz came running up behind me. "Oh thank God," she said. "Ya did dress like a gargantuan man."

"What?" I yelled at her.

"No, ya don't understand," she pulled me off to the side of the bar. "Scotty was really upset when I told him you were comin'."

I gave her a hurt look. "Doesn't Scotty like me?"

"Yes, yes," she said reassuring me. "He likes you just fine. Turns out…he doesn't like his brother."

"What do you mean?"

"His brother's a cad! A skirt chaser!" she said wide-eyed. "He's obnoxious and rude. For God sakes, he's been hitting on everything that moves since we got here. He and Scotty haven't even spoken in over a year. His father arranged this little reunion against Scotty's better judgment. Cecil is actually paid to stay in South America and act like a Playboy so he doesn't embarrass the family. I guess from what Scotty said, Cecil was a 'blemish on the family name' in Ireland.

I took a deep breath and let it out. "So, what do you want me to do Fitz? You want me to go home?"

"Not exactly," she paused. "I want you to keep him in line."

"What?" I asked. "How am I supposed to do that exactly?"

"Just keep him talkin' about himself. It's his favorite subject, so it won't be too hard."

I started shaking my head, "Fitz, I've had nothing but bad experiences with men since....sixth grade, as you pointed out, and now you want me to willingly throw myself to a man that you yourself, refer to as a lecher?"

"I need ya here, Janie," she said with pleading eyes. "Maybe if yer here and keep Cecil busy, he and Scotty won't fight. I'm beggin' ya, Janie. Please! I'll owe you a big one."

I had never seen Fitz look so distraught, and I'm counting the whole 'picked her up from her gay boyfriend's house so his lover wouldn't kill them both', thing.

I nodded, "Fine. I'll do it. But, you are aware of the fact that I'm marching towards Cecil like a virgin who willingly hurls herself into a volcano, right?"

"I know. And I love you for it. I really do," she said taking my hand and guiding me to the table where Cecil and Scotty sat.

Scotty smiled and stood when we approached, leaning forward to give me a hug. Cecil stood and shook my hand. He was, I thought, handsome like Scotty but not in the same way. He

had the same dark blue eyes but had sandy brown hair and a great tan. His white button-up shirt seemed to snug up in all the right ways and places to show off his sculpted body. He also had the same smile as Scotty. But his had a devilish quality. The devil does come in beautiful packages, I reminded myself. He had an air about him. I couldn't immediately tell if it was confidence or cockiness. I would soon find out.

We sat and engaged in conversation. Fitz was right. He did love to talk about himself. Within twenty minutes, I heard all about his beach-front Condo, his Yacht, that was named 'Deep Blue' for his eyes not the water, his Mercedes (that had cost a fortune to have shipped overseas) and the possibility that he may have fathered several children in South America. Letch didn't begin to describe him.

So after hearing all of this, I posed the question. "So Cecil, what do you do for a living?"

I saw Fitz go wide-eyed.

"What do ya mean?" he asked, with his Irish accent. "I'm part owner of the brewery."

"Oh," I said. "So do you do distribution in South America for the company?"

"Well, no. I just kinda leave that up to dad and my big brother here," he said, giving Scotty's arm a nudge.

"Oh, so you don't do anything?" I saw Fitz eyeing me to shut up, but this guy was a real asshole.

Cecil gave me a cocky grin. "Not so much. What do you do for a living?" he asked.

"I work in a coffee house," I said blankly.

"A coffee house, how ambitious!" he said, smugly.

I smiled, "Well, it's not much, but at least I EARN my living. No matter how petty it is," I returned his smug smile.

"She doesn't just work in a coffee house," said Scotty, through a tightened jaw. "Janie here," he turned to smile at me, "is a brilliant artist. In fact, she's a featured artist at an auction this Sunday night," he added, raising his glass.

I raised my glass back to him and said, "Thank you, Scotty."

"An artist?" Cecil raised his eyebrows. "Any real money in that?" he asked.

"If something sells," I told him.

He leaned over and put his hand on my knee, "Maybe I can help ya with that," he said winking. "I need some artwork for the Condo."

I gave him a sly grin and looked down at his hand. Was he trying to seduce me? Or trying to purchase me? I took his hand in mine, leaned forward and said, "What's your taste?" I gave his hand a gentle squeeze before returning it back to his own knee.

He winked and leaned back in his chair, locking his fingers behind his head. "I don't really know. I mean, I like what I like," he grinned.

"Spoken like a true art virgin," I said, leaning back in my own chair and crossing my legs.

We were sizing each other up. Fitz and Scotty looked like they were watching a tennis match during our conversation. When it ended, Fitz excused herself to the ladies room and asked me to accompany her.

"What are ya doing?" she hissed, as we entered the ladies room.

"What do you mean?"

"What do I mean?" she repeated, her eyes wild. "I mean, are ya flirting? Are ya fighting? What the Hell's going on out there? He's comin' on to you!" she blurted out, as if I hadn't noticed. "And it seems like yer comin' on to him, as well."

"I'm just figuring him out," I said, reapplying my lipstick. "I'm playing his angle."

"You don't like this guy, do you?" she asked, horrified.

I smiled at her and answered her honestly, "Not even a little bit."

"Alright, but it looked like he was gonna throw ya on the table and have his way with ya," she said.

"Not a chance," I replied.

We walked back to the table and the conversation stopped abruptly. Scotty was fuming mad. He put a kiss on Fitz's cheek and then asked if anyone would like another round. Cecil nodded his head, "That would be wonderful, big brother," he said. "Why don't you get one for Janie as well? Just have them put it on my tab." Scotty stared at him for a moment before walking to the bar. Fitz gave Cecil a glare and followed Scotty.

"What was all that about?" I asked.

Cecil smiled, "We were just talkin' business."

"I didn't think you had anything to do with the business," I said, eyeing him.

"Ya wouldn't understand," he winked again.

"You're right," I said slowly, holding his gaze. "Sometimes I forget that I'm just a woman and have no head for such things."

"Ya make it sound as if I think all women are beneath me," he cocked his head.

"You make it sound as if, one way or another...we all are." I wasn't going to back down or be intimidated by him. Truthfully, he was a great target for some much needed mental sparring. The thought of damaging him made me feel all warm and powerful. He, after all, was everything I hated about men. And knowing that he took great pride in this fact…was going to make this even more fun.

We held each other's gazes. He grinned at me, "Would ya like to dance?"

"Why don't we wait for a slow one?" I suggested.

"The slower the better," he agreed.

He was trying to seduce me. So what was so wrong with making him think it was working?

Fitz and Scotty returned with the drinks. He looked much

calmer now. The band started a slow albeit, but definitely not romantic song. If you actually listened to the words, it was about finding a dead body in a dumpster.

Cecil stood and held his hand out to me, "Ya owe me a dance," he said with a crooked grin.

Fitz piped in, "Janie doesn't like to dance."

"It's okay Fitz, I do owe him one," I said, never taking my eyes off his.

We walked out to the dance floor and he took me in a close embrace. I could feel every part of him against me. He tightened his grip on my hand and waist then spun us around. He was doing some kind of Latin moves. And, oddly enough, I was doing a great job of following them. His body was writhing and gyrating. His hand moved further down my body to rest on my ass. My eyes bugged out, but I quickly recovered my stature as a sexy seductress. Fitz saw the 'ass grab' and she narrowed her eyes. I took his hands in mine and slid them up to rest on my hips. I looked him deep in the eyes and growled, "Behave." He leaned in to kiss me. I let his lips barely brush mine before turning my head away from him.

He smiled, "Yer either a temptress...or a tease, either way, I'm having a great time," he said, spinning me around again.

"I haven't invited you to kiss me," I said, twirling in his arms.

"Am I readin' the signals incorrectly?" he asked, pulling me close against his body again, his eyes burning into mine.

I put my lips close to his ear and said in a warm whisper, "I thought we were just dancing?" He did a little body shudder.

When the song ended, I released him, smiled and walked away leaving him standing alone on the dance floor. He shook his head and followed.

As we sat down, he said to Fitz, "Our little Janie here is quite the dancer."

"Yes, OUR little Janie is," Fitz retorted, with a glare.

Cecil and I spent the rest of the night seducing each other. Laughing, making eyes and finding reasons to touch each other. I had never seduced a man before. Truth is, until now, I never even knew I was capable of it. I knew I could have him if I wanted. But, I had to remember that in his mind, he would always think that he had 'HAD' me. I couldn't allow that. As the night drew to a close Cecil offered to drive me home. I informed him that I never drink and drive. For that matter, I never rode with anyone who had been drinking, either. He offered to pay for a cab.

Fitz was not okay with this idea, but I assured her that I was fine and would call her in the morning.

Cecil and I got into the cab and drove the eight blocks to my house. When the cab stopped, he got out and walked around the car to open my door. The cab driver informed him that the ride was ten dollars. I stared into Cecil's eyes and said to the cab driver, "This isn't the only stop sir. My friend will need a ride to his hotel."

Cecil smiled at me and said, "Really? Yer just sending me on my way, huh?"

I nodded. "You weren't under the impression that I was easy, were you?"

He let out a deep sigh, "A man can hope, can't he?"

He did have a great smile. And, he was incredibly handsome and charming, but he'd have to settle for a kiss on the cheek. As I turned to go in the house, he asked in a joking tone, "Is that really all I get?"

I looked back over my shoulder and said with a grin, "From me, yes. After all, that's all you deserve."

I walked inside and shut the door. "Goodnight, Miss Janie,"

he sang.

A few minutes later there was a knock on the door. I wondered if I had played too hard. What if he was the kind of guy who wouldn't take 'no' for an answer, and I had teased him all night? I was starting to lose that powerful feeling I had just moments ago. I looked out the peephole and saw Fitz standing there. I unlocked the door and she practically flew through it.

"Where is he? Is he here?" she asked looking around.

"Of course not," I said offended. "I told you I had no intention of sleeping with him."

"Well, I couldn't tell. You weren't..." she searched for a word, "YOU tonight!" she huffed. "In fact you were actin'...like a 'sexpot', or like.......me. Or at least how I used to act before I got together with Scotty!"

"Well I'd like to think I found my inner Barrymore, but I know it was more your influence." Drew Barrymore was the epitome of cute, smart, talented, funny and you bet your ass, sexy! "Honestly who do you think I learned it from?" I asked, doing a palms-up.

"Yeah, but I did it cause I was interested in a guy and wanted to be with him."

"Oh, I get it," I said. "You were worried that I was acting like that because I actually wanted Cecil?"

"Well, yeah," she said, confused. "If not because you wanted him, then why?"

I started to laugh. "Are you kidding me?" I asked. "I did it to keep him from picking a fight with Scotty ...just like you asked. Remember? And....."

She stared at me, "And what?" she asked.

"And...I hate guys like that! Women users! Dream crushers!" I was shaking my head. "I wanted to make him want me so bad, and then...crush him like a bug."

Fitz was smiling, "I kinda like this new side of ya, although bein' honest, ya need a bit more sexiness to really 'Barrymore' it."

"You couldn't just give me this one? I mean, obviously I know it was a Barrymore fail."

"On the contrary, I think yer attempt was a total success," she said.

"Yeah, well the only thing I succeeded in was making sure he didn't get laid tonight. Even that remains to be seen. For all I know, he'll pick up a woman in the lobby of his hotel. I hate that some poor, albeit dumb, woman is prey for a guy like that."

"Yer a good friend, Janie. And I know as soon as I explain to Scotty what happened, he'll be grateful, too."

"Scotty's here? Why didn't he come in with you?"

"He, ugh," she stammered, "he thought ya might be bangin' boots with Cecil," she winced.

I just shook my head. "Well, you can inform him for me that I don't 'bang boots' on the first date, not that this was a date," I said quickly.

I told Fitz good night, and waved to Scotty.

I did feel kinda sexy and bold, tonight. Too bad I was just acting the part. Although, I thought, I was convincing enough. Maybe I do have a sexy bone in my body. Usually I described myself as not having one of those.

My answering machine light was blinking at me. I pushed play.

It was mom. "Crap," I said out loud.

"Janie, it's your mom. Have you given any thought to going out with Otis, the donut maker? I know you can't make dinner this week because of your 'little art thing'," she said, like I was doing crafts at camp, "but let me know about next week. No pressure," she said. "Bye."

The next was Betty.

"Puddin, I am so glad you liked your surprise. You know

you're a very special person. You deserve to have a special place. Maybe you can move your...what's that thing called...," I heard her yell to someone in the background. "Easel," I heard Walter say. "Yeah, yer easel, to the patio and paint out there. Anyway Puddin, I love ya. Have a great night."

My heart warmed.

The next was Mum. "Janie dear, don't forget yer comin' to the BarBQ tomorrow, around noon-ish. Please, don't bring any food. Marble and I have been cookin' all day. We have enough food now to feed a whole football team."

You're gonna need it, I thought. The Fitzpatrick brood was bigger than a football team.

I was exhausted. I couldn't figure out if I was more tired or hungry. I knew I was both, I just didn't know in which order. I grabbed my comforter off the bed and headed to the couch.

I couldn't help but wonder why I even owned a bed. I preferred the couch and spent most nights crashed on it in front of the TV. I went to the fridge and got out a bottle of Chardonnay, some cheese, sourdough bread and brought them back to my coffee table. I turned on the TV. as I passed by and headed to the bathroom to change into my jammies. I pulled off my jeans and the little Rune fell out again. I picked it up and stared at it. "How do you keep doing that? I know damn well I left you on the table," I said to it. I shook my head and set it on the shelf. "I'm gonna leave you here," I told it. I wondered why I didn't 'wonder more' about its ability to find a way into my pockets.

I went back to the couch, uncorked the wine that I intended to drink straight from the bottle in true wino-fashion, and made myself a dry cheese sandwich. It doesn't sound like much of a meal to most people, but I could live forever on cheese, good sourdough bread and wine. Once my tummy was full, I downed the wine and curled up. I was asleep within minutes.

16

SATURDAY: EIGHT DAYS OF DUMPED

I woke up and looked at my watch. I had six hours till I had to be at Mum's. I made myself a Latte and headed to my new patio.

Sitting in one of the wrought iron rockers, I took in the view. It was so beautiful and the best part was the seven foot high fence. Mr. Mendlebaum, being all of five-five, would need a ladder to see over the top. I had my privacy again. I still didn't think keeping my shades open was a good idea, at least not on the side of the house facing his.

I was enjoying my coffee and solitude when I heard someone trying to open my back gate. I saw a hand come over the top, searching for the pull-up lock. I figured that it was Mr Mendlebaum trying to spy. But this was just too bold, I told myself. I walked as quietly as I could to the side of the house and grabbed my garden hose. I kinked the hose and turned the water valve on full blast. The door sprung open. I pointed the hose and let out the kink. Water sprang forth in a gush. I was hoping this would put an end to the snooping Mr. Mendlebaum. But it wasn't Mr. Mendlebaum. There, standing in front of me, was a thoroughly soaked Cecil. He was yelling at me to, "Turn off the bloody hose." I aimed the hose at the ground and tried to shut off the valve as quickly as I could.

"What the hell?" he yelled. "Is this how you treat all of yer guests?"'

"I thought you were my nosey neighbor," I yelled back. "And, yes! This is exactly how I treat people who break into my back yard."

"I wouldn't have had to break in if ya woulda opened the damn door."

"So why didn't you just leave if no one answered? You do know its 7am on a Saturday morning, right?"

"Mum told me that you were an early riser, so I thought I'd invite ya to breakfast. Ya never gave me your number and I knew Fitz wouldn't give it to me, so I decided to just swing by, and then…" he trailed off.

"And then… what?" I asked, doing a palms-up.

"I was..." he stammered, "I needed to apologize, okay?"

I shook my head at him, "Why?"

"Last night, I didn't come off well."

I did the palms up, "So…you were gonna…what? Break in through my patio door?"

"Actually, I tried yer front doorknob," he winced, "and it was unlocked."

My eyes rounded, "So you just opened my door?"

"Yeah, about that," he said, "you should really lock yer door. No telling what kind of weirdos an unlocked door can attract."

"You're the kind of weirdo," I pointed out.

"Yeah, I was hopin' ya wouldn't focus on that… anyway, ya weren't in the house, so I figured you were in the back yard. But I figured it would freak ya out if I came through yer back door…"

"Uh, yeah, it would have. And don't ever use the term 'back door' to me again," I added.

"So I decided to go around and come through the gate, so…"

"So, you broke into my backyard and got sprayed down?" I said, trying to keep my laughter to a minimum.

"Yeah," he said nodding, trying not to smile.

I shook my head at him, "Come inside. I'll get you a towel."

I handed him a towel and told him I would throw his wet clothes in the dryer. "You can change in the bathroom." I pointed the way.

"This towel is too small. Unless that's what ya had in mind?" he winked.

I let out a little sigh and rolled my eyes, "There's a robe hanging on the back of the door."

He went into the bathroom and I heard him grumbling.

"Hand me your wet clothes," I said.

"Is this yellow robe the one yer talkin' about?"

"It's the only one I have," I sang.

"Oh, for the love of Pete," he moaned. "This is hideous. I mean real torture here."

He opened the door and I put my hand to my mouth to stifle a laugh of my own. The robe came up to his middle thighs and the arms holes were up to his elbows. He looked like a gay centerfold. "Oh God," I rolled. "I hope it doesn't look like that on me."

"Hey, I'd like to think I make this look sexy," he said, striking a pose."Oh, yeah," I laughed, "that's hot."

The towel fell off the hook behind him, he turned and was getting ready to bend over, when I screamed "No," and turned my head away. "I'll get the towel, just....go sit down or something. With your legs closed, please," I added, as he passed me.

I scooped up his clothes and put them in the dryer on high. I made him a cup of coffee and sat on the couch next to him.

"So, can I ask you a question?" I began.

He took a sip of coffee and nodded, "Shoot."

"Why are you here?"

He gave me a hurt look. "What?"

"What I mean is," I said, trying to be gentle, "I'm not gonna have sex with you, Cecil."

He grinned and stood up. He walked over and opened my front door. I thought maybe he was leaving…right there and then, with my Peep bathrobe on. He picked up a bouquet of flowers from the porch and brought them to me.

"These are for you," he grinned. "I just wanted to thank you for last night. It was the first time I can remember spendin' an evenin' with my Big Brother, without it turnin' into a fight."

"Oh," I nodded, feeling like a complete ass.

"Had I known that this," he said, looking down, "was what ya did to men bringin' ya flowers, I would have let the florist deliver 'em."

I laughed.

"And, as for the sex…" he said with a sly grin.

I raised my eyebrows, waiting for him to finish the sentence.

"…well, we'll just have to see. I'm not easy, ya know. I need to be finessed, wooed!" he laughed.

I hit him with my throw pillow. "Shut up!"

We sat and talked while his clothes dried. Turns out, he wanted to go back home to Ireland and work in the family business. He said that this news bothered Scotty.

"That's what we were talking about when you and Fitz came back from the ladies room. I don't blame Scotty for being leery," he said. "I've managed to screw up, and off, quite a bit in the last eight years. But, I want to stop driftin'. Start taking my life more seriously. And Scotty won't even begin to accept my apology for bein' such a selfish spoiled ass. I've missed home and my family. Believe it or not, I've done a lot of growin' up, but he still treats me like I'm incapable of change.

"So, why were you such a...?"

"Go ahead and say it!" he said.

"Conceited arrogant ass? No offense," I added quickly.

"That was a pathetic stab at my brother. Ya see, before ya got there, Scotty was schoolin' me on how I was supposed to behave. He was chidin' me like I was little kid. I know what I did was petty, but I hate it when he tries to act like he's my dad. He even told me whatever I did, not to act like me. Pissed me off, and I'm embarrassed to admit, I purposely did not 'rise above' his opinion of me.

I remembered the call I had gotten from Fitz asking me to please dress like a girl and not wear heels, and how I had done the exact opposite. I nodded to him indicating that I understood completely.

"Then," he went on, "I met you, and you are...somethin'. Ya called me on my shit. Ya tore me down a little and I loved it. You were just, you!"

"Well, kinda," I said with a crooked smile. "I have to admit something, too. That whole sexy act, well, it was just that. It was an act."

"What do ya mean?"

"I tried to 'Barrymore you'," I said, getting all fidgety.

He smiled. "You don't give yerself enough credit. We'll have to work on that."

I smiled, "Wait, you know what 'Barrymore-ing' is?"

"Please, Drew is drop dead hot. I assume it has something to do with inner sexiness."

I nodded. "Indeed. And I am a Barrymore fail."

"Yeah I don't see it that way," he smiled.

I went to get his clothes out of the dryer and heard Fitz's

'hello' ring through the house as she came through the door. I could only imagine the look of shock on her face when she opened the door and saw Cecil sitting on my couch in my Peep bathrobe. I heard Fitz scream and something crash. "Shit," I said and dropped Cecil's clothes on the floor. I ran to the living room, but no one was there. A shattered picture frame was lying on my couch, and I could see the chip in the wall where it had hit. The front door was wide open, and now Fitz began to yell.

"Ya think your safe hidin' behind Baby?" she yelled, chasing Cecil around her car. "She's fully insured, you lousy piece of shite! I'll put a dent in her myself, so long as I can put one in yer skull, too."

Cecil was trying to explain, but he was laughing too hard. This pissed Fitz off even more.

I tried to sway her attention. "Fitz...FITZ!" I yelled.

She turned to me, wild eyed. "How could ya Janie? I told ya he was a letch!"

"Fitz!" I yelled again. "Nothing happened."

Her eyes narrowed. "Nothin' happened?"

"Would I lie to you...about anything?"

She considered the question then she slowly shook her head.

She looked back at Cecil, who was still laughing. "Why is he wearin' yer bathrobe?"

I let out a deep breath. "Come in, and I'll explain everything over coffee."

Once I explained everything, Fitz was laughing her ass off. She and Cecil talked while I got ready for the BarBQ. It seems they had gotten off on the wrong foot. After he told her everything he had told me, they were acting like chums. She even offered to put in a good word to Scotty for him. Cecil shook his head.

"Thank you for the offer, Fitz. But, I'm going to have to

prove myself to Scotty, and to dad. It's time for me to stand on my own two feet," he added.

"Where is Scotty?" I asked.

"He's pickin' up his dad at the airport. We're supposed to meet up with them later at the BarBQ. "Yer comin' right?" she asked Cecil.

"I intended to," he said, nodding, "as long as Janie can control herself around me." He leaned over and pretended to whisper to Fitz, "She's been usin' my name and sex in the same sentence," he smiled at me.

I smiled back and shook my head, "This should be fun," I said, sarcastically.

17

THE BAR B.Q. FROM HELL

Mum and Da's back yard was a huge gathering place. It was big enough to accommodate three long family sized picnic tables, Da's grill, an eight stool wrap around bar and that was all just the patio. When you stepped down off the patio there was the lagoon style pool, complete with a lava rock waterfall lined with flowers. To the right of that, was the twelve man Jacuzzi, also done in lava rock. If you followed the winding path you'd be headed to Mum's Garden, as the sign read. She would spend hours out there, working, just her and her Scotch. When we were young, this place was a kid's paradise. Now that the grandkids were abundant, it was again.

Cecil had met Mum and Da the day before, so he was treated like family. With a hug and kiss from Mum and a hearty shake of the hand and clap on the back from Da. She pointed us to the drinks and told us to help ourselves to drink and food, or starve to death. "Take yer pick!" Mum laughed, "Oh, Janie, I want ya to meet Marble's boyfriend."

Cecil and I followed Mum over to the lounge chairs that Aunt Marble and her new boyfriend were occupying.

Aunt Marble was wearing a moo-moo with a bold and bright tropical design. I bet they could see her from outer space, I thought. Her boyfriend was a slight bald man with huge square glasses that covered most of his face. He was wearing a short sleeved button-up cotton shirt, and short pants that showed his knobby knees. His black socks were pulled halfway up his calves, topped off with white running shoes that were fastened with Velcro strips. I don't know how Aunt Marble did it, but she found an exact duplicate of her late husband, Ira. All the way down to the Chicago accent.

He stood as we were introduced. Him being all of five-two, we met damn near face to breast. He smiled and said, "Whoa, you could take an eye out with those things."

I couldn't help but laugh.

"The name's Benny," he said, holding out his hand. "Benny Schwartz. I didn't mean to offend ya kid," he said to me, "or your boyfriend."

"He's not my boyfriend."

Cecil introduced himself and said, "It's kinda sad how bad she wants me. I just won't give in," he grinned.

I shook my head and Benny looked at me, "I think maybe the lady doth protest too much?"

"Et tu, Benny?" I replied, laughing.

I introduced Cecil to all the Fitzpatrick boys (but Barry of course), their wives and children. Mona had come up to say how happy she was that I had brought a date. She hated to think of me alone and heartbroken.

"It's so sad to think of you being dumped again," she gave an overly expressed look of pity. "And I heard this time was particularly embarrassing for you."

I tried to smile through her obvious attempt to injure me, and was just getting ready to tell her that Cecil wasn't my boyfriend, but he cut me off.

"She was just holding out for the total package." Cecil flexed his biceps (which I must admit, were impressive even through a T-shirt), wrapped a muscled arm around my waist and shot her his perfect smile. It had the desired effect of shutting her up, so I just let it go.

Scotty and his dad showed up an hour later. I had never seen Fitz so nervous. But Martin, as I was asked to call him, was a warm, down to Earth, charmer. He was in his sixties, tall with broad bull like shoulders, a full head of silver hair and the same gorgeous smile as both of his sons. He took Fitz in a big bear hug and told her that she was now family. "Even if I have to marry ya, myself," he smiled.

Over lunch, Martin and Da regaled us with stories of their childhood. Something about bathing in the pool of Holy Water at St. Catherine's; seems Cecil wasn't the only bad boy in the family. We were having the best time until I heard my name being called from the back fence. I looked at Fitz, bewildered.

"Is that John?" I asked her.

"Janie, are you in there?" he yelled again.

I stood and walked to the back gate with Fitz in tow.

"John?" I said over the fence, opening the gate. There he stood. The guy that had dumped me a week ago was crashing a very dangerous party for him to attend.

"What are you doing here?" I asked, baffled.

"Ya have a hell of a lot of nerve showin' up here," Fitz bellowed, from behind me. "Ya really are as stupid as I always thought ya were!"

"Fitz, it's ok," I said, reassuring her. "I'll talk to him."

"She shot him a look of pure hate before turning to me and saying, "Alright Janie. But if ya need me or my brothers," she emphasized, "we'll be right there." she pointed. The Fitzpatrick boys had gathered to stand together, arms folded across their chest, waiting for a signal to pounce. They made quite a frightening sight, I thought. God I love 'em!

I watched Fitz walk off and then turned back to John. "Again, what are you doing here?"

"I made a huge mistake, Janie," he blurted out. "I can't believe that I did this to you...that I hurt you the way I did! It's just, you and I were talking about living together and I knew you wanted to get married," he rambled. "I guess I just got scared."

I stood there shaking my head. I couldn't believe this was happening, "So…what?" I asked. "I mean…did she dump you or something?"

He looked at the ground. "Well, yeah. She met some millionaire on the beach before we were supposed to leave. She told me that she had fallen head over heels for him and she was staying right there in Hawaii. But she was horrible anyway, Janie. She was whiney and rude and spoiled. She never wanted to do anything but lie on the beach and read magazines. She wasn't like you. You and I like all the same things. We..."

I cut him off. "Actually John, I don't," I said, shaking my head.

"Yes you do," he argued.

"No, I really don't." I took a deep breath. "I don't like sailing. And I don't like hiking through the desert. I don't want to go rock climbing. I did like the French Cooking class we took, but if I'm really being honest with myself, I would rather have taken the Italian course that I was signed up for in the first place." I was the one rambling now. "I don't like extreme mountain biking and I don't ever want to jump out of a plane. And most of all, I don't like being cheated on for months and then tossed aside like I never mattered in the first place!"

He looked confused.

"You see, John," I said gently, "I did all of those things just to be with you."

"See that's what I'm saying, Janie. You're the least selfish person I've ever met. You're the perfect woman."

"No, John," I shook my head, "I was the perfect doormat. But, I've done a lot of changing in the past week, believe it or not. And I really can't be a doormat for you anymore, or anyone. I'm sorry."

"You see, you're saying sorry to me when I should be begging for your forgiveness," he added.

"What I'm trying to say, John, is that it wouldn't make the slightest difference. I'm afraid I just don't love you." I paused then finally said it out loud, "I don't even know if I ever did."

"What? Look I know you're angry and hurt. You have every right to be, but to say that you never loved me? I don't believe that!"

I just stared at him. "I think I loved the idea of you, John. I wanted to feel complete. Somewhere in my mind, I thought that meant I needed to belong to someone…even if he wasn't the right one. I am sorry, John, because part of this is my fault too… for not knowing me better… but it really is over."

I turned and walked away, leaving him standing there.

I was almost to the pool when John grabbed my arm and spun me around. He put a lip lock on me, but I pulled away.

"No John!" I said, struggling against him. "It's over." I tried to pull away, but he tightened his grip around both my arms, holding them down at my sides.

"No, you love me," he yelled. "I know you do!"

"Let me go," I begged, as he squeezed harder. I could see the Fitzpatrick boys, Fitz, Scotty and Cecil running towards us. "Let go of me, damn it," I yelled. "You're hurting me!""I'm not leaving until we've worked this out," he yelled back. He tightened his squeeze on my arms and was shaking me hard.

Pulling me in front of him, he tried to use me as a barrier against the approaching mob. Fitz tore me out of his hands and pulled me aside. John threw wild punches at the brothers. He threw one that would have hit Fitz if she hadn't ducked. Unfortunately, this girl right here has to learn to duck a punch. I took the blow to my temple and dropped like a sack of potatoes.

18

PUNCH DRRUNK LOVE

When I came to, I was in the hospital. I didn't know exactly what happened, but the doctor informed me that I had a concussion and a contusion to my right temple. My head ached and my neck was too stiff to turn.

"I'll let your friends know that you're conscious."

I drifted off again. I came to when I felt someone kiss my forehead. I opened my eyes and saw Fitz. Standing close behind her was Cecil, looking concerned.

"Are ya ok, Janie?" she asked with watering eyes. "We've been so worried."

"I have a really bad headache," I said, holding my head.

"I bet ya do," she retorted. "Do you remember what happened?"

"Not really. I know John showed up and was freaking out. He had my arm." I looked down and saw a huge black and blue bruise darkening, "that bastard!" I said.

Fitz nodded. "He hit ya in the temple then you fell and cracked your head on the side of the pool. Just another foot the other way you woulda hit the grass instead."

"Where is he now?" I asked, feeling very groggy.

"The police arrested him. But not before he got the ass kickin' of his life."

"I guess you should tell the brothers 'thank you' for me."

Fitz shook her head. "Ya know, they would have loved to have kicked his ass, but there wasn't much left after Cecil got through with 'em."

I looked past Fitz and saw Cecil hovering a few feet behind her. "Cecil?" I said.

He walked forward and took my hand. "I'm so sorry I didn't get to him sooner, Janie."

I tried to shake my head but couldn't. I winced. "No, don't feel bad. I can't thank you enough for...what you did. I owe you one."

"See," he said, trying to smile. "There ya go.... talkin' about sex again. I may just have to give in and let ya have yer way with me, already."

I smiled, "Just when I thought we were about to have a moment."

"Please, Janie, Fitz is still in the room. Yer an animal," he growled at me.

I looked at Fitz. "When are you springing me?"

"Not tonight," she said, shaking her head. "You don't have any bleedin' on the brain, but you do have a concussion, and eight stitches on the back of yer head."

I moved my hand to the back of my head and felt the bandage.

"They wanna keep ya overnight for observation," Fitz said. "You'll probably be let out tomorrow."

"But the Auction?" I said, trying to sit up.

"Afraid not," she said, laying me back down. "I'll go and represent ya, if ya like, but you are to stay down for a few days. The doctor said you'd be groggy and not too steady on yer feet."

I gave her the pouty face. "My first showing and I'm gonna miss it because my ex-boyfriend knocked the crap out of me... while trying to win me back. Yep, that sounds like something that would happen to me," I gave her a weak smile.

She kissed my forehead again, and asked if there was anything I needed from home.

"A change of clothes for tomorrow would be great." She turned to leave, "Fitz?" I called. She looked back at me. "Not the spandex shorts, okay."

She smiled and left.

I drifted in and out of sleep. I wasn't sure how much time had passed. But every time I woke there was Cecil sitting in the chair next to my bed. He doted on me and tried to get me to eat something, but the pain medication was making me nauseous. I woke once, and saw that he had unfolded the chair into a make shift bed. Sleeping, body curled into a tight ball, and still his legs were hanging down onto the floor. I smiled at him as he quietly snored away. The next thing I knew I was being woken up to have my vitals taken and a breakfast tray placed in front of me. Powdered scrambled eggs and a round of turkey sausage, with dry whole grain toast. "No thank you," I said to the nurse. "I'll wait for a burger run."

Cecil woke and said he was starving. I offered him my breakfast. He took one look and said, "Maybe I'll go get us somethin'. How does a burger sound?"

I smiled, "Perfect."

When I woke again, I could hear two people arguing quietly. "She can't eat that crap," Cecil's said in whisper.

"We're not allowed to let people bring in outside food," the old nurse argued back.

"She doesn't like the sludge this place tries to pass off as food."

"No one likes it," she fired back. "But it's the rule!"

"Fine, I'll put her in a wheelchair and we'll eat on one of the benches outside."

The nurse shook her head at him with fading patience. "Fine, she can have the damn burger. Just close the curtain. And if anyone finds out…" she warned, "I don't know anything about this. You got that?"

"Got it! Yer a peach," he said, kissing the old lady's cheek.

She walked off, "Yeah, yeah."

He entered the room and started unpacking our burgers and fries.

"You really will hit on anyone," I joked.

"How long have ya been awake?"

"Just long enough to be grateful that you won't be wheeling me outside in this beautiful backless gown."

"Oh, that," he said with a wave, "hell, I woulda slept with her to make sure you ate somethin'."

"I know you would have," I said, taking a grateful look at the bacon cheeseburger. "You're good to me like that."

After we ate the doctor came in and told me he was having my release papers finished up. He was a slight man of East Indian descent. He reminded me of Gandhi. I loved that movie and was strangely attracted to the little man.

"You'll have to stay down and take it easy for a few days," he said in a thick accent. "And try not to get your stitches wet. I know it'll be inconvenient, but an infection would be more so. Here is a prescription for some pain pills. They'll take the edge off, but may make you groggy and nauseous, take them with food. Also, no alcohol while you are taking them."

I shot him a look of disappointment. Truth was I had never wanted a shot of whiskey so badly in my whole life. Blame it on my Irish bloodline.

"It thins the blood," he said, trying to drive his point home.

"And," he continued, "can intensify your inability to function, and doubles your chance of an overdose."

I groaned. I hated taking pills. My side effect from drinking whiskey weren't nearly as severe.

An hour later, Fitz came to pick me up. She handed me my 501's and a T-shirt. "Cecil," she said, "why don't you step out while I help Janie get dressed?"

"Oh, don't worry about me," he smiled. "I've already seen everything. Janie did a strip tease for me earlier while under heavy sedation. I'm not even sure she remembers, but...."

Fitz turned to him and pointed to the door, "Out!"

Looking like a scolded child, except for the devilish grin, he left my room. Fitz asked, "Has he been here all night?"

I nodded, moving towards the edge of the bed. "I think he feels guilty. Why? I don't know."

Fitz untied my gown for me, "I don't think so, Janie. I think he likes ya."

"I forgot what a huge turn on a wounded woman in a backless gown, could be."

"I'm not kiddin', Janie."

"Yeah, well, you said it yourself, he likes all women. And regardless of how awful I feel and frightening I must look, I still fit into that category. Besides, don't men like him always prey on the sick and the lame?"

"No," she shook her head. "I think this is different. I think he... cares for ya."

Her struggle for the word indicated how much the concept confused her, too.

I smiled and let her help me get on my jeans.

After a quick stop at the pharmacy, Fitz and Cecil took me home. I was weaker than I thought. My legs felt like rubber. The thought that people out there in the world paid good money to underground dealers to feel this way, baffled me. My first few steps were so wobbly Cecil scooped me up in his arms and proceeded to carry me to the door. As we stepped over the threshold he stopped and looked into my eyes. I don't know why, but it made me nervous. He carefully put a kiss on my temple before proceeding to the couch. He gently laid me down and said, "I'll go get yer comforter off the bed." Fitz stood there, gaping after him.

She started to say something but I stopped her. I held up my hand, "Not now, Fitz."

"Ok," she said with a smile. She came and put a kiss on my cheek, "But I want details later. Right now I have to meet up with the family for lunch, then go and get ready for yer art openin'."

I pouted a little. "Yeah, I hope it goes well."

"It will," Fitz soothed, as she headed for the door.

"Aren't you gonna drive Cecil to his hotel?" I asked.

"No," she smiled again, shaking her head. "He refuses to leave until yer feeling better."

I gave her a worried look.

"Enjoy!" she said, and closed the door.

As if I hadn't been nervous enough about Cecil's intentions, now I was to be left in his charge? Truthfully, I was somewhat grateful. I didn't want to be left alone. And, if it made him feel better to 'nurse me' then so be it. But, I couldn't help but wonder again...didn't wild beasts always go after the sick and lame? The thought occurred to me, at the moment, I was both. Cecil came back with my comforter and tucked me in on the couch. He brought me some juice, a glass of water and one of my pain pills.

"You don't have to babysit me," I said to him, before popping the pill in my mouth.

"Are ya gonna be a problem patient? Because I saw some

restraints hangin' on the back of yer closet door," he said, raising his eyebrows.

"Those are belts Cecil."

He shook his head. "I knew it was too good to be true," he winked.

I laughed despite the pain in my head. What could I say, my new pain in ass, was funny.

He went through my DVD's and picked out a movie. He held it up for my approval.

"You've Got Mail?" I laughed.

"Hey," he said in a hurt tone. "It may not be as manly as 'Fists of Fury', but it's one of my favorite movies. And," he added, "doesn't everyone love Meg Ryan?"

I smiled at him and nodded as best as I could.

We watched every Meg Ryan movie I had on VHS and DVD. I drifted in and out of sleep the whole day. He woke me at seven to serve me Mexican Food cheese enchiladas and tacos, with chips, salsa and beans).

"This is wonderful," I said, eating until I felt I might burst. "Where did you order this from?"

"I made it," he said, wiping his mouth.

I couldn't hide a skeptical look. "What? How?"

"I hope ya don't mind, but I borrowed yer car and went grocery shopping."

"No, that's not what I meant," I waved my hand. "What I meant was, how did you learn to cook Mexican Food?"

"I know how to cook all kinds of food," he said with a shrug. "I love to cook. Why is that so surprisin'?"

"I don't know," I said, eyeing him carefully. "I'm just peeling back the many layers of onion you apparently have," I concluded.

He raised his arm and smelled his pit. "Do I smell like an

onion?" he laughed. "Maybe I can use yer shower later? And your robe?" he grinned.

I nodded, smiled, and was back asleep before my head hit the pillow.

Next thing I knew, I was awoken by voices. I lifted my head and saw my father shaking hands with Cecil at the front door. Cecil was still wearing my floral apron, and I could see my father's eyes studying it. "So, you're the young man I owe a debt of thanks to?" my father asked.

"No sir, no debt at all. She's a lovely girl, our Janie. I wouldn't let anyone hurt her, if it's in my power to stop it." Cecil had lost his joking, jovial tone and seemed all too serious to be him.

"Yes, OUR Janie is a wonderful woman," my father emphasized.

Cecil smiled then and let his gaze fall to the apron. "Oh, I… ugh… I was just going to make Janie and me some tea. Can I get ya a cup?"

My father nodded as he made his way over to take the chair next to me. Cecil disappeared into the kitchen.

I tried to sit up, but my father prevented my ill-attempt. "No, no, Janie girl. Lie still. I came as soon as I heard," he said smiling, placing a gentle kiss on my forehead.

"How did you find out?" I asked. "Did Fitz call you?"

"No love," he inspected my temple. "I went to your showing at the Gallery. I didn't see Fitzy anywhere. I did have the luck to run into Mum, though. She told me what happened. What John did," he said gravely. "If I had been there...," he began, his face twisting in an angry scowl.

I patted his hand. "I know Dad."

He smiled again, took my hand in his and gave it a squeeze. "I would say lucky for him that I wasn't, but it seems your friend in there, a much younger version of me," he said with a grin, "took care of things in my stead."

I smiled, "I guess he did. I was unconscious for that part. What were you doing at the Gallery?" I asked. "Mom said that she wouldn't be there...."

"Janie," he began, "I made my peace years ago with who your mother is, and truthfully, I love her. Flaws and all," he added. "But there was no way I was gonna let my little girl's big night pass me by, while I sat on the couch watching boxing." Beaming, he brushed my hair from my forehead. "I am so proud of you, Janie Girl," he whispered. "And your mother is, too. You've become such a beautiful woman," his eyes welling with tears. "And a very talented one from what I saw. I feel a fool that I didn't know just how talented you are. Your paintings are amazing. You got that from your mom, ya know?"

My eyebrows raised, "Mom was an artist?" I asked.

He nodded slowly. "A pretty damn good one, too," he added.

"Why didn't she ever tell me...or show me her work?"

Dad smile broadened and his eyes dropped to the floor. "They're mostly nudes," he said trying to hide a blush. "And, a few of them are...uh...of uh...me."

This did explain why I hadn't seen them, and mental note, don't ever want to.

I just nodded and stifled a grin. "Oh," I finally said. "But they were good?"

"They were great, if I do say so myself," he smiled back. "I know she can be difficult, Janie. Maybe seeing you get your shot reminds her of a path of life she missed for herself."

I thought about it for a moment, "I think maybe her constant pushing to see me married with children is a way of saying she wants me to find the happiness she's found."

He gave my hand another squeeze, "I hope so, Janie. I'd like to think she doesn't regret the life she chose."

"I love you Dad."

"And I love you, my Janie Girl."

Cecil came back in with my tea pot and three cups, but my dad declined saying that it was time for him to leave and let me get some sleep. He raised his eyebrows to Cecil, "You'll take good care of OUR Janie Girl, wont ya?"

Cecil smiled, shook my father's hand and said, "Anything within my power, Sir."

"Drop the Sir stuff, son," my father said, clapping Cecil on the shoulder. "I'm not your boss." They exchanged smiles and I could see that my father both liked and approved of Cecil. That scared the shit out of me. He had never approved of any guy. I couldn't help but wonder, just what was Cecil's role in my life? Dad put a gentle kiss on my forehead, said a quick Irish blessing and headed for the door.

"Dad," I called after him.

He stopped and turned to face me.

"Tell mom I love her, okay?" I said.

He winked, "Will do, Janie Girl," he said, then closed the door behind him.I tried to stay awake, but couldn't. The next thing I knew it was morning and Cecil was bringing me a Latte. He obviously didn't have any trouble with my Espresso machine. He was wearing my Peep bathrobe, so I assumed he took a shower. I suddenly had a vision of him…lying in my bath tub, surrounded by bubbles, his hair wrapped in a towel, singing 'I Feel Pretty'.

There was a gift wrapped box on the table in front of me. "What's this?" I asked, pointing to the box.

"It's for you," he smiled. "Open it!"

I grabbed the box and gave it a shake, "You didn't have to do this."

“What makes ya think it’s from me?” he asked, with a sly smile.

I opened the box and pulled out a new robe. It was plush black, and I noted, many sizes bigger than my Peep robe.

“Just in case ya have visitors over,” he grinned. “Or gain 50 pounds and 5 inches.”

19

VICODIN DREAMS?

Fitz showed up a few minutes later. She was beaming and ecstatically bounded through my front door 'Tigger' style. "Oh my God," she yelled. "You'll never believe what happened at the Auction last night!"

"What? What?" I yelled, realizing two things. One: yelling made my head ache horribly. Two: It was definitely time for another pain pill. I grabbed my head and Cecil took his cue to pop the top off the Vicodin and hand me one of the God sent pills. I popped it in my mouth and quickly washed down the bitter tasting disk of pain relief. I then gave Fitz the 'keep going' hand roll.

"Well....they sold!" she blurted out.

"What?" I asked, unable to conceal my utter disbelief.

"Every one of 'em!" she yelled. "And there was even a biddin' war on one."

"Which one?"

"Mine!" she beamed, and did a little spin. "Scotty's Dad bought it for him. Right out from underneath some millionaire from Aruba. Ya won't believe what it sold for!" she said, wide eyed. She looked at the check again before handing it to me.

I looked at it, and my eyes bugged out. "Is this for one painting?" I questioned, in the highest pitched and squeakiest voice I had ever heard emerge from me.

"No, it's for all three. But more than half of it is from the one of me!" she exclaimed.

I was holding in my hand a check made out to me from The Rien Gallery, for $25,000.00. I started to hyperventilate. "Holy shit! For three paintings?" I repeated.

"For three great paintins'," corrected Fitz. "And there's more."

I wasn't sure my heart could take much more.

"Scotty's dad, Martin, wants us to come to Ireland. He loved your landscape paintins' so much, he wants to hire you."

I shook my head, not quite understanding what he wanted to hire me for.

"He wants ya to do paintins' of his Castle, and the Brewery. And he's offered ya quite a bit of money, I might add. And, not to mention, we'll be guests at his Castle for our stay."

I was shaking my head in disbelief. This was the pain medication. What great pills. But I was going to wake up any minute and find Cecil sitting in my recliner, wearing my Peep bathrobe.

Fitz was reading my thoughts.

"Still more," Fitz bellowed and twirled around in a circle again, like a little girl. "Martin wants me to be the face of Wiccan B Ale. I'm gonna grace all the bottles and packagin', everything. I'm gonna be Wiccan B's version of the St. Pauly Girl!"

"Oh my God," I said, trying to take all of this in. Martin wanted me, Janie O'Connelly, to be his personal artist, and Fitz to be... I guess the "spokes-face," for all of his products. I was so happily overwhelmed. “I'm so excited...I don't know what to say...or what to do!”

Fitz smiled and said, “Pack yer bags Janie O’Connelly....we’re goin’ to Ireland!”

THE END

Don't miss JANIE A BROAD
Available Now

The second entry in the zany, heartwarming* Janie Chronicles *finds Janie O'Connelly questioning her sanity. But what else is new?

Janie is offered the job of a lifetime painting the Callaghan Castle and Distillery in Ireland.

When she and Sarra "Fitz" Fitzpatrick move into the amazing 300-year-old castle, they think it's a dream come true. But when things start disappearing and stories don't add up, Janie and Fitz must use their less-than-impressive sleuthing skills to root out the culprit.

Soon, they wind up in odd predicaments and secret passageways that offer more questions than answers. Turns out batshit crazy is universal.

Turn the page for an excerpt from *Janie a Broad.*

1

AWAY WE GO

"Oh, my God, I'm late, I'm late!" I yelled, springing from my bed like the White Rabbit.

I was more than startled when Fitz sat up from the opposite side of the bed. "What are ya late for, Janie?" she asked calmly, while holding her hung over temple. Her Irish accent more pronounced with drink or in her case, with residual drink.

I let out a sigh, "I was dreaming that I was late for work."

"No Janie, yer not late. In five hours we fly to Ireland. Now get back in bed," she patted my empty space.

I curled back up in my spot. "Wow that was such a realistic dream. I was late and Dante didn't have keys, and the customers were lined up out front...all waiting for me."

"Yes, yes," soothed Fitz, "It all sounds horrible. Now just ya lie back down...and shut the hell up."

I lay back down trying to calm myself but a million thoughts were running wild in my head. I didn't fly well and was trying to avoid thinking about it. I instead tried to mentally focus on my packing skills.

"Fitz?" I said in a whisper.

"Huh?"

"Are you packed?"

"Aye."

"Did you pack razors?"

"Cream hair remover."

"Did you pack tampons?"

"Uh hum."

"Did you pack period underwear?"

"Why for the love of God, are ya so concerned with my hooha? Seriously Janie, I've kept her in check without anyone else's help for quite some time," Fitz said.

"It's just, I feel like I'm forgetting something. I keep going over everything I packed, but what if I forgot something?"

"But why are ya making ME go over everything I packed?" she questioned.

"Hints," I finally said.

Irritated, Fitz sat up, "I'm not going to play the 'Janie is neurotic', game. Be assured, they have stores in Ireland."

"What if I forgot something I can't get in Ireland?"

"Okay Janie, so this is the game we play instead of going over every damn thing in your bag." She looked me straight in the eyes and I could actually see the hangover on her face and recoiled a little. "What can ya not replace in Ireland?" she asked.

When she put it that way, the list was shorter. I thought for a moment and sprung from the bed again, "The Rune Diane gave me!"

As I headed to search my living room for the Rune, I heard Fitz say, "Wonderful," before she pulled the covers over her head.

I had met Diane, (a woman old enough to be my mother but certainly nothing like her) at a rebirthing ceremony thrown in my honor or horror. I still wasn't sure which. Turns out, I am the dating impaired. Fitz, (my best friend since before school had number grades) her mother, Mum, as we called her, and her batshit-crazy, tantra-sex-teaching, coke-bottle glasses wearing Aunt Marble, had brought the 'Ladies of the Moon' a coven of sorts, to the Pub so they could put me in a child's hard plastic kiddie pool and rebirth me with oil, flowers, salt, and who knows what else. But that weird incident, along with a "Getting to Know Myself," chat with Diane had pushed me to follow my dreams. I finally asked to display my paintings at the coffee house where I have worked since 10th grade. (Don't judge. I love that place) Which in turn led to a gallery owner seeing my work and having me fill a last minute opening in his auction. That in turn led to Fitz's boyfriend's dad, Martin, hiring me to do two paintings: One of his Castle and the other of Callaghan's distillery, in Ireland. The Rune, a small stone with the symbol of a lightning bolt, had been part of a mojo bag Diane had given me. Crazy, huh? Oddly enough, this tiny stone had found its way into my pocket on several occasions. I started to think of it as a good luck charm and didn't want it to have to cross an ocean to find me. Although, some part of me, the 1% that believed in magic, thought somehow... it would.

I took off as fast as my own slight hangover would allow and ran straight into Cecil, his exceptional build knocking me backwards. Catching me around the waist, he pulled me back towards him.

"Whoa there," he said, putting me right on my feet. "Where's the fire, Janie?" I was surrounded by Irish accents, (between Fitz's family and her boyfriend's) and they always made my knees a little weak.

His sandy hair a mess, he was shirtless and rippled in all the right places, wearing a pair of 501 jeans and a huge white smile. "Sorry," I said, trying not to stare at his well chiseled chest. I took a step back, and asked, "What are you doing here?"

"Ya don't remember?"

A wave of fear washed over me then I saw Scotty, Fitz's

boyfriend, and Cecil's big brother, asleep on the couch. "Not really."

Cecil wasn't exactly a stranger to my home. After we first met, I had taken a very short, but not-so-sweet beating from my ex-boyfriend, John. (To be honest, John was trying to win me back, after having dumped me in an airport terminal and taking a woman he had been having an affair with for six months to Hawaii, in my place. Yeah, that was seriously screwed up.) I was unconscious from hitting my head on the side of the pool at Mum's house, when Cecil gave him a whipping. Afterward, Cecil stayed at my house for a week, to babysit me, feed me, and make sure that I took my pain pills, instead of succumbing to my favorite form of numb, Irish whiskey. The second week, he stayed with me because he had grown fond of my bed and preferred it to his hotel room. Don't get too excited though, I slept on the couch.

2

THE FLASHBACK

It was coming back now...well, parts of it. I thought it was to be a Bon Voyage Party since Fitz, and I were headed to Ireland for an extended working vacation. I was to do the paintings, and Fitz with her flowing red mane, emerald green eyes and porcelain skin, would be the perfect spokesmodel for the Callaghan distillery and brewery. What it turned out to be was actually a combo Bon Voyage/26th Birthday for me. I showed up at the pub as requested, after a torturous birthday dinner with my parents. My mind yelled to me, "Start there!" so I did.

It was the usual painful hour or so, out of my every week since I had moved out on my own. My mother was...hard to describe. She had a dream-crushing way about her that extended to my life as a whole. My hair was cut and styled incorrectly, long and straight, usually in a ponytail. My make-up was always too much, or too little. "Whore of Babylon," or "Did you even bother to look like this?" I didn't dress girly enough, 501's being my favorite go to style. All of this could be fixed to suit her, but I was also too tall. She criticized everything I did, said and wore.

Even my thoughts, at times were invaded and judged. I loved her none-the less. None-the-more for damn sure, but none-the-less either. My father was my saving grace and the polar opposite of mom. I loved and adored him, more-the-more. There was talk of a fix-up, as there would always be, with a mother who had once tried to set me up with my cousin. Yep! You read that right. She only noticed the error of her ways, when said cousin, was fired from the lab he worked at, for stealing fecal specimens. I repeat, STEALING. FECAL. SPECIMENS!

Mom had started in again, as she passed the potatoes. "I just don't like you being a whole ocean away. Especially, with that Fitz, I mean, that girl just invites poor decisions right through the door."

I had heard this from my mother since kindergarten. I let out a sigh.

"What?" my mother asked, doing a palms up, like she had no idea how old hearing these things had become.

"Just stop, mom!" I said, shaking my head.

"I've said it before," she started.

I cut her off, "Yes, you have. And I'm tired of it."

"Well, you know, all the bad decisions you've ever made, have been..."

"Have been mine!" I interrupted. "Stop! Just stop blaming Fitz for my life! I made the decision to not go to college! I made the decision to continue working at the same job I've had since high school! I made the decision to move out and live on my own! Me! Not her! Stop trying to blame all the things I've done, that make me a failure in your eyes, on Fitz! Not only is it old, mom, it's inaccurate."

"Well, she..."

"No mom, it's time for you to realize, I'm grown. 26 today. You've done your job. Now you need to get a life that isn't about trying to control mine!"

My father, who had never seen me really talk back to my mother, stared at his plate awkwardly.

"Well, if you don't need me in your life..." she started.

"I do need you in my life, mom, just not trying to control it!"

It was the most uncomfortable birthday dinner, I had ever had. That included my seventh birthday, where Fitz started a cake fight that left my mother's bleach cleaned walls covered in chocolate. I felt horrible for fighting with her, but, I was trying to take control of my life. And that meant I'd have to wrestle it out of her hands.

3

TO THE PUB I GO!

As I walked into the pub, heads turned and applause began. It took a moment of me looking around, to know that this was for me. Quickly, I started to recognize the faces in the crowd as old friends. I smiled as they began to sing 'Happy Birthday'. Fitz came and wrapped an arm around my neck, kissing me hard on the cheek. Muahhh!

"Happy Birthday, Janie girl," she yelled over the crowd.

I hugged her, and smiled from ear to ear. I wasn't fond of crowds, but these were all friends and their mates, making this crowd a reunion. As I walked the bar, I stopped at damn near every stool and table to say hellos, give hugs and do a quick catch up. From somewhere in the crowd appeared a Black & Tan and a shot of Bushmills.

"Down it," I heard my old friend Ashley, yell.

I held the shot over my head, cheering to my old friends, and took it down in one gulp. One hand removed the empty glass as another handed me a full one. As I pounded the second shot, I reminded myself that I was flying to Ireland the next day and needed to take it easy. Mum appeared with a giant chocolate sheet cake ablaze with what I am sure was at least fifty candles. I made a wish and blew out every last one of them with one long breath. It took about an hour to make the rounds, but slowly people began to let their focus wander back to others. I could relax and enjoy my party without being the center of attention, which I was never really comfortable with. I had gone to Catholic school with most of these folks, and where you have a bunch of Catholics cutting loose you have yourself quite a party.

I was sitting at the end of the bar taking a breather and sipping my Black & Tan when I caught sight of Barry walking toward me.

Oh sweet God, I thought to myself. Barry was Fitz's youngest brother, which still made him three years older than us. Six feet tall, brown hair, green eyes and a body I tried not to think about. He had been my secret crush since we were kids. I had almost been brave enough to kiss him just a few weeks ago. But then, right before I could find and summon the balls needed to go all in, his psycho ex-girlfriend tried to assault me. During the altercation he told her the words that still hurt my heart, "She's a friend of my little sister's. I'm just being a good person to someone who's had a really bad week." He had tried to apologize. Whether it was for what he had said, or the ex, I still wasn't sure. But by then I was having a date related issue of my own, now known as the "Henry Incident." My sixty-ish year old Southern Belle landlord, Betty, had sent Henry my way as a set up of sorts. It didn't go well. Henry, although a gorgeous well built god who spoke fluent Italian, was also a jealous, somewhat delusional whack-job. Barry and I didn't get to clear the air before he left for Ireland for his best friend's wedding. He returned early so he could wish his little sister Bon Voyage. This was the first time I had seen him since he arrived home and my knees were knocking under the bar.

"Happy Birthday, Janie," he said. "May I sit?" His Irish accent made my knees knock harder.

"Of course," I extended my hand to the empty stool next to me. "How was Ireland?" I asked, smiling.

"Ireland is so beautiful, Janie. I never remember how much I miss it, till I go home. You'll love it. How long do ya think you'll be gone?"

"Not sure. However long it takes me to do the paintings."

He nodded and looked at his beer before saying, "About Ireland, Janie, I understand Mum shared the news with the ladies about me finding my soul mate."

I nodded, feeling either my heart dropping, or was it the whiskey rising? Mum had indeed told us that my biggest crush since I was five, had found the love of his life within twelve hours of being in Ireland.

"Well, I didn't know that you and Fitzy had become part of the group. I guess I should have assumed that at some point, you girls would be invited. But I didn't know that it had already happened."

He was speaking of The Ladies of the Moon. He knew about them? My mind began to twist. Did that mean he also knew about my embarrassing rebirthing ritual? Done as I stood dressed in frog boxers (with a caption that read, "Sometimes you have to kiss a lot of frogs" on the crotch) and a bra, in a little plastic kiddy pool? (Not one of my finer moments) The ritual that was held because I hadn't just been horribly dumped once again, I had been the dumpee in every relationship I ever had! I couldn't stand the thought of him feeling sorry for me and my pathetic inability to successfully date.

"I had no idea you knew about the group," was all I could say while trying not to blush.

"Sure," he said. "Mum's always been a little..." he searched for a word, different!" he smiled. "But, that's what makes her so incredible."

I nodded again, "I hear you found an incredible woman of your own, Calle right?" I said, forcing a smile. I had the mental image of some perfect Irish lass, hair blowing in the wind as she stood on a lush green bluff. Eyes all shiny and when she smiled, her teeth emitted a sparkle like diamonds in the sun.

"That's what I wanted to talk to ya about," he said.

I didn't want to be a bitch, had no reason to be either, other than of course, pure jealousy. But the thought of listening to him gush about her made me... yeah, bitchy was the word. I smiled as best I could and let him continue.

"Ya see Janie, Calle isn't exactly..."

Mum came out of nowhere and cut him off before he could finish his thought. Being the only unmarried son, Mum had been working overtime to get him to the altar. I even had my suspicions that she had tried to "Potion" him, like she had tried to do with me. Apparently, 'potion-ing' and 'drugging' are NOT the same thing, according to Mum.

"Oh, are ya tellin' Janie of yer girl in Ireland? Seriously son, when am I to meet this woman who has stolen my baby's heart?"

"Ummm," Barry stammered eyes darting from me to Mum.

"Yer not gettin' any younger, son!" she shook her head. Ya may want to be thinkin' of weddin' bells. Ya know, before I'm dead," Mum added. "In fact, I have some ideas I'd like to run by ya."

"Uh, well yeah Mum, I'd love to hear 'em, but..."

Barry was cut off again, "To be sure, you'll want to be gettin' married in Ireland," Mum's eyebrows raised.

"Well, yeah," said Barry. "I always assumed I'd marry back home, but..."

"Well, you can't put it off too long. Planning a weddin' in

Ireland will be more difficult from the States," Mum broke in again. "Ya can't be expectin' her to do it all on her own, and I have lots of ideas to run past ya," she beamed.

"I think I should go find Fitz," I said standing. "You two have a lot to talk about."

"Alright Janie girl," said Mum, pulling me down to her height so she could kiss my cheek. "Don't ya leave though without findin' me for yer blessin'."

Barry said, "I, ugh, I..." he looked back at his mother, "I guess I'll talk to ya a little later then, Janie."

I nodded, "Yep, sounds good."

I was grateful for the volume of the band, as I walked away. It was drowning out Barry and Mum's convo, as well as my own thoughts. Further down the pub close to the bandstand, Fitz sat at a table with Scotty, Cecil, and Mona of all people. Mona was Fitz's third brother Paul's wife. She hated me, but was kind enough to wrap her dislike in condescension and backhanded compliments. Fitz and I had come to the conclusion that maybe she and Paul had stayed drunk before their wedding and once upon a time, she wasn't a raging bitch. Since we had never seen her drunk, or nice, this was all theoretical.

As I approached the table, Mona said, with a drunken slur, "Well, Janie, there you are! You must be enjoying all the trouble MY family went through to throw you this shindig. You being an attention seeker and all," she snorted a laugh.

Fitz narrowed her eyes as I shook my head ever so slightly to her. Fitz was, for all practical purposes, not just my best friend, but my sister. And she didn't take kindly to someone talking ill of her family. Even by family forced on her by marriage.

"Unfortunately, you just blend into the crowd, don't you?" Mona asked. "Well you would," she laughed, "If you weren't man sized. But plain as you are I could still see you coming from across the bar," she did a drunken snort.

Finally, after years, our theory had been disproved. She was just a bitch, I thought. Five ten! I'm an inch and a half taller than Fitz, and this woman tries to torture me with it. Honestly, I had always wished my stature was a little less statuesque, but I wasn't about to back down from her. I had had just enough whiskey, and was in just enough of a mood, "Not all of us can be hobbit sized," I said, smiling.

"You know what they say," she retorted, "Good things come in small packages." She held out her hand to expose her 3 carat diamond wedding ring. "Like this," she slurred, "It came in a Tiffany's box. Look at it hard, Janie. It may the closest you ever get to one."

"I guess you haven't heard what else they say, then?" I replied, "GREAT things come in even bigger packages," I motioned to my boobs. In fact, I had three things she was jealous of: 1. A real spot in the Fitzpatrick family. The other two were my aforementioned C's.

She had her hand on Cecil's knee, and he looked uncomfortable with her over aggressiveness. Especially since Mona was married to Fitz's brother, Pauly.

"I hope you don't mind," she said, "I was keeping your boyfriend warm for you."

Cecil looked up at me widening his eyes. Cecil had introduced himself to Mona as my boyfriend when they met last week. Basically just so she would stop torturing me about being dumped by John. So I knew what her game was. But the look on his face was riddled with a 'Please Save Me' expression.

"Well, thank you Mona," I said. "But your assistance is no longer required," then I turned my back to her and plopped down in Cecil's lap, pinning her hand underneath my ass as I did so.

She pulled it free and huffed before grabbing her drink and teetering off.

Cecil smiled and put his arms around my waist, "My savior," he grinned and hugged me.

"Yes, you're safe now," I said, moving forward towards a seat of my own.

"Where ya goin'?" he asked, tightening his arms around me. "I like ya right where ya are."

"Not sure this chair is meant for two people, especially when one of them is a gargantuan woman."

"Never ya mind Mona's comments. She's a snake. And yer light as a feather."

I put a kiss on his cheek and moved to my own chair. "You know, eventually, she's gonna find out that you're not really my boyfriend. It may even make her back off of you."

Cecil asked, "Why do you put up with her?"

Fitz and I replied in unison, "Pauly!"

"Surely he knows she's a bitch?" he stated, matter-of-factly.

"I'm sure he does," I said. "But having us attack her would hurt him, so we hold our tongues."

"I hold my fists," Fitz uncurled her hands to show nail indents in her palms. "But, speaking of holding our tongues," Fitz said, and motioned to one of the cocktail waitresses hired to work the party. Fitz held up four fingers, the girl nodded and headed to the bar.

I laughed, "The cocktail waitress has been pre-programmed I take it?"

"Definitely! I wrote her a list of what we wanted, in which order, and told her I would display a finger count of how many we needed."

Next thing I knew four Redheaded Slut shots, four Bushmills shots, and four Black & Tans arrived. "Holding my tongue I can do all alone, but, you may be holding my hair later," I said to Fitz. "I think I better stick to beer from here on out."

"Nonsense," Fitz responded. "This is to yer Birthday and our Bon Voyage. Down the gullet," she yelled, raising her glass. We raised our glasses back at her, and shot down the Redheaded Sluts...followed closely by the Bushmills.

"Whoo," said Scotty, breathing sweet fire after the Redheaded Sluts. "I'm not used to things that sweet."

"I beg yer pardon," said Fitz, feigning offense.

"No," said Scotty, pulling Fitz on to his lap, "I am used to hot, sexy, 200 proof you!"

Cecil and I sat awkwardly, as their kiss turned into a moaning, hair pulling, just short of mauling moment. Just a few short weeks ago, Scotty could barely get up the nerve to speak to Fitz. Now he couldn't keep his hands off of her. And Fitz, not the dating kind, was smitten. I give the credit to Mum and Aunt Marble's potion. They had actually planned to set me up with Scotty. But their plan went to hell, when they reluctantly had to give the potion to Fitz's dad, (Da, as we all called him) instead of me. Turns out, Scotty had had the biggest crush on Fitz for quite some time. The "Push," (a potion of sorts) he had been given, had enabled him to finally voice his feelings to her dad. Thanks be given to St. Peter, Da had been potion-ed also, or Scotty's awkward declaration of love could have gone badly.

"Ya know," Cecil said to me, "We should make out too, and make them uncomfortable."

"It wouldn't make me uncomfortable in the slightest, little brother," said Scotty.

"Hush, big brother. I'm trying to convince Janie to lock her lips onto mine." He smiled at me, "No?" he asked.

I shook my head and smiled back, "No."

"Alright...but yer missin' out. I've heard from hundreds of women that I am great kisser."

I smiled again, but didn't have the heart to tell him that the hundreds of women was the problem for me. Cecil openly admitted that during his years spent on hiatus in South America he had “Had” several women. It was one thing to know your guy had exes. It was entirely another to know that he bedded half of a country. In all honesty, Cecil was someone I enjoyed. He had a great personality, was gorgeous, funny, smart, gentle, a great cook, quick witted, loved Meg Ryan movies, thought Drew Barrymore was the epitome of sexy, and let’s not forget, beat the crap out my ex, when he knocked me unconscious. But he had admitted to being a 'Letch in Recovery.' And with my horrible dating stats, I didn't think I should be his first encounter after giving up on sluthood. Plus, I wasn't a “Fling” kind of woman.

I was starting to feel the effects of the booze kicking in and told Fitz it was time for me to slow down. To that, she raised eight fingers in the air and grinned. This is where it all went downhill for me.

ABOUT THE AUTHOR

Edith Scheffer is a SoCal native, now blissfully transplanted to the Pacific Northwest. A gypsy at heart with the soul of a witch, Edith has wandered but never been lost. She loves sleeping under the stars and moon, walking in her bare feet, dancing to an eclectic playlist of favorite songs, and proudly parenting her exceptionally fierce and fabulous daughter, Brenna. Edith can mix the perfect drink (bartender by trade), massage your aches away (licensed massage therapist), and entertain you with her many novels (yes, she writes, too!). Her works include The Janie Chronicles, *Winged*, and *Fallen Gracefully*. You can discover more at edithscheffer.net.

facebook.com/AuthorEdithScheffer

goodreads.com/edithscheffer

www.ingramcontent.com/pod-product-compliance
Lightning Source LLC
Chambersburg PA
CBHW061556190726
48288CB00007B/2059

* 9 7 8 1 9 5 4 1 7 4 0 1 6 *